the hot shot

New York Times Bestseller
kristen callihan

Copyright © 2017 by Kristen Callihan

All rights reserved.

No part of this book may be reproduced in any form or by any electronic or mechanical means, including information storage and retrieval systems, without written permission from the author, except for the use of brief quotations in a book review.

This is a work of fiction. Names, characters, places, and incidents are the product of the author's imagination or are used fictitiously. Any resemblance to actual events, locales, or persons, living or dead, is purely coincidental.

Cover design by Sarah Hansen, Okay Creations

Cover photo by Michael Stokes

Digital Edition 1.0

All rights reserved. Where such permission is sufficient, the author grants the right to strip any DRM which may be applied to this work.

Those who upload this work up on any site without the author's express permission are pirates and have stolen from the author. As such, those persons will likely end up in the level of hell where little devils shove stolen books into said persons' unmentionable places for all eternity. Ye've been warned.

THE HOT SHOT

First we were friends.
Then we were roommates.
Now I want more...

What can I say about Chess Copper? The woman is capable of bringing me to my knees. I know this about five minutes after getting naked for her.

No one is more surprised than me. The prickly photographer my team hired to shoot our annual charity calendar isn't my usual type. She's defense to my offense, a challenge at every turn. But when I'm with her, all the regrets and darkness goes away. She makes life *fun*.

I want to know Chess, be close to her.
Which is a bad idea.

Chess is looking for a relationship. I've never given a woman more than one night. But when fate leaves Chess without a home, I step up and offer her mine. We're roommates now. Friends *without* benefits. But it's getting harder to keep our hands off each other. And the longer we live together the more I realize she's becoming my everything.

Trick is... Now that I've made her believe I'm a bad bet,
how do I convince her to give this player a true shot at forever?

AUTHOR NOTE

A few things…

The timeline for this story runs parallel to the one in The Game Plan. You don't need to read The Game Plan to understand or enjoy The Hot Shot, but I want to point out that Dex and Fi's story is playing out at the same time as Chess and Finn's.

In this book, I reference several versions of the song "Can't Help Falling in Love." They are:

- The original Elvis Presley
- The cover by Ingrid Michaelson
- The cover by Lick the Tins

You don't have to listen to these songs to enjoy the book. But they definitely set the mood, if you are so inclined.

ALSO BY KRISTEN CALLIHAN

THE GAME ON SERIES
The Hook Up —Book 1
The Friend Zone —Book 2
The Game Plan —Book 3

VIP SERIES
Idol —Book 1
Managed —Book 2

THE HOT SHOT

CHAPTER 1
♟ CHESS

When the promise of spending hours in the presence of hot, fit, and famous naked men fails to excite me, it's time to concede that I've hit a new level of apathy.

Last year, I'd been in a similar situation—all the naked men, so much hotness to immortalize in pictures— and I'd been practically jumping out of my skin with anticipation. Much like my friend James is right now.

"I think you're going to have to give me a 'bitch, be cool' lecture," James says, as he slowly blows a tendril of smoke into the air.

Curled up on a rattan love seat on the opposite side of my balcony so I don't get a face full of his cigarette smoke, I can't help but laugh. "And why is that?"

James, resplendent in a lime green suit, complete with acid yellow bow tie, rolls his eyes. "Don't be coy, Chess. It isn't a good look on you."

I'm mildly interested in knowing what 'coy' looks like on me, but I don't bite; I know perfectly well why James is freaking out. It's cute, though he'd hate it if I told him so.

Instead, I shrug and flick a dead fern leaf off the seat cushion. "You're seriously this excited because we're going to photograph a bunch of naked football players?" I shake my head, as if I'm completely clueless.

"We work with some of the most beautiful people in the world. The body is nothing more than shapes and shadows to me at this point."

Not that this will matter to James. The moment I'd told him we were doing a calendar shoot for New Orleans's NFL team, that all the top players would be participating not only in a photoshoot but a nude one, James had gone into fanboy hissy-fit mode. For him, that usually means chain smoking and talking non-stop.

At this point, James is so worked up, he doesn't seem to notice that I'm leading him along. He snorts as he takes another drag, squinting at me through the smoke. "Naked I can handle. Shit, I kept it together quite nicely when I had to stick rhinestones on Gianna's breasts, with her nipples all but staring at me while I worked."

"They were fantastic breasts," I admit, remembering the stunning model and how James had turned beet red up to the roots of his auburn hair.

James is in charge of makeup and styling for our models. He's a consummate professional, but he's not immune. Some of the models, be they women or men, turn him on.

Unlike me; I've been so apathetic this past year, I'm fairly certain a guy could wave his dick in my face during a shoot and I wouldn't respond. Professionalism aside, it's not exactly a good thing. In truth, it's a little worrisome.

Years of shitty dating experiences and not one glimmer of commitment have left me feeling defective and brittle. On the bright side, I have a job I love and a loft condo in New Orleans, my favorite city. My life is fulfilling and, frankly, just getting warmed up. Still, I can't seem to escape these bouts of lethargy.

James, unaware of my inner turmoil, nods as if remembering Gianna, but then sighs. "Tits are nothing compared to this torment, Chess. We're talking NFL players here. My home team." He fans himself. "Jesus, I might actually blush, or fucking stammer, or something equally mortifying."

"Ah, right." As if I'd forgotten what an extreme football fan James is.

During the season, he goes on about team records and playoff chances and who fucked up what play, or who is his complete hero because of one win, until I'm ready to tear my arm off just to hit him with it. "The struggle is real, eh?"

Something in my expression clearly gives me away because his mouth snaps shut and he gives me a long glare. "Bitch."

I laugh then. "You'll be fine, James. One week of naked football players parading in front of you and then it will all be a faint memory."

"Who says I want it to be a memory?" He wrinkles his nose. "I'm going to enjoy this. And so should you."

I hadn't wanted to do this shoot. James and I are overworked at the moment, and I've been feeling the tell-tale dull pressure behind my eyes that signifies a cluster of migraines are headed my way.

I shouldn't complain. Success has fallen into my lap these past few years. I'm a design major. Cyn, my college roommate, who now lives in New York, is a fashion major. I started doing photos for her fledgling collection, and people liked both of our work. Things took off from there, and I'm not looking back.

Were I not exhausted, I might be okay with reining in a bunch of overgrown, muscle-bound boys—because that's how the male athletes I've worked with before usually behave. But now I don't want to deal with any of it. I want to crawl into bed and sleep for a week.

Unfortunately, James, who also acts as my booking agent, insisted I take this job. It was for a good cause, rebuilding housing for flood victims not only in the area, but also in the greater US. And, because it would feature our city's football heroes in the buff, it was guaranteed to be a big hit.

"Besides," he had said over the phone last week, "they want you. Your naked fisherman calendar impressed them."

I'm fairly certain the fact that the buff fishermen images went viral is what impressed them. But I found myself saying yes. Damn it all.

"It's just a job, James," I tell him now. Because, honestly, I don't want to get excited over men I can't have. Famous football players definitely fall into that category. I just want an honest working Joe with a clever mind and a talented tongue. A cute smile wouldn't hurt either. Is that too much to ask?

"Right," James drawls. "And gelato is just another word for ice cream."

I gasp. "You hush your mouth, mister."

A faint pounding noise catches my attention. James lurches up as if he's been pinched. "Shit biscuits, they're here!"

He stands there, flapping his hands for a minute, before stomping on his cigarette and giving me a panicked look.

I smile, though I feel the strain on my cheeks. "Bitch, be cool."

"Huh. That was actually depressingly unhelpful." A small pout pulls at his full beard.

"If it will make you feel better, I can oil them up."

Outraged horror has his eyes going wide. "Take that from me and I'll salt your coffee for a week."

"That's just cruel!"

"Fair warning," he says with a sniff.

"All right, all right." I snicker and then get up. "I'll get the door. If you go, we might never get started with all of your fawning."

"Har." He rolls his eyes, but then straightens his suit. "I'll make some espresso. Do you think they drink espresso?" James is addicted. The upside of this being that he makes killer coffee drinks. Every morning, I'm graced with a creamy *café au lait*. Every evening, a bittersweet *macchiato*.

"I honestly have no idea." My knowledge of football players' likes and dislikes is nil. "Maybe stick with water for now."

"Chess, we can do better than that." He pulls a tray of charcuterie from the fridge.

"Jesus, it's a photoshoot, not a party."

"Those two are not necessarily mutually exclusive."

"If you say so." I leave him to fiddle with his tray. The stairwell to my loft is a vast echo chamber, and thus, before I'm halfway to the door, I can hear the guys clear as a bell.

"Maybe he's on the can or something," says a deep, snide voice.

"Great," drawls another. "We've gotta wait for a shit? That could be half an hour at least."

I slow my steps, fighting a laugh, and I hear a long-suffering sigh.

"Lord," says a guy with a Southern drawl, "these boys keep leaving themselves wide open for a smack down. It's almost too easy."

I agree, but nearly jump out of my skin when someone starts pounding on the door hard enough that I fear it might fall from the hinges. Really, that's just going too far.

"Dude!" Shouts an irate male. "Nip it off and open up!"

Someone mutters about having some class, but I'm annoyed now and stride to the door, ready to remind my impatient guests of their manners.

I whip open the door and find four enormous guys staring back at me. Aside from their impressive size, they couldn't be more different in appearance. The man-mountain directly in front of me, with his full beard, man-bun and tattoo sleeves, looks as if he'd be at home in the clubs I like to frequent. He also appears to be completely chagrined, which makes me think he was the one who'd been begging for the others to have some class.

Next to him is a good-looking, lean guy with an amused smile. Short dreads spike up around his head like a crown of thorns. He's shaking that head and giving the golden boy at his side a dry look. Golden boy is unrepentant in his glee, his light brown eyes shining with mischief.

They're all handsome in their own way; excellent subjects for what we're about to do.

But it is the guy behind them, looming in the background with a sour expression, who catches my eye and makes me pause. This guy is the cover model, blazing blue eyes and tanned skin. So gorgeous, he makes my teeth hurt. And he's looking down his perfect nose at me as if my presence offends him.

His face I know well. From TV ads to billboards, I've seen him smiling back at me, trying to sell me athletic gear, health drinks, and even home mortgages. He's the quarterback, the designated king of the football team, Finn Mannus or 'Manny' as the press dubs him. A strange nickname, since he's so damn pretty.

He catches me looking and quirks a brow as if to say, *"Yes, I know. I'm all that and a bag of chips, but don't even think about taking a bite; I've better things to do."*

And so do I. I cut my gaze away and study my other clients. They all look back at me with various levels of expectation or impatience. Dominance and testosterone radiate from them like sunlight. If I give them an inch, they'll take over this shoot. They probably wouldn't even notice they were doing it; they're clearly just that accustomed to taking charge.

I draw myself tight and try to remember what they'd been saying. Ah, yes, they were talking about shits. Lovely. It's time to assert some dominance of my own.

🏈 FINN

There's a lesson I learned early on in life; sometimes you have to suffer though shit. Best buck up and get past it as quickly as possible. As a football player, there's a lot of shit I suffer through: physical pain, mental exhaustion, mind numbing questions from the press, rigorous diets, lack of personal time. Looking at it from the outside, you'd wonder why the hell anyone would actually want to be a pro-football player. Answer: because it is the best fucking game on earth, and I kick ass at it.

But there are days like today, when I'm asked—ordered—by my team's marketing director to pose for a calendar, that I really question my devotion to football.

I've been told this is for charity, which is the only reason I agreed.

Even so, I give to charity. I use my face and my name to promote causes that protect children, the disadvantaged, and the abused. It's one of the best things about my fame. But striking a pose for a beefcake calendar makes me feel like a right fuckwit.

To top it off, I'm standing outside the photographer's door with three of my teammates, and he isn't answering. I pound on the metal door with the side of my fist, and the sound echoes in the wide stairwell. This is technically my day off. I could be napping, soaking in the tub—don't knock it 'til you try it—or playing Call of Duty on my PlayStation.

Then again, if he doesn't show, we don't do the shoot. No skin off my nose. "We get the time wrong?" I ask over my shoulder.

"Nope," says Dex, my center. "In fact, we're a few minutes late."

Perfect. We're sitting out here with our dicks in our hands. "The photographer had better not be having some sort of artistic huff."

Dex shrugs, looking bored. "Maybe he's on the can or something."

My starting wideout, Jake Ryder, seems more interested in cracking jokes.

Jake shouts at the door again, banging on it with his fist. "Dude! Nip it off and open up!"

If I wasn't so distracted, I'd be embarrassed. I pace and eye the stairs. It isn't too late to get away.

Unfortunately, the door whips open. A woman stands there looking pissed and kind of scary. She's thin and tall, maybe five foot ten, which still makes her six inches shorter than me. Her eyebrows are arrow straight, not something I'd normally notice on a woman, but it gives her such a fierce expression, as if she's an Amazonian ready to do battle, that it's hard to ignore. Or maybe it's that she's glaring like she's deciding which one of us she wants dismember first.

As if she hears my thoughts, her dark gaze snaps to me. And I swear I feel it down to my balls. She's not pretty. Her narrow face and high-bridged nose are too severe for pretty. Long straight hair, inky black at the roots and magenta at the tips, give her a Goth girl vibe. As does her black tank-top and jeans. A tattoo of dogwood flowers, done in black lines, runs along her left upper arm.

In short, she's the type of female who has stayed clear of me for my entire post-pubescent life. And I've stayed clear of her type as well. Call it cliché; I don't care. It's just a simple truth; women who look like her have never had any interest in guys like me, and I've never given her type a second glance.

Even so, my blood quickens. Her intense stare holds power. And power is something I respect.

I hear it in her husky voice when she finally speaks. "Nip what off, do tell?"

That's a sex voice, the kind that wraps around a guy's dick and tugs. I absolutely do not need to respond to a sexy voice right now. Especially since she clearly considers us nothing more than a bunch of unruly boys.

Take charge. Control the situation. It's what I do. Always. I step forward, bringing her attention back to me. "We're here for the calendar shoot."

Her upper lip curls. "Well, I certainly didn't think you were here for the little league group shot I have scheduled later."

Cute. Really cute. Wait. What?

"You're the photographer?" Dread punches my gut.

She scoffs with obvious annoyance. "Let's not be a cliché, eh, pretty boy?"

Prickly heat fills my gut. I've been called that my whole grown life. I'm used to it and don't really care when the guys tease me about my looks. But it pisses me off, hearing it come from this woman, as if I'm nothing.

Ryder snickers. "She's got your number, sweet cheeks."

No, she doesn't. Not even a little. But she thinks she does, which fucking irks. "Hey now, we were told our photographer's name was Chester Copper. Excuse me if I assumed it was a man."

She flinches as if smacked, and a little crinkle forms between her brows. "I go by Chess. I've no idea how your PR manager got my full name." It sounds as if she aims to find out.

I don't envy the poor sap who let her full name slide. But I do like that I'm getting to her too. *Turnabout is fair play, honey.* "Probably because they do background checks to weed out the freaks."

Chess responds with a bored roll of her eyes. Now that I'm close enough, I can see that they're bottle green, the color deep but crystal clear. I don't think I've ever seen eyes that particular shade, and it makes me want to keep looking.

I have no idea why I'm even noticing. Her appearance has no bearing on how she'll do her job. And that's the only reason I'm here.

At my side, Jake stirs, his brows pulling together. "Chester Copper... That's kind of like Chester Copperpot from *The Goonies*," Jake adds, looking around at all of us. "Remember that movie?"

Our photographer utters a ripe curse that has me fighting a grin.

"Yeah, that's a cool flick," Rolondo says to Jake. "Little dude who played the lead grew up and played Samwise Gamgee. Man, talk about a sad sap. As if I'm gonna toss myself into the fires of Mount Doom cuz I gotta boner for a hobbit."

Dex, who has remained silent until now, shakes his head with clear disgust. "He was on a quest to help Frodo save Middle-Earth from Sauron, chucklehead."

"Naw," Rolondo insists. "He wanted Frodo bad."

My grin grows. Get these guys talking about movies and they'll go off on a never-ending tangent. Something Jake knows as well. He makes a noise of impatience. "Hello? Can we please get back to *The Goonies* and Chester Copperpot? You know, that old dude they find all shriveled and crushed by a boulder?"

Chess flushes pink. "Yes, I know," she grinds out. "My parents met at a draft house viewing of the movie. They expected a boy, and since my grandma had already embroidered all my baby blankets..." She shrugs as if bored, but I don't miss the tension in those slim shoulders. She's pissed.

"And they actually named you after a Goonies character?" Dex asks, horrified.

"Yes." Her voice is tight and pained.

I'm torn between kind of loving her parents and thinking they're nuts. On the one hand, big points for originality. On the other, who does that to a girl?

Rolondo murmurs something about crazy white people under his breath, clearly not low enough because Ms. Chester abruptly turns and strides into the studio with those long legs of hers.

After exchanging looks, we follow.

The loft takes up half the floor of the building. It's an enormous space of exposed old brick, well-worn plank floors, and industrial black grid windows. There's a living area with brown leather couches and one of those coffee tables that are made out of a gnarly tree trunk. An old farm dining table is set opposite a gourmet kitchen.

It reminds me of my place, and I have an odd sense of homecoming. Some of the guys don't care about their spots as long as there's a massive TV and good couch to recline in. But I do. Our homes are our havens, and God knows we're barely ever there, so we should have a place we enjoy.

Chess stops by a big pedestal table that holds football equipment: pads, footballs, our team helmets, even some shin guards and tape.

I guess we're doing dress up, only I don't see any uniforms. The back of my neck begins to tingle the way it does when I'm about to get sacked.

A slim guy with a bushy red beard hustles out of the bathroom. He's wearing a yellow fedora and a lime green skinny-pants suit with brown pinstripes. Nothing out of place for NOLA. In an odd way, it makes me relax a bit.

"I'm James. Chess's assistant. Sorry about the delay. We were on the balcony having a smoke." He grins, and his gaze slides over Jake nice and slow. "Or I was. Chess was just keeping me company."

Jake frowns in obvious confusion, as if he's not sure if he's being checked out.

"They don't need a play-by-play excuse, James." Chess doesn't glance our way as she inspects the props. "Changing room is to the left. Strip down, and James will get you oiled up."

All the air sucks out of the room, and I hear a distinctive pop in my ears. My guys stiffen as well, their eyes going wide with obvious shock.

"Oiled up?" I can barely get the words out from between my clenched teeth. This is just fucking peachy. PR failed to mention anything about stripping. "You fucking with us?"

Her expression is bland as ever. "When I fuck with someone, he knows it, Mr. Mannus."

Oh, I bet they do. I wouldn't be surprised if she's left claw marks on some poor chump's balls. My own balls tighten in sympathy.

Jake, who has never been one for self-preservation, laughs. "I love this chick."

Green eyes flash beneath severe brows of justice. "I am not a chick, Mr. Ryder. I am a woman."

Rolondo makes a faint, mock crowd-roar, and Dex elbows his side to shut him up.

"With a job to do," she adds with such disdain that I can't keep quiet.

"Let me guess," I drawl. "You're obsessed with finally finding One-Eyed Willie."

Jake chokes on a smothered laugh, and Dex runs a hand over his beard, clearly hiding a smile.

"Man," Rolondo mutters. "You've gone and done it now."

I'm pretty sure I have. A hint of warning trickles down my spine, but I'm too irritated to heed it. We've been played, and now we're expected to strip like good little boys? I don't think so.

Chess slowly walks my way. I've had offensive coaches stare me down with less intensity. But they've never made my heart rate speed up and my skin heat. It's unnerving, but damn if I'm going to let it show. I set my hands low on my hips and wait for the inevitable explosion.

She stops in front of me, close enough that I catch a faint whiff of sunshine and earth, as if she's been sitting in a garden, soaking up the light. Our gazes lock. I expect her to rip into me, and maybe she's going to—her lips part as if she's about to. But she doesn't speak. She just stands there as if frozen in place.

A weird shift pushes through the room. I don't know what the fuck is happening. My focus narrows down to her, nothing else. The warmth of her body radiates outward and buffets mine. And it's as if she's easing a hot hand down my abs. The sensation is so intense, my balls lift and my dick grows weighty and full.

What the actual fuck?

I can't move. All my brainpower has gone south to take orders from my rising dick. And said dick is insisting that we get closer. He wants a formal introduction.

No, no, no. Not happening.

I pull in a deep breath, and my brain gets scrambled further by her scent. I am in serious trouble here.

I'm almost grateful when she finally speaks, but her bedroom voice doesn't help matters much. "Let's be clear, Mr. Mannus. You're in my house now. We have a job to do. I'll do my part, and you do yours." Her dark eyes search mine. "Make all the dick jokes you want. They won't save you."

No, I suspect they won't. Like an inevitable collision with a charging linebacker, I suspect Ms. Chess Copper is going to take me down and make me feel it. Bitch of it is, I'm not sure if I hate the idea or kind of like it.

CHAPTER 2
♟CHESS

Work flows as it always does. I cajole the shy, quiet big guy, Dex into relaxing. The showboat Rolondo, I simply shoot as much as I can while he poses in as many ways as he can. And I manage the flirty one, Jake, until he settles down. It's fun, all of it.

And, yes, James is a stammering, blushing mess the whole time. The guys take it in stride. It's clear they're used to walking around naked and they view their bodies as machines –for the most part.

Disrobing doesn't seem to bother them in the least. Dicks, however remain a sensitive issue. Surprisingly, the flirt, Jake Ryder is particularly worried.

"Shit," he mutters, as he drops his robe and a fine blush tints his cheeks. "What if I get wood? I mean, I'm not turned on or anything. Not, that you aren't really cute…Shit. I didn't mean that." He shuffles his feet, his hands moving to cover his penis before they jerk away as if he doesn't want to hide either. "I'm just saying. I'm naked and you're going to be looking. That usually tends to make him stand at attention."

The mere fact that he's not hiding his fear endears him to me. I keep my expression neutral and take a shot to check the light. "If he decides to give us a wave, we ignore him. Just like I do whenever that happens."

"Happens often?" he asks, brightening.

"I'm sure I don't need to tell you, Mr. Ryder, that penises can have minds of their own."

"Or lack of," he agrees with a little laugh.

With that, he relaxes, and we get along just fine. But all the while, there's a burr under my skin, the annoying thud of my heart against my ribs. Because, unlike Jake, I am not at ease. Not one bit. And I know who is to blame.

The Asshat. Mannus.

I could pretend I don't know why he affects me when the others don't. But it would be a lie. I'm attracted to him. And it is horrifying.

Usually, I need to like a man in order to feel a spark. Asshats who clearly think they're hot shit do not get more than a passing glance from me. And why should they? I'm around good-looking men all the time. Physical beauty is nothing more than an appealing package to gaze on. What's below the surface is so much more interesting.

The fact that Finn Mannus, who annoys the hell out of me, has been tickling the edges of my thoughts since I've set eyes on him is not a welcome experience. That he's up next and I'm going to have to see him naked, that I'll need to keep my composure and photograph him, is messing with my head. A lot.

My insides are stupidly fluttering and swooping. My fingers are cold, but my skin is hot. I'm so annoyed with myself, I want to take five and slap my own face. At this rate, I'm going to need James to give *me* a "bitch, be cool" lecture.

I just need to get through the day, and soon it will all be a hazy memory. I'll drink a glass of chilled white wine—or maybe an icy shot of vodka at this rate—and get ready for my date with…Shit, what was the guy's name? I blink, unable to remember.

Adam? Marvin? Melvin?

"Evan!"

"What?" Jake Ryder peers at me in confusion.

I clear my throat and lift my camera. "Nothing. Carry on."

The advice goes for me as well. There is no way I'm going to be distracted by a mouthy quarterback. No freaking way.

🏈 FINN

"You seem…tense."

I halt mid-pace and shoot Dex a look that would make most guys fuck off. The guy merely settles back in his chair, crosses his arms over his chest, and raises a brow. Since I've been trying to get him to be more involved with the team, I should be glad he's taking any interesting in talking. Because Dex rarely does. But now is not the time.

It feels like ants are crawling over the lining of my stomach, and it's all I can do not to claw them out. I haven't been this unsettled since my last college championship game. A game I fucking lost to his team, thank you very much. So I'm not in the mood to play.

"You're done with your shoot," I tell him. "Doesn't that mean you can go now?"

His smile is thin and knowing. "I drove all of us here, remember?"

I do now. Shit.

"And even if I hadn't," he continues blandly. "I wouldn't want to miss this."

"Miss what?" I ask, even though I know full well.

"You falling apart. It's fascinating. You get stiffer with each turn you take around the room."

I let my hands drop to my sides and order my shoulders to relax. My body ignores the directive. "Find something better to do."

"Can't. This is basic study," he says. "Now, I know what the signs are when you're close to losing your shit on the field."

As my center, the more he knows about my body language, the better. I tell myself this, but I really want to knock the legs out from under his chair.

"Dexter, when I'm about to lose my shit on the field, I'll tell you.

I have absolutely no qualms admitting when I need help during a game." Some QBs would rather swallow their left nut than show any weakness. But we're a team out there. And I believe in teamwork, not fucking up just to save face.

Dex tilts his head and inspects me as if I'm some sort of exotic bug that flew in through the window. Shit, I can't think of bugs. It pulls my attention back to the uncomfortable prickling in my gut.

"And now?" he asks. "You gonna admit what's getting to you in this situation?" The corners of his eyes crinkle. "I mean, I know what it is, but are you going to admit to it?"

Cursing, I lean against the rough exposed brick wall of the loft and let my gaze wander around Chester Copper's living area.

Chester Copper. Despite my discomfort, I want to smile. God, she's a handful—the type who will bite your hand off. It's kind of hot, in a pissed off gloom and doom way. I guess I'd be pretty pissy if I was a girl and my parents had named me Chester.

My smile fades. It's clear she thinks I'm an asshole. I'm usually better at charming women. My game is off today. But I was expecting an old guy name Chester, someone who I might have been able to talk football with and maybe convince him to take just a few quick photos before I fled. Not a blunt woman with dark green eyes that seem to flay my skin and see right under it.

She had assessed and dismissed me in a glance. While I'm used to being judged on my looks, I'm usually not found wanting. I shouldn't give one great fuck. And I don't really, except now I'm supposed to strip down in front of her and pose before the unyielding glare of her lens.

The photo studio is cordoned off by massive rolling wall panels that block my view of the photo session going on. I stare hard at those panels. The harsh lights she's using set the ceiling aglow, a beacon of my impending doom. Music throbs through the loft, some techno beat with a woman singing in a sultry voice. It started up as soon as Jake had begun his shoot.

"What the hell is that music?" I mutter.

"Goldfrapp," Dex says easily. "'Strict Machine' to be precise. Great song. But I expected Jake to go for AC/DC or something like that."

"This is dance music." I squeeze the back of my stiff neck. "I'm now imagining Jake strutting around on a catwalk."

Dex cracks a smile. "Don't give me that visual."

"If I'm haunted by it, I'm sharing." I roll my shoulders. "Jesus, why the music, anyway?"

"You get a choice. Whatever makes you comfortable." He shrugs again. "It was surprisingly easy."

"I feel like I'm about to be offered up like a side of beef."

"Grade A, prime, quarterback ass." This from Rolondo, who exits the bathroom, where we've been offered the use of the showers to clean off the oil they're rubbing all over our bodies. *Jesus.*

He huffs out a laugh. "You look like you're about to toss your Wheaties. What's the problem, Manny? Shit, you've given interviews in your birthday suit plenty of times."

Yeah, I have. Nudity is not the problem.

"Is it your junk?" Rolondo flashes a grin. "You worried it won't stack up—"

"You do realize I've seen your junk, Ro'. Worrying about stacking up is not a problem for me."

His grin only gets bigger. "So you *have* been looking."

Dex shakes his head at me. "You walked right into that one, friend."

On any other occasion, I might have smiled. Now, I only wave them off. "Play your reindeer games with someone else, boys."

"Shit," Rolondo says with a drawl. "You must be suffering if I can't get your ass riled up."

From the far end of the loft, I hear Ms. Copper tell Jake he did a great job. Which means James will be coming to get me any second. My heart starts to pound, and I run a cold hand over my hot face. "I'm uncomfortable with this, all right?" I tell my friends. "And I don't really give a shit what that says about me."

Silence greets me. Dex and Rolondo are both wearing somber expressions.

"Dude," Dex finally says. "If you don't want to do this, don't. We aren't machines. Say no."

I glance at the partition, and shift my weight, the urge to turn tail and run creeping up the backs of my thighs. "The team agreed, so I agreed."

"Woodson isn't participating," Rolondo points out. "Wife put her foot down."

"Woodson is a kicker. I'm the quarterback. I say no, fans get disappointed. Besides, I already committed. Backing out wouldn't be right."

It's too late, anyway. James strolls out from behind the partition. "Mr. Mannus," he says, all business now. "Let's get you ready."

"Great," I mutter.

I follow him to the changing area, and he gestures to a table covered with lumps of fabric, ranging from pale beige to dark brown. "If it makes you more comfortable, you can wear one of these."

I frown down at the lumps. "These?"

James picks up a light brown cloth and shows me.

To my utter, fucking horror, it's a thong. A man thong. "Oh, hell no."

"Why do you all say that exact thing?"

"Two guesses." I can't even imagine the shit the guys would dole out to any poor fuck caught wearing that nightmare.

"We'd edit it out," he assures, his lips twitching.

"And you think that's why I'm objecting?" I glare at the thong in his hand.

He tosses the thong back with the others. "To be honest, I'm with you. I've tried one on. I don't know how women stand it. Thing feels like the world's worst wedgie." He glances at the thongs, and then me. "Then again, it does great things for a tight ass."

I don't know if he's hitting on me or not. Something in his eyes tells me he wouldn't object if I offered to model one for him. It wouldn't be the first time I've had a guy try to flirt with me. Probably not the last either. Athletes and sex go hand in hand.

"As long as it isn't my ass in one," I tell him with a shrug.

He gives me a wry smile. "Right then. There's robes or towels you can use. When you're ready, just head to the studio space."

He leaves me to undress. The silence in the little dressing area presses in on me. The laughter of the guys rings out, but it only serves to put more distance between them and me. I tug off my shirt and try to shake the sensation of being exposed.

This is bullshit. Rolondo is right, I've never had a problem with people seeing me in the buff. I'm proud of my body. I've worked hard to perfect it and it works hard for me. But right now, I'm not asking it to perform a task. Right now, I'm expected to put it on display.

A year ago, I would have been fine with that. Hell, I'd probably have preened like the fucking cock of the walk. Fame and adulation can swallow a person whole, until it's all you think about. Until you believe its bullshit.

Funny how personal tragedy can strip the veil away so fast it will make your head spin. I'm no longer blind to the bullshit, and, frankly, part of me would have preferred maintaining my ignorance. Because now I feel empty, and the yawing space inside me keeps growing.

"Jesus," I mutter under my breath. "Just buck the fuck up and do your job."

I undo the button of my jeans and tell myself that none of this matters. Then James shows up to oil my skin, "So that the camera can pick up every swell and dip."

I really hate this day.

♟ CHESS

There's an old saying: the camera never lies.

Photographers know this isn't true. The camera—and by extension, a photo— lies all the time. We make it lie through manipulation. What looks one way in real life can appear completely different in a photo. Light and dark, negative space and angles…so many things come into play.

The concept of beauty changes with a camera. Some ordinary people come alive behind the lens. Something about the way the light hits them, and suddenly they are utterly beautiful. Haggard, craggy lines can be wondrous. And utterly breathtaking faces can fall oddly flat.

It is my job to find the story in a face, in a body.

I remind myself of this as James leads a sullen Finn Mannus into the studio.

From under my lashes, I watch Mannus move. There is no doubt about it; the man is put together well. So very well. Perfectly proportioned, bold features: a high-bridged and straight nose, a precise jawline, and sculpted lips.

That mouth. It's the kind of mouth that makes you think about kissing. Lazy, languid, deep kissing. Frantic, tongue-fucking kissing.

That mouth annoys the hell out of me, always quirking as if he's on the verge of a smug smile or about to say something snarky. Except for right now.

Right now, his lips are pressed together so tightly they nearly disappear. He glances my way, and our gazes clash. It is totally unnerving the way my heart kicks in response. And unwelcome. This guy is a jerk. I'm not supposed to get breathless when I look him in the freaking eyes.

I can tell myself that it's because Mannus has beautiful eyes. He does. Deep-set, shockingly sky blue eyes, surrounded by long, dark lashes. The color is so intense it's almost unworldly.

But I've seen pretty eyes before.

No, it's something else. Something about the way he focuses on a person. The power behind his stare is immense. Given that, when he opens his mouth, it's all smug teasing and easy charm, his intense gaze doesn't seem to fit.

I look away first. He's too pretty for my taste. I like quirky faces with strange lines. Glossy perfection doesn't interest me. But I'll have to find something in Finn Mannus's face that tells a story.

Or maybe I just go with focusing on the body.

Wearing a white towel low around his trim hips, his skin slicked up with baby oil to catch the light, most of that impressive body is on display.

Mannus doesn't have the super lean physique of a model. He is built in bold, tough lines. Somehow he is both cut but solid—well-defined in places, with big slabs of muscular bulk in others. At six foot four, he towers over both James and myself, his shoulders wide enough to blot out the sun.

His pecs twitch as if wanting my attention. They have it. Unlike most models I work with, he has an intriguing smattering of hair over his chest. After seeing so many smooth chests in my profession, it feels almost illicit to look upon him, as if he's somehow *more* undressed. My hands itch to glide over his torso and feel his textures.

I give myself a mental slap. Objectivity is needed here. *View him as art—just as you would any other client, you hussy.*

There's a tattoo down his right side. But he's facing me and the angle is wrong to fully view it. His right elbow is scraped and a few bruises pepper his forearm.

He walks farther into the room with a stiff and halting gait. By the scowl on his face, I'm thinking this is due to him not wanting to be here rather than from pain. But who knows?

"The hair is too tidy," I tell James. "I can see the comb tracks in it. Can you fix that, please?"

"The man attached to the hair can fix it himself," Mannus says, glaring in clear irritation.

"I'm sure you can," I tell him. "However, James is the stylist, so let's let him do his job."

Mannus doesn't look away from me. "Do you like busting balls in general, or just mine?"

"Since you're about to be standing balls out in front of me, I'd be careful, Mr. Mannus."

The corner of his mouth quirks, but the smile doesn't reach his eyes. And, when he speaks, his voice is strained. "Thinking about them already, are we, Ms. Copper?"

"Not really. I've seen three other sets today, so my mind is a bit full at the moment."

The smug expression falls from his face.

At his side, James snickers. "I think she just said her mind is full of balls," he says in a sotto whisper to Mannus. "Not that I blame her. Let's get you ready, and you can give her another eye-full, eh?"

Mannus pales. "Already?"

He sounds surprised, which is odd, given that he's wearing nothing more than a towel.

"Er… That's the idea." James makes a move to muss Mannus's honey brown locks, and the quarterback rears like a skittish horse. James freezes, glancing at me with wide, "what the fuck" eyes.

I am thinking the same. "Do we have a problem, Mr. Mannus?"

He flinches, his gaze snapping between James and me, and his jaw goes tighter.

Anger swells hot in my chest. "Do you have an issue with James touching you?"

As soon as I say it, I'm sorry. I never throw James under the bus. And it is absolutely shitty of me to do it now. But, damn if this guy isn't messing with my head.

Mannus frowns so hard, his brows almost touch. "What? My masseuse touches me all the time and he's a guy. Why the hell should I care as long as he does his job?" He glances at James. "Why is she asking me that?"

James clearly fights a smile. "I'm thinking it's because you're flinching like you're about to fly out of your skin."

Mannus's cheeks flush. "What?"

He looks so genuinely distracted and flustered, I pause and really study him. Sweat beads at his temples, and his pulse beats a fast tattoo at the base of his strong throat. Hands low on his slim hips, his knuckles are white where he's digging his fingers into the towel.

My heart gives a guilty lurch and then promptly goes soft along its hardened walls. He might have been an asshole with that One-Eyed Willie comment earlier, but he's still my client, and I'm not doing my job well if he's this unsettled.

I catch James's eye. "Can you get me a coffee?" I don't need one; it's our agreed upon signal for James to clear out whenever we're dealing with a panicky client.

"Sure," he says, easily. "You want anything, Mr. Mannus?"

Finn shakes his head once. "No, thanks."

James quietly leaves, and won't return until I call him.

Alone with Finn, the studio space becomes unnaturally quiet, and I can hear the conversations ebbing and flowing in the kitchen. I need to put the client at ease. Usually, I can do this without any problem. But that hasn't been the case here. Finn Mannus is surprisingly hard to read.

Setting my camera down, I move to the iPad that has my music setup.

Finn watches me with a guarded expression. "Please, not the music. I will lose it if you expect me to go all *Zoolander*."

He sounds weary to the core, and I give him a small smile. "I'm not expecting Blue Steel from you, don't worry. And no fast beats, I promise."

I glance toward the kitchen and then incline my head as if I'm confessing a secret. "It's just, I have a headache." Which is true; it's been building all day and is finally here to fuck with me. "Playing some low, easy music helps to drown out all the background noise."

Also true. But it will hopefully relax Finn as well. I select a slow song by Lana Del Ray.

The hard set of those broad shoulders eases a touch, and he nods shortly. "Half my life is fighting headaches. You have my full sympathy."

Looking at Mannus, it's easy to forget that he's more than a pretty face, that he uses his body as a tool, battering and stretching it to the limit for a living. I wouldn't be able to handle that kind of pain. But he does. They all do. It's that strength and vulnerability that I want to capture.

He turns more my way. "Is it bad? I have some ibuprofen in my bag."

Of course he does. I don't know how to deal with nice Finn. But I try. "I took something before you came in. But thanks."

He nods again, still uneasy, but focused on me, at least. "Should we reschedule this?"

So hopeful.

It's like kicking a puppy to have to say no. "I think it would be best for both of us if we just get through this, don't you?"

His blue gaze darts over my face, every muscle in his body going so tense, they stand out in perfect, glorious relief. Then he sighs, and his hard stance sags in defeat. "Yeah. It would."

But he doesn't move.

"You can keep the towel on," I say in the awkward silence. "We can do a torso shot."

That gets his attention. His brows snap together, and I'm treated to a focus that is laser-sharp. This guy, I can see leading a team down field. This guy is intimidating without even trying.

"It isn't that," he says, deeper now. More in charge.

"Look, I know we got off on a bad foot, but—"

"I hate photoshoots," he cuts in, color flooding the high crests of his cheeks. "All right? I don't know why. I just do. I know it's a part of my job, but it never gets easier. There's something about them that makes me feel…" His shoulders lift in a helpless gesture.

But his gaze is defiant, as if daring me to tease. Okay, I guess I earned that. I haven't hidden my disdain very well. But that's not what I'm feeling now. "I hate having my picture taken too," I tell him truthfully.

His quirks a brow at me, and I lift my camera with a faint smile. "Why do you think I'm on the other side of this thing?"

"Wanna trade places?" he asks with a little brow waggle.

I am not going to find that cute. No way. I have to focus. "I'm fairly sure no one is going to mistake me for you."

A slow smile lifts the corner of his mouth, and those pretty eyes warm. "Absolutely no possibility of that, Chester."

And there's the flirt I knew was lurking below the surface. My stomach flutters, and I kind of want to kick myself.

He runs his hand over his face so hard that I hear the scratch of his palm over his stubble. "Fuck it. Let's do this."

"Excellent. Do you want to wait for James to get back? Or start now?"

I'm guessing the latter. And he doesn't disappoint.

"No, I'm good." He clears his throat. Almost as if he's moving in slow motion, his hand goes to the knot of the towel and tugs.

And even though I've put on music, I swear it's so silent just then that I hear the towel slither to the floor.

Jesus.

Like that, my heart pounds against my tight ribs, and I want to sit down, find my breath, because it has fled. Heat swirls between my legs and down the backs of my thighs.

Professional. You are a pro-freaking-fessional.

The voice in my head is tiny and faint, drowned out by the rushing in my ears.

Mouth dry, I stare at the man before me. Our eyes lock, the silence so thick I can taste it on my tongue. I see the whole of him, utterly exposed, vulnerable yet so powerful that I can't think straight.

His skin is smooth and golden but holds a tinge of rose to it, like a man who's been out in the sun a bit too long, or one who might be blushing.

He's the third nude man I've seen today, and yet I'm the one who feels like blushing, as if he's the first naked man I've *ever* seen.

There's just so much of him.

Sculpted chest, strong thighs, tight calves, and elegant feet; I take all of it in with a glance. But that's not where I really want to look. Unable to help myself, my gaze glides down.

I've been trained not to stare at a man's penis while working. It's rude, objectifying, unprofessional.

Yet here I am, staring.

My cheeks burn, my heart thumping out of control. I grip my camera tighter than necessary.

He's beautiful. From a nicely trimmed nest of dark brown hair, his penis hangs thick, long, and dusky rose over a pair of weighty balls.

And that's enough, missy. No more gawking.

I take a deep breath, look away from the illicit view before I start imagining his cock getting thicker, harder, plumping up with heat and want…

A shiver goes over my skin, and I meet Finn's eyes. Guilt bites me, because he doesn't seem to have noticed I've been perving on him. His expression is intense, but pained.

"Talk to me." It's almost a whisper, husky and desperate.

It does things to my insides. Swoony, throbby inconvenient things. I stare at him, my limbs unmoving and heavy, my stomach clenched with anticipation and indecision. He needs a distraction, and I can't think of a thing to say. His eyes widen in a plea. I swallow hard.

"What's your best football moment?" It's a standard question. Get the client to talk about what they love, and they'll open up to you. But I truly want to hear his answer.

He takes a breath, and his gaze turns inward. "Freshman year of high school, I made the varsity team. It was just after our first practice…"

I take a picture. But he doesn't seem to notice. He's not looking at the camera but past it, as if he sees that day.

"Coach had us doing ladder sprints over and over. I was exhausted. My legs felt like jelly. My thighs burned like hell fire."

His thighs—those massive, beautifully muscled thighs—clench as if remembering that long ago pain.

"So there I was," he goes on in a soft, fond voice, "limping off the field with my teammates, the sun so low it lined the tree tops. And I just kind of stopped there at the edge of the field, listening to the guys joke and laugh, and I got this feeling." He pauses and smiles. "That this was it, you know? I knew right there and then that football was where I belonged. It just clicked."

He stands in the light, his feet planted wide, utterly naked. He should look ridiculous. But he doesn't. He looks like a warrior, a man completely at home with his body.

"And here you are," I rasp before clearing my throat. "You've attained the highest possible position in football."

A slow smile unfurls. "Yes, I have." Pride fills his voice, makes it stronger. But there is also joy.

I feel it reverberate in my heart. "That moment," I tell him. "That is what I want to capture."

He blinks, his body twitching. And then he's somehow standing taller. "You want the joy?"

I take another shot, not breaking eye contact with him. "I want you to remember that joy. It will shine through." Another shot. "Despite what you may think, that is what people respond to. That gorgeous body of yours is an expression of what you do, who you are."

When he looks at me now, it's with a slow burn of heat. "You think my body is gorgeous, Chess?"

My heart thumps against my ribs. I could lie to him, throw snark his way, but it would ruin the moment. I won't see Finn Mannus after this job is done. We will never be friends. And despite my superficial attraction to him, we will never be lovers. But right now, in this space, there is something pure between us. He's letting me see him, as he really is, no pretenses. I cannot hide in the face of that honesty.

I lower my camera. "Yes, Finn. I do."

For a second, I think he might reach for me. But he simply draws in a breath, his nostrils flaring slightly. His eyes never leave mine. "I'm all yours, Ms. Copper. What do you want me to do?"

So many ways to answer. But I'm calmer now. He's in my hands, and I will not fail him.

"Will you get on the floor?" I ask.

His brow quirks.

"People will expect a nice chest shot," I explain. "Maybe you holding a football over your—"

"Junk," he puts in with a slanting smile.

I expressly do *not* look at said "junk" but nod. "I get that this is supposed to be a nude calendar. But I don't want to objectify you." *Let's ignore the fact that you mentally ogled him like a perv.* "Your body is your instrument. If you're in an unexpected pose, it makes people look at you in a different way."

"All right, then." With the simple grace of a world-class athlete, he lowers himself to the floor.

I raise my camera and peer through the lens. "Can you roll onto your stomach and brace yourself on your elbows? I want a look at that tat."

Finn's lips twitch on a smile as he turns, planting his elbows and forearms on the floor. His biceps bunch as he easily lifts his torso up. Gorgeous. Utterly gorgeous. And his ass? It clenches as if he's….

I push the thought away.

The tattoo running along his ribs is a black outline of the state of California with the Golden Gate Bridge etched inside of it.

"Hold on a sec." Setting down my camera, I run over, adjust the lighting, and take a reading. Usually James would do this, but I don't want to break the spell by calling him in. Finn doesn't move but watches me out of the corner of his eye. Unable to help myself, I crouch down and gently tuck back a lock of his hair that's creating a bad shadow.

The second I touch him, I know it's a mistake. The air between us changes, drawing tight. A hum pulses in my bones, and his expression becomes intent, his focus never wavering from mine. In that instant, I know him. I *know* him. I feel like I've known him my whole existence, like I've been waiting for him to return from wherever he's been.

My muscles flex with the urge to lean in, feel his skin, rest my cheek next to his, to do... *something*. I see that knowledge reflected in his blue gaze, as if he wants the same. Blood rushes in my ears, my heart thudding like a warning drum.

But then he blinks and sucks in a light breath, and a wall comes down between us. I need that wall.

My head clears and, finally, I can breathe too, as if I've been let out of a trap. With a smile that is forced, I quickly stand and pretend that nothing has happened. "Perfect."

I hate the gravel in my voice. But neither of us acknowledges it. He merely gives me a tight nod. The weight of his attention presses on my back as I retrieve my camera.

Behind the lens, Finn is both smaller yet more detailed. I take my time focusing, setting up the shot, and giving us both a chance to settle. I don't know what the hell just happened, but I don't like it.

"Tell me about the tat," I say, snapping a picture.

His gaze goes to my arm. "Tell me about yours."

"I thought it would look pretty."

"That the truth?"

"Yes. Boring, but true."

He huffs out a laugh. "I like true."

"It was the most spontaneous thing I've ever done," I feel compelled to admit in the name of truth. Most people assume boldly colored hair and tattoos mean you're a wild child or frivolous, when sometimes it's just a simple act of self-expression. The tattoo had happened on a day I'd been too shocked to plan out exactly what I wanted in advance.

Finn's expression turns thoughtful, as if he's reading my face like a book. Silence rises between us and, for a moment, I wonder if he'll refuse to tell me about his tattoo. But then he speaks. "Went to Stanford for college. Before my first game, I drove into San Francisco and took a walk over the Golden Gate Bridge. Thought about all I wanted to accomplish, all I wanted to be. Got the tattoo that weekend."

I snap another shot. "And have you accomplished everything?"

A secretive light comes into his eyes. "Almost."

"Hmmm. What about the roses?" He has two vibrant red roses inked on the top and bottom of the state.

The corners of his eyes crinkle. "When I won my first and second Rose Bowl."

Such pride in his look. I capture it.

"And the diamond?" I nod toward the stylized diamond at the bottom of California.

"Freshman year, Coach told me I was a diamond in the rough. And if I ever made it to the pros, he'd consider me polished." His lips quirk. "Got that added the day after I was drafted."

"You love your job."

"Yes, ma'am," he says with a cheeky look.

"What goes through your mind just before a play?" I ask, snapping in rapid fire.

"You want me to walk you through it?" He seems more than willing to tell me, but also curious, as if he can't figure out if I really want to know or am just humoring him.

"No. I want you to picture the process."

Silently, Finn drops his head. His eyes close.

And my breath catches. Because he is stunning.

Stretched out on the floor, his intensity should be diminished, but it isn't. His body remains tight, his muscles almost quivering, as if ready to spring into action. But his expression is a different story. A look of peace falls over him, his lips soft, almost parting, the clean line of his jaw relaxed, and his brow smooth.

He is utterly at home within his skin, within his mind. It's as if I'm witnessing a man at prayer. A true believer.

And I feel transformed right along with him. Pure and revitalized instead of simply going through the motions. Again, that feeling of *knowing* hits me. Only this time it isn't terrifying, but a warm balm that makes me aware of my own skin, of each breath I draw in and let out.

I almost forget to take the shot. But when I do, I know it will be the cover. A covetous part of me resents that, as if this moment is private, something Finn Mannus has allowed only me to see.

But then I remember myself. It's just a job. And the job is now officially done.

CHAPTER 3
🏈 FINN

"I'll tell you one thing," Jake says, after taking a long pull on his beer. "Baby oil is great for my skin. I should have slathered myself in it long before today."

I have to laugh. "I was going to mention the way your face now resembles a baby's butt."

"This face," he says, "is going to get me laid after I finish my beer."

I just shake my head and relax into the booth we're sitting at. "Good thing you rubbed baby oil on it, then."

Personally, I hate the lingering feeling of the damn oil. I'd just as soon forget the whole day. But even as I have the thought, I know it's a lie. Once the photoshoot got going, when it had been just Chess and me, it had been… I don't even know how to explain it. Different. Unexpected.

For a small while, I'd stopped thinking about my job, about the various aches and pains plaguing my body, about the press, the team's record, winning, losing. I'd stopped thinking about anything, really. Somehow, Chess had done what I've only been able to accomplish on the field; she got me to focus solely on the moment.

Now it's over. My time with the combative Ms. Chester Copper is done. I'm used to people drifting in and out of my world. I meet new faces almost on a daily basis. So I shouldn't feel any sense of loss.

I do, though. But why do I?

I'd blame it on attraction. But I'm attracted to women on a daily basis too. I've learned to let it go and get on with my day. Truth is, I've felt off and alone since the thing with Britt. Which is something I really don't want to think about. Ever.

I'm frowning when the waitress sets a heaping platter of smoked oysters on the table. "Here you boys go." She adds a basket of hush puppies and another basket of fried shrimp to the mix. "Can I get y'all anything else?"

Her smile is wide and accommodating, and it pisses me off that I instantly wonder if she's flirting, that I've trained myself to immediately second-guess everyone's motives.

"We're good," I tell the woman.

Her smile fades a bit then comes back brighter. "Well, holler if you need me. For anything at all."

Jake tucks into the food, as she walks away.

"Was she flirting?" I ask him, as soon as she's out of hearing range.

"Why?" He sucks down an oyster. "Did you want her to be?"

"No." I run a hand over my hair. "I just can't tell anymore."

Hunched over his food, Jake looks up at me. "Messes with your head, doesn't it?"

Relief that I don't sound like a pompous asshole floods me. "Yeah, it does."

"Well, for the record…" Jake points his beer in the waitress's direction. "She was flirting."

"Maybe you're imagining things too." I pop a shrimp into my mouth.

"Finn," he says with exaggerated patience. "You're a starting pro quarterback in a town that loves its team. You can safely assume that even the dogs on the street are flirting with you."

"The landscape of your mind is a scary place, Ryder."

He grins, his mouth full of shrimp. "But a lot of fucking fun."

I'm laughing in agreement when it hits me; Chess didn't flirt. Not in the usual, please do me and then sign my chest kind of way I'm used to.

She didn't try to get anything from me other than a good picture, which is her job. She'd been utterly herself. And, for a few brief moments, so had I.

"What's that sour face all about?" Jake asks, cutting into my thoughts. "Got a bad oyster?"

I slouch back in my seat and toy with the soggy label on my beer bottle. Jake and I were drafted in the same year, to the same team. We suffered through having to do stupid singing skits during training camp, rookie hazing, fucked up buzz cuts with bullseyes on our heads, and the mental mind-fuck of transitioning from being top dogs in college to holding on by our fingertips as we made our way in the NFL.

He is my closest friend. And if either one of us gets transferred, I might actually break down and cry manly tears of sorrow. He's also my sounding board, as weird as his advice usually is.

"I was thinking about the photographer."

"Chester Copperpot?" He chuckles. "I don't think she liked you."

"She liked me fine." While she hadn't batted her eyelashes at me, there had definitely been moments of…something. I've never had *something* occur with a woman before, so I'm not sure what the hell it is or what it means.

Jake lifts up a hand. "Okay, I need to amend my earlier statement. You can rest assured that everyone in New Orleans, including the dogs, is flirting with you. Except for Chess Copper."

I resist the urge to chuck a hushpuppy at his head. "That's the thing; I know she didn't flirt. I kind of liked that."

He rests his forearms on the table. "Dude, be reasonable. The One-Eyed Willie comment killed it for you. Move on and knock on more welcoming doors."

"Hell, I'm not trying to get into her pants—"

"Bullshit," Jake coughs loudly.

"I just want to…" I trail off, not really knowing what the fuck I want. Being with Chess had been one of the most real moments of my life, and yet it also feels like a strange dream.

"Have a meaningful and deep conversation with the woman who took pictures of your junk all day?" he supplies. Not at all helpfully.

A hushpuppy pings his forehead dead center. My aim is a thing of beauty.

Laughing, he flips me off and wipes the grease spot from his head. In turn, I give him a salute with my beer bottle. "Look at it this way," I say. "At least she won't be distracted by trying to picture me naked."

"Worse, she's already seen you naked. So if she's not trying to get you there again, you know she found you lacking."

"Why do I tell you anything?"

"I don't know. I'm just going to sell it to the tabloids later."

It might be wrapped up in a joke, but he's giving me a good reminder; our lives aren't like normal people's. Finding someone to hook up with is easy. Having an actual relationship is a minefield. You never know whether the person likes you or your fame. And there's the hassle of easing someone into a life where they're under a public microscope, and you're either on the road for most of the season, or training, making appearances, and basically having no personal time. That's why most smart guys either marry their college sweethearts or connect with someone famous who knows what to expect.

And that's why I've never sought a relationship, but rely on hookups for my sexual release. One and done is as easy as it can get in our world. Usually.

Since I really don't like the direction my thoughts are taking, I move on to discussing simpler topics with Jake, such as college football and who will likely be a real pro contender once drafted. Jake and I eat our food and drink our beers. Every so often, fans come up and ask us for an autograph or thank us for a good game. This is my life. It's fucking fantastic.

I tell myself this as we leave the restaurant and walk down Iberville Street. I could have bought a house somewhere in Uptown. But it's just me, and who the hell wants to rattle around in a big mansion on their own? So I bought a condo just at the edge of the Quarter.

"Man." Jake nudges me on the side. "Never say I don't support you. Look over there." He points to a restaurant across the street. Sitting at the bar, her long purple hair glinting in the low light, is Chess Copper. She's traded her black tank for a silky gold top that clings to a firm pair of tits I could easily engulf with my hands. The thought flickers to life, and my fingers curl in response.

She isn't the sweetly pretty or stunningly beautiful kind of woman I usually spend time with. She's severe, elegant. It would be easy for me to say she isn't my type. But I'm fairly certain that goes both ways. And I'm beginning to think my "type" has just changed.

"I think fate is tapping on your shoulder," Jake says in a stage voice.

A weird surge goes through me, but I ignore it. "More like telling me to piss off. She's on a date."

Hard to miss the guy sitting with her, his body turned her way. He's just the kind of guy I'd have guessed she'd go for: beard, multiple tatts and piercings. Hell, he looks like a skinny version of Dex.

"Maybe he's trying to pick her up," Jake points out.

"It's a date. They're settled in. Her bag is on the back of his chair, and he's completely at ease."

Reading body language is second nature to us now. And Jake nods. "Good point."

I shift my weight, ready to move on. "Let's go before she spots us gawking like a couple of—"

Chess turns her head away from her date and hides a yawn in her hand. It could be that she's simply tired. But I see the boredom in her expression, and that strained, "when the hell is this going to be over" look in her eyes. I know that look because I've worn it too.

"You know," I say, still watching. "It would be rude if we didn't go in and say hello."

A slow grin spreads over Jake's mouth. "After we've spotted her and all."

I match that grin. "And we're nothing if not polite."

"Perfect gentlemen." Jake tugs the brim of his cap down further over his brow. "I'll take care of the date."

I clasp his shoulder. "Good man."

♟ CHESS

There has got to be a better way to find love. I take an anemic sip of my watery vodka tonic and try to search for something to say to Evan, my date for the night. As dates go, this isn't the worst one I've had. Not at all. It's just off.

Which is disappointing. I had high hopes for this one. Physically, Evan is exactly what I look for; soulful brown eyes, full tattoo sleeves, thick but trimmed beard. He had caught my eye last week when we both stopped to listen to a zydeco band playing on Royal Street. He'd been engaging then, witty enough to have me agreeing to this date.

Now?

I give him a smile that feels strained. "So, you're a tattoo artist." *Great, you've only mentioned his job twice before now.* "How is that going?"

Oh, holy hell, maybe I'm the boring one here.

His pinched expression says pretty much the same. "Can't complain. I live for skin."

That probably sounded better in his head.

I take a sip of my drink. I don't miss the way the bartender shakes his head as he puts away a glass. Yes, we're that pathetic. This date is going down like a week-old balloon. And it hurts. Not the loss of this particular guy, but the loss of a possible connection. Simple, basic connection. Someone to hold me, make me feel good. It's been so long since I've had good sex, I'm beginning to forget how it feels to be touched in reverence. And that fucking hurts.

Evan lets out a sigh, and I'm hit with a waft of garlic and stale cigarette smoke. That's the other thing; he has terrible breath. Why didn't I notice this before? Maybe it's just tonight? Should it matter?

Everyone has bad breath now and then.

"Chess?"

I blink out of my fog, ready to answer Evan, when I realize the voice that had spoken was deeper, laced in an innate sense of confidence and command. That voice grabs hold of my spine like a hot hand, sending prickles over my skin. No, God no, not *him*. He cannot be here to witness this fiasco.

And even as the thought runs through my brain, my stupid, traitor of a body begins to hum with happy anticipation.

Bracing myself, I turn and come face to face with my tormentor, my rescuer. Finn Mannus. *Of all the gin joints, in all the towns, in all the world…* From beneath the brim of a battered Mickey Mouse ball cap, his blue eyes twinkle. There's such sly humor in his gaze that I'm hard pressed not to smile.

"Fancy meeting you here," he says, crowding my seat. He isn't exactly insinuating his big frame between Evan and me, but it's a close thing.

"Who did I piss on in a prior life to deserve this?" I mutter, even as my body stirs with renewed energy. And, really, I'm full of shit because I'm happy to see him. My mouth can lie, but my heart knows the truth.

He's close enough that the warm length of his arm brushes against mine. "Some say my presence is a blessing."

"It doesn't count if you pay them to say that," I lob back.

He chuckles low and easy. "It was only the one time, I swear."

My lip twitches. And he sees it, his eyes bright with shared humor.

Jake Ryder takes the moment to make himself known. "Chess!" He bumps into both Finn and me. "Can you believe this coincidence?" He says it with such obvious exaggeration, that I give Finn a look.

He's got a good poker face, but the fact that he's even wearing one makes me wary.

"Is it now?" I drawl.

Again, Finn flashes a quick smile meant to charm and evade. He leans in a touch, and his voice rubs over my skin. "I was just nowhere near your neighborhood."

My heart gives a little kick. "I'd never imagine you'd quote *Singles*, Mannus."

A strangled sound to my right snags my attention. Evan is gaping at us like he's seen a ghost. Right. *Evan*. I'd forgotten he was there.

"Finn Mannus," he says in an awed voice. "Seriously?"

Finn gives him an easy, ah, shucks grin. "Yep."

"Wow." Evan's gaze pings from me to Finn and then back to me. "You didn't say you knew Manny."

"I don't. Not really."

Jake slings an arm around my shoulders. "Oh, come on, Chess. You've seen us naked. I'd say that counts as knowing us, don't you, Manny?"

Little shit. I roll my eyes, as Evan's mouth falls open again.

Finn glares at Jake. "Keeping it classy, Ryder?"

"You…" Evan looks at me. "They?"

"Naked," Jake confirms with a nod.

"They were in the studio for a photoshoot today," I explain, pursing my lips at an unrepentant Jake.

"Cool," Evan says, then does a double take. His eyes go wide. "And Jake Ryder too? Fucking awesome play on fourth and ten last week, man."

Jake grins. "Thanks. I try."

"I can't believe you know these guys." Evan turns to the bartender. "You see who's here? Finn Fucking Mannus and Jake Ryder."

The bartender, who is at the other end of the bar, pouring drinks perks up. "No shit." Soon he's sliding over, wide-eyed as a kid in a toy store.

I roll my eyes again, and my gaze clashes with Finn's. He's not paying his fans any attention, but is watching me. Amusement lightens his expression, and for one strange moment, it feels as though we're sharing a secret joke. "Bet you didn't know my middle name was 'fucking'," he murmurs as the bartender shakes Jake's hand.

"I'd have guessed 'asshat'," I tease.

Finn presses his big hand to his chest, now sadly covered in a white t-shirt. "You wound me, Chester Copper."

Shaking my head, I incline my head toward his. "The fact that you keep calling me Chester might have something to do with it, Finnegan Mannus."

"Actually, it's Finnegan Asshat Mannus."

"So I was right."

"You're the only one who's figured it out."

I hadn't realized how close we'd gotten to each other, that we were nearly nose to nose, him bent over me, his hand resting on the back of my chair. A loud laugh bursts the little bubble we've created for ourselves, and a man slaps a hand on Finn's big shoulder.

Finn's expression tightens for a second before he turns his head to look back at whoever grabbed him.

"Manny!" the guy yells in glee. "I can't fucking believe it."

"Believe!" I cry, waving my hands in the air.

Finn nudges my side with his elbow. "Cute."

I blink innocently, but don't miss the way he keeps his arm pressed against mine, as if we're together. His skin is warm and firm, and has my body's complete attention. Which is wrong; I'm on a date with… fuck, not again. Edward? Ethan?

"Evan," I mutter, pulling Finn's attention back to me.

"No, it's Finn," he says, smug as hell.

He's so tall, I have to tilt my head back to meet his eyes. "I'm on a date with Evan."

He lifts a brow, glancing at my date, who is gesturing wildly as he talks to Jake about football stats. "Looks like it's going well."

"Well, maybe if someone hadn't interrupted it…"

"You would have fallen asleep on your stool?" he offers, lightly.

I exaggerate taking a sip of my vodka, turning my back on him even as he chuckles low and close to me. The sound sinks into my skin, an unwelcome prickle that makes everything shiver.

But then he's crowded by more fans, getting more slaps on the shoulder. The loss of his attention is like being pulled out from under hot stage lights. It's cold and dark where he isn't.

I snort into my glass and keep drinking. I'm losing it around this guy. It must be his fame I'm reacting to. That's all. It's normal. *Normal.*

Except none of the other football players I photographed today did anything for me. And none of them sent giddy anticipation fluttering through my middle.

Manly, deep laughter rumbles around me, and then I hear it; the softly feminine lilt of a bunch of women on the prowl. Stiffening, I glance over my shoulder. Sure enough, four women have found their way to Finn and Jake.

These women aren't wide-eyed with fame. Oh, they've clearly recognized the football players, but they aren't fazed. No, they're sizing Finn and Jake up, looking for a good in.

Hell, I've been part of such groups, heady college days when we'd go out in search of cute guys. It was thrilling back then, the excitement of hooking up, maybe finding someone who I'd actually want to stick around afterwards. Now, the thought of searching makes me tired.

Pushing my drink away, I lean past Finn's wide shoulders and tap Evan on the arm. He's so caught up in fawning over his idols that it takes a couple of taps before he notices.

"I'm going to call it a night," I tell him.

Relief washes over his face, though he does try. "You want me to take you home?"

"No," I insist, wanting to escape and fast. "I'm good. You have fun."

I don't mention seeing him again. We both know that's not going to happen. He's already turned back to Jake.

Grabbing my purse and jacket, I slide off the stool. Finn, who has been mobbed by women, wrenches around and his gaze narrows on me. "You leaving?"

"Yep."

A brunette hangs on his arm, and he slips free of her before stepping back to give me room.

"Night," I tell him, needing a clean getaway. The longer I linger, the more I'll like him. And I know my time with Finn is akin to getting a glimpse of a shooting star.

He touches my elbow. "I'll walk you."

The heat of his fingertips sends little fissures of awareness skittering over my skin. I won't pretend the attraction between us isn't there. But it's superficial at best. Still, I'm not surprised he wants to act on it. From the second he appeared at my shoulder, I'd known his play would arrive, a foregone conclusion with the inevitable cliché ending; hot, cocksure, famous guy bags the woman who gave him shit earlier.

I don't think he's trying to be a dick. He's just following the script. Doesn't mean I have to.

Two women press in on both sides, wanting to be near him. I glance their way and give them a tight smile. Finn doesn't acknowledge their presence, but gives me an expectant look.

I put on my jacket then sling my purse over my shoulder. "It's all right. I'm perfectly fine walking by myself."

Finn lifts a hand the way cops do when they're about to give you shit. "Can't do it, Copper. I won't feel right not seeing you home."

"Don't go all caveman on me, Mannus."

The guy is like rubber, happily bouncing back with each volley I serve. "Didn't you know?" he says lightly. "All football players are part cavemen. Some more than others."

I'd never have thought a six-four, muscle-packed guy could be cute. But he is. And it's hard to resist him. "Be that as it may, I'm really fine."

We reach the door, and Finn opens it for me. "Okay then, walk me home."

"You?" Despite myself, I pause on the sidewalk, the humid night air wet on my skin.

Finn's tan skin glows purple in the light of the bar sign. "Yeah. I don't feel safe going it alone."

Such innocence in his expression. I bite back a smile. "And where do you live?"

He gives me my address.

Laughing, I shake my head. "Persistent bugger, aren't you?"

"Again, football player. We don't give up."

With that, I find myself being walked home by the quarterback. With the brim of his cap down low over his head and his hands tucked into his pockets, no one seems to notice who he is. He still draws glances; a tall, fit guy with a strong jaw line will always get attention. But we walk along unhindered.

Crossing Bourbon Street is a show, as usual. Music blares from all corners, country from one bar, rock from another, blues down the street. Drunks and gawkers flow past us like geese in a flock.

Finn steps closer to me, his arm brushing mine. "You see," he says, bending low to my ear. "I might have been swept up by the mob if you weren't here to guard me."

I snort. "I'm sure it would have been horrible. Dozens of strangers all vying to buy you a drink."

"Endless women showing me their tits," he says with an expansive sigh. "And me without any beads to give them."

"I doubt they'd mind."

The corners of his eyes crinkle as he looks at me from under his brim. "No. But I'd rather be with you anyway."

I'm not one to flush. I blame the heat in my cheeks on the balmy night air. "I'm not sleeping with you," I blurt out.

"All right."

"All right?"

A laugh leaves him in a huff of breath. "You expect me to beg?"

"No. Of course not. I just…that was easy."

His big shoulders lift in a shrug. "I'm an easy going guy."

"At the risk of sounding paranoid, this all feels odd. Like you're playing me."

His lips quirk. "You do sound paranoid. Tell me, does this paranoia affect all areas of your life, or is it just with men?"

We cross Canal at a brisk pace before the light can turn. "I've never been walked home by a man without him expecting something, Dr. Phil."

"You've been walking home with the wrong men, Chess."

No one knows this better than me. But I slow my steps. "Look me in the eye right now," I say to him. "And tell me that you have walked a woman home without intending to get in her pants."

He halts, which has me stopping too. From the bar on our right comes the sound of Elvis crooning about how he can't help falling in love. It's loud and sappy and fills the resounding silence between as we stare at each other in challenge.

Guilt skitters over his expression, but he tries to hide it. "I have walked a woman home without intending to get into her pants."

My eyes narrow, and his lips curl in a slow smile. "I'm doing it right now," he points out.

"You're impossible," I tell him with a laugh and start walking again.

"Charming," he counters. "You know, I don't actually have sex with every woman I talk to, Chess."

"You don't?"

"So dubious." He nudges me with his shoulder. "I do have some standards."

"And they are?"

He gives me a cheeky look. "Whether or not I want to have sex with them."

"Your vetting process is foolproof, I'll give you that."

Finn shrugs again. "Attraction is instant, for the most part. Whether it burns and grows or flickers out and dies after you talk to someone is the key."

"Look at you with your insight. And here I thought you had the all the wisdom of a fortune cookie."

"My wisdom is worthy of at least a pamphlet."

"Tell me something…"

"Anything," he says agreeably.

"If you only have one night stands, how can you possibly talk to someone long enough to know if the attraction will grow?"

He opens his mouth and then shuts it. A reluctant smile tugs at his lips. "Okay, you got me. My criteria basically consists of, can I stand her for the next two to four hours? But it still holds true."

"I want to call you a pig right now," I say with a shake of my head. "But at least you're honest."

"Most football players are. Our world is fairly blunt."

I've judged him. The realization is a slap to the face and not pleasant. Yes, he is blunt, which I knew from the start. And yes, his sex life is fairly shallow; he's admitted as much. But he's clearly intelligent and kind. Not the soppy sort of kindness that seems to be more about showing off than actual caring, but a quiet, unobtrusive thoughtfulness that's unexpected and lovely.

Too soon, we're at my building. Finn shoves his hands in his pockets and gives me a gentle smile. "Well then."

"Well…" My voice trails off.

The impact of Finn Mannus is immense. It's not the way he looks, although he is certainly blessed there; it's the intensity of his focus, as if you are the most important thing in this golden god's world. An illusion, but no less potent.

And no less awkward when our stare stretches on, neither of us saying another word.

He looks at me as though he knows exactly what's going on in my head; which is funny, since I don't have a clue. I don't want to leave this spot, and yet I don't want to invite him in either.

And he isn't exactly asking to come up. Irritation swells within my chest. For the first time in ages, I'm dithering.

"So," I say through stiff lips. "Thank you and good night."

That smile of his returns. The one that's slow and easy. The one that graces billboards and sells millions in athletic wear. "It's gonna be like that, huh?" he teases. "No, 'see you around' or 'let's have lunch.' Just 'bye'?"

I'm facing down the man equivalent of devil's food cake. But years of shitty hookups and bad dates have given me strength. "I also said thank you."

The lines of his face go tight for a second, and I wonder if I'm seeing disappointment. "You're welcome, Chess." He takes a step back, already becoming part of pedestrian traffic. "Sleep well."

I go into my building and don't look back. But I want to.

My day doesn't go well. At all. I'd tossed and turned all night long, finally falling asleep when the sky had turned dove gray. Having forgotten my phone in my purse, I overslept, not hearing my wakeup alarm. Which means I'm not able to take a shower before James arrives and, right after him, the next group of football players I'm supposed to shoot. So I'm stuck with lank hair and a stiff neck from sleeping the wrong way.

James somehow manages to knock over a light, breaking it and putting me out of several hundred dollars. He's so upset, I can't find it in myself to do more than pat his shoulder and refuse to let him pay for it.

The guys I'm photographing are nice and cooperative, which should put me in a better mood, but somehow it makes it worse. They remind me of Mannus. How can they not? These are his teammates, his friends. Every joke they toss out, every good-natured chuckle and charming smile they send my way, makes me think of him.

I imagine how he'd joke with them. How he'd take up the space in the room without even moving a muscle. The sad truth is he's doing that without even being here.

I don't *want* to think about him. But the man must have witchcraft in his veins, because he's managed to haunt me after only one day of knowing him.

Worse, I feel wrong for having left him at my doorstep last night.

It's ridiculous. He probably forgot about me before he even reached his home. We hung out for a few hours, made each other laugh. That's it. Move on.

One of the guys, a big wall of man flesh named Carson, idly jokes that if Manny oiled up for games, it would make him harder to tackle and, thus, his job easier.

Dubois, another offensive lineman, tisks at Carson. "Manny already is a slippery motherfucker. You just want to see him oiled up."

Don't we all?

I drop my camera. On my toes. "Shit!" I bend down to inspect my camera, thanking the gods that my poor throbbing toes spared it from damage.

Neither of the guys notice.

"Oil this." Carson grabs his crotch, now thankfully clothed, and hefts his handful.

"No one is oiling anyone or *anything* but me," James announces, which makes them all blush and stammer.

Foot hurting, muscles aching, I do my job, hoping to get everyone out of my house as soon as possible. But it's not until five in the afternoon that I'm actually alone.

Finally.

Except, for the cherry on top of my shitcake day, I get my period a *week* early, and don't have enough tampons left to get me through it.

Grumbling, I toss on some black lounge pants and my oversized Tulane t-shirt and head to the drugstore.

My head throbs by the time I get there, and my insides are writhing. I rest my hand against my lower stomach and grab a basket before calling James to complain.

"I swear," I tell him as I grab a bottle of painkillers. "It's like this entire day has been cursed."

He snickers. "Curse. Get it? Curse?"

I roll my eyes, even though he can't see me. "Laugh it up. Meanwhile, it feels as if someone is playing Battleship in my uterus."

"Poor Chessie bear. At least we know why you were in such a foul mood."

A flush washes over my cheeks. "Yeah." *Lie. Lie. Lie.* A tub of salted caramel gelato makes its way into the basket.

"Tell me you're getting some gelato," James says.

I smile. "Just grabbed it."

"Salted caramel?"

"You know it."

I find the feminine products aisle and search for my brand. "I'm going to go home, take a long bath with my gelato, and forget this fucking day." *Forget Finn.* "And then I'm going to go on Amazon and buying a freaking year's supply of tampons so I don't have to make these kinds of emergency runs anymore."

A low, deep chuckle rumbles from behind me, and all the tiny hairs lift on my arms.

"But you'll still need your gelato," a familiar—*fuck me, seriously?*—voice points out.

My insides swoop even as my cheeks burn.

"Who is that?" James asks in my ear.

I slowly turn on one heel. "The plague," I say, glaring up at Finn Mannus's smiling face.

"From asshat to plague." Finn scrunches up his brow. "I'm not sure if that's a step down or a tie."

"Who *is* that?" James nearly yells now.

I don't take my eyes off Finn. "I'll call you back."

James's squawks of protest cut off as I hit the end button.

"Are you stalking me, Mannus?"

Finn rests his hands low on his lean hips. "Having a healthy amount of conceit myself, I have to admire yours, but no, buttercup. My buddy Woodson lives a few blocks away. It's poker night. I'm stocking up on beer."

It's only then I notice a twelve pack tucked under his other arm.

"And tampons?" I ask, with a pointed look around the aisle we're standing in.

"Not tonight," he says easily. "Though we used to keep a pack of them back in college. Light flows were perfect for stopping up bloody noses."

"Now there's a visual." Somehow, I've taken a step closer to him. He's freshly showered, the golden brown strands of his hair still damp at his temples. And I wonder if he's just come from the gym or practice. "So back in college you went and bought these tampons?"

"Nah," he says with a cheeky smile. "I'd ask one of the girls hanging around to get me some."

"Of course you did." My nose wrinkles with annoyance.

"Give me a little credit, Chess. I'd buy them now if I had to."

"Hmm…" I eye him, trying not to return his smile. If only because it's more fun when he teases. "So why are you in this aisle now, if not for potential nosebleed needs?"

"That's easy." He steps closer, a warm wall of muscle and clean scent. "I heard your voice."

For a second I just blink. "You recognized my voice?"

His gaze darts over my face as if he's trying to get a read on why I'm gaping at him. "Not to be…ah…rude, but you're loud when you talk on the phone."

"Yeah, but… You recognized it." We've only just met. It occurs to me that I'd recognized his both times he'd snuck up on me. Then again, his voice is distinctive, flowing like hot honey when he's relaxed or hammering down like iron to rock when he's taking command of a situation.

A soft flush of pink tints the tips of his ears. If I wasn't staring at him, I might have missed it. He shifts his weight. "Was I not supposed to?"

"No. Yes." I shake my head and laugh. "I don't know."

He grins then. "You're cute when you're flustered."

"I'm not flustered." *I am.*

As if we've come to some silent agreement, we head down the aisle to the register, drawing a double take from some skinny guy buying a bag of M&Ms. The cashier gapes at Finn, but doesn't say a word as she rings me up. She also misses the bag by a foot when she attempts to put my gelato in it. I help her out by bagging my own stuff so she can continue to stare at Finn. He takes it all in easy stride.

Out on the street, Finn nudges me with his arm. He does it gently, barely a tap, and yet I feel the strength in him. "This makes two times now we've run into each other," he says.

"I'm still not convinced about the whole stalking thing."

He leans down a touch, so we're nearly face-to-face. "I think it's fate telling us to hang out."

"Hang out, huh?" The truth is, I don't want to go home now. I want to linger on this humid sidewalk and hear what ridiculous thing will come out of him next. But I have gelato melting. "I don't know why. We've been at each other's throats since we met."

"Ah, Chessie, that's just the way we play." He nudges my shoulder again. "Tell me you haven't had any fun with me. Come on."

I can't. And he knows it.

His smile turns soft. "I like you."

He likes me. I want to grin like a twelve year old. I imagine this is how it feels to be passed a note by the hottest guy in school.

"Is that so hard to believe?" he asks.

Not hard exactly. More like unexpected and strange. Yesterday, he was just some dickhead jock giving me shit. Now he's telling me we should hang out. And what does that even mean?

I've been silent for too long because he speaks again, soft, cajoling. "I think you like me too."

Hell. I do. That's the most unexpected thing of all. He's unlike anyone I know. A challenge and yet easy to talk to. He's also a famous, extremely hot football player who has beautiful women throwing themselves at him. In a world full of bad bet men, he's at the top.

"I'm just not sure what you expect to get out of this," I explain. "A date?"

Finn rubs the back of his neck, looking as perplexed as I feel. "I'm fairly crap at dating, Chess."

Disappointment hits me like brick to the chest. But I nod in understanding. "I'm fairly crap at hookups," I tell him. "I've run through that playbook and don't particularly like it."

His brows lift with a pleased expression. "Look at you using football terms."

"I thought I'd speak to your level." I bite back a laugh.

His amusement slowly slides away. "Last night, I did see you from the street. I went into the bar to talk to you. Even before that—at dinner—I was thinking about you."

I make a sound of shock.

He doesn't seem to notice. "I dreaded that photoshoot. You turned it around and made it bearable. All the bullshit just went away."

"That's part of my job," I say, lamely. It isn't a lie. But with him, I'd stopped thinking about getting a good shot. And though we've just met, he appears to know that too.

"And last night at the bar?" he counters. "Right now? You aren't working."

"I..." *Shit.*

"Everyone in my life is connected to football. I don't get true interactions very much. And, if I do, they're fleeting. But I have them with you." A line creases between his brows. "Does that make sense?"

I might not be famous, but I feel the same sense of isolation, as if I'm going through life underwater and everything is muffled and distorted. When I get within a few feet of Finn Mannus, there is clarity. It scares the hell out of me, because I need stability too. But I can't lie.

I clear my throat. "It makes sense."

He smiles then, pleased and happy. And it takes my breath. His expression turns earnest, his eyes scanning mine. "I want to know you, Chess Copper. I don't know why. I just do. I could make a play to get in your pants. But I don't want to. A one night stand with you doesn't appeal to me."

"Oh, well thanks." It's one thing to agree that sex is a bad idea. It's another be told you're unappealing.

Finn shakes his head as if I'm slow. "Pay attention, Chester. I said I want to know you. I don't get to know my hookups."

"So we're going to…What? Be friends."

He looks almost boyish then. "Yeah. We are." His eyes spark. "Fair warning. I'll still be picturing you naked half of the time. So get used to a bit of leering."

"You just had to go and ruin the moment, didn't you?"

"Probably should get used to that too."

CHAPTER 4
🏈 FINN

"So?" Jake gives me an expectant look.

I have to hand it to him, he waited a whole two minutes before pouncing, the nosy bastard.

"So what?" I maneuver my pickup around a plodding bus.

Jake snorts, because he knows as well as I do that I'm stalling. "You tap that, Manny?"

"She's not a keg, Ryder."

"Okay, fine." He rolls his eyes. "Did you hook up with Ms. Chess?"

"Nope."

"Bummer."

"I told you I wasn't trying to get in her pants." I feel his stare drilling into me, and I glance over. "What?"

"You're attracted to her. Anyone with eyes can see that."

I give him a lazy shrug as we stop at a red light. "Not denying it."

"So you want me to believe that you're fine with striking out?" He says it with such incredulity, as if the possibility of not having sex with a woman is sacrilege.

"I didn't strike out. I didn't even try. She made it clear she wasn't interested."

"I'm pretty sure you could have persuaded her to change her mind."

We pull up in front of a squat cinderblock building on St. Charles. "I don't want to persuade a woman into bed. Jesus."

Jake nods. "You're right. It's not like either of us has to go searching for it." He looks me over in clear confusion. "So you just walked her home and that's it?"

"You're awfully curious about my business."

"I know, right?" He grins happily. "I'm like a kitten over here."

"I think I'm going to need an antacid. Where's my bag?" I reach behind me to grab it, and earn a flick on the ear. My head rears back. "You did not just…"

Jake flips me the bird. "Bring it, Manny pants."

Things devolve from there as we give each other smacks on the head.

"Okay, fuck, I give!" Jake yells when I get him in a headlock. An older woman walking by peers into the cab of my SUV with suspicion. I give her an innocent smile and let Jake go. He pushes off me, adjusting his shirt with a mutter. "Touchy priss."

Grabbing my bag, I get out of the car, and he follows, getting his own gear.

"When's the last time you hung out with a woman," I ask. "One that wasn't trying to take a selfie with you or rifle through your stuff when your back was turned?"

Jake's expression scrunches up as we head for the building's entrance. "Uh, freshman year." He laughs. "Of high school."

"Exactly." I pull open the door, and we enter the freezing haven of air-conditioning. "Chess is just Chess. I don't need to fuck her. I just want to *be* and not have to explain it."

"Frankly," he says, as we jog up the stairs. "I'm more surprised she even talks to you. I could have sworn she hated you."

"I grow on people."

"Like fungus."

My reply is lost to the ringtone blaring from my phone. Since I've assigned all the people closest to me a tone, I know who it is right away, and my insides clench at the sound of "Bohemian Rhapsody."

It's an easy thing to hit "ignore." But it doesn't halt the guilt.

Jake frowns. "You ignoring your mother now?"

Yes, I am now the son who sends his mother straight to voicemail. "This from someone who ignores his mom all the time?"

"My mom usually calls to complain about my sisters, and I end up getting stuck in the middle of one of their heinous fights. Have you ever had to deal with five pissed off women? It's not a pretty sight. Your mom, on the other hand, feeds me and tells me how cute I am. She's like Martha Stewart and Betty White rolled into one adorable package."

I try to visualize that, but decide it's best not to for the sake of my sanity. "All this because she sends you care packages after you made up some sob story about being a starving bachelor."

"It's the truth. I am a starving bachelor." He pulls open the door of the studio we're going to spend the next hour in. "Her snickerdoodles are prize worthy. Besides, can I help it if she loves me? At this point, I'm fairly certain she wants to adopt me. Hell, she needs to baby *someone*."

His words send a bolt of pain straight into me. It squeezes my chest with hard hands, and I suck in a breath. Immediately Jake pales. "Oh, shit, man. I didn't—"

"It's okay," I cut in, lifting a hand. I don't want to talk about that.

Lips pinched, he nods shortly.

"She wants me to come home for *Thanksmas*." There are some seasons when I'm stuck playing a game on Thanksgiving or Christmas. My mother came up with the idea of celebrating both during one of my bye-weeks and calling it *Thanksmas*. It's a ridiculous name, but one that usually makes me smile.

Now, I dread it. My mother always means well with her meddling ways, but she has all the subtly of a bulldozer. "She married Glenn off, so now I'm her pet project. And I do not have the energy to deal with it."

"You want me to come with you?" Jake offers. "I'm an excellent distraction. I can moan about not getting enough to eat and how I'm wasting away." He runs a hand over his chest where he's put on about ten pounds of lean muscle during the off-season. Not that my mother will care; she'll feed him regardless.

"Thanks," I say, toeing off my shoes. "But that will only give her two of us to fixate on."

Jake stows his gear in a cubby and stretches his arms overhead as three women walk in. Barely dressed, their bodies lithe and graceful, they eye us with familiar, playful interest. Jake tracks their movement through the room. "Best fucking day of the week," he says with a feral grin.

"I actually enjoy coming here, Ryder. So don't fuck it up by dipping your wick in this particular wax."

Jake snorts. "Too late."

"Jesus. Who?"

"Rachel."

Which would explain why the little blond keeps sending covert glances our way.

"And Sheila," he adds, as Sheila of the bouncy curls and death glare stomps by. Thankfully, a guy can't actually lose his balls with one look, or we'd both be hurting right about now.

"Oh, for fuck's sake. You're a fucking menace."

He laughs, totally unrepentant. I wonder if this is how I come off to Chess. It isn't exactly flattering. If that's the case, I can't blame her for wanting to stay away.

Shaking my head at Jake, I pull out my phone. Thoughts of Chess make me want to talk to her. We've agreed to be friends, exchanged numbers, and then I'd left her to her night. Not an easy task, considering she'd said she was going home to soak in a tub.

Would it be within the bounds of friendship to ask how that bath of hers went?

"Who are you texting?" Jake tries to peer over my arm.

I elbow him away. "Isn't there another female you could be posturing for?"

Jake squints as if contemplating. "Probably not a good idea. I think I'm pushing it as it is."

"Oh, now, you come to that realization?" Snorting, I tap out a message to Chess.

And she answers immediately. We fire a few texts back and forth. No matter what I throw her way, she volleys right back with sass.

"You should see your face right now, Manny," Jake says. "You are in total smit."

"Smit?"

"Yeah, smitten. Totally fucking smitten." He looks almost sorry for me.

Chess pings me back, and I grin and answer, only half aware of Jake.

"This does not bode well for you, my friend," he says. "Clueless shits like us should stick to hookups."

"Not everything is about sex," I tell him, only half believing it. I type another message to Chess, as Eleanor spots us and heads our way with a look in her eye that promises she'll be making us sweat and burn.

"You're right," he says with a grin. "There's football. Sex and football. What more could a guy want?"

Six months ago, I'd tell him nothing and give him a high five. Now? I don't know the answer.

♟ CHESS

I'm putting on my makeup when Finn texts me.

GQ: Hey. Who are you shooting today?

I can't decide if it's the fact that he texted me or that I'd named him GQ in my contacts that makes my day suddenly a little sunnier. But there's a smile tickling my lips as I pick up my phone and respond.

CC: Porter. Worchowsky. Redmond. Phillips, Mr. Nosy.

We're actually doing two calendars. One featuring the offensive team and the other with the defensive team. Today, I'm working with guys on the defense.

GQ: I don't know this Nosy. Careful. He might be a spy.

CC: Very cute.

GQ: I try. ;)

CC: Aw, and you do emojis too. Such a cute QB.

GQ: Am tempted to send the finger emoji...

My laughter rings out in the relative silence of my loft. I find myself unable to sit still anymore and head for my balcony.

CC: :-* Where are you?

GQ: On my way to ballet class.

Okay, what? Not what I was expecting.

CC: Ballet?

GQ: Yes. Ballet.

CC: Ballet?

GQ: Are we talking in circles here?

Biting my lip against a grin, I rest my forearms on my balcony rail and answer.

CC: No. I'm trying to convey my skepticism.

GQ: You know, for an independent career woman, you're awfully old fashioned in your outlook, Ms. Copper.

CC: Fine, I'm exposing my double standards. Send a picture as proof.

GQ: So untrusting. Here's your proof, Mrs. Doubtfire.

He sends me a selfie. Wearing a tank top and baggy gym shorts over tight compression shorts, he's in front of a mirror wall with a barre bar attached to it. Jake is with him, and they're both making goofy faces, their tongues sticking out like Gene Simmons from KISS. Between them stands a thin and elegant, older woman in a leotard. She grins with pride, her arms around the two men as if they're her boys.

I laugh, and tap out a quick message.

CC: My mind is officially blown.

GQ: Is that all it takes? Should have done a pirouette for the shoot.

CC: Fairly certain would have resulted in panties going up in flames when that got out.

GQ: You say the nicest things, Chester.

Since I know he's doing it to irk me, I let "Chester" slide.

CC: I'll bite. Why are you taking ballet classes?

GQ: Jake found out about it when he pulled a hamstring and had to limber up. It's great for flexibility, balance… stamina.

GQ: It's GREAT for stamina.

CC: You keep repeating that like I'm supposed to be impressed.

GQ: Oh, you will be.

Cheeky, little… I start to type out an answer but he sends another text.

GQ: Plus, all the women in class are very eager to help me

maintain my form. ;-)

The happy fizz in my belly instantly goes flat, and I'm left with a sour stomach instead. If that isn't a sign to put the brakes on this, I don't know what is. I have plenty of male friends. None of them inspire jealousy.

CC: Don't strain something while you're at it.

GQ: If I do, will you give me a rubdown?

Right there. That's flirting. I put down the phone and pace away. Who am I kidding? We've been flirting from the start.

James walks in the door and drops his key in the dish. He immediately spots me wearing a groove in the floorboards. "Well, someone has lost her happy face."

"What did we agree on about reminding me to smile?" I warn, not stopping my pacing.

"To not to," James says happily. "But then we both know I ignore most of your directives, oh mighty queen."

The phone dings again. I eye it like a snake.

James unwinds the orange scarf wrapped around his neck. It clashes horribly with his hair and beard, but I suspect he likes that. "All right," he says. "Who is harassing you? Is it that diva Maria? Tell her the camera can perform certain illusions, but it can't wash the bitch out of her hair."

I choke back a laugh. Maria is a model we worked with a while back. She had insisted that I'd shot her in unflattering angles. Not true. She is gorgeous. But insecure. And a complete pain in my ass.

"Thankfully, I haven't heard from her since I told her there was a tornado warning in effect and to look out for flying farmhouses."

James snickers as he makes a cappuccino. "So then who is texting your knickers in a knot?"

"Finn."

He almost stumbles, foam sloshing over the rim of the cup. "Finn?

As in Finn, he's an asshat and I totally hate him, Mannus?"

"I don't hate him. We just got off on the wrong foot. Finn is fine."

"Yes, he is."

"Not what I meant."

A slow, evil smile spreads over his face. "And now it's Finn, eh?"

"That is his name," I deadpan.

"Mmm…" He hands me the cup and turns to make another cappuccino for himself. "Why are you in a snit over *Finn*? Is he harassing you?"

"No." I grab the phone but don't look at the screen, so I won't be tempted to answer. "He's flirting. *I'm* flirting. And I like it." I flop my arm in exasperation.

"I don't think I've ever seen anyone be put out by good flirting." James sips his coffee and studies me with a frown. "You sure you're feeling okay?"

The phone dings again.

GQ: Was that too much? Or has the possibility of massaging my fine ass made you faint?

A snort escapes me.

CC: Yes. You got me. The terror was too much.

GQ: It's okay, Chester. A lot of women can't handle this much hotness at once.

James's voice turns droll. "You know, I don't think I've ever seen that expression on your face."

"What expression?" I wait for Finn's reply.

"Besotted."

"Besotted? Have you been reading historicals again?"

"Yes. And stop trying to burn a hole in my head with your eyes. There's nothing wrong with liking this guy. You've had shit luck with men. Finding one you're actually excited about is a good thing. Why are you fighting this?"

Heat churns in my chest. "Because he isn't interested in dating," I grit out.

"Then take a ride on that hot body of his and enjoy yourself."

The heat moves from my chest to the back of my neck. "He doesn't that want that from me either."

James gapes at me in confusion. Which doesn't help my bruised and confused ego. "Not possible. I saw the way he looked at you."

"Oh?" *Ignore the flutter. The flutter is a cheap, attention whore.* "And how's that?"

"Like you were the Vince Lombardi Trophy covered in honey."

"I don't even know what that is."

"Super Bowl, Chessie. Best you bone up on your football knowledge now."

Cute. "However he may or may not have looked at me, Finn made it clear he didn't want to hook up. He said he just wants to, and I quote, 'know me.'"

"Huh." James taps his fingers on the counter for an annoying few beats. "Well, maybe it's best not to overthink things. You like him, that's clear. Just go with it."

"Go with it." How helpful.

"You never know what can happen."

I'm rolling my eyes when someone knocks on the front door.

James snaps to attention. "Ah, speaking of that…" He fiddles with his polka dot bowtie. "I've…er…met someone."

"I presume this someone is at the door?" I ask, bemused. James has never really introduced me to anyone. Not in a formal way. I've gone out on double dates with him, but those were casual, and I rarely ever saw his date again.

"Yes." James flushes. "I was going to tell you, but got caught up in your 'dare I do the quarterback' drama."

I shoot him a quelling look. "Are you going to get that? Or do you want me to?"

"No, no. I'll get it." He hustles over to the door as if he's about to jump out of his skin.

Which means it's serious. Suddenly, I feel as unsettled as James looks.

I quickly tap out a text to Finn because I don't want to be rude to James's guest.

CC: James is here. I have to go. Talk later?

Why did I feel the need to ask?

He answers quickly.

GQ: Nxt Tuesday is my day off. You available for lunch? Lemme know when U get a chance.

I don't answer. James leading his new love into the loft, while giving me a soppy smile. And he called me besotted? The man is practically floating along.

I had expected him to introduce me to a model, either male or female. Tall and stunning is James's preference. But that's not the case here.

"This is Jamie," James says, holding his arm around a short, slender man with a halo of blonde curls and wearing heavy, black framed glasses. "Jamie, met Chess."

"Chess." Jamie leans in to offer me a hand, and from beneath a cute blue argyle sweater vest, I see the soft swell of breasts. "I've heard so much about you."

Since James has been closed-mouth as shit, I can't say the same. So I simply shake her hand, but I lose hold on my smile. "James and Jamie, eh?"

James actually flushes. "I know. It's awful, isn't it? We'll be one of those couples who dresses alike and finishes each other's sentences." He looks completely happy about that prospect.

"You're halfway there already," I point out, eyeing James's brown argyle sweater vest.

Jamie laughs. "And we didn't even plan it."

"I'm feeling very Bert and Ernie right now," James says, running a hand down his chest.

Jamie laughs again. "If we want to be really obnoxious, we could get a dog and name it Jimmy." Her nose wrinkles. "Never mind. I forgot. I once dated a girl who had a dog named Jim."

"I always wanted to meet a boy named Sue," James musses.

Jamie smiles up at him. "We could name the dog Sue."

"Okay," I cut in, "you guys *are* annoying."

They both grin wide.

"I brought beignets." Jamie holds up a big bag from Cafe du Monde, the bottom of it spotted with grease stains. And I swear my mouth waters. "James says they're your favorite."

Definitely serious if kissing up to the best friend is involved.

God. I'm jealous. I'm actually jealous.

Snap out of it, you shrew!

The woman is wearing a sweater vest and a blue bow tie, for Pete's sake. How can I not find this endearing?

"I love them. Thanks." I take the bag from her and get us some plates. "Let's eat on the balcony."

And so, on the balcony, I listen to James and Jamie finish each other's sentences as they tell me how they met at a jazz club. I laugh along when they tease each other about how they fought over whether Duke Ellington or Ella Fitzgerald was better—neither, by the way; they're two sides of the same coin. And I stuff two beignets down my throat to keep from butting in with my own James stories. Because Jamie doesn't need to hear that right now.

They're so cute together it makes my jaw ache and my heart contract.

James is in love. I never thought I'd see the day.

He brushes a nonexistent crumb off Jamie's chin, as she states that she should get going. "I know you have a shoot to do."

"You can stay and watch," James offers, his voice so gentle, I almost don't recognize it.

"Oh, no," Jamie says with a laugh. "I don't think I can watch you oil up a bunch of big bruisers and not get jealous. Besides, there's an art gallery around the corner from my place that I've been wanting to visit."

"Do you live in the Quarter?" I ask her.

"I live in New York," Jamie says, sharing a quick look with James. "I'm just here for a week."

A week? They fell for each other in less than a week?

James picks at a seam in his trousers. "She's going back next Monday."

"I keep telling him he should come with me to get a taste of New York life," Jamie teases faintly.

"And I keep telling *you* I have to work," James shoots back with false playfulness. There's pain in his voice, and he can't hide it.

An awkward silence descends. My mouth is filled with puffed dough, a coating of powdered sugar turning to paste against my tongue. James is my best friend. But I am also his boss. At times, the gulf between friend and boss feels as vast as the distance from here to New York.

I swallow down my bite with difficulty. "We only have one more shoot for the calendar after today. I can do the smaller jobs on my own. You should go visit. Take some time for yourself."

James's pale blue eyes meet mine. And it feels like a hug. I smile back weakly. Was he worried I'd say no? I'd never deny him his happiness.

But while James sees Jamie off, I stare out over the balcony rail, watching cars pass by and, in the distance, the Mississippi rolls along like a wide, brown snake against the land. I feel empty.

Pulling my phone from my jeans pocket, I text Finn.

I'm good for Tuesday.

He answers a few seconds later, as if he's been waiting.

GQ: It's a non-date. ;-)

I still don't know what I want from him, but I can't deny that the sight of that silly winky emoticon makes me feel a little warmer inside.

CHAPTER 5
♟ CHESS

I quickly find out that Finn loves seafood. As in, he'll happily drive to an out of the way roadside restaurant to get his fix. He takes me to Middendorf's, overlooking the lake, for what he promises will be a feast.

We sit on the patio, and soft breezes coming off the water stir my hair. It's one of those perfect Louisiana fall days when the temperature is in the low 70s and the sun is shining brightly. I relax with a sigh of contentment.

Finn, on the other hand, is practically twitching with the anticipatory promise of food. "Their thin fried catfish is why we're here." He eyeballs me. "You do like catfish?"

"Can't comment one way or the other on it," I tell him. "I don't remember the last time I had any."

"Well, you're in for a treat." He rubs his hands together like a little boy. "Do you want a white wine?"

"Please don't tell me you're one of those guys who thinks everyone who has a vagina must drink white wine." It's fun to tease him. He never gives in.

"It's a pussy, Chess. Save vagina for your OB." He flashes a quick smile. "And, no. Just so happens that every *pussy* I've taken out orders white wine. Or a club soda with lime." He frowns, perplexed. "What's with the club soda thing, anyway?"

"I have no idea." I look over the menu. "I'm getting a beer."

"Excellent." His glee over our impending meal is contagious.

The waitress shows at that moment and practically trips over herself when she sees him. I don't blame her; a happy Finn is almost too pretty to take in at once. You have to brace yourself and look at him in stages.

Oblivious of our covetous stares, Finn orders the beers and catfish. "Oh, and some oysters and crawfish. Could you bring it all at once, please?"

"I hate oysters and crawfish," I tell him, as our waitress leaves.

He gasps and sags in his seat as if weakened. "Sacrilege, Chester."

"Fried oysters are fine," I say with a light shrug. "But raw? Nope. Salty snot pellets."

Finn glances up at the sky. "Lord, she knows not of what she speaks."

"And crawfish tastes muddy to me."

"A good muddy," he counters.

"There is no such thing as good mud."

"Girl on girl mud wrestling." His expression dares me to argue.

"Guy on guy mud wrestling," I amend.

He salutes me. "Fair enough."

The waitress soon returns and sets down two icy bottles of beer and our food. The rich scent of fried seafood rises up, and my mouth actually waters. I take a bite of paper-thin, golden catfish and moan.

"Right?" Finn says with an approving nod.

Crispy and light, it is fried-food mana. "I'm in love," I tell him.

The corners of his eyes crinkle, and we sit there eyeing each other like happy thieves. "You know what's weird," I say in a low voice, as if, by whispering, I'll make the moment last longer.

Maybe he feels the same because he answers just as softly. "What?"

"I'm having more fun on this non-date date than I've had on all dates this past year." Maybe longer.

Finn's gaze warms. "Me too."

Somewhere around the region of my heart, everything gets all tender. I feel like I'm falling, lightheaded and confused. My fingers curl around the edges of the table just to hold on.

Finn clears his throat and takes a large bite of his fish. "So," he says around a mouthful. "Dating sucks for you?"

"You saw the horror of the last one."

"Yeah, that was painful." Snickering, he bites into a fry. "How is Edward, by the way?"

"His name isn't Edward. It's…" Fucking hell.

He grins.

"Evan," I announce with a near shout as I remember. "His name is Evan. And I haven't talked to him since. Thank God. He told me he lived for skin."

"That's kind of creepy, Chess."

"I thought so too." I take a bite of fish, then swallow it down with cold beer. Heaven. "Sad thing is that wasn't even my worst date."

Finn grabs the Tabasco and dashes some on an oyster. "All right then. Give me your worst."

"Only if you tell me yours."

"I don't have dates. Only hookups."

"The lazy man's date." I munch on another bite.

"True," he says with a laugh. "But if you want to hear about them, I'll tell you."

"We're really going to do this?" I ask. "Go full girlfriend mode?"

Finn shrugs lightly. "Hey, if Kevin Costner can paint a woman's toes in Bull Durham, then you and I can gossip like girlfriends."

I try not to picture Finn painting my toes. I bet he'd be thorough.

"Worst date I've been on…" I close my eyes and lift my face to the warm sunlight before looking back at Finn. "It started out fine. Guy was attractive, witty—"

Finn makes a dubious noise. I ignore it.

"The conversation was flowing, but he kept looking over at the bar. Finally, I glance that way and notice a woman watching us."

"He was checking out another woman while on a date with you?" Finn snorts and shakes his head. "Fucking douche move."

"Yeah, if only." I can laugh about it. Now. "I assumed the same. But dude is horrified at the assumption. No, no, he tells me. It's totally okay. The woman is his wife."

"What, like his ex?"

"No, his wife. They liked to watch each other be with other people. And was I into the idea of coming back to their house and letting her watch us have sex? Because I looked like the type who would be."

I smile at Finn's shocked expression.

"Well that's…" He huffs out a laugh. "Fucked."

I shrug and sip my beer. "It's not my kink, but whatever floats their boat. I'd have appreciated a little upfront honesty, though."

"You're not really selling this whole dating thing, Chess."

"I haven't even mentioned the guy who came back to my place, locked himself in my bathroom for an hour and tried to have a conversation with me through the bathroom door while he was…indisposed."

"Are you sure he wasn't one of my teammates?" he asks, snickering.

"You're not really selling hooking up with football players."

"Not if they play defense," he says blandly, but then winks. "Those guys are freaky."

"I'll make sure to tell them you said that." I eat a fry. "Okay, your turn."

Finn sits back, and the sunlight caresses his skin, making the angle of his jaw both sharper and warmer. And I find myself wanting to paint him, capture the way he dominates the space around him without even trying. His presence is immense and effortless. Compelling.

I haven't painted since college, but my fingers remember the feel of the brush. A picture is taken in one click and then it's over. To paint someone is to linger over them, live in their skin for a while. I miss that intimacy.

My distraction ends when he finally speaks. "Let's see. Two stick out in my mind. There was the time I got up to use the bathroom—"

"Oh, my God, please tell me you didn't get all Chatty Kathy with your date while in there."

He rolls his eyes. "Yes, that exactly what I was going to say. How did you guess?"

"Right. Sorry. Go on."

"I thought my…er…date was out for the count, so I didn't bother fully closing the door."

I eye him warily, having no idea where this is going.

"So there I am, taking a piss, when this hand, holding a phone pushes past the crack of the door—"

"No!" I lean in with a gasp.

Finn nods. "Yeah, she was trying to take a picture of me."

"Peeing?" I plunk back in my seat. "What the hell?"

Finn smiles, but it doesn't reach his eyes. "That's what I said. She claimed she was just curious, and that she wasn't going to show anyone."

"What a freak."

"Total freak. But that's not the worst one."

"I'm almost afraid."

Finn takes a long drink of his beer as if to brace himself. "There was the chick who started crying during sex."

"Because you were so bad?" I tease, with mock horror.

"I left myself wide open for that, didn't I? But, no, chuckles. I'd barely gotten started when she starts sobbing, like full out snot-fest, chest heaves." His lips twist. "I was fucking horrified. Was I hurting her? Was she traumatized?" Slowly, he shakes his head. "Between sobs, she says she just couldn't believe Finn Mannus was fucking her. That she had 'Finn Mannus's dick in her.' And, maybe, could we film it?"

I'm gaping. I don't know what to say. He's fidgeting with the edge of his napkin and giving me a pained smile as if he wants to make a joke out of this, laugh it off, but can't summon the energy. And why should he? I get that hookups aren't going to be the most meaningful encounters. But those women were using him. Blatantly.

"Hey," he says in a low voice. "I didn't tell you those stories to get you to feel sorry for me. They're supposed to be funny."

I swallow hard. "Do you find them funny?"

He winces, lifting one, big shoulder. "When I told the guys, yeah. We laughed our asses off. But when you look at me with those big, pained eyes? It feels…shitty."

With a breath, I shake myself out of it and rest my arms on the table. "You're not allowed to feel shitty."

"I'm not, huh?" The easy expression is back, his stiffness fading.

"I forbid it. They are the ones who should feel shitty. I want to hunt them down and slap some sense into them."

"You're kind of scary when you're pissed." His gaze slides over me in a slow stroke. "Scary hot."

"I didn't realize there was such a thing."

"Oh, yeah there is." His expression is sin and promise. "Wonder Woman is scary hot. She can kick your ass, tie you up, and make you spill the truth. You know, beg for it."

He says it with such zeal, my breasts grow heavy with the image of him tied to a chair, those firm muscles of his straining against the ropes. I suck in a breath, let it out nice and slow. "You're into begging?"

"I'm into hot women who know their minds." He gives me a cheeky grin. "And Wonder Woman. I'm definitely into her."

"I used to have this fantasy that Spider Man wrapped me in his web and had his way with me," I confess in a stage whisper.

Finn looks delighted, which makes me feel better. I didn't like seeing the happy light in his eyes dim or that I'd made him feel shitty. We're probably flirting too much for supposed friends. But if feels light, fun. I am the first to admit I can be too serious.

"Saucy, Chess." He leans close so we're facing each other over the table. "So is it just the dates that suck? Or the sex too?"

The fact that he has to ask puts us on totally separate planes. I don't have sex with crappy dates. He clearly does. I give a little laugh and shake my head. "It's been so long since I've had good sex, I swear I heard the mournful sound of 'Taps' coming from the vicinity of my vagina last night."

He chokes on his beer, spewing a fine mist over the table. Coughing on the remnants, he wipes his mouth and then the mess, before glaring. "I can't believe you said that to me."

I sip my own beer, hiding a smile. "Did my use of vagina offend you?"

"Yes," he deadpans, then rolls his eyes. "I'm a guy. Now, I want to fix the problem."

The heat in his eyes has me squirming in my seat. Not that I show it. "We're friends. You can't fix it."

Finn's expression could only be described as a leer. "Oh, I could fix it, all right."

I grin wide, pretend that my heart isn't beating harder, that my nipples aren't perking up with interest. "But you won't because that would ruin this fragile and new friendship."

He snorts, then takes a long drink of his beer. "So don't tempt me."

Is that what I'm doing? Maybe I am. Maybe I need my head examined. Any time I get within sight of him everything grows warm and slow, swollen and tender. Except my heart and my breath, those quicken with impatience and greed. How would it be to fuck him? Would it be as combustible as my body believes? Would he wreck me for all others?

For one heady moment, I entertain the thought of giving in, of telling him, "Fix me. Until it hurts to walk." But what if sleeping with him falls flat in the face of expectation?

And there is the unavoidable fact that he has flatly stated he doesn't want to hookup with me. Despite his easy flirting, I know he was being honest. And, really, I don't want a hookup either. So I'll treat him just as I treat James.

Under the table, I nudge his knee with mine. "Come on. You don't talk about sex with your friends?"

He gives me the stink eye, but he's clearly fighting a smile too. "In general, guys never admit that their dicks are singing sad songs. Kind of messes with the rep."

"Heaven forbid."

"Seriously, though," he says. "I'm having a hard time believing you don't have guys lined up waiting for a chance with you."

Warmth blooms in my chest. "Well, aren't you the sweet talker."

"I'm stating a simple fact." His brows draw together. "You didn't have a bad experience, did you?"

"Why do men always assume the worst?"

"You're getting it wrong. Men assume to every problem there is a solution. So state your problem, and I'll find a solution."

The tilt of his chin is so imperious, I want to laugh. But the earnest concern in his eyes is kind of cute. With a sigh, I tell him the truth. "Sex for me is complicated."

"You confused about what goes where, darlin'?"

"That was payback, wasn't it?"

"A little bit." He grows serious. "Why is sex complicated?"

I draw a fry through a puddle of ketchup. "I have a problem with latex."

"A problem?"

"It gives me a rash." I glance down at my lap with meaning.

A look of sympathetic horror washes over his face. "Oh, shit." He shifts around in his seat. "Yeah, say no more. Please."

My lips quirk. "It started a year out of college. Suddenly, it was like my body was turning against me having casual sex." It turned against me in more ways than that, but he doesn't need to hear everything.

"Killed the free love, eh?" Finn steals one of my fries and eats it. "There are non-latex condoms, you know. Some of those ultra thin, barely there brands? They feel great…" He trails off with a slight flush. "The point is, options are available."

I snort on a laugh. "Yeah, I know. But it became a kind of mental thing. I'd see dude rolling on a condom, and my lady bits would seize up in remembered horror."

He winces, and I nod.

"I knew those condoms wouldn't irritate me, but my lady bird was all, nope. That's a no fly zone."

Finn snickers, but his gaze travels over me with thoughtful appraisal. "So that's it for sex? God, please don't tell me that."

"No, but it's become…"

"Complicated," he finishes for me.

"I can protect myself from getting pregnant. And I do. But now I have to trust the guy when he says he's clean. He has to trust me when I say I am too. It's just not a good casual sex situation."

Finn nods in sympathy.

"Stop looking at me like that," I say. "I still have sex. Just not casual hookups. Which is a good thing, since I actually want to get to know the guy before having sex with him. I *want* a relationship."

"I hear you." But he still stares.

"I'm not a pity case."

"Didn't think you were."

"I'm going to ping you with a fry if you don't get that look off your face."

Finn's lips curl, but his gaze turns calculating. "You know I'm clean—"

"No."

"Consider it a friend helping out a friend service—"

"No," I say with more emphasis.

He grins. "Worth a shot."

"I think we should refrain from talking about sex from here on out." In truth, I have no interest in hearing about his hookups.

Finn lets out an expansive sigh. "Thank God for small mercies. I'll keep thinking about your mournful pussy and want to comfort it."

He looks so disgruntled that I roll my eyes and chuck a piece of fish at him.

Finn catches it midair, pops it into his mouth, and munches away without remorse. "Hey, Chess?"

He steals another fry off my plate.

"Yes, thief?"

"We're hanging out again."

The urge to giggle like a smitten schoolgirl is so strong, I have to bite my lip. What the hell? I'm a badass woman. A rock in the face of hot quarterbacks with cheeky smiles.

And yet here I am, flushing with happy pleasure and grinning wide. "Yeah, we are."

Lord help me, I'm in trouble.

"These shots are gorgeous, Chess."

"Thanks. I'm happy with how they're turning out." I'm on the phone with Dani, the graphic artist who is laying out the charity calendar, and Meghan, who is in charge of publicity for Finn's team.

Currently, we're going through a set of photos that include Ethan Dexter, Rolondo Smith, Jake Ryder, and Finn. My first shoot, and the group of men who Meghan seems to be most interested in featuring.

"These *guys* are gorgeous," she says now with little, breathless laugh. "We really should have a shot featuring Manny flanked by his offensive line."

I stare at the image on the massive screen I use when editing photos. Finn stares back at me. It's a fairly tight shot, from the waist up. He's caught in a laugh, his smile self-deprecating and wry. There's a light in his eyes, a charisma and confidence that draws you in and makes you want to get closer just to bask in his perpetual energy.

It's been days since I've seen him. Enough time that I'd almost convinced myself our lunch by the lake had been a one off. A nice memory for me to pull out every once in a while and think about fondly. Except he keeps sending me texts at random times—quick inquiries about my day or cute anecdotes about his.

I've come to live for those texts, each one of them sending small zings of happiness through me. Looking at his smiling face now, I find myself missing him. Which is ridiculous. I barely know Finn Mannus.

I want to know you.

My fingers curl into a fist so I won't touch the screen. What had Meghan been saying? Finn and his linemen. Right. "We can schedule a group photo session if you like. Might make for a nice cover."

"I was thinking of having the option to choose your favorite player for the cover," Dani says.

While Megan and Dani go over the costs involved for having various options, I tap my trackpad and move on to a shot of Ethan Dexter, so I don't have to keep staring at Finn's smiling face.

The image of Dex is a good one. Set against a red background, he's crouched down, fingertips braced on the floor, as if he's about to rise up and sprint. Every muscle on his big, impressive frame is tensed and corded.

It's enough to stop the conversation between Meghan and Dani.

"Look at those tats," Dani says with appreciation. "They really pop here. I love that you went for color instead of black and white with these, Chess."

I study Dex with detached focus, looking for flaws in the overall image. "Seemed the right choice. Black and white softens things too much. These guys should be shown in living color, bruises and all."

"He'd make a good Mr. December with all that red," Meghan puts in.

"I thought so too," I say.

"We want to send a couple of shots to the press," Meghan goes on. "Whet the public's appetite and drum up some excitement."

"The Dex shot would definitely work."

"Agreed. Love the quiet intensity of him. What else to do you have?"

I click again, and a collective sigh runs over the phone line. As for me, it's as if a wave of heat has slapped into me. Because it's *the* shot: Finn, his hard, golden body stretched out in a plank position, his expression serene yet intense, almost as if he's on the verge of coming.

I swallow with difficulty, trying to pull in a breath.

"Wow," Meghan says. "If this got out, I think we'd have a riot on our hands."

"Yeah." Dani sounds queer, as if she's struggling to maintain a steady voice. "Given that he's all…" She clears her throat.

When I'd taken the shot of Finn, I'd been transfixed by his face, the expression on it. But Dani's comment has my attention sliding down.

Violent heat suffuses my cheeks. The photo is unedited; I haven't had time to crop out certain things. It doesn't take a genius to know Dani is staring at Finn's cock, hanging low, the wide tip just touching the floor.

"Ah…" Meghan, huffs out a sound. "Is he… Um?"

The heat in me churns, pushing at my skin and clogging my throat. Finn's cock isn't hanging limp but is at half-mast, thick and curving a bit as if it's about to get a whole lot thicker. God, I hadn't even noticed at the time. And now? I am painfully aware that two other women are looking at it; violating Finn's privacy.

"He's getting there," Dani whispers.

The heat in me boils over into something vengeful and dark that feels like possession but is stronger. It crashes over me, followed by a punch of recrimination and shame. I put this picture up without checking. I let them see this. Instantly, I shift the image toward his torso, zooming in on it so that his lower half is out of view.

Somehow, I find my voice, but it sounds halting to my ears. "It happens sometimes when the guys don't have clothes on." I don't know if I'm defending Finn or myself. Neither of us has any reason to be ashamed, but I don't want these women assuming the worst. I push on before they can answer, as if the subject of Finn and his dick is nothing more than a blip. "We'd do something more like this."

"Too bad," Dani murmurs, but then says in a stronger, more professional tone, "I think we should at least bring it down to his hips. Although I'm happy to Photoshop it, if you want to go lower, Meghan."

No fucking way. You don't get him.

"I edit my own work," I say, tightly. "You can crop the picture however you think best after that."

Fuck. I don't even want her manipulating Finn's image. I don't want anyone looking at it again.

"Okay, sure," she says, clearly trying to bring things back to the light and easy level we'd been on before.

I need to get a hold of myself.

On my second monitor, I pick out a shot of Rolondo laughing as he holds a football over his crotch. I move the image over so that it shows up in our chat room. "This is a good one for publicity," I offer. "Rolondo's smile is infectious, and he's playing really well right now."

Thank you, James, for your constant football prattle.

"Love it," Meghan says. "But back to Manny's shot. Maybe we should lead with that one."

I'm not bringing it back on screen. No one else is seeing the unedited version again. I shake off the possessive feeling that's clinging to my neck.

"It's up to you, obviously, but I think it'd work much better as a surprise. Everyone is going to want to see Mannus. He's your star quarterback and team leader. Keep him under wraps and you feed the need."

Part of me is internally laughing at all the bullshit I'm spewing, and wondering if they'll see right through me. The other part hates that I'm even in a conversation that revolves around how to best use Finn's fame.

But Megan makes an agreeable noise over the phone. "I like it. Let's go with Dex and Rolondo for now."

"I can send them over in about an hour," I promise. "I'm just going to touch up a few shadows." Shadows being a set of balls, but she doesn't need to hear that.

"Great. I'll plan to get them out with a press release today."

Thankfully, the call finishes fairly quickly. As soon as I hang up, I let out a breath and hold my head in my hands. What the fuck is wrong with me? I just hissed and swiped over Finn like some territorial she-beast. I have the horrible suspicion that, if I had been in the room with Dani and Meghan at the time, I'd have bared my teeth at them.

Total she-beast.

Finn isn't mine, and he can take care of himself. Then again, he didn't want to be seen as some piece of man-meat. You were right to protect him.

Running my fingers through my hair, I flip the heavy mass back over my shoulder and take a long, cleansing breath. I have work to do. Thinking about Finn Mannus isn't part of that job. The sooner I remember that, the better off I'll be.

The thought barely settles when my phone digs, and my stupid heart gives a happy leap. It's embarrassing how fast I grab for the phone. Maybe even more so when my grin wavers, as I see that it isn't Finn but James.

JamesTTwerk: You almost done for the day?

CC: Just finishing up

JamesTTwerk: Cool. You want me to pick you up on Friday?

It takes me a second to remember what the hell he's talking about. When I do, I sigh. James is back from New York, and we're supposed to go to our friend Malcolm's annual "Cocks and Cocktails" party. I slump against my chair. Same people, same conversations. Why that has suddenly lost its appeal, I can't say, but just the thought of going exhausts me.

I'm tempted to tell James I don't want to go, but I know he'll just nag and cajole me to go anyway. And I clearly need to get out of this loft and out of my own head for a while.

CHAPTER 6
FINN

Things some people might not know about my job. I am a chess player. You might think I'm just standing there in the huddle, or on the line of scrimmage, shouting out instructions passed down to me by the coach. In reality, it's more than that. I'm reading the defense, arranging my guys like pieces on a board, reacting and plotting. And I'm given about five seconds to do it.

I am a cheerleader. I don't have pom-poms, and while my ass is admittedly cute, I don't shake it—much. But I am absolutely cheering my guys on. Pride is a powerful motivator. So is loyalty. I create both when I tell them how fucking brilliant they are on good plays, for them to keep pushing, never let up.

I am a leader. They look to me to set the tone, to take the game in hand. Even if some of them will never admit it.

And I am an actor. If I fold, if I show fear, it's game over for my men. There isn't a play in which I'm not faking the defense out, putting up a good front, and playing mind games.

On the field, it's mind, body, and sprit working in perfect harmony.

As I said, best job in the world.

And then we have the other days of the week.

I suppress a sigh and flip through the massive binder on my lap. In the armchair next to me, is my backup QB, Dillon. Wooster, the third string quarterback, is sprawled on the couch. Not sure why that fucker gets to lie down. But house rules regarding seating has always been first come first serve. Somehow Wooster always gets to the couch first.

Altman, our offensive coordinator is droning on, explaining the new play calls that I can read for myself if he'd end this meeting and let me. One hundred and thirty new play calls, to be exact.

Did I mention I'm also a student? Every week, I study, learn, memorize. Playbooks are my life. I read over them at night, during breakfast, whenever I get the chance. But right now?

I want out.

My head isn't in it. It's past five on a Friday, I'm fucking tired, and we've have been here for hours, reviewing footage and now the playbook.

Fingers snap, the sound catching my attention. Altman's cold blue eyes bore into me. He's about fifteen years older than I am, once a backup quarterback who got traded around toward the end of his career. It's the thing we fear most, being tossed aside, scrambling to find work, and finally realizing no one will pick you up.

But Altman made the most of it. He's an excellent offensive coordinator and will probably be a coach one day.

"You got something to share with the class, Manny?" he asks now.

This is my second year working with him. I can read him well and know he isn't pissed. Yet.

I give him an easy smile. "Yeah, I've gotta use the can."

"Can't hold it in, Manny?" Dillon teases.

"Heard it's bad for the prostate," I say blandly.

Wooster snorts. "Wouldn't want Manny to lose his shit on the field, now would we?"

That's exactly what he'd love. But, despite what people might think, we're not exactly enemies either.

Even so, I give him the finger. "Spin on this a bit, *Rooster*."

Altman snorts. "Dick around on your own time, kids."

But he lets us go. Thank fuck.

As soon as we're out in the hall, Dillon is on the phone, making no effort to keep his voice down. "Hey, baby," he croons. "Just got out. Yeah. Yeah." He nods along to whatever his wife is saying.

I know it's his wife because he always calls her after meetings, and he always calls her baby.

I walk a little ahead of him, trying to get out of earshot but maintenance is buffing the floors and it's slow going.

"She sleeping yet?" Dillon asks his wife. There's a pause, and then the man truly croons. "Baby girl. That's right, it's Daddy." The sound of a babyish squawk comes from the vicinity of the phone, and he chuckles.

I move around an equipment hamper, but get caught up at the door to the gym. Dillon ends the call with his wife, promising to be home soon. The look on his face is so contented and softly joyful, it feels like I'm invading his privacy.

But he catches my eye and grins wider. "Vera's starting to stand up now."

Vera. Right. I knew that. "She's about a year?"

"Ten months." He pulls a photo up on his phone and shows me.

Dillon's wife is blonde and beautiful in a homecoming queen sort of way. Their daughter is a perfect blend of them, her hair a riot of tight brass-colored ringlets, her skin light brown and dewy with youth. Bright hazel eyes shine as she smiles at the camera, displaying two front teeth.

It almost hurts to look at her, she's so cute and happy. "She's beautiful, man."

"I know this," Dillon says proudly. He gives me a friendly clasp on the shoulder. "Best thing in life, man, having a family. No matter what shit these guys tell you."

The family men are always trying to convert us poor, soulless singles. Jake claims it's so they feel better about being trapped. I used to agree. Now, I'm not so sure.

Dillon heads out, and I'm left rubbing the tightness along my chest. The place is fairly deserted right now, most of the guys having long since gone home. I turn the corner and enter the gym on the way to the locker room. The familiar scent of metal, rubber, and lingering sweat soothes a little.

Rolondo is working the leg press, his muscles straining as he huffs and pushes his legs out straight.

"You should be working with a spotter," I tell him. "At least if you're going for the free weights."

"Yeah, yeah." The weights clank as he lowers them too fast. He grabs a towel and wipes the sweat from his face. "What you doin' here, Manny? Everyone else has scattered like roaches to the light."

I laugh. "I could ask the same of you."

He rises with a groan and then stretches. "Lost track of time."

Wooster walks in, wearing the smarmy expression that he never truly seems to drop. "You guys hear about Dex?"

"I heard." Rolondo shoots him an annoyed look.

"I haven't." Concern makes my words sharp. "What's going on? Is he all right?"

"He's fine," Rolondo says. "It's nothing but some nonsense bullshit."

Wooster ignores Rolondo. "PR released a few photos of that beefcake calendar you all are in."

Beefcake? I feel an eye roll coming on. But it's news to me that PR sent out photos. I'm guessing I'm not in them or I would have heard. I think about Chess looking over the shots we took and feel exposed all over again. Shaking the sensation off, I wave my hand at Wooster to continue.

"Press was all over Dex's photo." He glances at Rolondo with a glint in his eyes. "Guess they found it the most interesting."

Rolondo makes a lazy jerk off gesture.

But Wooster goes on. "Dex's old college rival gave an interview, claiming that Dex is a virgin. Next thing you know, some crazy ass dating service got wind of the story and is offering a bounty of his virginity."

For a second, I can only stare, my mind spinning. "What the hell?" Seriously, what the hell?

"How did I miss this?" I ask no one in particular.

"Too busy searching for your own press?" Wooster throws out.

I glance at Rolondo. "He okay?"

"He's *fine*. Like I said…" He gives Wooster another nasty look. "…It's just some dumb bullshit."

I doubt Dex is as okay as Rolondo claims. Dex covets his privacy like a miser hoards gold. Not that I blame him; none of us exactly relish our private life being exposed. I make a note to call Dex as soon as I'm alone.

"I heard the photographer is a woman," Wooster says, cutting into my thoughts.

My head snaps up, my gaze narrowing as something hot surges in my gut. "What the fuck does that have to do with anything?"

Rolondo starts shaking his head. "Man," he mutters under his breath.

Wooster, however, clearly sees blood in the water and is just that stupid. "Guess it doesn't. Just heard that she was hot in a *The Fast and the Furious* kind of way."

I take a step in his direction. Blood pounds in my head. "Fast and the Furious?"

"Yeah, you know a low rider hood ornament that you fuck fast and furi—"

My hand is wrapped around his throat before he can finish. I don't remember moving, but I'm not letting go. "You want to keep that tongue," I grit out, "I suggest you shut the fuck up."

Wooster claws at my arm, but he can't get free. But then he relaxes with a smile. "I get it. You're fucking her. Nice, man. Bet she's getting around with a job like that."

Two steps forward, and I'm slamming him into the wall. "You need to shut the fuck up, asshole."

Rolondo steps between us, but he's looking at me. "He's not worth the fines, Manny."

Debatable. But I loosen my grip.

Wooster shakes me off and then smirks. "Can't forget that paycheck, can we?"

Rolondo makes a noise of disdain. "Stop playin' as if a fine won't hurt you more than it does either of us, punk ass. And stop disrespecting women. Didn't your momma teach you better?"

"Pretty sure you'd be singing a different tune if you had any interest in women," Wooster drawls.

Rolondo is gay. He's never hidden it, but until now, I haven't heard anyone give him shit.

"What the fuck did you just say?" I lunge for Wooster again.

Rolondo blocks me, his expression almost serene as he stares down Wooster. "I'd say suck my dick, but I have standards. Now get the fuck out of here and worry about improving your weak-ass game."

Wooster bristles, as if he's about to reply, but his gaze cuts between us, and he backs up. "No fucking sense of humor."

"Oh, yeah, it's our humor that's a fail here." I take a page from Rolondo's book and make a quick jerk off gesture. "We're done."

Without looking back, I head to the free weights. I want to leave, but I'll be damned if I let Wooster chase me away. Rolondo joins me, as Wooster flips us off and stalks out of the room.

"Man…" Rolondo starts.

"I know," I say over him. "I shouldn't let that asshole get to me."

"Good of you to remember. Now."

I stare down at the weights, not moving to pick them up. "He give you shit before?"

Rolondo lets out a half laugh. "You worried about me, Manny?" He sounds amused.

I lift my head. "You're my teammate."

I don't have to say more; Rolondo gets it. But his expression remains passive. "Guys talk smack. Doesn't matter about what. Either you take their shit or you don't." His gaze bores into me with unsettling depth.

"I'd lock down whatever it is you have going on with the photographer. Guys will be talking about her for no other reason than she's taking pictures of them naked."

The truth irks. I resent that she's seen any dick on this team but mine, and I resent that the guys view it as some sort of joke they can snicker over. But there isn't a damn thing I can do about it.

"Chess is my friend." I gesture toward the direction Wooster left. "I don't let people talk shit about my friends."

Rolondo slowly grins. "I see that."

I give a short nod.

"Just one question," Rolondo asks.

"What?"

"Your dick know you're just friends?"

He laughs, as I swipe at him, easy evading the hit. "That the best you got?"

We duck each other's half-hearted swings for a few, both of us needing to shake off the pall Wooster threw over the room.

Laughing, Rolondo reaches for his pack that he'd left by the leg press. "I'm heading out."

Strange how his words seem to highlight how damn quiet the place is. In the far distance, a phone rings then cuts off. I'm not creeped out, but I don't want to linger in a ghost town either.

"What are you doing now?" I ask him.

"My ma's in town."

"No shit?"

"Yeah, I'm taking her to *Commander's Palace* for dinner." He grins. "The woman's been after me to go since she got off the damn plane."

"I know how that goes. My mom was the same. Had to go there and to *Galatoire's*."

Rolondo chuckles. "Went there the other night."

We both laugh. And suddenly, I miss my mother. Which doesn't make a bit of sense, since I'm a grown man, she's been annoying the hell out of me lately, and I've been avoiding her.

Rolondo goes to shower, and I'm left staring at the weights without really seeing them. I don't want to be here. I don't know where the hell I want to be. But one thing is clear.

I pull out my phone.

> **BigManny: Can I interest you in a po'boy?**

Chess answers almost immediately.

> **ChesterCopperpot: Do you actually know any poor boys?**

> **BigManny: Cute. Fine, can I interest you in eating a sandwich with this here rich boy?**

> **ChesterCopperpot: I'm actually at a party right now. Dinner in the form of finger foods and cocktails**

Disappointment swims in my chest. I swallow past that self-pitying lump and man up.

> **BigManny: Another night then. Have fun, party girl**

I head toward the locker room where I've left my keys. I'll grab a po'boy and watch some basketball. Tired as I am, a night lazing on the couch sounds about right.

I'm almost at my car when my phone buzzes.

> **ChesterCopperpot: You should come here. There's plenty of food.**

I halt, staring down at the screen. Chess texts again.

> **ChesterCopperpot: I promise no one will grope you unless you ask.**

I smile at that.

> **BigManny: Will you grope me, Chester?**

> **ChesterCopperpot: No but James would. He's a huge fan. ;-)**

> **BigManny: I'm happy to give him an autograph. But that's as far**

as my call of duty goes.

ChesterCopperpot: Fair warning… If he asks you to sign his ball, run away.

A laugh breaks free, filling up all the empty spaces in my chest. God, I want to see this girl. But I hesitate; a party isn't exactly how I want to spend my time with Chess.

The phone rings in my hand.

"Chester," I say with a smile.

Her husky, sex voice competes with the sound of chatter and music in the background. "So? Are you coming or what?"

"Longing to see me, are you?"

"Yes," she drawls. "I need to reconfirm that your head truly is that big."

I'm grinning wide now, even though she can't see me. "Which head are we talking about?"

"I'm hanging up…"

"All right. I'll behave."

"Sure you will." Someone shouts loud and shrill in the background. Then Chess speaks again. "So?"

"You sure you want me there? I don't want to disrupt your evening."

Chess is silent for a second. She speaks again and sounds stiff, reminding me of the first time we met when she thought I was an asshole. "I don't extend false invites, Finn. But you don't have to come. Honestly, it's okay."

I think about sitting comfortably at home with a sandwich versus sitting next to Chess in a room full of people I don't know. There is no contest. "Give me the address."

After a quick shower and change at home, I head out to meet Chess. The party is at a house in Uptown, near Audubon Park. Light, misty rain is falling by the time I pull up before the double gallery home, every window blazing with light. Louis Armstrong's version of "Don't Get Around Much Anymore" drifts through those windows and, for a second, it's as if I've stepped back in time.

You get that a lot in New Orleans. Old jazz, older houses, cracked pavements, and gnarly oak trees that drip with moss pull you out the modern world and leave you feeling haunted by history. I push past the short wrought iron gate and make my way up to the door.

It occurs to me that I'm nervous, as I ring the doorbell and find my hands clammy. And I have to laugh at myself. I'm grilled by reporters at least once a week and never break a sweat. I've won national championships with a crowd of one hundred thousand people screaming down at me and didn't flinch. Yet here, I'm nervous as a teen on his first date.

A woman wearing a purple 50s style dress opens the door. For a long second, she stares at me.

"Hey," I say, when she doesn't speak.

She blinks and then shakes her head as if coming out of a fog. "Please tell me you're a stripper."

"Stripper?" I repeat, half-amused and a little confused. Behind her, the house is full of people in dresses or suits, and I wonder if I have the wrong address.

"We've never had a stripper at a C&C before," she explains in an excited rush. "But I am totally on board with this development."

C&C?

"I'm looking for Chess Copper."

Purple Dress frowns as if she's never heard of Chess, and I'm about to drop the whole thing and leave when James suddenly appears, all but tumbling into Purple. "Manny," he exclaims with a happy smile. "You're here."

Relief eases my stance. "Hey, James."

He grabs my arm and tries to tug me in. I could have told him I'm too big to be randomly pulled, but I just step inside. Purple Dress makes a disappointed sound. "So, not a stripper?"

"Stripper?" James sounds appalled. "This here is The King. Show some respect."

"He needs a crown then," a woman with poufy hair and wearing a green dress says as we walk past her.

Inside, it's crowded and close with people. The furniture is nineteenth century, with gilded framed portraits hanging on the walls. Cigarette smoke hovers overhead, several people smoking in groups and holding cocktails. And I swear, I feel a moment's trepidation, as if I actually did fall into some freaky time warp.

"Why is everyone dressed like they're auditioning for a Mad Men reunion?" I ask James.

"It's standard attire for Cocks and Cocktails," he says, as we stop at side table set up with a bar. "Want a beer?"

"Sure, but... Cocks and Cocktails?"

James hands me a bottle of beer before fixing himself a gin and tonic. "It's a cocktail party. Only you wear your best vintage duds." He sweeps a hand over his black and white pinstripe suit, topped with a hot pink bowtie. "Point is to be the sharpest dressed cock of the walk, so to speak."

Given that I'm in jeans and a plain, gray long sleeve shirt, I'm grossly underdressed. Since I'm also about a foot taller than everyone here, I stick out like a sore thumb.

"Don't sweat it," James says, clearly reading me well. "When someone looks as good as you, no one gives a damn how the window is dressed."

I eye his suit again. "Somehow I think this will go over your head, but sometimes it's nice to get lost in the crowd."

James smirks, taking a sip of his drink. "Maybe. Then again, if that were true, you wouldn't have someone looking at you the way that particular lady is right now."

I turn toward the direction of his gaze, and there she is. Any response I can give James is gone; I'm at a loss for words. Up until now, I've seen

Chess in jeans and casual tops. This version of Chess is like a present.

She makes her way to me, and my heart knocks against my chest like it's trying to break free. Her usually stern expression is lighter, green eyes smiling. "Trish was babbling about some GQ model looking for me," she says in greeting. "I assumed it was either you, or it was my lucky night."

"It was both," I finally answer, too aware that my voice is thick.

She's wearing a dress, a black velvet bodice that hugs her slim torso and hangs off the curves of her shoulders. The skirt is a white cloud that ends mid-calf.

"You're staring, Finn."

"*Rear Window*," I blurt out, making her blink. "That dress. Grace Kelly wore a dress like that in *Rear Window*."

James laughs. "Holy shit, I can't believe you picked that up."

I take a sip of beer to wet my dry throat. "It's my mother's favorite movie."

I don't add that I might have had a small crush on Grace Kelly when I was a preteen.

A soft flush of pink colors Chess's cheeks. "Most people haven't figured it out. They expect the ice blonde hair too."

Her ink black hair is swept up in one of those twisty buns pinned to the back of her head that exposes the long line of her neck. She is fucking beautiful, and I tell her so.

The pink in her cheek deepens, but she shrugs off my compliment. "You find the place all right?"

She seems flustered, her gaze darting around to the people staring at us. At me. The attention prickles on the back of my neck. I ignore everyone but her.

"Yep." I dip my head, and the light scent of her perfume tickles my nose. "I could have dressed up too, you know."

Her cherry red lips pinch. "I'm sorry, I didn't even think about it when we were texting."

I can't resist teasing her. "Hmm... And here I thought maybe you were afraid I'd back off once I heard, 'Cocks and Cocktails'."

The corner of her mouth quirks. "Well, maybe not the cocktails part."

"It's okay, Chester." The urge to touch the soft curve of her cheek has me gripping my beer. "Thanks for inviting me."

Chess fiddles with the strand of pearls around her neck. "Come on. I'll introduce you to Malcolm, our host. He's an antiques dealer."

"That explains the decor. I thought I'd fallen into the nineteenth century."

Her eyes gleam. "Wait 'til you meet him. The man talks as though he lived here five decades ago, when I know he grew up in Cleveland."

Malcolm turns out to be a middle-aged man sporting a thin, black mustache. He's wearing a white suit with a black bowtie, and tells me he's going for a Clark Gable *Gone with the Wind* look, but the image that comes to mind is Colonel Sanders. I keep that to myself as I shake his hand.

"You look familiar, Mr. Mannus," he says, peering at my face. "Are you a model, perchance?"

The Colonel image gets stronger, and I have the sudden urge to eat fried chicken. "No, sir, I'm a quarterback."

He gives me a blank look. "I could have sworn you were one of Chess's boys."

Chess's boys? I glance at her, and she makes a face. "I don't have boys, Mal."

He waves a hand. "You know what I mean. Your model friends." He stares at me again. "A quarterback, you say?"

James cuts in. "Christ on a cracker. He's a pro football player. And the reason he looks familiar to you is because there is a massive billboard of his smiling face on Canal Street."

I cringe. That freaking ad. I hate driving by it. I see myself in the mirror every time I shave; I don't need a fifty-foot reminder of what I look like haunting me every time I drive around town.

Recognition dawns over Malcolm, and it's clear that billboard has haunted him too. "Football. Ugh." His mustache twitches. "I loathe football. All that grunting and sweating. And no actual sex involved."

"Hits a little too close to home, does it?" a man at his side quips.

"You should know, Robert." Malcolm rolls his eyes then zeroes in on me again. "Please tell me you have other interests, Mr. Mannus."

Chess gives me a quick, worried look. But I don't mind. I'm around sycophants enough as it is, and there's no malice in his tone.

"Oh, sure," I say lightly. "I like baseball and basketball too."

He stares back at me, and I return his look with a bland smile. His lip twitches. "You're cute."

"I try."

Purple Dress joins us. "I thought he was a stripper."

I'm beginning to think this chick has a one-track mind.

"Strippers wear a costume, Trish," Robert says with an exasperated drawl. "If he'd shown up in a football uniform, I'd give you that. Otherwise, it's just wishful thinking on your part."

Trish glares, but then gives a lazy shrug. "I wasn't too far off, though. If he's a football player, then he has been stripping for Chess."

"Jesus, Trish," Chess mutters.

Malcolm and Robert both perk up.

"We're doing a charity calendar," she explains, not at all flustered but clearly annoyed at Trish.

"I saw the photo of that big guy with all the arm ink on the news," Trish says. "Too bad he didn't show up. So freaking hot."

Dex wouldn't have made it through the front door of this place before turning tail and running.

Chess shoots me a hesitant look. "Did you see the photos?"

I take a sip of beer. It's getting warm and flat. "No. But I heard about them."

Why didn't I hear about them from you? It shouldn't bother me that Chess didn't say anything. But it does. It seems like a something a friend would definitely tell a friend.

But you aren't friends, are you? One lunch and a couple of conversations makes you little more than brief acquaintances.

"They came out well, I think." Chess is babbling now. "Meghan wants to use Dexter's photo for December."

"You gonna put a Santa hat on him?" I quip.

Her body jerks, and instantly, I feel like a shit. But she doesn't reply. A woman bumps into her and they start chatting. I'm left to my beer and the curious stares of people circulating the room.

I'm starving. Smoke stings my eyes and fills my mouth. My feet hurt from standing, and I'm starting to feel like an old man because all I want to do is sit down where it's quiet and comfortable. When yet another person bumps into me, giving me a double take, I excuse myself and head to the bathroom.

"Use the one upstairs, darling," a pretty, older woman tells me when I discover the downstairs one is occupied. "Malcolm won't mind."

I find the bathroom with ease, but I don't really need to use it. It had been an excuse to get away.

At the end of the hall, a set of French doors lead out to the upstairs gallery—a wide porch that runs the width of the back of the house. I step outside, closing the door behind me, and draw in a deep breath. Light from two wall sconces illuminate the space. It's quiet here, the sounds of the party dim. I take a seat on a wooden porch swing and let it slowly rock.

I shouldn't be up here. I should find Chess and... Go? Stick it out? I don't know if I'm just feeling off tonight or if I imagined things about her that were never there.

The door opens, and I stiffen. But it's Chess. And it isn't a fluke, the way my pulse kicks up whenever I see her. Because it does it again, and all my senses attune themselves to her as if she's my True North.

"There you are," she says, stepping onto the gallery. "I was wondering if you'd run away screaming."

Almost did.

I stand. "Just getting some fresh air."

"I don't blame you. Sometimes I forget how much people smoke at these things." Chess comes close, and I see that she's holding a plate covered with a napkin. "Makes my throat hurt."

Her skirt rustles and froths as she sits on the swing. I sit next to her.

"Here," she says, handing me the plate. "I brought you some food."

Surprise makes my movements shaky as I take it from her. "You didn't have to do that."

But I am so fucking grateful she did, I'll eat every damn bite, no matter what it is.

"Of course I did," she says, as I lift up the napkin. "I dragged you out here. I'm not going to let you starve." She leans in. "It's a sandwich."

"I see that." Actually, it's several sections of what looks to be a *muffuletta*. I eat one section in two bites. Yep, definitely a *muffuletta*.

A small groan of appreciation escapes me.

Chess smiles. "Oh, wait." She stands, and plunges her hands into the folds of her wide skirt, which obviously has hidden pockets because she pulls out a can of soda and something wrapped in another napkin. "A coke, and a brownie for dessert," she says proudly.

I nearly propose right there.

She sits quietly as I eat, and shakes her head when I offer her a sandwich section. Because I'm hungry, and because I don't like the idea of her having to wait for me to eat, I wolf down my food. The brownie follows with a few, quick bites. I wash it down with the coke.

Wiping my hands on a napkin, I set the plate and empty can on a side table, and then let out a contented sigh. "Thanks. I needed that."

Her smile is small and quick. "I should have fed you as soon as you got here."

"I'm good now."

Chess braces her hands on the seat and leans forward to watch her feet as we slowly rock the swing. Silence descends, thick and awkward, and for the first time in her presence, I'm at a loss for words.

I don't know this girl. Not really, and yet I've inserted myself into her life with a determination I usually reserve for winning games. Except I have no endgame here. I told her I want to be friends. But how does that work for us?

Our friends and lives couldn't be any more different. Parties for me are self-congratulatory events, filled with people whose sole focus seems to be bolstering my ego, followed by me searching for a quick hookup. And my friends are all part of football in some way. We talk football or sports. It's a narrow focus life, but it's my comfort zone. That chafes too, knowing I live a life that seems wild and free to outsiders but is actually small and structured on the inside.

The silence has stretched too long. I should go. But I don't move. If I go, I know it will be the end of whatever this is. Embarrassment will have me avoiding seeking her out again. Likely, she'll do the same. And that will be that.

The knowledge sits like a stone on my chest.

"I'm sorry about my friends," Chess says. "They can be uncomfortably brazen."

"So can mine." I shrug. "Your friends are…fun."

Her lips pull tight. "They can be. But they were definitely giving me—and by extension you— shit tonight." She bites her bottom lip. "I don't think they know what to make of you."

"So I wasn't imagining things."

"'Fraid not."

The novel sensation of being a fish tossed into the wrong pond grows. I've taken away Chess's fun by coming here, and I'm sorry for it.

"I shouldn't have asked you to come here," Chess says in a low voice.

She's only echoing my thoughts but the stone sitting on my chest pushes harder against my ribs.

Chess makes a small sound, as if she's trying to laugh but can't. "Parties suck when you arrive halfway through and don't know anyone."

"I know you," I point out, quietly.

She turns and the porch light illuminates her face. Green eyes met mine and hold, as a slow, true smile curls over her cherry lips. Something inside of me shifts and slides. I want to kiss Chester Copper. Haul her onto my lap and make out with her like we're teenagers hiding at our parents' party. But that's not what she invited me here for.

"I wanted to see you," she confesses in that husky morning voice that goes straight to my cock. She turns away and stares out into the darkness. "It's weird, you know? But hanging out with you was so unexpected it kind of felt like I imagined the whole thing."

I know exactly what she means. My hand settles next to hers, close enough that our pinkies touch. That small point of contact sparks along my skin, makes me want to move closer. I hold steady because I don't trust myself not to act.

"I wanted to see you too," I tell her. "It's been a long, fucking day."

I hadn't planned to admit that, but it feels good to confide in her.

Chess eases back against the seat and then curls her fingers over mine with a light squeeze. The unexpected touch holds all my attention. It's nothing more than a simple offer of comfort, and here I am twitching in my seat as if she'd cupped my dick instead. I'm in so much trouble here because this woman is getting to me in ways I don't know how to navigate. But I don't pull away. Not one fucking chance of that.

Chess speaks, pulling me attention back to our conversation. "So tell me about it."

I can't remember the last time anyone asked me to tell them about my day. Likely, no one ever has.

So I do. And with every word that leaves my mouth, a little bit more of my stress eases. No, I don't yet truly know Chess. And yes, our lives are different. But there's no way I'm ending this. Because when it's just her and me, everything else falls away. I'm not going to let myself forget that again.

CHAPTER 7
♟CHESS

When people say they're busy, they usually mean they have a lot of work that piles up while they spend a few hours watching TV and lamenting how busy they are.

Hell, I've been there, done that, have the couch divot.

When Finn says he's busy, he means it. Workouts, team meetings, practices, games, press conferences, television tapings, sponsor obligations, charity meetings and visits... I can't keep up.

I hear from him in random spurts. Texts between his travels from one obligation to the next. Phone calls when he finally gets home, his voice soft with exhaustion.

Sometimes, I have to order him to get off the phone and go to bed. Because I can practically feel him fading.

"I'd rather fall asleep talking to you," he always responds.

And I won't pretend that it doesn't make me all warm and fuzzy inside. Days pass into weeks. Before I know it, Finn has become a fixture in my life.

One rare free Saturday afternoon, he takes me to the aquarium.

"I've never been here before," I tell him as he collects our tickets.

"Let me guess," he says. "You haven't been to the zoo either."

"I haven't been to a zoo since grade school."

"Where you from, Chess? You've never said."

"Neither have you."

"La Jolla, California," Finn says with pride.

"Wow. Surfer boy, eh?"

"How do you think I developed my awe inspiring balance and sense of timing?"

"That ego of yours inspires something. But I believe it's heartburn."

He slings an arm around my shoulders and gives me a squeeze. "We'll get you an antacid inside. Now tell me where you grew up."

"Brooklyn, New York."

"No shit?"

"Yep. But my dad is from here. He bought my loft as an investment property, but gave it to me after I graduated." It is the one big surprise from my parents that I actually found myself extremely grateful for. Usually their gifts were well meaning, but involved some sort of drama that I'd need to clean up. "I took out some equity on the loft to pay for my camera and equipment, which really helped as well."

"Your parents still in New York?" Finn asks.

"No. I think they're in Oregon right now. Or Idaho. I can't remember. They sold their townhouse and bought one of those tiny houses that you can tow all over the place."

A startled laugh escapes him. "Really? You ever watch that show with the tiny house buyers?"

Cringing, I can't meet his eyes. "Mom and Dad are on an episode."

"Holy shit. Which one?"

"Nope. Not telling."

"I'll just do a search on their last name," he warns.

"Damn it."

Snickering, he gives my shoulder another squeeze before he looks me over. "So, Brooklyn, I'm guessing you know how to handle yourself in a rowdy crowd."

There's something in his tone that has my steps slowing as we reach the main aquarium lobby. "What are you up to, Mannus?"

He hesitates, rubbing the back of his neck. "Nothing much. Just that you'll have a couple of chaperones on this outing."

And by a couple, he means thirty. Ranging from the ages of six to thirteen, the crowd of school children gives a big cheer and cries, "Manny!" when we round the corner.

For his part, Finn gives them all high fives, learning each one of their names. Then he turns, surrounded by kids, the tallest one barely reaching the center of his chest, and beams at me. "Guys, meet my friend Chess. She's never been to the aquarium, so we'll have to make sure she doesn't get lost. Let's give her a big welcome."

Feebly, I wave as all of them shout, "Hi Chess" with various levels of enthusiasm.

Finn winks at me before turning his attention back to the kids. And I grin like a loon because he's adorable with them, like an overgrown kid as excited as they are at the prospect of seeing a shark or maybe petting a stingray.

A blond woman in skinny jeans and a t-shirt with a schoolhouse logo on it comes to stand by me. "I'm Ally, the program director. Thanks for joining us."

"Sure. Although I don't really know what all of this is about."

"We're an after-school sports program for children, sponsored and funded by Mr. Mannus..." She flushes a bit. "Finn, I mean. He keeps telling me to call him Finn. Anyway, this outing is one of many Finn takes the kids on throughout the year."

We chat as Finn leads his crew to find the sharks. But as soon as we stop, I find myself pulled into his orbit. His big hand engulfs mine, as he tells the kids that his favorite shark is the hammerhead. This is met with much approval.

"What's your favorite, Ms. Chess?" a boy, who's probably around eight, asks me.

"Hmm..." I pretend to think about it. "I'm going with the whale shark."

The kid looks unimpressed, but a couple of others pipe up to agree that the whale shark is awesome.

They race on to the next viewing window. Finn and I follow. He hasn't let go of my hand. But I don't mind. His is big and warm, the strength in his fingers tempered now by a gentle clasp. A hand worth around fifty million dollars in the eyes of pro-football. And it's holding on to me as though I'm the valuable one.

"Sorry I didn't warn you," he says at my ear.

Little shivers dance along my skin. I ignore them. "I'm beginning to think you like surprises."

"I do."

"Thanks for letting me be a part of this. You're great with them."

"Kids are easy. Completely unfiltered and ready to have fun. Kind of like football players." He gives my fingers a light squeeze. "So you don't want to run away screaming?"

I'm not certain if he's referring to the kids or football players. Either way, the answer is the same. "Only if you try to get me to touch a stingray."

"Now, Chess, that's basically a dare."

Before I can answer, we're swarmed by the kids, who've realized their hero isn't in their midst anymore. Finn doesn't let me go, and I'm swept up along with him.

By the time we're done, I know more about fish and sea life than I probably need to, and have been infected by a bit of Finn Mannus hero worship myself. How can I not be? When he lifts each kid who asks up for a better view. When he takes the time to shake employee's hands and put them at ease when they get flustered.

Parents show up, and Finn takes a picture with anyone who asks. Each time, he grins wide as if he's standing next to a good friend.

Finn might hate posing for professional cameras. But he clearly loves this part of his life.

He ends the tour by handing out t-shirts with his jersey number on them.

"You didn't give one to your girlfriend," a solemn six-year-old girl points out. "You'll hurt her feelings."

I'm trying to figure out if it's worth it to clarify that I'm not Finn's girlfriend and my feelings won't be hurt, when Finn catches my eye. A teasing smile plays on his lips. "You're right, Maisey. But I'm out of shirts." He takes off his baseball cap with his team logo splashed over the front. "Think she'll be okay with this?"

"If she doesn't want it," an older kid drawls, "I'll take it!"

Finn shakes his head. "You got your shirt, Darrius. My girl here needs something special." He looks over his flock. "Girls like special things."

A bunch of boys gag. But a few girls giggle.

Me? I'm both trying not to blush and restraining myself from rolling my eyes at his antics.

Finn's expression, however, is soft and sincere as he sets the hat on my head, deftly tucking strands of my hair back behind my ears. The cap is too big and sits low on my brow. I probably look like an idiot, but I'm not taking it off.

A little cheer rings out. And, before I can blink, Finn swoops in and gives me a playful peck on the cheek. I feel the warm brush of his lips like a stamp on my skin, pressing there long after he's moved away.

🏈 FINN

Losing sucks. Losing when you're a quarterback sucks sweaty balls. And I don't give a shit what they say; if the offense is crumbling, it's the QB's fault. Fucking fair weather reporters jump all over that: Has Mannus lost his touch? Can he handle the pressure? Is this just an off night or a sign of things to come?

I'm lying on the grass, a three hundred pound slab of lineman sprawled over my hips. My head rings, white lights popping behind my eyes. *Fuck, that hit hurt.* I can't breathe for a second. My entire body has seized with an internal shout of *what the shit?!?*

Davis, the lineman who'd plowed into me like a tank powered by nitro, lifts his head and grins at me as if I'm his new bitch. I want to get to my feet and show him that his effort failed, but my head is still swimming and I can't feel my legs.

"Can I have some fries with that shake next time?" I ask lightly.

His grin dies a swift death, and he jumps to his feet—show off.

I'm not so quick, because I hurt like a motherfucker. "Nice hit, bro," I say, extending my hand out. *Help me up, asshole.* But I smile like it's all good.

Have I mentioned that part of the art of playing football is to mindfuck your opponent? It's actually one of my favorite aspects. I might get knocked down, but you better believe I'm going to take the wind out the motherfucker's sails in retaliation.

Slightly confused, Davis silently helps me up and then shakes his head with a laugh.

I laugh too, ignoring the pain in my ribs—I'm gonna feel that shit tonight—and give him a friendly slap on the shoulder before he jogs off.

Only when my guys surround me do I let my smile fall. "Dex," I say to my center, "I don't know what bug crawled up your ass, but get it together and pay attention."

He's been addled the whole game and completely misread the defense on this last play. Resulting in me being sacked before I could blink. I'm fairly certain the press digging into his personal life is getting to him, but we have a job to do.

Glumly, he nods. "On it."

I slap his helmet. "Good man."

But it's a lost cause. Whatever is going on with Dex spreads like a disease through the line. Soon, everyone is fucking up. Jake and Rolondo both drop passes. North, my tight end, can't gain yards. Moorehouse, my running back goes down with a bad hit, and they haul him into the locker room for evaluation.

As for me, I'm battered like a goddamn piñata. I try to focus, try to rally. I might as well be attempting to hold water in my hands. All the while, Coach and my coordinators are having apoplectic fits. Most of which ring in my ears through the mic in my helmet.

That this is an away game and the crowd is completely loving our defeat doesn't exactly help.

The distinct shout of, "Eat turf, pussy boy Mannus!" somehow makes it through the din of the crowd. Excellent.

It is, as Chess would say, a complete shitcake of a game.

By the time we hobble off the field, defeated and deflated, I am ready to sink into a hot bath and swallow down a mouthful of painkillers. But I'm not going to get to do that. I'm going to get reamed by my coach and then reamed by the press.

I'll have to stand at a podium, lights shinning on my face, and answer insightful questions such as, "Do you think you could have done something better?" Yeah, I could have fucking won. Or, "Do you think you lost because you failed to score during the second half?" Considering this game is won on a points based system, I would say not scoring had something to do with it.

In the dank, echoing hall that leads to the locker room, I turn to Jake, who walks wearily at my side. "Give me a reminder."

Since I ask this question every time we have a shit day, he doesn't miss a beat. "Fifteen million signing bonus."

"I'm going to have to put that aside for new hips when I'm forty."

"When you're thirty-five," he counters easily. "And are we getting solid gold hips?"

I laugh. "I'm going full on cyborg. Try again."

Jake smirks. "Willing women in every city."

"I'm too tired to screw."

Jake shoots me a glance. "Man, you are a sad sack today."

He's right. I'm in full on pity-party of one mode. "I'm depressing myself," I tell him.

"Which is why you need to let off some steam. I'm going out as soon we get back. You want to join me?"

I'm already shaking my head. "I'm going home, taking a bath, and getting some sleep."

"Jesus, you really are an old man now."

Maybe I am. But the prospect of going out and looking for a quick hookup is utterly unappealing. I'd rather call Chess and see if she's up for dinner. And right there is what truly makes me a sad sack.

I don't get to dwell on that any longer. Because we reach the locker room and the reality of my job snaps back into place.

Grimly, I walk through the locker room doors and prepare to defend my performance and my men.

♟ CHESS

I'm mopey. Finn is at an away game, and James is in New York with Jamie again. It's his second visit, and I gather things are getting serious between them.

I've received two texts from James. One selfie of him and Jamie in Central Park by the Bethesda Fountain, the other of them all smooshie-faced in Times Square on the night they went to see Hamilton, the musical—the lucky bastards. A wave of homesickness had hit me, seeing those pictures.

New Orleans is home for me now. But there are days I miss the fast moving rhythm of New York. Sometimes, I'll hear a car horn and close my eyes and think of cabs and cars and trucks all vying for road space. I'll remember the shouts and bangs and rattles as the city pulses around me.

But then I'll sit on my balcony and breathe in the warm air, fragrant with the basil that's growing high, despite the fact that it's fall, and I feel restored.

Doesn't stop me from being lonely.

I have other friends I could call. Girlfriends I haven't seen in a while. But that's not who I really want to see.

Finn has called and texted fairly regularly. But it's not the same. When he's in the city, we can find times to meet up, even if it's for a quick bite to eat. When he's gone…

I feel it.

Today, he sent me a package of gelato. Packed on ice and delivered by courier, there were a dozen flavors to choose from. It's the best gift I've ever received.

A little flip of joy goes through me as I survey my stock of gelato. There's a flavor called *Amarena,* which, upon discovery, turns out to be sweet cream and sour-tart cherries, swirled with glossy crimson ribbons of cherry sauce.

I eat it with a spoon, straight from the carton, slowly savoring it on my tongue. I love gelato, but this stuff? It tastes like sex. I lick the cold metal curve of the spoon and think of cherry cream rivers running down tight abs.

"Jesus," I mutter, flushed and jittery. "I need to get laid."

From out in the hall blasts the almost manic sounds of Miles Davis, played on full volume. My neighbor, Fred, is a jazz lover. And apparently nearly deaf. I glare toward the direction of the door, and help myself to another spoonful of cold, creamy sin.

A shriek and a whiff of ozone barely register. But then the sudden loss of Miles Davis and the blare of fire alarms have me turning.

Fred yells, the sound an echo in his loft.

I tense, ready to investigate, when a series of loud pops goes off near my kitchen. In a blink, sparks fly from several outlets. And then it's like I'm inside a live firework. Sparks explode outward, fire flares in hot lines as it races along plaster and up the ceiling.

For one horrible second, I am frozen in shock. *Electrical fire* and *you're fucked* flit through my head, and then I jump up. My heart rises in my throat, as I grab the laptop sitting by my side on the counter and clutch my spoon in the other hand.

Alarms screech. I race for the door and run into a wall of black smoke. Fred's loft door is open, the space engulfed.

"Fred!" I choke on smoke, the flames pushing me back. I've never felt heat like this. The strength of it sears my skin and burns my eyes.

If he's in there, I can't help him. The thought fills me with horror.

Crouching low, I stumble down the stairs, my spoon clattering to the floor. Overhead, the sprinklers start up. Water falls with stinging force, and the concrete stairs turn slick. I grip the metal banister and fumble along.

Another man joins me on the first floor, and we travel together, going as fast as we can. We're nearly at the bottom, when Fred comes racing up the stairs, face covered in soot, his ratty brown bathrobe flopping around his thin legs.

"My records," he cries, wild eyed and crazed.

I hold out my free hand, trying to stop him, but he slams into me and we both go down hard. My computer flies in the air, my hand reaching down to catch my fall.

The impact of hitting the ground is so fast and furious I can't get past the pain. It spikes up my wrist and ass in the same instant, white light exploding behind my lids. My breath escapes in a gasp. I can't move my arm. Fred's bony knee is in my gut. I might die here, smothered by smoke and Fred's cheap chenille bathrobe.

Fuck you, Fred.

Then black smoke and blazing heat rolls over me, and all thoughts of Fred flee, leaving only one truth: I really might die.

CHAPTER 8
🏈 FINN

"I hate flying," Dex grumbles at my side. "And I hate wearing a suit."

Having come directly to the plane from leaving what will now be known as The Game of Suck, none of us had time to change out of our suits. Most of the guys have ripped off their ties. Dex has his jacket wadded up on the armrest between us and is currently digging his big elbow into it as if he can somehow grind the poor thing into dust.

"Flying sucks." Make no mistake, we have it good in first class. The seats are big, and the food is all right. But it still wears on you. There's a loneliness to it. Especially when you're coming home to an empty house. I used to like that. I'd crave alone time after being with my team for all hours of the day. Now, I think of walking into my dark place, reheating some chicken and rice to eat in front of the TV, and it just... sucks.

"But every time I want to bitch about the suits," I say to Dex, "I think about what women wear and shut the fuck up."

Dex grins, which makes him look downright mercenary with that thick beard of his. "Yeah. The heels are for shit. I don't know how they do it. Although, I think I might straight up cry if they stopped wearing those pretty bras and panties."

There's a slight flush on his cheeks that makes me think he's got certain sets in mind.

"You thinking about your girl, Dexter?" I grin, giving him a nudge.

Dex leans his head back and closes his eyes as if in pain. "I try not to. Makes it worse, you know?"

I almost tell him that I do know, the response so immediate that I actually gurgle. Because what the fuck? I don't have a girl.

Then who the fuck have you been thinking about all week? Why is it that your empty apartment now feels like a tomb instead of a refuge?

Facts must be stated.

I miss Chess. I miss her like I'm being denied air.

Running a hand over my face, I stifle a groan. Doesn't do any good. My mind is still filled with Chess. God, I actually sent her a care package of gelato. And got giddy as a preteen wondering if she'd like it and which flavors she'd try first.

"So your girl," I say to Dex. "She's Ivy Mackenzie's sister?" Ivy Mac, as our world knows her, is an up and coming sports agent and the wife of Gray Grayson, a brilliant tight end who, unfortunately, does not play for us.

"She is." Dex's expression can only be described as moony. I wonder if I'll soon be wearing that same face. Maybe I've worn it already. *Shit.*

Dex stretches his massive hands wide, then curls his fingers into a fist. "First saw her in college. At Ivy's house. Knew she was it for me right then."

"But you're just hooking up now?"

Dex slides me a glance. I get it. We don't usually talk relationships. Hell, Dex doesn't usually *talk*. But he doesn't ask me why I'm so interested, for which I am grateful. Instead, he shrugs one massive shoulder. "Timing wasn't right. I told myself it was for the best, that I wasn't ready, all that shit."

Quietly, I nod.

"Now that I've... That we've..." Dex actually flushes and clears his throat. "There's zero hesitation on the field. Seems fucking stupid to hesitate in life."

He's right. I've never hesitated in football.

Staring at the seatback in front of me, I feel as if I've been suddenly caught doing something wrong. I shift in the narrow confines of my seat, trying to find room that isn't there. "What if..." I lick my dry lips, too aware that Dex is quietly watching me. I huff out an uncomfortable laugh. "What if you don't know what you want? Only that you want something more than what you have?"

"You talking about Chess?" When I shoot Dex a look, he quirks a brow. "I guess you're not aware of how much you mention her."

The heat on my cheeks is because it's hot as fuck in the plane and I'm wearing my stupid suit jacket. Nothing else.

Dex has the stare of an agent on Draft Day.

"Okay, yeah," I blurt, then sigh. "I think about her. A lot." *Always.* "We're friends but—"

"You want more," Dex cuts in with a solemn nod that I'm pretty sure is his version of "duh."

"Well, that's the thing." I rub my tight neck. "Chess is looking for a relationship with someone. God knows she deserves it. Yes, I want her." *Understatement.* "And I know a one-off isn't going to cut it."

I'm not stupid, nor am I ignorant of my dick's needs; you don't lust over someone to this level and think it's going to die out with one fuck.

"But..." Dex prompts.

"When I try to imagine past that, my mind goes blank. And I can't breathe." I'm not proud of this. But it's the truth.

I force myself to look at Dex, and find him watching me with a small frown. He doesn't say anything, and I swear the bastard does it to make me sweat. I'm about to tell him to forget the whole conversation, when he finally speaks.

"She mean something to you?"

"Yes."

"Without the sex?"

"Jesus. Yes, all right? I'm not a total pig."

He nods again. "Then leave it alone until you're certain. Otherwise you're just fucking with her head and that ain't right."

The muscles in my chest draw tight, and the stuffy air of the plane closes in on me. "You're right."

It hurts to say it. There's a voice in my head that is protesting the fuck out of agreeing with Dex. It's probably my dick, since he's a selfish bastard. But it's the region around my heart that aches.

The plane dips and turns on the final landing leg. Below, New Orleans is a faint glitter to one side, the enormous spread of Lake Pontchartrain an inky blot on the other side.

Home.

Chess is down there. My hand twitches with the desire to pull my phone out and text her. But the flight attendant has already chastised Gruben for texting. And I really should heed Dex's advice, pull back from Chess for a while. Not seeing her every chance I get will probably help clear my head.

Then again, Dex had been warning me off sex, not friendship. I can still be Chess's friend.

As soon as we land, every guy pulls out his phone and is on it. Including me.

BigManny: Just landed. What you up to, Chester?

She doesn't answer.

I tuck my phone away and try not to be impatient. It's evening. She might be eating. Or out. On a date. Yeah, not liking that idea.

I pull out my phone again. Nothing.

BigManny: You out?

Nothing.

I want to leave it alone; she's under no obligation to respond. But it feels wrong. Like something's off. Frowning, I stalk down the gate, my teammates chatting around me.

Rolondo is glued to his phone when he halts. "Shit," he says, turning to look at me.

That quickly, my skin prickles. "What?"

"Isn't this your photographer's place?" He hands me his phone, which is running news footage.

The bottom drops out of me. Because Chess's building is an inferno. I can't breathe. For a second, I can't even see.

I start running, my heart in my throat. *If she's gone...*

No. Nope. No. No.

She has to be okay. She *has* to be.

♚ CHESS

So this is what shock feels like. I've always considered myself a fighter. Life slaps at me, I slap back. And yet here I sit, smelling of smoke, unable to do more than stare a rusty blot on the floor. Is it blood? Iodine?

Pain radiates along my wrist at a steady rate. My right butt cheek is so sore I lean to the left to alleviate the pressure. I'm guessing there's a massive bruise forming but no one looked, and I don't really want to either. Everything else is numb. The bustle of the Emergency Room hums in my ears. The sounds are strangely detached from where I sit behind the thin curtains that surround me. A woman starts retching. My stomach roils.

I've been here for hours. Everything moving at a snail's pace. But I'm finally patched up and free to go. But here I sit.

I can't stay here forever. But I don't move. I can't. I have nowhere to go.

Panic skitters at the edges of my mind, trying to claw at my skin. I push it down deep where it can't get me.

I won't cry. I won't cry. I won't.

But I am afraid. I have no home. No one to comfort me. Loneliness is a gapping maw threatening to swallow me whole. A slow shake starts low in my belly, spreading upward and outward.

In the hall, someone is running, soles scuffing on the linoleum. My curtain pulls back with a trilling ring.

Finn strides in, wearing a frown and a perfectly cut navy blue suit.

The urge to cry surges up my throat. I swallow it down, blinking rapidly.

"I broke my laptop," I blurt out lamely.

He doesn't stop until I'm wrapped in a giant hug. "Honey," he says in my damp air.

Don't cry. Don't cry.

I lean my head against his crisp suit jacket and draw in the scent of wool and soap. He's so warm and solid, the ice around my heart instantly starts to thaw. He strokes my hair and then eases back to look me in the eyes. The compassion I see in his twists my battered heart. "You all right?" he asks.

No. Not even a little.

"Fractured wrist. I'll live."

I just don't know where.

Finn touches the temporary cast they put on me, then his fingers drift down to skim across my knuckles. "It hurts, I know."

"How did you know I was here?"

Why is he in a suit? God, he looks good in a suit.

"Someone started watching the evening news when we landed." Finn's expression turns haunted. "They were covering your building."

"Ah." I don't want to relive that picture.

His fingers tighten on my shoulders. "Scared the shit out of me, Chess. I didn't know if you were in there…" He trails off and gives me another hug. Fiercer this time. "Your neighbor, some guy named Fred, was still outside. He told me where to find you."

I guess I have something to thank Fred for.

Finn peers down at me when I give a small huff of laughter. And his mouth tightens. "You should have called me."

"I forgot to grab my phone when the fire started." I laugh again, but it doesn't feel good. "I don't know a single fucking number. Isn't that pathetic? Couldn't even remember James's number, and I've known him for ten years. Not that it would matter since he's in New York right now." I bite my lip to keep from babbling any further.

A sympathetic smile tilts Finn's mouth. "I'd be fucked without my phone."

I snort, fighting the burn behind my lids. "Well, I'm certainly fucked."

He grimaces, ducking his head. "Shit. I'm sorry. I'm crap at this."

Personally, I think he's pretty perfect right now. "It's okay. I know what you meant. I'm just wallowing."

"No, honey," he says with force. "You feel whatever the hell you want to feel." He looks like he wants to say more, but simply rests his massive hand on my shoulder, engulfing it with warmth. "You all clear to go?"

I nod toward the clipboard on the rolling table. "I have to fill out some forms first."

He glances at my hand, half encased in the cast, and then picks up the clipboard. He rests his butt against the bed, pen at the ready. "Give me the answers."

A lump rises in my throat, and I swallow with difficulty, tasting ash. Slowly, I answer the questions, and he diligently writes them down.

The next thirty minutes swirl like a fog around me: Finn going off to talk to the nurse, give her my forms; Finn collecting my broken laptop, his hand at my lower back, guiding me out; the slap of fresh air when we leave the ER; Finn opening the door of his SUV and helping me climb in.

It isn't until we're driving, my bruised body softly embraced by luxury leather seats, that I find it in me to talk. "Where are we going?"

"Home." His grip tightens on the wheel. "My home."

I nod, not knowing what to say. I'd planned to go to a hotel. A small voice inside me cries that it wants to go home. I've never been homeless before. It feels like I've lost a huge piece of my identity. I take a deep breath and focus on the road before me. If I don't, I'll think about all my things now burnt or water logged, and I will lose it.

At the edge of the French Quarter, Finn pulls up before a converted factory building that overlooks the Mississippi. A doorman hurries over, and Finn hands him the car keys.

By the time we get to his condo, my wrist feel like it's being crushed in a vise. I hold it against my chest and follow him in. Finn's apartment reminds me of mine with exposed brick, wide and worn floorboards, and high ceilings. But where mine is—fuck, *was*—a loft, his has been divided up into rooms.

With a hand on my lower back, he guides me down a wide foyer into a living area. It's a man cave, but refined: reclaimed wood coffee table, big leather club chairs, a gray couch you could swim in, and a massive TV with what looks like three separate gaming systems. Arched windows frame the river, glinting with moonlight.

"Are you hungry," he asks, pausing.

"No, just tired."

He nods as if he suspected as much, and leads me down another hall. The first door opens into a bedroom. At first glance, I think it's his because it's so large and it is fully decorated. But there's a slightly feminine touch in the lacy white duvet and multiple throw pillows on the pretty carved mahogany canopy bed that I just can't see Finn choosing for his bedroom. Nor can I imagine him sitting on one of the delicate little linen covered armchairs set up before the fireplace.

He sets my busted laptop down on a sideboard. "My mom uses this room when she visits. There's a bathroom here." He opens a door, and I get a peek at a clawfoot tub and more exposed brick walls. I'm suddenly aching for a hot bath.

Finn clearly notices the direction of my gaze. "Want me to start a bath? It'll take a bit to fill."

"Okay."

While he fiddles with the taps, I stand in the middle of the room. I want to sit, but everything is so pretty and clean, and I stink of soot and smoke.

Finn bustles back in, full of nervous energy that makes me want to hug him. "Right, so there's a coffee maker." He opens the doors of the sideboard and pulls out an automated espresso maker on a tray. "And a fridge as well."

The small fridge is stocked with cream and juice and bottled waters. Just like a luxury hotel. I blink several times and nod, as he looks over his shoulder at me to see if I'm getting everything.

"It's perfect," I assure him, my voice thick.

He stands and shoves his hands in his trouser pockets. He seems larger in this room, his masculinity somehow highlighted against all the frilly touches. An elegantly dressed bruiser with a sensitive heart. "Towels and a robe are in the bathroom… And, right…" He moves to the tall dresser by the closet. "Clothes."

"Clothes?" I croak. On stiff legs, I go to him, as he pulls open a drawer.

Shirts of various colors, jeans—blue and black—sweaters… They're all neatly folded, tags still on them. I blink again, more rapidly, my throat swelling.

"You got me clothes?"

His eyes meet mine. "You needed them."

I can't speak.

"It's just to get you started," he goes on as if I'm not about to lose it right here in his cozy guest room. I find bras, panties, socks and nighties, in a rainbow of colors, resting nicely in another drawer.

"Bra size was a little harder to guess. I mean, I was pretty sure about cup size but 34? 36? I have no idea what that's all about…" He meets my gaze, and the tips of his ears pink. "Ah…yeah…so anyway…"

A smile pulls at my lips. "I could always go without."

"Please don't," he teases. "I'm trying hard enough as it is to not ogle your tits."

My chest is so tight it hurts to laugh. I suck in a shaky breath at the end of it. "When did you do this?"

He couldn't possibly have had the time.

"As much as I'd like to take credit," he says, sliding a drawer closed.

"My assistant, Charlie, did it. You'll meet him soon enough." Finn goes to turn off the water. "He works for a bunch of us guys, and when I heard about the fire, I called him in to help."

"Finn…" I don't know what to even say. Slowly, I walk toward him. "All of this…" *Shit, I'm going to sob.*

He shrugs again as if it's no big deal. "I wanted to give you what I could."

The bathroom is warm and humid, the air fragrant with the vanilla-lemon bubble bath he added to the water when I wasn't looking.

Finn gazes down at me, his expression so tender, I might break. I can't. If I cry now, I don't know if I can stop.

"Look, you don't have to stay more than the night," he says in the quiet. "But I wish you would. I've got some away games coming up and will be traveling for a couple of weeks, so you'll have the place to yourself."

"Okay," I whisper.

The stiff way he holds his shoulders eases, and he lets out a breath. "Good. Go on and have your bath. I'll get the meds the doc prescribed."

"You'll get my meds?" God, all I'm doing is parroting him now, but my mind has scrambled.

Finn rests his hand on my shoulder. "Chess, honey, I'll get you anything you need."

He becomes a blur as my eyes fill. I blink back tears that cannot fall. But my resistance crumbles. With a shuddering breath, I step into his space and wrap my good arm around his waist. "Finn," I croak.

Immediately, he gathers me up, holding me close, his lip pressed to the top of my head. I lean on him and wallow in the feel of his body, strong and firm and warm. It's so comforting, part of me wants to pull away, afraid that I'll come to need this too much. But I can't move.

"I think I love you right now," I tell him, my voice muffled on his crisp shirt.

Those massive arms of his tighten a fraction, even as his chest shakes on a laugh. "Only right now, eh?"

"I'm sure you'll eventually say something to remind me why that's a bad idea." I don't bother lifting my nose from his chest. The silk of his tie presses against my cheek, the scent of fine wool and clean man surrounding me. Finn in a suit is devastating. But I miss his t-shirt and jeans.

"Probably," he agrees then sighs. "I'm glad you're okay, honey."

A fine tremor goes through his body. And I realize, he isn't nervous, he's upset. I snuggle closer. "Thank you for coming to get me."

"Always, Chess."

He says it with such fierce sincerity that my knees go weak. I think about the loss of my house, my work. Jesus, my Nikon D5 DSLR. I took out a loan to get that baby. Not to mention my lenses. My beautiful lenses. Gone. Melted.

Panic claws up my throat. If I let it in, I'll ask him to take me to bed, make me forget for a few hours why I'm so scared. I can almost hear myself begging, almost feel my hands moving down to cup the fat bulge in his pants.

He'd be willing. I know this well. Finn has never hidden his attraction to me. And it would be so good. I know this without a doubt. But morning would come and I'd still be a woman without a home, facing the only friend I have close right now with all the awkwardness and regret that comes with a one-night stand.

I force myself to loosen my hold on him, to step back and find some distance. Finn's arms fall to his sides as he watches me back up. The loss of him makes me cold and off balance. I clutch my arm to my chest.

"I should take my bath now."

"Sure." He leaves me to bathe, closing the bathroom door behind him.

At some point, while I soak, I hear him return and leave my pain meds in the bedroom. By the time I crawl into his soft guest bed, the sheets smelling faintly of laundry detergent but stiff with disuse, I'm shaking.

I cry with my face buried deep into a pillow so he won't hear.

CHAPTER 9
🏈 FINN

I'm one twisted bastard. My girl has had one of the worst nights of her life, and here I am, fucking content because she's in my home.

It rattled me to the core when I thought of her hurt, or worse. The time it took me to get to her had felt endless. And when I'd finally found her, all bruised and dazed, her green eyes so wounded and scared, it had leveled me. I'm still shaking deep inside my guts.

With a grunt, I push my body up, my weight resting on my fingertips. Sweat trickles down my temples and into my eyes. Slowly, I lower myself until my nose almost touches the floor. Up, down, the burn in my arms and chest is a welcome distraction. But not enough.

Chess had been crying last night. And it fucking killed me. I'd wanted to go to her so badly, I'd leaned against her door, my heart in my throat, my hand pressed to the wood. The only thing that stopped me was that she had obviously waited until I'd gone to cry. She hadn't wanted me to witness her pain.

That hurt too. I want her trust. I want to take care of her. Badly.

An oddity I don't fully understand. Because I have never taken care of anyone but myself. Never wanted to until now.

Yet it felt good last night, knowing that I was providing her with safe harbor, seeing to her comfort. Which brings me back to feeling like a bit of a bastard. She's hurting and I don't know how to make it better.

I'd have made her breakfast, but it's going on eleven and she's still not up.

I grunt again, picking up the pace. A strangled squeak has me pausing.

Chess stands in the living room, gaping at me. "Holy hell." Her gaze slides over my bare torso like greedy hands. "Is this one of the perks offered at the House of Mannus?"

With a little more flare than necessary, I leap up from my plank position and land lightly on my feet. "Daily viewing times are at ten to eleven, barring travel blackout dates."

"Excellent. I'll set an alarm from now on." She grins, and I feel a little dizzy. When Chess smiles, she lights up—even as she is now, hair tangled around her shoulders, eyes bruised by lack of sleep and crying. To make her smile feels like a reward.

I set my hands on my hips, not bothering to towel off. "You've seen me naked and didn't bat an eye, but watching me do pushups is a treat?"

"I was working. It would have been unprofessional to ogle the client." Her gaze touches on my chest, and I swear I feel it. "Now, I might just make some popcorn and settle in. You have popcorn, right?"

"Sorry, I hate popcorn. But feel free to watch me any time."

"How can you not like popcorn?" Chess shakes her head as she folds her long limbs onto the couch. She's in black leggings and a t-shirt with my name and jersey number on it. Not her usual attire, and I know Charlie bought the shirt, but damn if it doesn't give me a possessive thrill to see her wearing my name.

"Gets in between my teeth. Drives me nuts." I grab a bottle of iced water from the kitchen counter and take a drink. "But I'll stock some for you."

Chess looks around, taking in the living room, small den area, and finally the kitchen with its black cabinets, brass fixtures, and concrete countertop. "You had someone decorate this place, didn't you?"

"Realtor recommended a decorator friend of hers." *Ah, Jessica and Janet. Nice women.*

Chess narrows her eyes and I suddenly feel caught out.

"You slept with her, didn't you?"

How the hell?

Show no weakness. I give her an easy smile. "The realtor or the designer?"

"Oh, God, both of them?"

Jesus, is she a mind reader? "Not at the same time."

She scoffs like I've chumped her Cheerios. "For fuck's sake."

"I mean, I might have been down with that if they'd asked," I tease, because it's fun to get her riled.

But she looks more horrified than amused. "They were friends. You don't think screwing each of them would cause problems?"

I'm beginning to feel like a worm just waiting to be hooked and cast in a lake. "I didn't ask."

"Because you never saw them again?" It isn't really a question, though. Condemnation is written all over her face.

I head into the kitchen and take out a packet of chicken breasts I'm going to cook. "You aren't going to get all righteous on me about sex, are you, Chester?"

She rolls her eyes and follows. "Don't worry, I'm not clutching my pearls. I'm just reminding myself why I'm glad we didn't hookup."

The chicken package lands on the counter with a slap, as her words punch through me. It's surprisingly painful knowing that she thinks I'm a bad bet. And yet… "So you have to remind yourself, eh?"

A pretty pink flush colors her cheeks. "I'm here at your house. You're you. Can you blame me for being guarded?"

Now I'm pissed. I feel it rising, and I grind my teeth against the urge to snap at her. My hand spreads wide on the cool counter, as I take a deep breath. But then I catch a good look at Chess. She seems smaller somehow, tightly coiled within herself, her expression wane and her eyes a little wild.

"Are you trying to pick a fight?" I ask. Despite her prickliness, I know she's fragile right now.

For a second, it looks as if she might snap at me, but her shoulders sag on a breath and she puts her face in her hands. "I'm sorry. You don't deserve this. I'm all persnickety, and... I don't know what I'm saying. Ignore me."

I want to give her a hug, but she holds herself tight, eyeing the hall as if she might cut and run. "You need to get back to normal, is all."

She nods, but there's no energy left in her.

"Here's what we'll do," I say. "Let's have lunch—"

"Lunch?" She makes an amused sound. "It's only eleven."

"Elevenses, then," I amend. "I basically eat like a hobbit."

She cranes her neck and peers over the center island that stands between us.

"What *are* you doing?" I ask with a laugh.

"Checking out your feet."

I wiggle my toes, still encased in sneakers. "They aren't hairy, but they're very large." I lift a brow. "I'm well-proportioned."

Chess scoffs, but she's no longer slumped in defeat. "Yes, I know, big guy. I've seen you naked, remember?"

"How can I forget when you keep bringing it up?" *I can get naked now, if you join me.* "If I didn't know better, Ms. Copper, I'd think you were fixating."

"Good thing you know better." Chess rounds the kitchen island and comes up beside me. She's so slight, compared to me, her wrists delicate and fine. The black cast covering her right one is bulky, running up over her hand, leaving only her fingers free. I don't miss the bruising on her forearm, and the way she's been limping makes me believe she has bruises elsewhere.

I want to demand that she show me her hurts, let me gather her up and tuck her back in bed, where I'll feed her lunch, rub her sore muscles, do anything she wants. But I know she'll refuse. And I don't think it would ease her worries, which is what she truly needs right now. Never mind the fact that, if I get into a bed with her, my control will crack; no way can I hold her now and not keep my hands at neutral.

I push the thought of exploring Chess out of my mind. "So after elevenses, we'll go and buy you a new camera and some equipment. Get you set back up for work."

She rests her slender fingers on the edge of the counter. "Thanks, but I don't get a check from the insurance for a few weeks."

"Which is why I'm buying."

A frown works over her face, and I lift a hand. "You can pay me back when you get your check."

"Or I can wait," she argues. "I'm already staying here. You bought me clothes. I can't take more—"

"Chester, I make an obscene amount of money and spend it on very little. You and I both know that. So let's not pretend you're putting me out monetarily."

"We're talking about nearly thirty-thousand dollars of equipment, Finn."

"I am aware. Makes no difference to me." When she rolls her eyes, I lean in. "Helping you get back on even ground makes me happy. All right?"

"Maybe I don't want to be on even ground. Maybe I want to mope."

I don't buy it for a second. I see the anticipation in her eyes. The girl is dying to get a camera back in her hands. "Too bad. The House of Mannus also has an anti-moping law in effect. Violators are subject to noogies and loss of TV time for one day."

Chess looks at me as if I'm full of it. Which I am. But she clearly likes that. "Any more rules I should know?"

"They're all in the playbook located on your bedside table." I open the fridge and pull out some roasted beets, goat cheese, and bulgur salad.

Chess watches me with bemused interest. "This looks…elaborate. You cooked all this?"

"I can cook the basics, but the team's nutritionist has a chef on staff who sets us up with a few of our weekly meals. You know, elevenses, lunch, second lunch, and so on."

The doorbell rings, cutting off whatever Chess wants to say. I hustle to get it and find Charlie, box in one hand, a massive bouquet of flowers in the other. The spray of orange roses is so big, I can barely see his head. "Charles," I say, as I let him in. "You shouldn't have. I'm more of a plant man."

Before Charlie can give me shit back, Chess walks in and makes a sound of wonder. "Wow."

Charlie steps past me like I'm not even there. "These are for you." He sets the ridiculous bouquet on the hall table because it's too damn big for her to hold. "They're from the offensive team."

My guys went in on flowers and didn't tell me? Those little ass-kissing shits. I could have told them that Chess isn't the type to get impressed by flowers—

"Oh!" Her face glows with pleasure. "How lovely."

Wait. What?

"Well," I say, trying not to grind my teeth. "That's how we do."

Chess sniffs a rose, as she reads the card that's covered in signatures. "Stop trying to get a gold star, Finnegan. I don't see your name on here."

Biting back a grin and pointedly not looking my way, Charlie holds out the box in his hand. White and sleek, it doesn't hide what's inside. A freaking MacBook Pro? "And this is from the defensive team."

She looks stunned.

Chess will never take it. No way.

But then she smiles, all wobbly and misty-eyed. Just like she did last night. "That's so…sweet." She clutches the box to her chest like it's precious.

I'm torn between gratitude to my teammates for putting that look on her face, and feeling the urge to punch them all in theirs because I didn't get her a computer first.

I close the door with a little more force than necessary. "Chess. Meet Charlie Beauchamp." *Resident turncoat.* "When not helping me and some of the guys out, he's a junior, studying at Tulane."

"You play football, Charlie?" Chess asks.

It's a valid question. At six five and two hundred and eighty pounds of bulky muscles, he could easily be a defensive end.

Charlie, used to the question, gives a wry smile. "No, ma'am. Much to my chagrin, I have two left feet and they're made of lead. Or so says every coach I've tried out for." His Haitian accent thickens a bit. "I'm majoring in Sports Management."

"I wanted to thank you," Chess says. "For buying me those clothes and things. I'm so grateful."

Charlie's cheeks turn the color of rosewood. If I weren't standing here, I wouldn't have believed he was capable of blushing. He's an unflappable island of calm around *me*. "It was the least I could do, ma'am. Though I apologize if anything doesn't…" He clears his throat. "If certain items aren't your usual style."

A low, laugh escapes Chess's lips, and even though there's nothing suggestive in her expression, the sound is pure sex to my ears. "You did just fine."

I find myself picturing her wearing one of those uninspired panties Charlie picked out and nothing else. Pure white cotton, stretched over that toned, pert ass, hugging every curve and dip.

Jesus. Charlie might be onto something. I shift my weight and try to think of something unsavory, such as the way Dawes never washes his socks during playoffs.

Yep, that'll do it.

"It was a novel experience," Charlie is saying. "Buying women's underwear."

"I'm sure you'll get to do it again under better circumstance someday," Chess assures, barking up the wrong tree.

Charlie gives her a small smile. "I don't think any of the guys I date would be into that, ma'am."

"Probably wise of them," Chess says without missing a beat. "Bras aren't the most comfortable attire."

I really don't want to start thinking about Chess wearing a bra. Or going without. "We're about to eat," I say to Charlie. "Want to join us?"

Before he can speak, Chess hooks her arm around his. "You must."

"Let the guy answer for himself, Chess."

She shoots me a reproving look. "I'm trying to make him feel welcome, *Finn*."

"He knows he's welcome. I just asked him to join us."

Charlie chuckles, interrupting us. "You two sound like my grandparents."

"Surely not as old as that," I exclaim in mock horror.

Chess tisks at me.

Charlie flashes a grin. "I mean the way you two go on like you've known each other forever."

The words invade the room like the drunken uncle no one wants to acknowledge but can't ignore. Chess and I eye each other for a long moment, neither of us knowing what to say. But then she purses her lips as if mildly entertained.

"Sure feel like it sometimes," she mutters before turning heel and striding toward the kitchen, her long dark hair swinging like a pendulum over her pert butt.

I watch that jiggle and sway, and my dick twitches in response.

Next to me, Charlie makes a choked sound of amusement. "Man..."

I glance his way. "Yeah, I know."

♟CHESS

"I cannot believe you didn't call me," James scolds over the phone.

I open another one of Finn's cabinets in search of a platter. The man has ten different sets of beer glasses, yet barely a serving tray or bread bowl to be found. "Did you miss the part where I said I lost my phone?"

"You could have borrowed one!"

"Am I the only one who doesn't have people's numbers memorized?" I mutter, moving on to the next cabinet.

"Good point." Horns blare in the background, and I wonder if he's outside.

"Where are you?"

"Headed toward the MoMA." He's slightly out of breath when he speaks again. "Don't worry, as soon we're through, I'm booking tickets home."

Finally, I find a cheese tray and a few shallow bowls that might be used for crackers or bread. The price stickers are still on them. I have a vision of Finn's mom buying him these, stocking his kitchen for parties he'll never have.

"Don't do that," I tell James, as I pick off the sticker on the tray. "There's no need."

"What do you mean there's no need?" he exclaims. "Your freaking home just got crisped. Of course I'm coming back."

"No, really, James, I'm all right. Stay with Jamie. Have fun."

He lets out an audible huff. "I'm coming back. What kind of shit friend do you think I am?"

Setting the tray down, I get to work on unwrapping my cheeses. "I'm fine. Seriously. I have a temporary place to stay, and the insurance company is actually being very helpful."

"What about work? Or the calendar?"

"The computer guys were able to get the files off my busted laptop and transfer it into my new one. So I can easily finish up the calendar work. I've had to drop a few jobs…" Which is going to sting financially. "But I bought enough basic equipment that I can work the Ducain wedding, which I really can do on my own. And we don't have anything major for another month."

James makes a noise of assent. "What about the loft? How long until you can go back?"

"It's destroyed. I'll need to find a new place. Frankly, I want to pull a Scarlett and not think about that today."

"I always thought you'd make a great Scarlett. Snapping green eyes, inky dark hair, creamy skin—"

"Perfect resting bitch face?" I offer with a snort.

"Exactly."

"So listen to Katie Scarlett and stay, wallow in love and all that sappy shit."

"Sappy, hmm?" James makes a suspicious sound in his throat. "Tell me, Chess, does the fact that you're shacking up with an insanely hot quarterback—and I'm still jealous of that, by the way—have anything to do with your insistence that I stay longer in New York?"

"Your suspicions hurt, Rhett." I grab a bread knife and start hacking at the fresh baguette I'd picked up at a bakery. "Here I am, generously supporting your newly found love—"

"Pfft."

"And you accuse me of having ulterior and nefarious motives."

"You sound like a thirties movie villain," James drawls. "And I'm accusing you of ulterior and hedonistic motives, to be clear."

"Bah." I arrange the bread slices in a shallow bowl, then flick away a few crumbs.

"So," James asks in a sing-song voice. "What's manly Manny's place like? Does he have a Red Room of Pain?"

Smiling, I roll my eyes. "At first I thought he did, but it turned out to be a home gym."

"Bummer."

Glancing at the clock, I carry the bread and cheese out to the coffee table. "Yeah, but I can attest to its pain inducing powers."

James laughs. "Joke all you want, Chessie bear, but you can't hide from me. You like being sexy Manny's roommate."

A denial dances at the edge of my tongue. But I can't force it out.

I could fall for Finn. Irrevocably. I know it. I already feel myself teetering, and we haven't known each other for that long.

My insides clench in protest, and I move my hand to my lower abdomen before I can stop the action. My stomach is flat for the most part, but I'm not a fan of sit-ups, and I have a soft little swell just below my navel.

I have a love-hate relationship with my little pooch. When I'm standing up, I find it kind of cute and sexy, a bit of feminine softness on my body that, in all other areas, runs to thin and gangly. But when I sit down in a bikini and everything kind of pillows, I hate it.

Right now, I cradle that vulnerable spot. "James? Do you ever feel…" A shuddering breath leaves me. I should shut up. Right now. But I have to ask someone. And James is my closest friend. He'll never judge me. "Defective? Like damaged goods?"

Instantly, my face heats with shame and annoyance. I've shown my underbelly, and I don't like the sensation. But James's soft voice comes through the phone. "Chess, I'm bisexual. I get shit from all directions. I'm either a liar or deliberately choosing to be as I am. Defective in the eyes of both camps."

Even though he's a thousand miles away, I want to hug him. "They're the ones who are defective, not you."

He's silent for a moment. "There is nothing wrong with you either, babe. Not one fucking thing."

"That's the messed up part. I know I am not defined by what I lack but by who I am as a whole. And I'd probably kick someone's ass if they tried to tell me differently."

"But?" James prompts, because he knows me well. "Something's not clicking in that head of yours. What is it?"

"Sometimes…" I lick my dry lips. "Sometimes I wonder if my heart hasn't gotten that message. That maybe I sabotage myself with men. You know, what if, when they learn everything there is to know about me, they decide I'm not worth it."

I don't even know what I'm trying to explain. Only that, despite my best efforts, there are days when I feel flawed. When it feels like my fault that I'm single and have never had a boyfriend.

"I used to think that too," James says quietly. Which is a shock, because his sense of self-confidence has always been enormous. "And at the same time I had thought that there was no one perfect enough for me."

I give a little half-hearted laugh at that, because, despite my insecurities, I fully admit to being picky as fuck over men. "Yeah."

I hear the smile in his voice. "Now I know that there is someone perfectly imperfect for all of us."

"Yeah, I guess."

"And if that person for you happens to be a six-four, hot as fuck-sweat quarterback, then I'll love you forever."

I snort. "You'd love me forever anyway."

"True. But I'll forgive you when you turn into a PMS rage demon from now on."

"So magnanimous. But I wouldn't hold my breath if I were you."

"Then tell me I'm wrong. Go ahead, I'm waiting."

I look down at the coffee table I'm standing in front of. Cheese platter, baguette rounds, a plate of cured meats, a bowl of wasabi peas and roasted almonds are arranged just so. And a couple of Abita beers are chilling in an ice bucket. My cheeks heat.

At home, I often make myself a little happy hour for one—or two, when James sticks around. Life is short, and I like to enjoy the small things as well as the big events. But this spread isn't for me. It's for Finn.

He's been gone for over a week and is due to arrive home at any time. What will he think of this? Is it too much? Girlfriend territory? I don't know. All I know is that I want him to be happy coming home. I want to do things to show my appreciation. But maybe he won't like this. Maybe it will freak him out and make him think I'm angling for something else.

Panic has my chest growing hot and tight. Shit.

"I gotta go," I tell James. "I'll text you later."

"I knew it! He just get home?"

I ignore the teasing lilt in his voice. "No. Girl issues."

It's our long established code for me admitting I have to use the bathroom. And nothing will get rid of James faster.

As soon as I hang up with him, I reach down to clear the table. But the lock on the front door turns, and before I can move, Finn walks in.

There's no more panic about cheese trays and beer, because he sees me and smiles. And, damn if it doesn't light me up like one of those old-fashioned pinball machines. I'm grinning back so hard my cheeks hurt, while those little zings of giddy pleasure bounce around in my chest.

He's wearing gray track pants and a black Henley, which should make him look like a slob. He doesn't. Those clothes hug that hard, fit body of his, showcasing every ripple, every bulge. I envy those clothes.

Finn tosses his gear bag onto the floor, never taking his eyes off me. "Honey, I'm home." He says it like a joke, but his voice is thick and rough.

Exhaustion? Or something more? I can't think. I should say something witty or light, but the only thing that comes out is, "Hey."

Finn's smile only grows. He heads straight for me, as if I'm the happy end of a very long day. And I can only stand there, shifting my weight on my feet, my fingers curling at my sides with the repressed need to grab him.

Before I can say a word, he's sweeping me up in a big, bear hug, my nose pressed in the small space between his hard pecs. The scent of clean cotton, warm skin, and potent as hell male pheromones washes over me like a sigh.

Finn's voice rumbles in his chest and warms the crown of my head. "I've missed you."

The simple declaration slides through my defenses with such ease, I don't have time to brace myself. I close my eyes and give him a gentle squeeze, unable to form words, because I am not a sentimental girl. I don't know to say sweet things.

Maybe Finn senses that. Or maybe he's just tired of hugging me. Either way, he sets me back on my feet. "How've you been settling in? Is your wrist still hurting?" He peers at my face as if trying to make sure I'm okay.

When he's away from me, I forget how blue his eyes are. Azure blue. I'm a fan of brown eyes. Yet here I am, staring up at his eyes like I've never seen the color blue before.

And, holy hell, I don't recognize this moony person I've become.

I take a step back and get some much-needed space. "I'm fine. The swelling has gone down and the pain is nearly gone."

He nods but then glances behind me, catching sight of the food. Surprise registers first. His big body gives a little jerk. And then he blinks as if trying to clear his sight.

I grow uncomfortably warm, my arms twitching with the desire to swipe the table clear.

But then his gaze meets mine. "You did miss me."

The heat inside me grows. "What a thing to say. Of course I did."

That soft expression of his expects too much.

"I should probably warn you..." I gesture toward my damn cheese tray. "I like to do this in the evenings."

The corner of his mouth kicks up. "You think I'm going to complain?"

I shove my hands into my back jeans pockets. "James says it's very nineteen fifties domestic."

Finn chuckles.

"But this is the only thing I do that can be considered domestic," I warn. "So don't expect me to greet you with dinners or—"

"Cocktails?" Finn supplies, pulling a beer out of the ice bucket.

Fuck.

"Yeah..."

He laughs again, and then swoops in, giving me a quick kiss on the cheek. "Relax, Chester. I'm not expecting anything. I won't be asking you to fetch my slippers. Although, if you want to..." He wags his brows. "I won't try to stop you."

"Asshat." I give his arm a slap. It's like warm granite.

With an expansive sigh of contentment, Finn plops onto the couch, twists the top off his beer and takes a long drink. He sighs again and rests his head against the back of the couch. His lids lower like a relaxed cat's. "Gotta admit," he says in a near purr. "Coming home has never been this good."

"Glad I could—" I yelp as he takes hold of my good wrist and tugs me onto the couch with him. "Easy there, Superman."

Finn cuddles me up next to him, draping his arm over my shoulders. "Sorry. But you were standing there all twitchy and shifty like you'd been caught stealing or something."

The laughter in his voice is unmistakable. And I elbow him, trying to ignore that his fingers have threaded through my hair, lightly stroking the strands.

"You colored your hair again," he murmurs, playing with the tips that now have glints of teal, gold, green, and magenta throughout the black.

A shiver of pure pleasure goes through me. His body is warm and solid, and I'd like nothing better than to rest against it without care.

"It's called an oil slick effect." Why am I telling him this? He doesn't care about color techniques.

But he lifts a whole section and slowly lets it sift through his fingers. "It brings out the green in your eyes."

It feels good. Too good. And wrong. I don't cuddle with James. I've never wanted to. I don't cuddle with anyone. Ever.

What we're doing here is dangerous. Because it would be so easy to turn my head and nuzzle the heated hollow of his throat, to lick a path up to the curve of his jaw and the soft turn of his lower lip. It would be as easy as taking a breath.

I'm living with him now. Hitting on my host is a definite *faux pas*. And stupid.

I edge away, causing Finn to frown slightly.

"Hey, Chess?"

I don't like the quiet, serious tone of his voice. "Yes?"

"When are we—"

The doorbell rings. We both flinch as if snapping out of a daze, and then Finn glares at the door. "Who the hell?"

"You don't get random visitors?" I tease, rising.

Finn sits forward on the couch. "They have to get past the doorman. My assistant Charlie has clearance, but I happen to know he's hanging out with Rolondo and Gruber right now."

The bell rings again.

"I'll get it," I tell him. "You have your beer. *Dear.*"

He smirks at that, but stands. "No, way. I don't know who the hell got past security. I'm answering the door."

We both go, bickering along the way. Which is ridiculous, but I can't seem to let it go; I have this weird sense that Finn shouldn't answer the door.

But he does, swinging it open as if he'll gladly pummel anyone who's here with ill intent. That all changes when he sees the woman standing in the hall.

At his side, I halt, my skin prickling in shock. Because the woman is stunning. White-blonde, silky hair, ice blue eyes, tanned skin, and the kind of bone structure artists commit to marble. It's my job to photograph women like her. And though I've never worked with this woman, I know who she is immediately. Britt Larson. A supermodel whose face currently graces the cover of Vogue.

She and Finn stare at each other as if nothing else exists.

It drops the bottom out of me. These two are golden people. The kind of pairing that media and fans alike eat up and sigh over.

"Britt." Finn's voice is a rasp.

She leans toward him but stops, her gaze falling on me.

The back of my neck tightens. Finn flinches as if he's forgotten I was there. I don't blame him; if I liked women that way, I might have forgotten too.

"Britt. This is Chess. Chess, Britt." It sounds like he's chewing on nails.

She gives me the barest of nods. "Hello."

"Chess is a photographer," Finn says, as if explaining something.

Britt's features tighten a fraction. I'm small time. And she knows it. "Yes. The calendar photographer. I've heard. Must have been a big deal getting to shoot you and your team."

Nice. I could say something snide. But it isn't worth it. Finn looks as if he'd rather the floor swallow him whole. He still hasn't moved back from the door or offered to let Britt in. She stands there awkwardly, clearly at a loss, and clearly expecting more.

"I was hoping we could talk," she says then, another glance in my direction.

Finn straightens then as if coming out of a fog. "Ah…yeah."

His neck is so stiff, I have to wonder if he's actively trying not to look my way.

Enough is enough.

"I'm just headed out," I announce, grabbing my purse and keys, both of them thankfully sitting on the hall console. Then I remember my phone. "Let me just get my phone…"

I jog to the kitchen, my temples throbbing.

Finn and Britt haven't moved from their spots by the door. But Finn frowns my way. "You don't have to—" He shuts his mouth abruptly, then grimaces. "Thanks, Chess."

The apology in his eyes irks. The hell if I'll let him see that. I give Britt what I hope is a pleasant smile. "Nice to meet you."

"Same," she says with about as much sincerity.

She's going to eat my cheese.

I hate her.

I leave without looking back.

CHAPTER 10
FINN

My feet seem to have grown roots. I can't make them move. My body is one dull throb of old pain and new shock. Dimly, I take note of Chess walking out, her dark, glossy hair swaying like an agitated flag down her back.

Don't go.

I want to call her back. It would be easier that way. I could shut the door on Britt's face and tuck Chess back against my side. But that's the coward's way out.

Britt makes a small sound, and I snap out of my fog. My parents taught me better than this.

"Come in." I step back to let her pass.

She leaves a trail of expensive and too flowery perfume. That scent stuck to my skin and gave me a headache when I'd fucked her.

Not something I want to think about.

I follow her into the living room and watch her as she strolls around, taking in the space. When Chess had done the same, I'd been filled with a strange need for her to be pleased, to like my place. With Britt, I just want her to spit out why the hell she is here.

Britt stares down at the coffee table with the appetizers Chess set up so prettily, and I am hit with a sense of wrongness that she's here and that Chess is out there somewhere.

I have never had anyone welcome me home before. Never knew I needed it until I walked in the door and saw Chess standing there, so fucking pretty in her casual jeans and black v-neck top. And so adorably nervous and prickly about doing something nice for me.

Maybe it's true that she always has a little personal happy hour. But she clearly had included me in her plans tonight. That makes all the difference.

"You're living with the calendar photographer?" Britt asks.

Seems like a petty distinction, calling her a calendar photographer when she's more than that. But I let it slide. "Chess is staying with me, yes." It's none of Britt's business. But I'm not trying to hide anything.

Britt nibbles on her bottom lip.

"How do you know who she is, anyway?" I ask.

"They are showing pictures of you two. At an aquarium. Food shopping together." Her smooth brow barely wrinkles. "They've been taking pictures of her coming in and out of your building all week."

Great. Chess will love that.

"You seem to know a lot about it."

Britt shakes her head as if I'm naive. "I envy your ability to tune out the press. They're everywhere, Finn." Her lashes sweep low. "They photographed us once too."

Annoyance skitters up my spine and claws my neck. "They took photos of everyone at that party. It was fashion week."

Fact: football players troll fashion shows and parties for models. Not because they like clothes. When you're a rookie and you get invitations to hang out with the most beautiful women in the world, you go. Hell, you're ecstatic.

Models, actresses, pop stars, they love us. We're fit, rich, and most of us aren't looking for complicated. Is it a shallow set up? Sure. But as long as no one gets hurt, why should it matter?

Only sometimes, people do get hurt.

"Why are you here, Britt?"

She lowers herself onto the edge of the couch, picks up a piece of cheese, frowns at it and drops it back down. I almost snap at her not to touch anything; that's Chess's meal. But then Britt gives a little sigh. "I don't know. I saw the pictures and thought of you. You're getting on with your life."

Is that what this is? Some guilt trip? Worse thing is I don't know if I should feel guilty or not. "Was I not supposed to?"

"No. Yes." She shakes her head, the simple movement stunning on her.

I'd been so blindsided by this woman's looks when we met that I'd turned stupid.

"I'm sorry," she says. "I don't know what I'm saying half the time."

And like that, I do feel guilty. "It's all right, Britt."

She utters a half-sob, half-laugh. When she looks up, her eyes are wide and a little hesitant. "Your mother has been calling me."

She couldn't have shocked me more if she'd slapped my face.

"What?"

Seriously. The fuck?

Britt's chin lifts a touch. "She invited me to your house for Thanksgiving…" Her nose wrinkles. "No, that wasn't what she called it."

"Thanksmas," I get out through clenched teeth. Blood rushes in my ears. I am going to kill my mother. I don't care if it's a crime. I don't care if my dad kills me in retaliation. The woman has gone too far.

"Right, that's it."

"Britt." My voice is hard. I can't control it. "No. I'm sorry, but no."

Her mouth falls open, her eyes welling as if she'll soon cry.

"My mother means well," I press on. "But this isn't the right thing for either of us." It sure as shit isn't what I want or need.

Britt staggers to her feet. I reach out to steady her but she shakes me off. "I thought…" She takes a breath. "I thought maybe she was speaking for you."

"No," I say, trying to soften my tone. Because she's a victim of Mom's meddling too. "I'm sorry."

"It is because of the photographer?"

"Chess," I remind her.

"Chess. Is it because of her?"

"No." It's the honest truth. Chess has nothing to do with why I don't want Britt celebrating holidays with me. "I just can't…" Fucking hell, what do I say that doesn't make me sound like a complete dick?

"I understand," Britt says, saving us both. She takes a breath and stands straight. "I do. I apologize if I made you uncomfortable."

Uncomfortable? God, there's so much uncomfortable between us, I feel like I'm choking. I rub the back of my neck. "No. I'm sorry if I was abrupt. I'm no good at this."

Her smile is wry and bittersweet. "Well, who would be?" She moves toward the front hall, and I hustle to open the door for her. Britt pauses and looks up at me. "Take care, Finn."

I can barely look at her anymore. It's wrong of me, I know. But feelings rarely listen to reason. "Goodbye, Britt."

I close the door and lean against it, wanting Chess back here more than my next breath. But she'll probably ask questions. And I don't know if I have it in me to give her the answers.

♟ CHESS

One of my favorite things about the French Quarter is that you can always find a bar no matter what time it is. And not some dank, gloomy dive—although there are plenty of those— but ones with high, pressed tin ceilings, walls of windows, and cute mixologists like my new friend Nate here who kindly slides a perfect sazerac in front of me.

I take a cool sip and listen to Ella Fitzgerald muss about being bewitched, bothered, and bewildered. It's almost enough to soothe the weary soul.

"That's an awfully big sigh," Nate observes, as he wipes his spotless mahogany bar.

I'm no longer a fan of nosy Nate.

"I wasn't aware I sighed," I say, taking another sip of my drink. Good man, Nate, despite being nosy.

"Practically blew back my hair," he jokes.

I eye Nate's shaved head, and he laughs.

"I need a short term place to live." Sadness swamps my chest. I don't want to find a new place. Which just proves I really need to find one.

"You just moved here?" Nate asks.

"No. My place burned down."

"Man, that sucks."

I think of Finn running into the ER to find me, the way he brought me home and made me feel like it was my home too, for as long as I needed it. And then I think of Finn up there right now with Britt, and the way he looked at her. They have a history, and it clearly isn't a simple one.

My cocktail chokes going down, a sticky sweet burn on my tongue. "Yeah."

Nate moves closer until he's standing opposite of me. "I can keep an ear out for you. If you want to give me your number."

I stare up at Nate with his shaved head, gauge in his ears, and cute suspenders over his shoulders. There's interest in his eyes.

"You want my number?"

The interest turns to heat. "I'm great at consoling."

I bet he is.

Finn is better.

Finn is in his apartment with a supermodel.

I hand Nate my phone, and he punches in his number.

Not even a glimmer of anticipation in my belly.

"So," he says, happier now. "You want another drink, pretty little lady?"

Pretty little lady? I'm regretting my decision more and more. "Another drink and I'll be buzzed. Better give me a menu."

"Let's get you fed, then." Nate grins. I know he thinks I'm lingering because of him, but I can't return to Finn's any time soon. Short of walking around, I have nowhere else to go, which utterly sucks.

I eat my dinner and chat with Nate and a few patrons who sit down at the bar until my butt is numb and I'm fairly certain I'm leading Nate to a very wrong conclusion.

When he's occupied, I leave some money on the bar and slip out into the fading light. And then I do walk around, until it's dark and I can't stall anymore.

At Finn's place, I turn the lock to his front door as quietly as I can.

Please don't let me hear them. Please let them be in his bedroom. God, the horror of actually seeing them makes me pause, my heart thundering in my chest like cannon fire.

Like a thief, I creep in. The living room is dark, and I heave a sigh of relief as I ease my way toward my bedroom.

"What are you doing?" Finn asks from behind me.

With a stifled yelp, I pivot and press a hand to my heart. "Jesus, sneaky much?"

Finn raises a brow and gives me a pointed look.

"I was trying not to disturb you." It's only now that I notice the TV is on, pressed to pause on one of his games. Finn is in sweats and an old Nike tee with the words "Just Do It" splashed across his broad chest.

"I'm disturbed that you're tiptoeing around like some cartoon villain," he says with an eye roll and then heads for the couch, a sports drink clutched in one hand.

Setting my purse down on the side table, I follow him. "I wasn't tiptoeing. I was being quiet."

Finn snorts and plops on the couch before peering up at me as if I'm full of it. Which I am. "You've been gone a while."

It sounds like an accusation.

"You had company." Shit, that sounds like one too.

Finn turns back to the screen. "Not anymore."

There's a tone in his voice that gives me pause. Sorrow or bitterness. It's hard to tell.

I make my way over to the couch and hover by the arm, not sure if I should sit down or leave him alone. Finn doesn't bother to look up, but takes a long drink from the bottle in his hand. The faint lines that fan out from the corners of his eyes are deeper now, tight and unhappy.

"You eat?" he asks, setting his sports drink on the table. "I had to put the cheese away. It was getting sweaty. But I can pull it back out."

I clear my throat. "No, I'm good. I ate at a bar."

Quietly, he nods and then reaches for his game controller. I turn to go when his voice stops me.

"Stay." He glances up, and I nearly rock back on my feet. Because he looks haunted. Angry. Lost.

I find myself sitting beside him, close enough to feel the warmth radiating from his body, but not close enough to risk leaning on him. "You all right?"

His expression shutters. "Just tired."

The finality in his tone makes it clear he's not going to answer any more questions. I'm almost relieved. The last thing I want to do is console him on his love life. Even so, I don't like that he's hurting.

He glances my way but doesn't meet my eyes. "I can put on something else if you want."

"No." I kick off my shoes and set my phone on the coffee table before curling up more comfortably on the couch. "Let me see you kick some ass with your big guns of fury."

The corner of his mouth twitches. "Are you throwing shade, Chester?"

"Me?" I blink innocently. "I would never."

Finn hums as if dubious, but his expression is lighter as he starts up his game. Content to sit next to him and watch him play, I zone out, my body growing heavy and warm. Two hours I've been gone, and I've missed him like it's been weeks. I'm so screwed.

He finishes the game and turns on regular TV, flipping through the channels.

"Oh, wait," I cry out. "Stop here."

"'Friends'? Really?"

"Don't give me that look. It's funny!"

"It's like... what? Twenty something years old."

"You're a twenty something," I point out with some asperity. "Should I not watch you on TV?"

His brows rise at that. "Do you watch me on TV?"

He sounds both hopeful and skeptical.

"James is a huge fan. I've been watching you play since the beginning."

For a long moment, he says nothing, his gaze darting over my face as if he's trying to figure out if I'm being truthful. But then a slow, pleased light fills his eyes. "It's unnerving how much I love knowing that."

It's all I can do not to squirm. "I should clarify that it was mostly out of the corner of my eye, and you were not much more than a padded up dude hiding under a big helmet."

Finn shakes his head and tisks. "You're not going to ruin this for me, Chess. You've seen me play. End of story." He sprawls out, his long legs slanting over the coffee table, like some lord of the manner.

"Are you going to let me watch my show or keep crowing all night?"

"I'm good," he says a touch too happily.

"I'll make a convert out of you with this show, just wait."

"I've already seen it. Dex is a fan." He grabs his drink. "You remember him from the shoot? The big guy with the beard and tats—"

"And piercings," I cut in. "Yeah, I remember, all right."

A choked, gurgle gets caught in Finn's throat as he jerks his head up. "Jesus, Chess."

"What? The man has his dick pierced. It's kind of impossible to ignore. Or didn't you know?"

His brows meet over a dark scowl. "It's not the kind of thing I *want* to notice."

God, it's hard not to grin; he sounds so put out and aggrieved. But the devil in me can't resist poking the bear. "I'd think a piercing like that would be the talk of the locker room."

As predicted, he reacts with an agitated scoff, but then turns back toward the TV. When he speaks, his tone is almost sullen. "Dex is your type."

Oh, we're going to talk about type now? After I've come face to face with Ms. Golden Goddess Pouty Lips?

"I suppose he is," I agree. Because Finn is right. Dex is one hundred percent my usual type. We'd even discussed our mutual love of art and painting when I'd taken his picture. And yet I hadn't felt anything past a gentle fondness and the need to put the big guy at ease. "Are you trying to set me up with him?"

I'm pretty sure I'll have to kill Finn if he starts trying to get me to go out with his friends.

The corners of Finn's mouth tighten. "Sorry, but he's taken."

"Good for him." And I mean it. I like Dex.

Finn grunts in response and shifts his position on the couch, moving his legs around as if he can't get comfortable. We're both out of sorts, and I can't tell if we're trying to fight or not. The thought makes me tired and depressed.

"You need a big ottoman to rest your feet on," I say, distracted.

"Usually I stretch out on the couch." Finn glances at his coffee table then at me. "But you're right. An ottoman would be better. We should go buy one."

We? Oh, hell. I curl up tighter into the corner of the couch. "You don't have to go through all that. I can always sit on the chair and give you the couch."

"Or you could sit on my lap."

"Cute."

"I thought so," he agrees.

It's our typical back and forth, but everything feels off. I'm tense as hell, and he's lacking his usual easy charm. The glow of the TV paints his face in flickering blues and reds. The lines of his face are pinched, his shoulders held tight. His hand rests between us, large and wide, the nails trimmed.

I know that, when stretched wide, his hand is ten and three-fourths inches from the tip of his thumb to the tip of his pinky. They actually measured it for the Scouting Combine before he was drafted. Because, as Finn had once laughingly told me, hand size matters. Perhaps to the NFL it does. Right now, I'm more worried about the way he digs his fingers into the cushions as if he needs to hold on to something.

I want to pick up his hand, trace the bumps of his knuckles and the fine fan of bones that lead to his wrist. But it isn't my place to do that for him.

"I'm glad you're home." His voice is low but strong, and it resonates through my bones.

Our gazes meet. Looking directly at him aches, makes my head light and my heart heavy. A petty, small part of me wants to yell at him for having a life that doesn't involve me, for so clearly being gone on a woman who *isn't* me. And I hate myself for that hypocrisy. He isn't mine. I can't make those demands.

But the tender, needy part of me wants to crawl into his lap and rest my head on his shoulder. That's all I'd need right now. Just that. "Me too."

That seems to please him, but the solemn expression doesn't ease. "You didn't have to leave, you know."

"Yeah, I did."

His gaze slides away. "Not for hours, you didn't."

There's a heaviness about him now, a slowness that isn't the Finn I know. And I realize it's pain. He's in real pain. My throat closes in on me and it's hard to say the words. "She broke your heart, didn't she?"

Finn flinches then holds himself utterly still, his lashes lowered. "I guess she did in a way."

I officially hate the woman.

"I thought you didn't date," I blurt out like an idiot.

The corner of his mouth quirks sadly. "I don't."

He doesn't expand on that, and I'm left confused with the hard hand of jealousy pushing down on my chest. Clearly, I'm not good enough at hiding my feelings because, when he glances at me, he does a double take, his brows knitting together. "Chess—"

My phone pings with a text and then another one. Finn reaches for it as if to hand it to me but freezes when he sees the screen. His nostrils flare on an indrawn breath. "Who the hell is Nate?"

I have absolutely no reason to feel guilty. I snatch the phone out of his hand. "A bartender I met tonight."

"Tonight," he repeats as if it's a bad word. "And what does he mean when he says you didn't tell him what kind of place you were looking for?"

I can almost hear his teeth grinding. My fingers curl around my phone. "I'd rather leave before I overstay my welcome. That's just awkward, you know?"

My joke falls flat. The muscle in his jaw bunches. "I said you could stay as long as you wanted, and I meant it."

"And I appreciate that. So much." A cold, sticky feeling lines my insides. "But I'm in your away. Tonight—"

"Jesus," he snarls, standing to pace away. "Is this about Britt showing up here?"

My face flushes hot. I officially hate her name too. "I've had roommates in college, Finn. I don't want to relive listening to hookups while stuck in my room."

He scowls. "You think I fucked her? Is that why you stayed away so long?" He snorts, an ugly pissed off sound. "What am I saying? Of course it is."

"I was being polite," I snap.

"Polite," he scoffs. "First off, I never bring a hookup to my home. Ever. I don't want them knowing where I live. The last thing I need is a stalker situation."

"Well, that's...bleak."

"It's reality, Chess. Mine." He sets his hands low on his hips as he glares down at me. "I didn't fuck her. I haven't fucked anyone for six damn months, if you want the truth."

"Wait, what? Why?" And, what? How can that be? Has he *seen* himself?

His expression turns pugnacious. "That's my business."

"Then why tell me?" I grit out.

Finn turns away, his face flushed, before pinning me with a look. "I know I joke about hooking up and it gave you the impression that I'm a player. That's on me." He takes a step in my direction, and the lines of his body grow hard. "But you're talking of leaving because you think I'm some revolving fuck door, and that's bullshit."

"I'm not judging you, Finn."

"Yeah you are," he says with a bitter laugh. "At least have the guts to admit that much."

"I freaked, okay? I didn't expect a woman to show up here because I never picture you with other women." *Only with me.* "Not because I think you're some walking sex act."

Finn blinks, his brows lifting high. An awkward silence falls over us, and it's all I can do not to escape to the safe harbor of my room. But I can't do that. "I'm sorry if I offended you," I tell him. "I don't know how to navigate this roommate situation and it's confusing."

He gives a tight nod, then blows out a breath. "This isn't a prison, Chess. I can't make you stay. And, frankly, I don't want you to stay if you're uncomfortable."

"I'm not uncomfortable—"

"But if you want to know how I feel about it," he cuts in. "I want you here. My life is better with you in it. I look forward to coming home. To *you*. And I really don't give a shit if that makes me a selfish bastard." With that, he turns and heads for his room. "If still you want to move, I'll help you find a place in the morning."

CHAPTER 11
FINN

I wake with a stiff back and throbbing head. It's par for the course after a game. Doesn't make it more bearable, though. The pain is bad enough to have me limping to the shower. Five pain killers and thirty minutes of standing under blistering hot water helps me feel almost human. I'm still sore, and my skull feels like cracked glass, but I'll manage.

What isn't going away is the shitty heaviness in my chest when I think of last night. I was over the line when I lit into Chess. Britt's appearance had thrown me for a loop, and I took it out on Chess instead. The burning bolt of jealousy I'd felt when I saw *Nate's* text didn't help.

Nate? Seriously? She goes out for two hours and she has some guy named Nate texting her?

Of course she has. Chess is magnificent. A guy would have to be deaf, dumb, and blind not to notice her. And he'd have to be stupid not to make a play if he got her talking to him. No, if he got her to *confide* in him.

I rub my chest, as I hobble to my dresser. Fuck, it irks knowing she told some charm boy bartender that she needs a new place to live instead of coming to me with her concerns. Cursing, I tug my clothes on and slam the dresser drawers shut.

Fact is, I'm the stupid one. I want Chess. I've wanted her since the beginning. But I got caught up in old habits and let her think I was a bad bet, good for only one night. And she's made it clear she has no interest in taking a chance on me. Hell, I orchestrated it so that she wouldn't.

Why did I do that?

I don't have an answer, but now I have to face her, and tell her what? *Hey, Chess, I know I've never dated a woman, but the thought of you leaving fills me with fucking dread. Because I don't want to be your friend anymore. I just want to be yours.*

Yeah, that would go over well. She'll probably cut and run.

It occurs to me that this is why I don't do relationships; I know fuckall about how to handle one.

Maybe start by apologizing for flipping out on her last night.

Since Chess usually sleeps until ten, I decide to get her some breakfast as a peace offering. Apparently, she's a sucker for beignets. I'll jog over to Cafe du Monde and pick her up a bag.

As I turn the corner into the main living space, I halt in my tracks. Chess looks up from her spot at the stove. "Hey!" she says with forced brightness. "I'm making French toast. With sausages. Do you like French toast?"

Hey, Chess, I don't just want you. I need you. I need you so much it hurts. I'm pretty sure if you leave it will end me.

I clear my throat. "I love it."

"Good." She waves her spatula in the direction of the coffee machine. "Coffee just finished, if you want some."

I'm staring at her even as I'm pulling down two mugs and pouring the coffee. It feels like I'm walking through deep water. Meanwhile, Chess bustles around, flipping the French toast and dipping new slices into the egg batter she has set up in a shallow bowl.

I add cream for Chess's coffee and two sugars for mine, then hand her her coffee. "This is new," I say, with a nod toward her breakfast.

Chess glances at me from beneath her long lashes. Those clear green eyes hold a hint of regret, and my heart starts thudding. Is she moving out? Is that what this is? My fingers wrap around my mug, pressing into the heated ceramic.

"You've done so much for me," she says, sliding the spatula under a golden brown toast and putting it onto the finished stack. "I just wanted to do something for you too."

"You don't have to."

She looks up at me, so fucking beautiful, I almost lean in and take a taste of her. That husky, sex voice of hers sounds small and sorry. "I want to."

Her lips are delicately drawn, a soft pink shade that reminds me of candy. I want to press my mouth to hers. Again and again. And again.

Jesus, I'm waxing poetic like some lovelorn sap while she's looking at me as if I'm touched in the head. And I realize I've been silent for too long.

"Are you staying?" I croak out.

Chess drops her gaze to the stove, and her fingers tighten around the handle of the spatula. "I like it here."

I lean against the counter so I don't make a fool of myself and fall to my knees. *I love you here.* I clear my throat. "You keep making me breakfast, and you can stay here forever."

She snickers. "I'd hold back on that declaration until you've tasted your breakfast. I'm not known for my cooking."

Then I'll make you breakfast forever.

I dip my head over her shoulder and peer into the egg mix. "Is that a shell?" I tease, pretending I'm immune to the clean scent of her hair and the warmth of her slim body.

"Shut up." Chess elbows me in the gut, and it's all I can do not to pull her against me.

My control is so shot, I can't stop myself from grasping her upper arm and holding on. She stills, not moving, not saying a word. My grasp is gentle, my palm pressed against the smooth warmth of her skin. I'm close enough that, whenever she breathes in, her shoulder blades almost brush my chest. A phantom touch. And yet I feel that contact as if it were real. It shivers over my skin, and I want more.

And, Jesus, who is this guy I've become? I don't recognize him; he is feral, hyper-aware, and yet so tenderhearted it disorients me.

Chess's head is bent, her eyes on the pan. Butter sizzles, a soggy piece of yellow, battered bread slowly browning. Neither of us moves, my hand cradling her arm, our breaths in sync. In. Out. In. Out.

It feels as though I'm fucking her.

The strange thought tilts through me, makes me a dizzy. I sway into her, and my cock, heavy and hot with need, kisses the curve of her ass.

Everything goes a little hazy.

I need. I need.

My fingers twitch on her arm, sinking into soft flesh.

She makes a sound, not pained but undone.

I draw in a hard breath, my lungs burning. "Chess—"

The blaring tones of "Bohemian Rhapsody" cut through the room.

Mom.

It's more effective than a blast of cold water. Instantly, I step away, my head clearing and my dick wilting. With a curse, I grab the phone and shut it off. Chess's stare is a brand on my back, and my neck tightens.

"Who are you ignoring?" she asks in the thick silence.

With a sigh, I scrub my hand over my face. "My mother."

With that one confession, I know I'll have to tell Chess everything. I could keep hiding it, but I want Chess in my life, which means I have to let her all the way in, as painful as that might be.

♟ CHESS

Saved by Finn's mother. I never thought I'd be grateful for that. And yet it feels true. Because a second ago? Jesus, I'd been blindsided by unexpected and unwelcome sheer lust.

Aside from his grip on my arm, Finn hadn't even touched me. Didn't matter. I'd felt every inch of him behind me, a wall of vibrating heat and intent.

I'd never experienced awareness like that. As if every nerve ending of mine were attached to his. He breathed, and I breathed with him. It had been all I could do not to beg him to touch me, slide his hand down into my pants so he could seek out the sensitive, swelling flesh that was slick and throbbing.

It still is. And I'm thankful for this new distraction. "You're ignoring your mother?"

Finn does not seem like the type to avoid family. But his expression turns mulish and guilty.

"I've heard that ringtone at least a half-a-dozen times since I've moved in," I add. "And you never pick up."

"You're right," he bites out finally. "I'm a total dick."

He looks so forlorn yet tightly angry that I can't find it in myself to even tease.

"When we first met, I might have agreed," I say carefully. "But I know better. You're one of the good guys, Finn."

"That doesn't sound like a compliment," he mutters, glaring off and rubbing the back of his neck.

"But it is. What's going on with you?"

For a second, it seems as if he might not answer, but then he lets out an expansive sigh of defeat. "Fuck it. I want to talk to you about this." Blue eyes full of pain meet mine. "I do. I just don't think I can have this discussion here or I'll lose it. I need some air."

Ten minutes ago, I'd wanted to lick him like warm honey. Now, it's all I can do not to hold him like a wounded animal. But if he's anything like me, he'll balk at that. I keep my voice neutral. "Well, then, let's take a walk."

We go to the river walk where the sun shines bright and cheerful and the breezes off the Mississippi are stiff enough to carry painful words away in a flash. We're silent for a while and pass a man playing "The Sunny Side of the Street" on the trumpet. Farther down, a group of completely ragged musicians who are probably my age sit on the ground, practicing bluegrass.

Finn's fingers touch my hand, and I edge away out of knee jerk habit. He makes a noise of irritation. "Take my damn hand, Chess. I'm not going to fucking cry or anything." His long fingers seek mine out again and secure them in a snug grip.

"I didn't say you were, Mr. Grumpy." I thread my fingers with his. "There? We're holding hands."

"Finally," he mutters.

I let that go and just walk alongside him, waiting for Finn to speak. When he does, his voice is tired and strained. "About eleven months ago, I went to a party and hooked up with Britt."

Okay, not what I was expecting. And not something I want to hear about. But I don't say a word.

"It wasn't even one night," he goes on. "We fucked in a bathroom and then went back out to enjoy the rest of the party."

Well, that's classy.

"Yeah, I know," he says as if I've spoken out loud. "I was high on an important game win and here was this supermodel begging to suck my—" He clears his throat. "Four months after that, Britt shows up at my door."

"Please tell me you recognized her," I blurt out, unkindly. Damn it.

Finn shoots me a repressive look that I absolutely earned. "Yes. But I'll be honest; I wasn't exactly thrilled to see her. Sex with Britt had been kind of…bland."

Only Finn would tell me sex in a bathroom with a supermodel had been bland.

He swallows hard and stares out over the river. "She was pregnant, Chess."

I stumble on a crack, and he tightens his grip on my hand to steady me.

"What?" I croak.

Finn's jaw bunches. "From high school out, they warn us about knocking women up. Never believe them when they say they're on the pill. Always wear a condom. Today's screw can be tomorrow's screw up."

"Lovely."

"But true," he says with a shrug. "I wore the condom. And I wasn't so naive that I didn't ask for a paternity test. Britt agreed. She didn't want money. She has more than enough of her own. She just wanted me to know because it was the right thing to do."

I suddenly feel small and petty for being jealous of the woman.

Finn lets go of me and shoves his fists into his pockets as we slowly walk along. "Tests came back. I was the father."

"How... I never heard a word of this in the press. And James watches Sports Center religiously."

"We kept it quiet and were fortunate that there were no leaks. Jake is the only friend on my side who knows. Well, him and my family. They know too."

He draws in a deep breath. "Anyway, I manned up, offered to marry her—"

My stomach turns with a violent lurch. If he's married...

"But Britt said no."

Relief and panic war within my chest. *He could have been married. I'd have never known him this way.*

"We hammered out how to handle custody, things like that..." He trails off and stares down at his shoes as we walk.

"So, you have a child." I can do the math. The idea that a little Finn offspring is somewhere out there stuns me. God. A father.

"Five months in," he croaks. "Britt miscarried."

"Oh, Finn."

He stands hunched against the wind, his expression blank. I touch his arm and find it vibrating with tension.

"I'm so sorry, Finn."

His nod is vague, the barest lift of his chin. "We'd just found out she was a girl, you know?"

My fingers curl around his arm. "Finn…"

He takes a deep breath as if he's sucking all his pain back into himself, and his shoulders straighten. When he looks up, his jaw is hard and set. "The whole time Britt was pregnant, I told myself that this is what real men do. They take care of their mistakes." He snorts, a broken sound. "That's what I thought of my baby as, Chess. A mistake. My baby girl."

His eyes well, and I can't stand still anymore. I step into his space and hug him tight. And he instantly hugs me back, squeezing with enough force to bruise, his face burrowed in my hair. For long moments, he shudders, fighting for control, while I press my palm to his back and coo nonsensical noises under my breath.

His rough voice is close to my ear. "I didn't even know how much I wanted her until I saw her in that sonogram." Another tremor slams through him. "But there she was, ten fingers and ten toes, flailing around like she was running in place, and I wanted her. I wanted her. And then she was gone."

"Oh, Finn." My heart breaks for him. For Britt. I've never been in their situation, but I know how it is to have something you never thought you wanted ripped away from you. And how that loss changes your life and haunts your future.

I think about that irony and a deep sorrow washes through me.

I don't know what to do for Finn except keep holding him. But he doesn't allow it for long. Soon enough, he pulls away and stands tall. The rims of his eyes are red, but he's tucked away his anguish. I've done the same thing so many times, a part of me admires how well he hides himself. The other part of me knows you can't heal that way and wants to comfort him longer.

"Britt went home to Sweden. She didn't want to see me. And, frankly, she reminded me of…everything, and I was glad she went."

"Was yesterday the first time you'd seen her since?"

He nods. "Shocked the shit out of me."

I feel myself growing distant, as if I'm breathing through layers of cotton wool. I can't shake the sensation that I've lost something I didn't know I had. All this time, I'd thought of Finn as a shallow bowl, not stupid by any means, but not someone who had much of a life beyond football and partying. And I feel so fucking small for assuming that.

"What did she want?" I can guess. She'd looked at Finn, as if he were her salvation. I swallow back the lump in my throat. They have a history I will never understand.

Finn sighs, and we start walking again. "My mom invited her to spend the holidays with us."

No need to for him to say how he feels about that. If looks could kill, his mom would be in grave danger right about now.

"What did you tell Britt?" The idea of them spending the holidays with each other doesn't exactly make me happy. But I have no claim on Finn. To demand one now would be hypocritical and petty.

"That I didn't want her there." He winces. "I know it sounds bad, but we were never friends. Just…I don't know, teammates with a common purpose. But my mother… I went home after it happened. She was with me at my lowest."

"And now you're avoiding her?"

"Because she won't let go of the notion that she needs to fix me." He moves to run a hand through his hair but feels his hat and flings his arm down. "No matter how many times I tell her that I'm okay, she keeps trying to set me up with some daughter or friend of so-and-so, as if finding the right woman will make it all better."

I bite my lip to hold back a smile. "Mothers can be well-meaning like that."

He snorts. "Last time I went home, Admiral Foster's daughters came to dinner practically every night. The both of them smiling pleasantly as if it were up to me to pick my favorite and take her. It was awkward as fuck. But this…" He lifts a hand in exasperation. "This is too much. Not only did Mom piss me off, she embarrassed Britt."

"So tell her that."

"I'm ridiculously bad at telling off my mom," he grumps.

"Well, avoiding her isn't going to work."

"I know that. Shit." He scowls so darkly, the woman walking by us does a double-take and quickens her step. Finn doesn't seem to notice. "I have to go home for Thanksmas."

"Thanksmas?"

"It's kind of a winter holiday catch all," he explains with a roll of his shoulders. "When my schedule has games on or too close to Thanksgiving and Christmas, my mom has Thanksmas on one of my bye-weeks."

"That's adorable."

"That's my mom." It's easy to tell that, despite his disgruntlement, he misses his mom and loves her deeply. He glances down at me. "Chess…"

"What?" I say, edging away. "I don't like that look."

Finn blinks, all innocence. "What look?"

"The same look you used the other week when you'd put my bras in the washing machine and it twisted them all to hell."

"I was trying to be helpful."

"As I said then, keep your helpfulness away from my bras and panties."

A brilliant grin lights his face. I'm happy to see it. This is the Finn I know, the one who doesn't leave me confused and bleeding for him. "It was totally worth getting yelled at," he says.

I roll my eyes. "Were you going to ask me something?"

He sobers a bit but there's a hopeful light in his eyes. "Come to California with me."

"What? For your family holiday?" I squeak like a startled mouse.

"Yes." He nudges my shoulder with his. "Come on, it'll be fun. My family will love you. And my mother is a great cook."

I eye him with suspicion. "What aren't you saying?"

The lobes of his ears pink. "Okay. While we're there, I was thinking we could tell her that we're together."

I halt so fast, Finn walks a step for before noticing to stop.

"Oh, fuck no," I say, shaking my head.

His brows rise as if he has no fucking idea why I'd object. The liar. "Come on, it isn't that bad."

"It's worse. You want to lie." My fingers curl into a fist. "To your family."

"Yes, I do. Because she won't stop, Chess. Not as long as she thinks I'm this poor, broken-hearted sap who needs a woman to mend him. It doesn't matter what I say, she has a fucking bee in her crazy bonnet."

"Well…"

He takes a step closer. "The press is already circulating pictures of us together. Of you living with me."

"What?" My skin prickles with horror.

"Surprise," he says with weak humor. "Britt told me. And I'm sorry for that, Chess. I didn't think about them invading your privacy."

"It isn't your fault." I swipe my hand in the air as if I can push away the whole shitcake of photographs of me with Finn being spread around like bad tabloid copy.

"Regardless, my mom follows my press religiously. She's kind of proud that way."

His mom is definitely adorable.

"She'll have seen us together, which is probably why she called this morning. If I tell her we're just friends, she won't believe it anyway." Finn ducks his head and makes a sound of frustration before looking back up at me. "If we say we're dating, she'll finally accept I've moved on with my life. And I can enjoy my mother's company without wanting to run away screaming."

A reluctant smile pulls at my lips. Who am I to criticize how he handles his family? I love my parents but they annoy me so much that I haven't even told them about the fire. Not something I'm proud of, but not something I want to remedy either. "So you want me to be your lady beard?"

He blows out a breath. "I want you to go home with me because I want to spend my favorite holiday with you. Life is more fun with you in it, Chess."

I'm in serious danger of melting into a sloppy Chess puddle. Thankfully, he keeps talking.

"But if you're so inclined, then, yes, I would appreciate it if you could play the part of doting girlfriend for the duration."

"You know, it never goes well when people pretend to be in a relationship for the sake of the parents," I tell him. "It's rom-com law. Next thing you know, you'll be on stage somewhere, confessing your well-meaning lies into a mic while dozens of strangers look on."

Wind sends strands of hair whipping around the edges of his cap, and he steps a little closer, his body blocking the cold, as his eyes search mine. "It doesn't have to be pretend, you know."

My breath halts then leaves in a rush. "What?" The question is more of shock than confusion. But he answers it anyway.

"You and me. We could be real." The blunt tip of Finn's thumb brushes back a wild lock of my hair and then lingers along my cheek. "We could stop dancing around this and enjoy each other."

Panic claws up my chest. "Finn..." I try to draw in a breath. "I'm living with you..."

He smiles, his thumb still stroking. "Which makes things convenient."

"No." I cup his hand and still his touch on my cheek. "It makes it stupid."

Finn's expression shutters.

"Most nights, I cry myself to sleep," I blurt out.

Finn sucks in a sharp breath, his brows knitting. "Chess—"

I hold him off when he tries to hug me. "I'm not telling you for sympathy. I barely want to admit this to myself. But losing everything has thrown me, Finn."

"Honey. Fuck." His other hand cups the back of my neck with a gentle squeeze. "You should have told me."

"I'm telling you now. Because the one bright spot in all this, the one anchor I have, is you."

A distressed, almost angry sound leaves him, and he rests his forehead against mine. "Honey, I can't..." His eyes squeeze shut. He seems a loss for words.

My fingers curl around his wrists, holding on. "I don't want to risk that. Not when I feel so..." Lost. But I can't say it.

I don't have to. He pulls me close, despite my protests and tucks me into the shelter of his chest. "It's all right, Chester. I'll never push you. We're good, yeah? Everything will be okay."

"Don't coddle me," I mutter, even though I can't find the strength to move away. "I don't need it."

Finn hums in his throat. "Yes, I know. You're a total badass. But you've got this wrong. You're coddling me. I have needs, woman."

A broken laugh escapes me. "I'm already regretting my confession."

"Chess?"

"Yeah?" My voice is a rough mumble in his sweater.

"Shut up and let me hug you."

With a sigh, I give up the ghost and lean fully into him, because hugging Finn should be a total body experience. And, despite my weak-ass protests, he soothes the ugly jitters that have started up in my chest and belly.

I'm not certain how long we stand there. Long enough for me to grow warm and soft in his arms. Then I clear my throat. "I'll be your lady beard."

Finn draws away enough to look me in the eye. I hate that his expression is strained and worried. "No," he says. "It's a stupid idea."

"Well, it's not your best," I agree with a weak smile. "But I see the logic. If it helps your mom relax, and thus you, it's worth doing."

Finn frowns, but I can see he wants to accept.

"Come on." I nudge his shoulder. "We can do this. A couple of cuddles. I'll tell your family how much I worship you—"

"I do like the sound of that." With a laugh, he wraps his arm around my shoulder and turns us back down the walk.

When I first met him, I'd have never had guessed he was easy going. I know his behavior then had been caused by stress and panic. But even so, he seems to be another person with me. There's no bullshit with

Finn, just open honesty.

He put his trust in me and revealed his pain. It isn't something I take lightly.

I wrap my arm around his waist as we walk along. "I'm sorry about the baby, Finn."

His step falters a bit, but he doesn't let me go. "Yeah," he says low. "Me too."

We walk a bit before his voice cuts through our silence. "It's not going to go away for me."

My arm slides from him as I look up. "What isn't?"

Finn's expression is solemn, but when he catches my eye, the corner of his lip quirks. "Wanting you."

I'm not aware of stopping but suddenly I'm standing still, unable to speak.

The look in his eyes is almost self-deprecating. But there's a thread of stubbornness beneath his gentle tone. "I said I wouldn't push you, and I meant it. But one day, Chess, you're going to feel safe enough to let go. And I'm going to be there to catch you when you fall."

CHAPTER 12
♟ CHESS

Finn is waiting to catch me. The thought haunts me more than I want to admit. It runs through my head in the weeks that lead up to our trip to California. It looms large when James finally comes home and slyly offers to let me stay with him, both of us knowing full well that I'm not going anywhere.

I like living with Finn. And though I want my condo back desperately, living anywhere else doesn't appeal.

Actual Thanksgiving rolls around. James and I spend it with Finn and his friends. Finn's team plays that day, but he gets us tickets, which nearly makes James cry. Wrapped up in team scarves and woolen caps, James and I sit at the fifty-yard line and scream ourselves hoarse.

At one point, Finn taps his fist to his chest and salutes in our direction. Which causes the crowd around us to go wild and speculate why he'd singled out our section; James, however, wraps his arm around my neck and gives me a happy noogie.

"Who's caught the quarterback?" he sings.

I do a very bad job of pretending to be annoyed. And don't even try to hide my joy when Finn and his team win the game.

Dinner is catered and better than any Thanksgiving meal I've ever had. Since Finn's dining room is an unfurnished space he uses for exercise, James, Jake, a lineman named Russell, Finn, and I crowd around his coffee table, sitting on the floor to eat.

Shoulder to shoulder, Finn and I laugh and eat and trade jokes. He is a warm presence at my side the whole time. But, true to his word, he doesn't try anything. And his promise keeps spinning in my head. *I'm going to be there to catch you when you fall.*

Now we are in San Diego where the sun shines lemon yellow and the sea air is a warm kiss on my cheeks.

Finn has rented a lime green convertible jeep and put the top down.

"This feels very nineteen eighties," I say over the noise of the wind.

His teeth flash white within the tan of his face. Jeep could sell dozens of these vehicles just by using a picture of him driving. "Too much?" Finn asks me.

It is; my hair whips around me like a lash, even though I started out with it in a secure ponytail. But it's also fun. After hours of being stuck in a stuffy plane, the open sky and fresh air acts like a balm. "It's perfect," I yell back.

He laughs and then guns the jeep up the curving road that hugs the coast. The scenery is stunning, with massive homes carved into the coastline, their endless glass windows glinting in the afternoon light, and the Pacific stretching west like a dazzling sapphire and gold-studded canvas.

Finn pulls up to a gated drive and punches in a number.

"I had these installed after I was drafted," he tells me, somewhat grim. "Dad didn't like the idea, but I liked the idea of some crazed fan trolling around even less."

"Someone would do that?"

"Someone *did* do that." The gates slowly open. "Young woman last year tried to break in. She was looking for my old room."

"Jesus."

"She was harmless, but someone else might not be."

Finn heads up the drive. It isn't very long but hides the house from view until we round a bend. Finn's parents' house is an L shaped, sprawling sixties California style ranch painted soft gray and trimmed in bright white that overlooks the ocean.

As soon as we pull up, the double doors to the house open and a slim, tall blond woman comes out.

"Finnegan," she cries, hurrying over to him as he steps out of the car. His reply is muffled in her hug.

I smile at the scene, shamelessly watching. But my car door opens, and I'm face to face with an older version of Finn. There are differences: this man's eyes are light brown instead of blue. His skin is swarthy and weathered from what is clearly a life lived under the sun. And his posture is arrow straight even when apparently relaxed.

He gives me an easy smile, more of a curl of the lips and a deepening of the crinkles around his eyes. "Ms. Copper, I presume?"

"Yes, sir." Because this man exudes authority without even trying. "You must be Finn's dad, Captain Mannus."

He helps me out of the Jeep even though I don't need it, and then shakes my hand with one firm pump. "Finn has never brought a woman friend home before. Which means you're special, Ms. Copper. Call me Sean."

"Sean. I'm Chess."

With a nod, he gestures toward the house. "This way. Meg will be fawning over her boy for a good while more."

"I heard that," Finn's mother says from behind us.

Up close, Finn's mother is beautiful in that golden, eternally youthful way of Californian women. I don't know if it's something in the air or all the excellent plastic surgeons who live here, but I want to look half as good when I'm her age.

"Finn's been telling me all about you, Chess. I'm so glad you could make it."

Finn got his blue eyes from her. And her smiling mouth. We are of the same height, and when she shakes my hand, her smile is genuine, but her eyes search my face as if looking for internal flaws.

I don't resent her for being protective. I know she loves her son.

But having never met a man's family before, I find myself wanting to squirm. I can only imagine how she sees me, pale skin, black hair with colored tips, tattoo on my arm. My white halter top and rose patterned A-line skirt are feminine, but they're no match for the casual elegance she manages to pull off with her cream-colored slacks and linen top.

"Thank you for including me in your holiday." There, that was polite. I can do polite and mannerly.

Finn rests his hand on my lower back. "All right, all right. Can we get inside? I'm starving."

"You ate a fish taco on the way here," I say with a half eye roll. In truth, it had been impressive the way he ate those tacos while driving. Not a drop spilled or his attention from the road compromised. But then his hand eye coordination is better than most. And Finn *never* wastes good food.

"That taco was tiny, Chess. It was gone in two bites."

"Well, with the way you ate it, yes—" I cut myself off, remembering belatedly that I'm meeting his freaking parents.

But Sean merely gives me a wink so quick, I almost miss it.

I let out a breath and tell myself to relax. I'm nervous, which is a new experience for me. Not one I like. Doesn't stop me from wanting to make a good impression.

Inside, the house is open and airy, with vaulted, beamed ceilings painted white, shiplap walls, and multiple picture windows framing the sea. The furniture is big and comfortable, California casual. It's like we've stepped into a design magazine. And yet there are signs of a well-lived life everywhere. Framed pictures of family on the tables, knick-knacks from exotic ports of call.

"It's beautiful," I tell Finn's mom.

She smiles wide. "Thank you, Chess. Let's get you situated and then we can have drinks on the patio."

Finn is back at my side, proprietary hand on my shoulder. "I'll show her, Mom."

There's an awkward beat of silence in the room, and I truly want to elbow Finn in the gut. I have no idea if his mom had planned to room us together, but the fact that he's made it clear that we are is mortifying. And, sadly, something I hadn't really thought about with this whole relationship farce.

"Ah…yes, of course," Meg says, with a small smile my way.

Wrapping my arm around Finn's waist, I smile back like a dolt, even as I surreptitiously pinch his side. He twitches, then presses his arm against my hand to keep me from attacking again. Nice block, but I'll get him in the room.

Aware of his parents watching us go, I keep quiet as he leads me down a long hall and into a bedroom at the far end of the house. I have a quick impression of clean, white furniture, and blue sea views before I pounce, pinching his little nipple.

"Ow!" He dances away scowling as he closes the door behind us. "What the hell is up with all the pinching?"

"You might as well have peed on my leg back there," I hiss.

Finn rubs his chest and frowns some more. "What are you talking about?"

"Out there." I gesture to the door. "Did it occur to you that your mom might have wanted to place us in separate rooms?"

"What are we, sixteen?" He looks appalled. "We're supposed to be together. There is no way I wouldn't be sleeping in the same bed with my girl. Mom knows that."

"Are you sure about that? And your dad is military…"

Finn laughs, looking genuinely amused. "Dad is a sailor at heart, Chester. He's the last person who would try to put you in the guest room." Finn peers at me as if noticing something, and I have the annoying urge to check my face for dirt.

"You didn't think we'd be sharing a room, did you?" he asks, smugly smiling.

"I knew." I glance at the bed. It's a queen. Not nearly big enough for us to share. Not when Finn is the size of a tree.

"Uh-huh." He takes a step closer. I don't like that twinkle in his eye. It spells trouble. "You know we're going to have to be a little affectionate toward each other, right?" Another step. "Remember? Cuddle, gaze at me with utter adoration."

"I don't think I'm that good of an actress," I mutter, refusing to back up, though I want to. I'm beginning to feel like a juicy piece of steak, the way he's eyeing me.

His warm, slightly callused palms skim up my arms. Little shivers of pleasure follow the motion. His lazy gaze lowers to my mouth, and I swear my lips plump in happy appreciation.

Finn makes a sound at the back of his throat. "I'll probably have to kiss you a few times."

My lids flutter, my lips going soft and full, as I try not to sway. He's close enough to feel his warmth. My body wants him to breach the tiny distance and take. But my brain is filled with blaring klaxons. I suck in a breath, and hear him do the same.

"If you were my girl, I'd definitely kiss you any chance I got," he whispers, dipping closer.

"Try to kiss me now," I murmur, my lips nearly brushing his. "And I will bite you."

A huff of laughter brushes over my skin. "Oh, Chester, you really shouldn't dare me."

I lift my lids and our gazes clash. He hasn't moved away. The heat in his eyes makes my thighs tight. For a mindless second I want to taunt him, really dare him to do it. Kiss me. Make me forget my name.

But then his mom's voice slices through the thick air between us.

"Finn," she calls from the hall. "Hurry up! Glenn is here!"

Finn doesn't move, but his grimace is swift and pained. Slowly he straightens, holding my gaze the entire time. "I'm beginning to think that woman has some sort of sixth sense." With a wry twist of his lips, he takes a step back. "Come on then, you heard the woman. Glenn is here!"

I should be grateful for his mother's impeccable sense of timing. But I'm not. I glance back at the bed as we leave the room. She won't be around at night. And I really don't have much faith in my will power anymore.

🏈 FINN

Awkward is a grown man hobbling out of his childhood bedroom, trying to tuck away his hard-on so he can face his family without causing anyone mental trauma.

And while part of me wants Chess to see the effect she has on me, I've pushed her enough already. I'm fairly certain Chess would have no compunction about kneeing me in my tender balls and taking the next flight home.

I haven't been doing a good job of keeping away from her. I know this. I've told myself this more times than I care to count. Problem is, I want her with a ferocity that aches low in my gut, and I find myself reaching for her without thought, only to restrain myself at the last second. Because she is not mine.

My body insists otherwise and is fairly pissy with me at present. Aching dick, bruised heart, twitchy hands, I'm an undisciplined wreck.

And then I had to go haul Chess off to my room. A stupid play. I have no idea how I'm going to keep my hands off her when we're stuck sleeping together in that small ass bed. Jesus, I haven't been this torqued for release since the seventh grade, when I caught sight of Angel Ramirez's boobs in gym class.

Pathetic.

"What did you say?" Chess peers up at me with suspicious green eyes.

"Nothing." I open a pair of French doors and lead her out to the patio.

Seated at a grouping of rattan chairs are my brother and his wife, Emily. They both stand, and I notice the small swell of Emily's belly. I take a hard step, the ground meeting my foot too soon.

Because she's right beside me, Chess bumps into my shoulder. But then her hand slips into mine, her grasp secure and firm, and I know she's seen Emily too, that she understands exactly. A lump rises in my throat.

I squeeze her hand in return and then ease my hold as if I'm merely a guy leading his girl out to meet his family.

Glenn meets me halfway. My brother is five years older than me. Though he is two inches shorter, with blond hair instead of brown, and thicker about the waist—because he doesn't have a job that requires him to work out until he drops—we still look a lot alike.

Glenn was a running back in college, but didn't make it to pros. Doesn't mean he isn't still strong as an ox. He nearly knocks the air out of me as we hug, thumping my back hard enough that I cough.

"Good to see you, man," he says, stepping back, his gaze darting to Chess.

I make the introductions, give Emily the standard hello kiss and ask how she's doing with her pregnancy. Yes, I knew. I just hadn't seen the visual proof until now. Soon enough Chess and I are tucked together on a love seat, as my family not so subtly grills us for information.

"So," my mom says, margarita in hand. "How did you two meet?"

"I took nude photos of Finn," Chess says before biting into a tortilla chip, loaded with guacamole.

Mom chokes on her drink, as Glenn laughs, and my dad holds back a smile.

Chess pauses, mouth filled with chip, and her creamy skin goes brilliantly pink. "Shit," she mumbles around her food, as I start to laugh. "I didn't mean…"

"I was posing for a charity calendar," I tell them, taking pity on Chess. "Chess is a professional photographer."

Weakly she nods as she takes a bracing sip of her drink.

"Finn must have made a good impression," Emily teases with a wink.

"Jesus, Em," Glenn blurts out, still laughing.

"What? All I'm saying is that a girl can get a little sidetracked seeing a naked guy."

"Oh, he wasn't the only one nude," Chess assures, then catches herself again and grimaces. "I mean, I saw a lot of other dicks—Shit."

My father loses it and starts laughing in that low, wheezing way of his.

"Fucking hell," Chess mutters, now tomato red. The cuss words seem to make her even more mortified, and she buries her face into the crook of my shoulder. "Let me die now."

My heart gives a weird sort of lurch at her unexpected turn to me for comfort and protection, and I wrap my arm around her slim torso, snuggling her close. "Maybe have a few drinks before you speak again," I tease, pressing my lips to her hair. "You know, to loosen up your tongue."

Her small fist punches my abs. "Shut up," she says into my shoulder, her breath heating my shirt.

Because she's my girl here in this moment, I grab her fist, press it to my heart, and then kiss the top of her head. I don't even notice my family gaping at me until I lift my head.

The look on my mom's face is so relieved she's almost weepy with it, and it sends an uncomfortable prickle of guilt down my neck. That look tells me she'll no longer worry that I'm lonely, but it's too hopeful. She glances at Emily, and her happy smile grows.

She's finally getting her grandbaby.

At my side, Chess is still bemoaning her big mouth.

"Don't worry, Chess," my dad says, leaning forward to give her a gentle pat on the knee. "You'll fit in here just fine."

Chess lifts her head, brushing the inky strands of her hair away from her face. I miss the contact immediately.

"Somehow, I doubt you continuously stick your foot in it," she says to my dad with a wry smile.

"No," he agrees with a chuckle. "But Finn certainly does. And we've decided to keep him around."

"That and, whenever he loses a game, I get sympathy drinks at the bar," Glenn adds with a wink.

Absence has made me forget what a dickhead Glenn can be.

Chess takes a cool sip of her margarita before replying. "You must not get many free drinks, then."

It's right there, on my parents sun-baked patio, with the tart taste of margarita on my tongue and the sound of Chess's husky voice in my ears, that my heart, brain, and body comes to one simple agreement: this woman is mine.

Dad starts telling Chess about places she should visit in San Diego, and I help my mother take in the empty chip bowl. She doesn't need the help, but I have a few words for her.

As soon as we're in her sunny kitchen, she rounds on me. "All right, let's have it then." She braces herself against the counter.

"Oh, you mean the part where you invited Britt to stay here without asking me?"

"I can hardly ask, Finnegan, when you don't answer your phone."

Zing.

With a sigh, I lean against the opposite counter. "I said I was sorry. I shouldn't have avoided you. But you can be stubborn as shi… as hell."

My mom snorts and turns to put the dishes in the sink. "You can say 'shit,' Finn. I am a grownup."

"Mothers aren't grownups. They are part chaste saint and part eternal nag."

"Ha."

I steal a mango from the fruit bowl and go in search of a paring knife. "I'm fine now, okay? Happy even. So, please, let it go with Britt. Let the scab heal."

"Consider me done with meddling," my mom vows with a lift of her hand. "A wise woman knows when to say when."

I let it go that she missed that mark by a few months. Wise men know when to back away slowly.

"So…" My mom says in a voice that is distinctly meddling. "Chess is nice."

A smile pulls at my lips. "Nice isn't how I'd describe her."

"Oh? And how would you describe her? Here, use a plate."

Perfect. Fuckable. Stunning. Funny. Mine.

Mine.

Mine.

"Great." I put the mango on the plate. "She's great."

Mom sighs in exasperation. "Men. None of you know how to properly describe your feelings."

She makes me grateful for every sunrise. Because I wake up knowing she's in the world.

I set the knife down and face my mother. "Just…be nice to her, okay?"

"Finnegan Dare Mannus, I am never rude to my guests, and you well know it."

"That's not what I meant. She's had a rough time. Lost her house, her workplace. Her best friend is off in a new relationship. I don't think her parents are in the picture." I run a hand over my face. "She needs a little care, okay. It's important to me."

Mom's eyes meet mine. God, she's welling up again. "Oh, Finn, you've gone and done it. You've fallen in—"

"Jesus. That's it. No more heart-to-hearts with you for at least five years."

"Just remember, Finnegan," she says, ignoring my protest. "Love with your heart, not your head. Think about things too much and it all turns to shit."

I grimace, hoping to hell Chess doesn't hear her. Even so, I fight a smile. "Thanks Mom, and don't say shit. It offends my delicate sensibilities."

Before she can snap me with a towel, I grab my plate of mango and head out to find Dad. And some much needed testosterone-injected conversation.

♟ CHESS

Finn's old room is not a shrine to all things Finn as I'd expected it to be. There are a few tasteful black and white photos of him throughout his career, including a ridiculously cute peewee football shot, where Finn is basically an oversized helmet and pads walking around on tiny legs.

Aside from that, the room is done entirely in ethereal blue and creamy white. The ocean, I know, is just beyond the massive windows that are open a crack to let in the breeze. But it's dark as pitch out there now.

Finn and I dithered and stalled, talking around the fire pit long after dinner had ended and his family had trickled off to their beds.

Sitting huddled together under a blanket in front of a crackling fire seemed like an equally bad idea so I had announced my intent to head to bed. Unfortunately, Finn decided to come with me. Not that I can fault him for it. We *are* sharing a room and it *is* late.

Now, I dither yet again in the little *en suite* bathroom, rubbing coconut oil over my dry elbows and brushing my teeth twice. But a girl can only stall for so long without making it obvious.

I find Finn tucked up in bed reading on his iPad, and thankfully wearing a t-shirt and whatever he has on under the covers. The bed looks dainty beneath his big frame and broad shoulders. The space left for me to lie beside him is a tiny sliver of bed real estate that promises prolonged bodily contact.

Well, fuck.

Finn looks up and studies me with a passive expression on his face. I can tell he's examining all angles of this, trying to figure out how to put me at ease, wondering if I'm about to bolt. The idea calms me, and I lean against the bathroom doorway.

"I expected your room to be covered in plaid and gleaming with school trophies," I tell him.

"Plaid?" He snorts. "I'm of Irish stock. We call them tartans, and you won't be finding them on me walls."

"That is the worst Irish accent ever."

Finn grins, his eyes impossibly blue against the sky colored sheets. "My parents remodeled the house three years ago. It's double the size now and every room has been redone. Glenn and I took what we wanted out of our rooms and packed up the rest to stuff in the garage."

"Ah, the end of childhood," I say with an expansive sigh. "It's always so wonderfully brutal."

"I'm guessing your parents did the same when they bought the tiny house?"

"Pretty much. Only they sent me a box of what they thought I'd want and gave the rest away."

"Jesus. They didn't warn you?" Finn scowls, which somehow causes his biceps to bunch. It's a good look for him.

"We are talking about people who named their daughter Chester because they thought it was a good meet cute story." I shrug, hugging my chest tight. "My parents are loving, generous, and flighty as fuck. I was the one who remembered to take out the trash, buy groceries, and do the laundry. They taught me to dance the waltz and fingerpaint on walls."

Finn's blue gaze rests on me, and I shift my weight onto my other foot. "They aren't horrible," I ramble on, aware that my voice is far too shaky. "But reliable, they ain't."

When he speaks, it's in a gentle, even tone. "Are you going to get in this bed, Chess?"

I stand a bit straighter and huff out a breath. "That's all you have to say?"

His lips part as if he'll speak but then he closes his mouth before opening it again. "In the spirit of friendship, I feel I should point out that your nightshirt is transparent when backlit by the bathroom light."

I jump out of the bathroom doorway, flicking off the light as I go. With a glare, I hustle my ass into the bed, sliding under the cool covers as Finn laughs low in his belly.

"Asshole." I pull the comforter up to my chest. "You could have told me sooner."

"The struggle was real," he admits, turning to face me. His impish smile fades. "How else was I going to get you in bed?"

With a sigh, I snuggle in, trying to get comfortable amidst the pillows. Finn turns off the bedside lamp and then settles down as well. We're so close, shoulder-to-shoulder, his knees bumping mine, my cold toes wiggling over his, that there is no escape.

I should be panicked but it feels nice. Safe. At least in this moment.

Finn's voice is a murmur in the near darkness. "I'm sorry you had to go through that, Chess. It couldn't have been easy. I've always wondered…"

"What?" I whisper thickly.

Finn rests his head on his hand. "You're so strong."

"Hardly."

"You weren't intimidated at all by us when we showed up at your place, hollering and acting like a bunch of rowdy boys."

"You're a bunch of overgrown puppies."

His teeth flash in a quick smile. "True. But I think you're used to dealing with shit. Having a name like Chester must have been a nightmare in grade school."

I tuck a pillow under my cheek and stare up at him. "Kids learn fast. Word gets out that taunting me will earn a punch on the lip, and they're not so quick to tease."

"But they still did it." He sounds so protective, it hurts my heart and makes my skin twitchy.

We're both fully aware that Finn calls me Chester. But, when he says it, somehow my name becomes simply me, something that I don't need to hide from or cringe over. After a lifetime of feeling as though an essential part of me is nothing more than a sad joke, it is a gift I never knew I needed.

My fingertips sink into the down pillow as I try to get a hold of my emotions. "We've all had shit to deal with in childhood. Frankly, I think most of us deserve a freaking medal for surviving it." I lift my head slightly and narrow my gaze. "Or did you coast through wound free?"

Finn worries his bottom lip with the edge of his teeth. "My ears grew bigger before my head could catch up. And I had acne."

"Get out of town. Pretty Boy Mannus?"

"Back then they called me Pimple Boy Mannus." He husks out a laugh. "At least when I wasn't throwing TDs."

"I bet the girls liked you anyway."

We're speaking in hushed tones now, and the words have a weight between us.

"I was the quarterback. Of course they liked me."

"That's not the only reason why."

"What's the other reason?" Somehow, he's gotten closer. I never saw him move, but we're almost nose to nose now, his forearm pressed against mine where they rest on the mattress.

I smile, the barest curve of my lips. "Like I said before, you're one of the good guys, Finn. People can't help but like you."

His eyes search mine. In the dim, they glint like dark skies. "I want to hold you."

My breath hitches, catching in my throat.

Finn presses on, his voice a rumble against my skin. "Just that, Chess. Let me hold you while we sleep."

I'm not aware of making a conscious decision, but in the next breath, my cheek is pressed against the firm swell of his chest, and my body is tucked securely along his lean length. His arm wraps around my waist and he clasps my nape.

He's so blissfully warm that I close my eyes on a quiet sigh.

"Thank you," he whispers into my hair.

It shouldn't be so easy to melt into his hold and fall asleep.

But it is.

CHAPTER 13
♟CHESS

Finn's gone when I wake. Not surprising since he's an early riser. After a shower, I head out in search of coffee.

Sean, who I still want to call Captain Mannus or sir, is in the kitchen pulling what looks like turnovers from the oven.

"Meat pies," he tells me, as I pour myself a cup of coffee. "Try one."

He puts a golden pie on a plate and hands me silverware and a napkin before setting my meal on the kitchen island. I settle on a metal stool and cut myself a bite.

"Delicious," I say around the hot, buttery pastry filled with savory meat and vegetables.

"There will be more where that came from this afternoon." With elegant efficiency, he moves around the kitchen, putting turnovers on cooling racks, setting another tray of them into the oven.

Having never spent time around military men, I wasn't certain what to expect from Finn's dad. I thought perhaps he'd be hard, a stern man who kept to himself or grunted behind the newspaper he was reading.

It certainly wasn't this man who exudes a quiet calm that makes you want to please him, who wears a "Good Lookin' is Cookin'" apron while preparing a holiday meal for his family.

"Finn got you that apron, didn't he?" I say.

The lines at the corners of Sean's eyes deepen. "Yes, ma'am, he did." He glances up from his work. "You know my son well."

I shrug and finish another bite of turnover. "His humor anyway."

Sean grabs a kitchen towel and wipes his hands. The more I watch him, the more I see a lifetime of military training in him. Not a single movement is wasted or hesitant. He manages to be utterly graceful, yet proudly commanding.

He reminds me of a less impulsive Finn.

"You haven't asked where my son is," Sean remarks.

"If I had to guess, I'd say he was out running."

Sean's lips curl in a smile that is very reminiscent of Finn's when he has something on me.

"It's eleven," I feel obliged to point out. "He always exercises at ten. Before returning starving and in search of food—"

Finn breezes into the kitchen, sweaty and flush. Gym shorts ride low on his hips, the white tank he's wearing sticking damply to his skin. "Do I smell meat pies? Man, I could eat a dozen."

Sean catches my eye before grabbing another plate from the cabinet.

Finn pours himself a massive glass of orange juice and comes over to stand beside me. He smells of sun and sea and sweat. "Chester." He kisses my cheek. A sweet gesture that makes my skin tingle. Memories of being wrapped up with his long, hard body flutter through my mind, and it's all I can do not to lean into him now.

From the speculative look he's giving me, I'm guessing he's remembering things as well. "I see Dad's taking care of you."

"Very well," I agree, focusing on my coffee. His gaze slides to the food on my plate and turns absolutely covetous. Rolling my eyes, I offer him and bite, which he takes without hesitation.

"Fuck, that's good," he says with a little groan that I find way too appealing, given that it's over food.

"You're stinking up my galley, Finnegan," Sean says mildly. "You know the drill. Shower before meal service."

"Aye-aye, Cap!" With a waggle of his brows to me, Finn grabs his glass and hustles off.

I'm left alone with Sean who looks at me as if he knows something I don't. He's astute enough to keep silent. But inside, I am a storm of guilt and uncertainty.

Finn's family adores him. Their joy over him being in a relationship is so lovely it threatens to break my heart. I don't want to lie to them.

But I don't get to discuss it with Finn. We are effectively swept up in family activities. Starting with putting up the Christmas tree.

Gathered around in the big living room, Meg, Emily, and I watch as the men pull sections of a white, artificial tree out of boxes. Sean's quiet commands keep Finn and Glenn from arguing while they try to figure out what goes where. Soon, the ten-foot tree is assembled before the picture window and plugged in to glow in softly lit splendor.

"I know fresh trees have that lovely scent," Meg says to me. "And some traditionalists sneer at artificial, but I just love my white tree."

I take a picture of Finn and Sean adjusting a few branches. "I have a silver tree. Or had one. I suppose it's melted now."

My laugh sounds brittle, even to my ears. Meg gives me a gentle squeeze around the shoulders, a move so much like her son's that it's eerie. "Well, I'm glad you're here to enjoy this tree."

I almost don't know what to do with the Mannus brand of tactile affection. My mother would have recited a poem about loss and patted my hand before drifting off. As new as it is for me to be cuddled and hugged, I find it comforting. Especially since they never cling or make me feel pathetic.

Meg announces that she's going to make her "special nog", which has Finn and Glenn snickering, and I really don't want to know why.

"You shouldn't be working," Emily tells me, as she starts opening up ornament boxes. "Come relax and trim the tree."

Glenn's wife is petite, her curly hair so dark brown it's almost black, her skin a deep, even tan that speaks of Hispanic descent. Silver bangles around her wrist tinkle as she works.

"I actually prefer this," I tell her. "Putting up ornaments makes me tense. I'm never satisfied with where I place them."

"Glenn is the same."

My expression must convey my surprise because she gives me a wry smile. "He's a landscaper. Everything has to be just so, the visual balance just right, or he's twitchy. Whereas, I teach fifth grade students, so I've learned to go with the flow."

I glance at Finn's older brother, who is currently trying to get Finn in a headlock. I take a picture of that. "You've been with Glenn for a while."

"How can you tell?"

"The way you two interact with each other. It's fluid. Like you've been together so long that you know which way the other will go before one of you even moves."

Emily beams. "That's lovely."

"Just an observation."

Finn walks up with a glass of nog for me, and a glass of what smells like hot cider for Emily. "Sorry, Em. Meg's special sauce is not good for the baby."

Emily laughs. "It isn't good for anyone." She glances at me. "Watch yourself. That stuff is lethal."

When she heads toward the tree, I lean closer to Finn. "I like your family."

"Good. They like you too."

We're alone now, off to the side of the action. But I keep my voice low. "I like them too much to lie to them."

Finn does a double take at that. "You aren't."

"I am."

He doesn't roll his eyes, but his tone implies he wants to. "Have you said to them, I'm in love with your son and we are having wild monkey sex?"

"Who says crazy crap like that to someone's family?"

The corners of his lips twitch. "Well, it would be kind of awkward, I'll give you that."

"You are annoying me. Stop being purposely obtuse. I came here playing the role of your girlfriend."

This time he actually does roll his eyes. "I'm trying to make it simple. Stop thinking of it as playing a role."

"But it *is* a role." I take a drink of nog to keep from yelling at him. And immediately regret it. "Holy lighter fluid, what the hell is in this drink?"

"Fireball cinnamon whisky." Finn calmly pats my back. "You're here because you're my girl. Sex doesn't change that fact."

Throat burning, heart threatening to turn to mush, I can only look at him and sigh. "Finn, what am I going to do with you?"

His smile is an easy glide, but his eyes hold mine a beat too long. "Keep me. I'm pretty sure I'm good for no one else."

Before I can answer, he's off again, helping with the tree, joking with Emily and Glenn. I take pictures, eat the stuffed mushroom caps that Meg sets out on the sideboard, and gingerly sip my nog from hell.

My tongue turns pleasantly numb and my limbs nice and warm. I'm taking a close-up of the little elf man who lives on the shelf—why kids actually want an elf who's supposed to come alive at night, hanging out in their house is beyond me— when Finn peeks over my shoulder to look at the camera screen.

I nearly yelp but settle down, trying my best not to lean into him. He smells like cinnamon and spiked eggnog, which I find exceedingly delicious at present.

His breath tickles the sensitive skin on my neck. "Can you do selfies with that thing?"

"With a bit of awkward juggling," I concede.

"That's what I thought." The warm wall of his chest presses against my back, as he swings his arm in front of us, holding his phone. "Say, hey!"

He snaps a picture. "And the humble iPhone triumphs over the fancy Nikon."

I'm still blinking, as he brings the phone up to look at the picture and utters a quickly stifled laugh.

I catch a glimpse. "Ack! No!" One of my eyes is closed, and my mouth is open.

Finn hums under his breath. "You look like a confused fish."

I make a grab for the phone, but he holds it away, chuckling.

"How on earth did you manage that, Chester?"

"Delete it or die, Mannus."

"All right, but I need another one to replace it with." Finn's grinning face is so close, the flecks of navy in his irises are visible. Those happy eyes full of mischief. That smiling mouth that I find endless fascinating.

"Okay," I say. "Do it again."

He adjusts his grip on the phone, lifting it right in front of us. As soon as I feel his arm tense to take the picture, I kiss his cheek.

Finn gives a small start, his breath hitching. Before I can move away, he turns, his eyes a little wide. I've shocked him, making first contact.

A smile wavers on my lips. "How was that—"

Finn presses his mouth to mine. The kiss is sweet and swift, a touch of lips to lips, a slight exchange of air. And it still manages to stop my heart and send heat flaring up my thighs.

He backs away just enough to meet my eyes. For one tight second we stare at each other, breathing a bit faster, deeper, as if we're not sure what just happened. And then he kisses me again. Another soft peck as if to make certain this time is real.

The third kiss is mine. His lips are firm and smooth, addicting.

Finn makes a small noise at the back of his throat, his lips lingering as if he's simply enjoying the feel of me.

We're barely touching, barely kissing even, yet it feels almost frantic, as if we have to take what we can get now. My hand rises, fingers clutching his shirt. *More. Give me more.*

"Yeah, enough of that," Glenn—the rat bastard—says, suddenly in front of us. "We have a tree to trim and Mom's hooched up nog to drink."

Finn's glare is scary, and I'd run if I were Glenn. But the man seems immune. He gives us a shit-eating grin and backs away, holding up a silver ball ornament like a taunt.

Shaking his head wryly, Finn turns back to me. Meeting his gaze is too much. I can't kiss him again. Not here. Not now. I won't be able to stop.

"Kissing in front of the family accomplished," I blurt out, hating myself as I do.

Ugly heat prickles on my cheeks, as he simply looks at me. I expect to see disappointment. But it's worse. His expression is one of affection and gentle amusement, as if he's silently saying, Oh, Chess, who do you think you're fooling?

"I think," he says after a long, hellish moment, "we'll have to practice that play some more."

With that, he leaves me. And I want to follow.

🏈 FINN

Sunset at Black's Beach is one of my favorite places to be. It's almost surreal, this canvas of gleaming oranges, hot pinks, and turquoise blues. The cliff face flares tangerine in the fading sunlight. The air is cooler now, tinged with briny sea spray.

A few surfers are enjoying an evening ride. I know some of them, but thankfully they haven't yet recognized me. I need a few moments alone.

Which is why I didn't invite Chess along, even though I want her to see this place.

I know what her lips feel like now. We've kissed. If you can even call what we did kissing. It was PG-13 stuff, quick pecks on the lips. And fuck if those stolen touches, the almost frantic fumblings with her, weren't the hottest thing I've done in recent memory.

First touch of her lips and I was hard. The second, I'd wanted inside her. I'd *needed* it.

Crazy thing is, it had been so unexpected—her kissing my cheek, me snatching a little taste of her mouth in return—that I'd been coiled tight as a spring, unable to move or do anything but steal a few more kisses like a greedy, horny bastard afraid of having the whole opportunity ripped away from him.

And then it was. She pretended the whole thing was just for show.

Bullshit.

Question is, what do I do about it? Call her on it? Let it ride?

I've never been struck by this level of indecision. In football, you hesitate, you're done. We train, run drills, and practice until reaction is muscle memory and instinct. There is comfort in that. Hell, there's comfort in knowing that you're one of the best at something. I know I'm not the best quarterback in the world. Not yet. But I'll get there. Perfection in this sport comes with experience and finding your groove.

But with Chess, I might as well be in the peewee leagues. I'm bumbling around, not knowing the plays or how to read a line. It's frustrating as fuck. And I cannot fuck up. Not with Chess. She's too important.

I'm at a crossroads here.

A small voice inside me is whispering to cut and run while I still can. That's the easy solution. No failure there. I can back off, treat Chess as a casual friend. The kind I call every couple of months when I have some free time and nothing to do.

That was Dex's advice, and the man is a master strategist.

Leave Chess alone. Go back to being alone.

I watch a surfer paddle out, calling to his buddy. Their voices are thin on the air, the surf crashing to the shore. Sun glitters off the curve of a wave, turning it murky, turquoise blue.

I feel old. Not yet thirty, not yet in the full groove of my career, and suddenly I feel so fucking old. Apart from everything. I could have been a dad.

Would she have had my eyes? Would she have hated green peas like

I do?

My fingers dig into the sand. It's cold and rough just below the surface.

The sound of my phone ringing has me dusting off my hands.

I reach for it, expecting Chess. "Hey, I'm down at the beach."

"Ah, okay."

It isn't Chess.

"Britt?" I actually look around as if expecting her to pop out of the sand.

"Yes, it's me." She pauses. "You thought I was someone else?"

Well, obviously. "What's up?"

I have no idea why she's calling, but I don't like it. It feels like one of those woman traps that end with her crying and me generally feeling like a heel.

"I…ah…" She clears her throat. "Look, I don't like how we left things."

This is why I'm terrible with women. Because I have no fucking clue what she means. She asked me if my mom had invited her to spend the holidays with us. I told her no. What else is there?

My silence must have gone on too long because she makes that sound again, as if she's trying to push her words past some blockage in her throat. "There were things I wanted to say, Finn. But I got distracted, upset." A soft, half laugh escapes her. "It was difficult seeing you again."

Again, I feel like a shit for rushing her out. I pinch the bridge of my nose. A headache is coming on. I need to get back to my parent's house. I've been gone too long, under the guise of making a wine run.

"I know it's hard," I tell Britt as gently as I can. "I was… I was just thinking of her."

A lump rises swift and painful in my throat, and I swallow convulsively.

"You do it too," she whispers thickly.

"Sometimes." My fingertips press against the hot skin of my eyelids. "At random moments."

"The other day, it hit me that she would soon be old enough to start eating baby food." Britt's voice trembles. "And I had to pull over my car and cry."

"I'm sorry." I don't know what else to say.

The beach is cold now. I get to my feet. I don't want to be here anymore. I need to get home.

Chess had gone off to take a nap, jet lag catching up to her. But she'll be awake now.

"Could we meet for lunch or something when you come back?" Britt asks, pulling me back to the conversation.

Fishing my keys out of my pockets, I rest the phone on my shoulder, holding it in place with my cheek. "You're still in New Orleans?"

"Yes. I'll be here for a while."

It makes no sense. Britt's home is in Stockholm.

"I'm in California for the week."

"I'll be here next week," she says.

When I don't say anything, she presses again. "I want to see you. And I…I'd rather not talk about it over the phone."

I don't point out that she called me. This feels off. No, it feels like she's working her way up to asking me out. "Britt, I don't…"

"We share something, Finn. There is no one else in our lives who understands it the way we do. I don't have anyone else to talk to."

The desperate pain in her voice is too much for me. With a sigh, I turn on the jeep and pull out of my spot. "All right. Text me next week and we'll set something up."

As soon as I hang up with Britt, I toss the phone on the car seat. I'm not looking forward to that meeting at all. Sharing with her doesn't make me feel better. There's only one person who does that. I turn onto the main road and head for Chess.

I can't let her go. It's too late for that now. But I can give her space.

Either she takes that distance and pulls away. Or she'll find it as unnatural as I do now. Instinct tells me it will be the latter. I fucking hope so.

CHAPTER 14
♟CHESS

It is fairly horrifying to realize how well Finn Mannus can play me. For the rest of the day, and into dinner, he keeps his distance. He isn't cold or anything. Hardly that. He's a great host. Solicitous, including me in conversations, making sure I have enough to eat.

And that's the problem. He's treating me like a guest. Gone are the light touches, as if he can't keep his hands off me. Gone is the way he somehow always manages to be standing close enough that our arms brush. And gone are the teasing glances that dare me to reach for more.

I hadn't truly noticed he'd been doing these things until he stopped.

The result being, I seek him out. I'm the one finding ways to stand closer, to touch his wrist or the curve of his biceps. And though he doesn't say a word about it, I know he'd predicted with unnerving clarity how I would react.

I don't know if I should admire his skills or be annoyed.

Both, is the answer.

My annoyance grows when he gives me space and heads out to get wine for dinner without inviting me to come along. He's gone for over an hour.

I'm pissed at myself. For being a coward where he is concerned. For pretending that what we are to each other isn't evolving. I know he cares about me. He makes certain I feel his care every day. He won't hurt me. Not intentionally.

And I need to apologize because how I reacted to kissing him was hurtful and unfair. But I don't get the chance. Between Finn distancing himself and his family intent on being good hosts as well, we are never alone.

Before dinner, Finn and his dad settle down in the den for a game of chess.

"I didn't know you played," I say to Finn, as I sit next to him on the couch to watch.

"We never really got to the 'hey, by the way, I love playing chess' stage of our relationship," Finn says with a sly wink.

I nudge his shoulder. "Smart ass." God, I'm doing everything I can to be close to him. It's ridiculous.

Even more so when my heart gives a little leap as he nudges me back, softly chuckling. "You play chess, Chess?"

I resist sticking my tongue out at him since Sean is watching with avid interest. "No. I admit it's over my head."

"Then watch and learn, my friend."

"I'll watch, but all I ever see are pieces being moved around, seemingly at random."

With a snort, Finn hunkers down and studies the board. The stern, absorbed expression on his face is adorable, and frankly hot. It's even sexier when I realize he's actually good, really good.

I lose track of time as he and his dad play with the intensity of men at war.

Eventually, I end up reclining on the couch to read. Without taking his attention away from the board, Finn puts my feet in his lap and rests one warm hand over my ankle. I keep reading, but I love it. I love that, ever so often, his thumb strokes my skin in an absent-minded but tender caress. Whatever is going on between us, I know he isn't angry with me. And some of the tension flows out of my body.

After dinner, I go back to the room and change into comfortable lounge pants and an oversized light sweater. Then Glenn, Emily, Finn, and I head for the family room to watch a movie.

"I feel like I'm in high school," I say to Finn. "Watching a movie with a boy while his parents are in the other room."

He gives me a knowing look. "You gonna let me cop a feel under the blankets?"

I don't answer, leaving him to catch up, his eyes narrowed on me.

The family room is a large but cozy space with a sectional couch near the back and two big recliners grouped together off to one side. A tumbled stone fireplace fronts the space.

"Where's the TV?" I ask.

Glenn picks up a remote. "Right here."

A movie screen starts lowering from the ceiling.

"Wow."

"Finn's last *Thanksmas* present to my dad," Glenn says. "I'm still waiting for mine, the cheap ass."

"Hey," Finn protests with a laugh. "I keep you flush in athletic gear."

"You get that stuff for free."

"Don't listen to Glenn," Emily says to me. "He wouldn't take a gift like that even if Finn snuck it into our house on the sly." She heads for a recliner. "My back is killing me."

"Damn it, baby," Glenn complains. "You know I like the couch."

"Then snuggle up with Finn and Chess." She relines the chair with a happy sigh. "Or would you rather carry this baby?"

"Yeah, because arguments based on total fantasy always work," he grumbles and plops down in the other chair.

"Sucker," Finn says, sprawling on the big corner of the couch.

I walk by him, intent on curling up on the opposite corner, when Finn reaches out and takes hold of my good wrist. And I pause, staring down at him. His grip is warm and secure, as he meets my gaze with steady eyes.

It's my decision, whether I cuddle up with him or move on. If I tug on my arm, or take a step, he'll let me go. I sink down. And he moves with me, turning his body and tucking me at his side. My legs drape over his, my head resting on the couch pillow beneath his chin.

Neither of us says a word as he reaches back and grabs a thick throw to cover us. Nestled against the firm expanse of his chest, I don't think I'll ever be able to go back to sitting alone. Not when he is near.

Finn grunts as if to say, about time, and then wraps his arm around my waist.

"What are we watching?" My voice is breathy.

"*Die Hard.*" Finn's words rumble against my shoulder blades. "Christmas classic."

"Come out to the coast, we'll get together, have a few laughs…"

His lips graze the shell of my ear. "I promise not to blow anything up."

Glenn messes with the remote again, and the lights go low. I've seen *Die Hard* a dozen times. I know the lines by heart. I hear none of them now.

The room is dark. Glenn and Emily are silhouettes against the screen. Tucked on the couch, Finn and I are in another world. I can't even pretend I'm watching the movie. Images flash, words are spoken, but my attention is on the man behind me.

He shifts a little, moving so that we're fully spooning. The wall of his body is rock hard yet it melds against mine, warm and comforting. Or it would be. Only my awareness is too keen now, sending little flips through my belly. Something stiff nudges my ass.

"Is that…?" My voice is a ghost in the dark.

But he hears it. "Yes," he says at my temple. "You get near him and he wants to say hello."

Ducking my head, I smile into the pillow. The devil in me has me arching my back just a bit, pushing my ass into his hardness.

Finn grunts low in his throat. His hand spreads wide over my belly, holding me still. So slow, it's barely a movement, he rocks against me. The rest of our bodies lay absolutely still. Oh, but my heart beats like a mad thing, violently pumping within my breast.

Finn's breath chuffs out as if he can't quite control it. His lips rest on my hair. "God, you smell good. You always smell so fucking good."

It's such a low murmur, I barely hear it over the sounds of the movie.

"It's the coconut oil I use on my skin," I whisper back, pretending everything is casual, that my sex isn't starting to throb and my breath isn't growing light.

Finn breathes in deep and lets it out slowly. "It's you. All you."

A shudder wracks him, and he seems to go tight all over, as if he's trying to hold onto his control. The hand at my belly is stroking now, small, leisurely explorations.

My breasts grow heavy, my nipples drawing tight. The screen grows blurry. I can't think.

Finn's hand slips beneath my shirt. His fingers are rough with calluses but feather light against my skin. A ripple of pleasure dances over me, and I suck in a breath, silently urging him on. Up and down he traces, the edge of his thumb touching my belly button, the tip of a finger glancing along my waistband.

His hand moves higher, and the blunt end of his thumb grazes the bottom curve of my breast. We both freeze. The shudder that moves through Finn is almost violent. His thumb presses into my bare breast, and he shakes again, a near-silent groan leaving him.

My lids flutter, desire making everything heavy and hot. I press my cheek against the couch pillow, waiting, willing him to explore me. A gust of breath stirs my hair, and then his touch slides up. The warm weight of his hand over my breast feels so good, I gasp.

Finn's body jerks, shoving against mine. As if in a dream, he palms my breast, rubbing in gentle circles. So good. Such a perfect tease. My breath grows shorter, my thighs trembling. In the dark, hidden beneath a blanket, he fondles me, lightly playing. The tip of his finger worries my nipple, toying with the stiff tip.

When he talks, his voice is hot smoke along my neck. "I want to see you." His finger skims back and forth. "Suck you here."

A light pinch. Luscious tension sparks down my belly, pooling in my sex like wet heat.

I can't take it. Moving in a fog of need, I roll onto my back, my body resting in the circle of his arms. The action sends Finn's hand skimming over to my other breast. He kneads it with possession, as our eyes meet. Neither of us speaks.

I want to kiss him. I want it so badly my lips are swollen with the need to feel his. But we can't kiss. Not here. It would be too loud, and they'd notice. And when I kiss Finn, I know I won't stop there. When I kiss him, I want to consume him. I see that understanding reflected in his eyes. This is killing him, but he loves it. He's reveling in it.

Gaze hooded, he fondles me, tugs my poor, achy nipple—teasing.

It feels good to be teased, to let the anticipation build and simmer. But he's getting away with it far too easily. Carefully, I ease onto my side and face him. He watches me move, a light of expectation in his eyes. Holding his gaze, I slide my hand under his shirt.

Finn's tight belly flexes beneath my palm as if he's ticklish. God, he's warm, his body hard but his skin soft. I rub him there, enjoying his textures and the way he twitches as if he can't decide whether to pull away or press in closer.

Closer wins out when he cants his hips and shifts his thigh between mine.

With a happy sigh, I lean into him. My lips touch the smooth curve where his neck meets his shoulder. He smells delicious, clean like soap, and spicy like sex and pheromones. The fragrance of Finn goes straight to my head and makes it light, while the rest of me becomes heavy and hot.

I lick that curve, and he grunts—a breath of sound. His grip on my breast tightens a fraction.

Smiling, I tug the button of his jeans, and they pop open. Finn goes utterly still. He's fairly humming now, he's so tight.

Delicious. I want to eat him up.

My hand slides under the waistband of his boxer briefs. His cock rises to meet me, fever-hot, silky-smooth. He's so hard he pulses. I give him a long, easy stroke.

Finn's breath comes out in quick, light gusts. He's shaking now, but he barely moves, as I quietly jack his cock. Up and down, squeezing just a bit at the tip. Finn's free arm snakes beneath me and gathers me closer.

We're wound together, my face tucked in the warm hollow of his neck, my hand stroking his dick, as he plucks and toys with my nipple. He can't do more. We can't move too much without being noticed. The huge muscle of his thigh, notched between my legs, flexes rhythmically in a maddening push-release against my clit.

Trembling, he rocks his hips, slowly fucking himself in my grasp. I run my thumb over his crown, tease the ridge of the wide head. The tremors increase. I don't know who is shaking harder now. I could come like this. But I want his release more. Straining against him, I find the sensitive skin at his neck and suckle it, as my grip tightens on his dick.

The sound he makes is tortured, almost a whimper, and then he jerks so hard, I nearly lose hold of him. Wet heat spills over my fingers. We both shudder then, gasping as he works through his orgasm.

Finn sags against me, his breath stilted and damp on my neck.

The world around us returns—the loud explosions on the screen, the reflective lights of the movie flickering over Finn's skin.

As if coming out of a deep sleep, Finn blinks at me, his lashes fluttering. And then his gaze clears, zeroing in on me with a force that makes my breath hitch.

Watching me, he takes my hand and wipes it clean on his shirt. And I am a twisted woman because part of me wants to tug my hand free and taste him on my fingers.

I don't know what he sees in my gaze, but his nostrils flare. His lips barely move, his voice so low only I can hear it. "Bedroom. Now. Or I take you here."

I move like water, rising up and flowing to my feet. My limbs don't feel like my own anymore. Somehow he's claimed them, and I'm left this throbbing mass of need. My nipples are so stiff they hurt. I need him to pinch them harder, put his mouth on them and suck...

Blood rushes in my ears, and distantly I hear myself saying goodnight to Glenn and Emily

Emily is asleep.

Glenn waves me off without looking back.

I know Finn is following. He's coming for me. The knowledge is cool heat on my skin, a pulsing pressure between my legs. My thighs clench with each step.

I don't make it far. The darkness of the hallway closes in, and then his warm hand is there, wrapping around my arm, pivoting me.

Silently, he presses me against the wall, one hand in my hair, the other cupping my chin. But he doesn't kiss me. Not yet. Our breath mingles in rasping pants, as we stare at each other in the shadows. The line of his jaw bunches. I'd think he was angry if it wasn't for the intense look in his eyes. As if he's hurting.

Need.

That's what that is. Because I feel it too.

I lift my chin, nudging at his hand, leaning into his touch.

His thumb strokes the edge of my jaw. His voice is barely a whisper but hard and stern. "Tell me again that I'm a bad bet. Because I can't wait to prove you wrong."

Anticipation shimmers through my belly. "Prove it."

All the tension leaves him with a breath, replaced by something more intent.

When he kisses me, it isn't rough or impatient; it's deep and consuming, as if he's been given air after so much denial. Or maybe I'm the one who feels deprived, because that first touch ignites me. Nothing compares to kissing Finn Mannus. It is glorious, delicious. Perfect.

With a rough noise, he settles into the kiss, feeding me his tongue with easy glides, coaxing mine to play with his. And I do, tasting, taking. I draw in a quick breath, plunge in again, working for those gruff, pained sounds he makes, as if he's dying and only I can save him.

I'm so attuned to him at this moment, every rapid thud of his heart against his ribs reverberates through my body. My fingers curl into the loose fall of his shirt at his back. I'm shivering with heat, my lips swollen, my jaw aching.

As if he feels my need, his grip on my hair tightens. He takes my mouth with soft, nibbling kisses, and deep explorations. All the while walking us toward his room.

Hands fumble behind me. He gets the door open, and then we are in the cool quiet of the bedroom. Standing in the center of it, I watch him close the door, pull his dirty shirt off and toss it to the side. Blue moonlight plays on his shifting muscles as he moves. I drink in the sight, my fingers clenching with the need to touch.

Finn's eyes gleam as he reaches out and flicks a switch. The bedside lamps turn on, and he grins, a slow curl of his lips. The look in his eyes is predatory.

My belly does a little flip. "Afraid of the dark, are we?"

He takes a step farther into the room. He looks as undone as I feel. Hair mussed and eyes glazed. "Needed to see this in full color."

We speak in hushed tones, as if neither of us wants to break the quiet spell.

He stops close enough that I feel his warmth, see the way his pulse beats a rapid tattoo at the base of his throat. His lids lower in lazy perusal. Softly, he traces a line down my neck, sending little shivers in his wake.

His finger hooks on the edge of my shirt and plucks it. "Take this off."

It's a low murmur that rubs like velvet on my skin.

Holding his gaze, I pull the shirt free. Cool air buffets my skin.

Finn's breath hitches. He stares at me without blinking, his chest lightly lifting and falling. "That first night," he rasps. "You were wearing a gold, silky top. I wanted to slip my hands under it, cup these perfect tits."

The backs of his knuckles graze the side of my breast, and I twitch, moving closer.

Finn makes a rough noise in his throat. "I knew they'd be so fucking pretty, Chess." His thumb brushes over my nipple. "I wanted to suck these juicy nipples right there. Right there at the bar. Right through your little top."

I sway a little.

Finn's eyes meet mine. "Take the rest off. I want all of you."

My hands go to the waist of my lounge pants. "You too. Let me see you."

Our eyes hold as he unbuttons his jeans and pushes them down with an impatient thrust. He's naked before my pants touch the floor. And then there is only us. And this Finn is just for me, his cock jutting out hard and long, a little pearl of need glistening at the tip. That big cock sways a little under its own weight as it twitches and preens for me. He grasps that beautiful dick in his hand, giving it a light stroke.

"You're beautiful," I tell him.

Finn's eyes gleam. "And you're my fantasy come to life."

I move to him, sliding my arms around his neck, melding my lips to his. He wraps me up in his warmth, his hard against my soft, his tongue dipping into my mouth for another taste.

Stumbling back, he takes me with him, his mouth never leaving mine. He lays me down on the cool bed, kissing his way along my neck. Big hands glide over my skin like a dream, slow, soft.

I squirm as he licks his way down my breast, seeking the tender bud of my nipple. All that time on the couch, he played with me there, working me up, getting me so sensitive, the slightest touch now is almost too much.

Finn knows this. It's there in the way he looks at me from beneath his lowered lids, all covetous and hot like he's planning illicit things. "So fucking gorgeous."

He goes at my poor, stiff nipple with short, leisurely licks, testing my flavor, getting himself acquainted with my textures. Just enough pressure to make me feel it, to want more.

A satisfied hum from his lips buzzes straight down to my clit.

I can't take it.

"Will you…" I swallow convulsively, my body jerking as he gives my sensitive flesh a little kiss.

"What?" he whispers, idly dragging the flat of his tongue over my nipple again.

"Suck it," I rasp. "Please. It aches so bad."

A groan tears out of him, almost pained. He cups my breast in his big hand, plumping my flesh up for his pleasure. The first wet pull of his mouth has me biting back a whimper. My back arches off the bed, but he holds me fast, sucks me with rhythmic tugs.

"Finn." My voice is thready, desperate. "Please. Suck them."

He mutters hot, frantic words, his breath coming quicker. His mouth moves to my other nipple. Teeth nip, and then the wet glide of his tongue before he sucks. It feels so good, I'm going to melt into a fucking puddle of heat.

My hips rock against the bed as I whine, needing more.

"Shhhh." He kisses my nipple gently. "You don't want to wake my parents."

That sly whisper goes straight to my core. We shiver, sharing the illicit fantasy of pretending we might get caught. It makes everything more intense. The room seems darker, his skin on mine hotter.

Slow, lazy kisses pepper over my chest, as clever fingers drift down my trembling belly. His fingers are thick and long, and by the time he gently slides them over the swollen bud of my clit, I nearly come.

Finn rubs his cheek against my breast, his fingertip tracing the opening of my sex. "I want to fuck you now."

I think I whimper. My hands claw at his shoulder, the back of his head. I need him closer.

He gives the curve of my breast a soft kiss. His voice is dark honey.

"Will you let me, Chester? Will you let me fuck you?"

An incoherent sound leaves me. It's enough for Finn.

Shadows shift as he rises above me, and then he moves into a shaft of lamplight. God, that body, golden and taut, I want to lick every inch of it. I need to feel it on top of me more.

He settles between my parted thighs, and he feels so hard and firm, his skin damp with sweat and emanating heat that I groan again.

"Shhh," he whispers in my ear. His body trembles. "God, you feel so good."

My hands glide down his back, mapping the hard terrain of his body. I need him in me. I'm so empty it aches.

But he just touches my hair, looks down at me with eyes that show too much. "You okay with this, Chester?" The tenderness in his voice wraps around my heart and squeezes. "Me going bare?" Another caress along my cheek. "I can get something."

"No." I lick my swollen lips. "Just you. Now."

His lashes lower in a sweep, and then he's staring at me as if I'm Christmas. The round tip of his dick nudges my opening. And…

"Oh, fuck," I moan. I feel that body move and all those muscles clenching as he pushes in, making room for himself inside me. So thick. So perfect. My sex grasps that hardness, holding onto the pleasure.

A helpless whimper breaks the silence. It is Finn.

Pausing halfway in, Finn braces himself on his elbows, his breath harsh. "Okay?"

Okay? I lift my hips, spreading my thighs wider. "More."

"Oh, fuck yes," he groans. One firm push and he's balls deep, so big it hurts.

I want the pain. "More. More."

Filthy words tumble from his mouth as he starts to move, giving me what I want. But it isn't fast. It's slow and savoring. Finn works me as if he's memorizing every damn second of it. And I love it.

"Talk to me," he pleads, moving in a slow, steady fuck.

"Talk?" I can barely think. My world is a heavy glide of muscles and cock.

"Your voice," he says. "Pure fucking sex. Love it."

What this man does to me. I cup the sides of his damp neck, kiss my way along his jaw. "I love your cock."

He trembles. "Yeah?"

"The first time I saw it, I imagined…"

Finn stills, pulsing inside me. "What? Tell me."

"Sucking it."

He groans deep, rocks against me. Sweat trickles down his temple. His breath is heat at my ear. "Fuck. More. Tell me more. How would you suck it, Chess?"

Slow shivers dance over my skin. "I'd put it in my mouth when it's still soft. Feel it grow hard as I sucked it."

"Oh, fuck." He pounds into me—three hard thrusts that hit so deep I grunt each time—before he slows, deliberately dragging that thick, glorious cock of his in and out in that same evilly steady rhythm. His cheek nudges mine. "Then what?"

"I'd want you writhing while I sucked you off. You'd lie there and take it, clutching the sheets, almost whimpering as I'd pull on your dick with my mouth." God, I want that.

"Jesus." He shivers, dips his head lower. Soft lips brush my shoulder. His voice is a deep rumble. "You gonna tie me up?"

In and out goes his cock, invading retreating. I swallow hard, try to concentrate on the words. "No," I whisper. "You'd have to hold still on your own. Your willpower against my tongue. That's part of the fun."

He moans low and pained.

I run a hand down his back and cup his ass, push him into me. The muscles flex under my palm. "I'd milk you dry like that, Finn. Your thighs parted, your body strung tight."

He grunts this time, his thrust a little less controlled, a little more greedy.

"After you come, I'll keep you in my mouth until you got soft," I whisper against his cheek. "Then nurse that dick hard again."

"Oh, fuck." Finn loses control with a groan and thrashes against me. "Oh, fuck."

He pumps without finesse, without thought, hard and fast. The tight coil of pleasure within me grows almost unbearable. I arch against him, keening as I come. And he's right there with me, his mouth open and wet on my neck.

He stays with me until the trembles die down and our breath cools. And then, with a pleased sort of grunt, he rolls us to the side, his dick still deep in me. We lie wrapped up in each other, limbs twining.

For a long time, neither of us says a word. I draw circles through the smattering of hair on his hard chest, and Finn runs his fingertips up and down my arm.

"We should have been doing that since the beginning," he says.

I smile against his skin. "The beginning, huh?"

"Yeah. I should have set aside my towel. And you should have put down your camera. And we should have fucked under those hot lights until we forgot the world around us."

I huff out a laugh. "Aren't we supposed to do it until we forget our names? Isn't that how it goes?"

"Nope." He kisses the crown of my head. "I want you to know exactly who's fucking you. And I sure as hell am never forgetting that it's you I'm with."

Gently, he cups my cheek and tilts my head back so his gaze meets mine. "I'm with you, Chess. You know that, right?"

He looks different now, as if the intimacy of sex has exposed a new layer of him. Or maybe it's simply freed a part of him that he's kept hidden. This Finn looks at me as if I'm his, as if he's mine. This Finn is irresistible, because I can touch him however I want, whenever I want. So I do.

I kiss his lips, the crest of his cheek, the stubborn edge of his chin. "I'm with you, Finn. All the way."

CHAPTER 15
🏈 FINN

I take Chess to a restaurant on the beach. We sit on a huge terrace strung with lights, our table right beside the glass railing, and watch the sun set over the ocean, as Chess drinks a fruity cocktail and I nurse a beer.

"What's good here?" she asks me.

For a moment, I can only stare. Her skin glows with a light tan that makes her green eyes brighter. The ocean breeze kicks up the silky strands of her dark hair, making them dance around her slim shoulders. She looks happy, relaxed, and well satisfied.

I did that. I gave her that soft, content look. I gave her those kiss-swollen lips.

And because I now can, because she's right here, I lean in and kiss her again. A gentle, lazy exploration of her mouth with mine. She tastes of tequila and passion fruit. And I could gladly kiss her all night.

I pull back just far enough to see her smile, those green eyes light with happiness, and I smile too.

I want to tell her things. Important, emotional things that I've never said to anyone else. But this shift between us is too new and the place too public. Besides, she wants to order food.

"Get the lobster tacos," I tell her with another soft kiss.

She hums against my mouth and, when I sit back, gives me an

assessing look. "Why do I suspect that you come home for tacos almost as much as you do to see your parents?"

I laugh. "Because I do. They're the best in SoCal."

"Pretty sure there are taco lovers who would defend their own hometowns."

"They can try." I wink. Looking her over, a swelling sense of rightness fills me. I've had moments I thought were perfect. They were preludes to this. To truly being with Chess.

"Our first date should have been like this," I tell her.

Chess quirks a brow, but she's still smiling. "I thought this was our first date."

"Our first date was eating fried fish and talking about bad sex. We just didn't realize it yet."

"We didn't?"

"Nope." Slowly I shake my head. "It was a date. But the execution was all wrong. I shouldn't have made it a friend thing. I should have gone up to you and said, 'I like you at lot, Chester Copper. Will you go out with me for, like, real?'"

She snickers, but it sounds suspiciously like a happy giggle. "How do you know it would have worked?"

God, I love her smile. I want to keep teasing her just to see it bloom again and again. "It would have worked. I would have kissed you the way I'd wanted to since we met, and you would have been mine."

"Oh really," she deadpans, but I see the knowledge in her eyes.

"Really. I was made to kiss you, Chess."

She goes soft at that, giving me those bedroom eyes. And her voice grows husky, making me hard and tight with anticipation. "Maybe I was the one made to kiss you, Finn."

Emotion rushes through my chest, taking my air, and I have to breathe deep. "You were."

The waitress arrives to take our order.

When she's gone, Chess looks out over the water, giving me her profile. She's flustered, her fingers tapping the glass in her hand.

Neither of us have been in a relationship, me because I didn't want to, Chess because she never found anyone she wanted. In a way, I'm glad that we're both new to this. We can be each other's only. But part of me wishes we both knew more, or at least one of us had some knowledge of how to play this.

But it is what it is, and I'm content to drink my beer, watch the sunlight dance in my girl's hair. Our food arrives and we eat with gusto, talking about nothing in particular. The sun sinks behind the horizon, and the string-lights twinkle overhead.

A dance floor is set up on one corner of the patio. Mostly older patrons are slow dancing to a Sinatra song. Chess watches them, the corners of her lips tilted up. "I wish I brought my camera. That couple there…"

I glance back and see a man and woman who must be in their eighties. He's dressed in a light gray three-piece suit, an honest-to-god red carnation tucked into his lapel. The woman's dress looks like something out of the 40s. They move together in perfect harmony, his hand in hers as they smile at each other.

Chess glances at me but then her gaze goes back to the couple. "What must that be like? To spend an entire lifetime with someone, and the threads of who you are have become so interwoven, you can't part without unraveling."

I don't know. But I want to find out.

The song ends and another begins. It's slow, the woman's voice filled with tender love and bittersweet nostalgia as she sings along to the piano. I listen to the lyrics and start to smile. "This song was playing when I walked you home that first night."

Chess's brows draw together. "It was?"

"Elvis was singing it then."

Her expression clears as she listens. "'Can't Help Falling in Love.' I remember."

I put my napkin down on the table and stand. "Dance with me."

Chess blanches. "What here?"

"That's the idea, yeah."

Her gaze darts from the dance floor to me.

I'm patient. But I'm not letting this go. Not when it's this song, in this moment. "Some things you don't take a picture of, Chess. You live them." I reach out to her. "Take my hand."

For a second, she just stares at me as if she's never seen me before. I don't move, don't look away. Chess licks her lips and slowly she puts her hand in mine.

The world shifts there and then, and it's as though I'm taking my first breath. I hold her hand and lead her to the dance floor. She moves into my embrace, and then there is nothing else. Just Chess. The scent of sea and sun in her hair, the smooth satin of her skin. I am a fucking goner. A man capable of cheesy poetry and big gestures.

I don't even care. Bring it. I want it all.

We flow together, barely dancing, just swaying and listening to the music. Her cheek rests against my chest, her arms wrapped around my waist as if she doesn't want to let go. I hold her closer, smoothing my hands up her arm, down the narrow slope of her back.

Part of me wants to get to my knees before her. I press my cheek to the crown of her head and breathe in, let myself fall. A white light flashes, and for a second, it doesn't register.

There is another. I turn my head, and spot the guy holding a camera phone aimed at me. Rage punches into my gut so hard I make a sound. Chess stops, moving back a step, her gaze zeroing in on the guy too. Her body stiffens, and it kills me.

I'm used to getting my picture taken without my permission. But that fucker didn't just violate my privacy, he violated Chess's.

I take a step, and her hand presses against the small of my back. "Don't," she says in a low voice. She looks at me with pleading eyes. "It's not worth trouble."

My thumb strokes her chin. "He does not get that piece of us."

Another flash, and now my eye is twitching. No fucking way.

"Trust me, it will be all right." Giving Chess a tight smile, I take her hand and head toward the asshole snapping pictures of us.

Dude stiffens as soon as he realizes I'm actually coming for him. I almost feel guilty about the way his gaze darts around and his mouth trembles, as if he can't decide to smile or bolt. Physically intimidating guys weaker than me is not my style. I make it easy for him.

"Hey, man." I hold out my hand. "Finn Mannus."

He glances at my hand for a second, as if trying to decide whether I'm going to rip his off. But then he relents and gives me a weak, quick shake. "Hey."

When I don't do anything aggressive, his grip gets a little stronger. "Manny, I knew it was you. I fucking love you, man."

Yeah, no shit. I nod, giving him an easy smile, as Chess hovers at my side, gripping the back of my shirt. I drop dude's sweaty hand, but my smile remains. "Saw you taking pictures of me and my girl."

Just like that, dude gets stiff again, thrusting up his chin. "You're in public."

And you're kind of a dick.

"Sure. I was wondering if I could get a copy." I nod toward Chess, as I wrap my arm around her. "It's our first date. Be nice to have a memento of it."

I can feel Chess's stare. She's wondering what the hell I'm doing. It makes my smile a little more genuine, because I love the sound of her chiding voice in my head.

Dude's date, who hasn't said a word until now, perks up. "Oh, that's so sweet. Dougie, isn't that sweet?"

He gives his girl an annoyed look, as if to say he's in charge, but then puffs up his chest a bit. "Yeah, sure, Manny."

"Cool. Can we have a look?" Another fake smile. "My girl really wants to see them."

Dougie is not entirely stupid and hesitates.

I hold out my hand and stare him down, but keep my pleasant expression. If he says no now, he comes off as a complete dick in front of his girl and his supposed idol.

Finally, he hands over his phone. Jesus, he took a lot. My anger rises. At my side, Chess's fingers dig into my arm. But she doesn't let her emotions show. "Your eyes are closed in that one," she points out lightly.

"I like slow dancing with my eyes closed," I tell her with the same levity, as I highlight the photo and a half a dozen more. They're grainy or overdeveloped with the flash, but every image shows what I'm feeling for Chess with perfect clarity. And while I'm not the least bit ashamed of that, the idea of them being all over the internet—and I have no fucking doubt that's where these are headed—makes me want to crush the phone in my hand.

A sense of violation coats my insides like hot tar.

Dougie, the little fucker, also recorded the last bit. I don't play it because I'm not sure I can keep my temper if I do. I send the entire lot to an email address set up for Charlie to check, with the code I use to let Charlie know it's from me as the subject line. He'll keep them safe for me and then block Dougie's email address later.

Dougie sees that I've sent the pictures on, and starts to fidget in his seat. Because I'm still holding his phone. It's clear that he's worried I'm going to delete them.

Chess tenses, obviously thinking the same. I could do it. Easily. It would take a tap of a button and there is no way Dougie could stop me. I have at least seven inches and about thirty pounds of muscle on him. But I've played the game long enough how that would go down.

I give him a thoughtful look. "Would you like a selfie with me?"

He brightens, letting out a breath. "That would be awesome."

My cheeks fucking hurt with all this fake ass grinning. "I see you're wearing my team cap. Could sign that for you too."

Dougie loves that. "Shit, yeah."

"Cool." I straighten to my full height. "All I ask in return is that you delete these."

His happy face falls.

I nod toward Chess. "See, this is our first date. I'd like my girl to keep her privacy."

He swallows hard. "I wasn't going to share them."

Sure you weren't.

"Still," I say. "It's hard to impress a girl when she's worried about photos."

Again, I hold his gaze. *Come on Dougie, don't make me toss this phone into the Pacific.* I know one thing: I'll try the nice route, but he isn't getting this piece of Chess and me.

Dougie rubs his chin like cock of the walk. I lean in a bit, noting how he stiffens. "Besides," I say in a low, confiding voice that's just between him and me. "I'm pretty sure the guys would appreciate that selfie more than me dancing with a girl."

That does it. Weakly he nods. He still wants those pics, that's obvious. But he won't push it. I delete them, relief rushing through me like air, then pose for new pictures with Dougie. My scrawl on his cap is quick and messy.

"Well, then," I say, trying not to toss his hat back in his face. *Be nice. Be nice.* "Have a nice night, guys. Dinner's on me."

His girlfriend beams. "You really are so sweet. We love you, Manny."

I wink at her. And then I'm grabbing Chess's hand and taking us away from the couple as fast as I can. Heading toward the hostess stand, I explain that I'm leaving and give her enough money to cover our bill and Dougie's.

The whole time, Chess stays silent, her hand in mine. She doesn't say a word as I take her down to the beach, my stride brisk, my heart still pounding with unleashed rage and regret. Stopping only to take our shoes off, we walk away from the lights of the restaurant, the sound of laughter and music slowly giving way to the crashing of surf.

The moon hangs overhead, bright enough to illuminate the beach and shimmer off the ocean. I slow to a stop. Moonlight gleams white on the inky strands of Chess's hair.

Her eyes are big and worried as she stares up at me. "You didn't have to pay for that rat's dinner."

"He didn't have to give me those pictures. But he did."

"He was a creep to take them." She scowls at the ocean. "Jesus, I know I said I wanted my camera when we watched that older couple. But I wouldn't have actually done that. It's an invasion of privacy."

I sigh, letting the anger leach out of me. "He's a fan. It's what a lot of them do."

Her gaze returns to me, and a small smile curves her lips. "You handled it well. I would have just smashed his phone and told him off."

A humorless laugh huffs out of me. "Yeah, well, I was tempted. But that would have caused a shitstorm. It's easier to manipulate the situation with kindness."

"You're amazing," she says. But her expression is troubled.

I touch her cheek, tucking back a stray lock that whips in the wind. "I'm sorry about that. I wish I could say it won't happen again, but I can't guarantee that. Fuck, it probably will."

Chess curls a finger into the belt hoop of my jeans. It's a small touch, but it anchors me. Again, she watches the waves. "They've already taken pictures of me. Remember?"

I wince, my skin drawing tight. "I know. I'm sorry about that too."

"I know you are." Chess glances back at me. "It really upset you tonight, though."

My insides roll and the anger returns. "We were dancing, for fuck's sake. It was…nice. I hate that some asshole ruined it."

She doesn't look away from me. "How do you stand it? People always wanting a piece of you?"

Oddly, no one has ever asked me that. "The payoff is worth it. Usually."

She bites her bottom lip. "I don't know if I could stand it."

It's as if she's pulled the rug out from under my feet. I actually clutch her wrist to keep steady. "I'll try to shield you from it, Chess. The best I can."

"But you can't, Finn. Not really."

I don't know what to say. She's right. And it scares me. I hate being afraid. It isn't an emotion I want to be familiar with. She could leave over this. And could I blame her?

Her brows knit. "It's something I'll have to learn to deal with on my own if I'm with you."

My face feels stiff, my voice stuck in my throat. "I guess it is."

She nods again, staring at the sea.

Arguments, persuasive and impassioned, flow through my head. But I don't say a word. I'm stuck there, standing in the sand. Some things I cannot change, no matter how much I want to. The fame that comes with football is one of them. If I do my job correctly, fame is something that will stick with me for a long time. And I would be lying if I said I didn't want that, even if fame comes with hassles. Because fame means I'm still in the game, that football still needs me.

I want to explain these things to Chess. But I can't find it in me to speak.

She's so still, I have no idea what's going on in her mind. But then she moves, and I'm strung so tight, I almost flinch.

She takes a step closer and her hand cups my cheek. I find myself leaning into her touch as she rises on her toes and brushes her lips over mine. "The payoff is worth it, Finn."

I release a breath, and then haul her into my arms. I lean down, nuzzle the warm curve of her neck. "I'll do everything I can to keep you believing that, Chester."

CHAPTER 16
♟ CHESS

JamesT.Twerk: Can we have dinner tonight?

I look up from my phone to Finn, who is at my side as we drive home from the airport. It feels strange now, coming home. I don't really know what to expect. It was one thing when we were friends dancing around our attraction to each other. There is safety in pretending.

How do we go on now? We're both amateurs, really. Finn with a long history of casual sex, and me with my inability to go beyond one or two dates with a man.

"What's up?" he asks me, his attention mainly on the road. He has a deep tan now, the ends of his hair almost blond from the sun.

"James wants to have dinner with me tonight." I tell Finn because I know that's what couples do: inform each other of their plans. But part of me feels stifled. Do I have to gain his permission?

Finn glances at me, and a wry smile tugs at his mouth. "Why are you glaring at me? You think I'll object or something?"

Grimacing, I lean my head against the window. "I don't know." My hand reaches for him, resting on his strong thigh. If he's near, I want to touch him. Even when my mind is a mess. "I don't know what the hell I'm doing here."

He sets his warm hand over mine and gives me a squeeze. "You think I do? The likelihood of me fucking up here is fairly high."

I smile. "Thanks for the warning."

He gives my hand a pat. "Remember that when you get the urge to yell at me later."

"Maybe I'll be the one to fuck up."

"Maybe," he agrees, a cheeky grin lightening his expression. "Be forewarned, I like to dole out punishment in the form of cunnilingus."

A laugh bursts from me. "Consider me forewarned."

"I'd like to say it will hurt me more than it hurts you, but that would be a lie."

He makes it too easy to smile, to laugh. Because he's there, and he's warm and strong, I rub my thumb along his thigh. I love the way it tenses and he moves closer to me. I watch those big, long thighs part and my gaze goes to the swell between his legs. He fills out his jeans so nicely.

My naughty half wants to move my hand there and rub that big bulge, make him hard. I picture it, leaning down, taking him out of his jeans—

"Chess." Another squeeze on my hand. "You're going to get us run off the road."

My gaze flicks up to his heated expression and then back down to where he's growing thicker. I lick my lips, and he groans.

"Chess..."

"Sorry." I take my hand away from temptation.

Finn gives me a sidelong glance, as he shifts a bit in his seat. "Don't ever be sorry about that. If I had any confidence that I could actually drive safely while you sucked my cock, I'd be all over that."

I laugh. And it feels good. But my mood quickly sobers. "My insurance money came in. All of it. I can buy a new place now."

The car goes quiet. Finn clenches the steering wheel. "You waited until I was driving to tell me this, didn't you?"

"Why would I do that?" But guilt rushes over my skin like a hot, itchy rash.

His long speaking look makes it worse. "So I wouldn't be able to persuade you with my best weapons."

He's right. Whenever he gets his hands on me, I can't think straight.

I glance at the road, watching traffic. "You'd try to persuade me?"

He makes a noise in his throat. "You serious? I've been dreading you leaving. You think that would change now that we're together?"

"No. But maybe I—"

"Don't say it," he warns.

"Should move," I finish. "Things can get complicated."

"Then let's keep them simple."

So stubborn.

"We just got together," I say. "We should take time to get to know each other. What if we start living in each other's pockets and find out we get on each other's nerves?"

He scoffs. "We've lived to together for weeks, Chess. That discovery time has come and gone. We're awesome as roommates and even better as lovers."

The traffic comes to a stop when we reach a red light, and he turns to face me. His big body overwhelms the space. I can scent the soap he used in the shower this morning. The soap I lovingly ran over every tight muscle while I'd showered with him.

Finn's eyes meet mine, and I see the knowledge of what we do to each other in there. I see other things as well, feelings that make my chest tight and my cheeks heat.

"I'm crazy about you," he says softly. "I don't need time to figure that out."

"I'm crazy about you too," I whisper. "I'm just scared."

Before I can blink, he leans in and gives me a firm kiss. It's more tender than sexual. I need that more right now. How does he know to do that?

He pulls back and cups my cheek. "We're going to be okay."

A horn honking makes us both jump. Finn's smile is brief. "See?

Discussing this in the car sucks. I'd totally be taking your clothes off if we were at home."

"My regret is an ocean."

"Smart ass."

"Besides," I say, "I'm going out to dinner with James when we get home."

"Right." Finn can't hide his disappointment. But it doesn't last because the man is definitely not a quitter. He nods as if deciding something. "I'll just have to fuck you later tonight."

"God." I laugh, shaking my head, even as heat licks up my thighs. "I've created a monster."

"Babe, you have no idea."

I should have known something was up as soon as James told me he was treating me to dinner at *Lüke*. He knows full well I love the desserts there, and that I become a contented, purring pussycat after eating one.

But no, I'd been so distracted by my anticipation over said desserts that I let myself be lulled into a false sense of security.

"Look at you," James says, as we sit down at a tiny table by the window. "You're freaking glowing."

"It's a suntan." I scan the menu, bypassing the dinner section. "Oh, they have steamed chocolate tonight." *Orgasm in the Form of Chocolate* should be the dessert's formal title.

"No...it's not the suntan."

James peers at me for too long, and I fight the urge to lift my menu in front of my face. Instead, I return his stare with a bland expression. But it doesn't work. He suddenly beams.

"You fucked him!"

A table of older businessmen turns our way.

I glance at the men now snickering at us, give them a death glare that has them looking away, before leaning in to hiss at James. "Would you keep it down? I like this restaurant. And you cannot tell I had sex with Finn just by looking at me."

"You're blushing bright red," James points out.

Fuck.

"All right, Miss Marple, I had sex with Finn. Can we eat now?"

"We don't have any food to eat yet. And if you're going to make me a Christie detective, make me Poirot."

"I knew you had a Poirot thing! With all those hats and bowties."

James gives me a level look. "Are you sure *you* aren't Miss Marple?"

"Truthfully, I'd love to live a Miss Marple life when I'm older. Settle down in a quaint English village, rife with murder and deceit and afternoon teas."

James rests his chin in his hand. "I've missed you, Chessie bear."

"I've missed you too."

James has been in New York more than he's been in New Orleans. At this point, I see Finn more than I see James.

"That's it?" James says now, his feathery red brows lifting in outrage.

"What are you talking about?"

He huffs. "You're not going to tell me anything about Finn?"

"God. When do I ever give you details?"

I swear the man's bowtie trembles with ire. He practically leans across the table. "Since you nailed Finn Mannus."

"At least you whispered this time," I mutter. "Please tell me this isn't about Finn being famous."

"You wound me, Chess." James sniffs. "This is about you finally getting what I know you've wanted since you met him. The fact that I've had a tiny crush on him for years is just frosting on the cake. But can you blame me for wanting to know? I mean, come on, have you *seen* him?"

"Oh, I've seen him," I can't help but say, fighting to maintain a straight face.

"Bitch," he says with a smile.

"Do I have to remind you that you're in a relationship, James?"

His teasing expression fades. "No."

I glance at him sharply, and James fidgets with his bowtie. "What?" I say, because that fidget never bodes well. "God, did you break up?"

"What? No." James sounds horrified. He exhales as if pulling himself together. "No, nothing like that… Chess." He reaches for my hand.

I pull away, my heart suddenly thumping. "Why are you saying my name as if someone died?"

"Chess," he says again, pained. "I'm moving to New York."

The words hang over us like a fug, as I stare at my best friend in frozen silence. My face feels too hot, my eyes scratchy. "You're moving?"

"Yes. I love Jamie. I don't like being away from her."

"You're moving."

I'm stuck on repeat, but can't seem to snap out of it.

He takes my hand then, and I feel how clammy his skin is. "I found my person, Chess. After all the searching. After empty nights of wondering if I should swear off women or swear off men, I found someone. I don't want to wait or take things slow. I want it all now."

"All?" My mouth is dry. I hear him. Of course, I hear him. But my mind won't move past the fact that he's leaving.

James gives me a small but hopeful smile. "Marriage, a dog named Sue, maybe even kids."

James is telling me this. James, who has scoffed at convention his whole life. James, who once said having kids wasn't for everyone—wasn't for people like *us*, he'd implied. I run a hand through my hair and find my forehead damp.

In silence, James looks back at me, his eyes wide, his skin pale against the red of his hair. He's leaving me. He won't be here if things don't work out with Finn. He won't be here if things do. I won't have him to talk to when I work or when I'm worried.

"Chess…"

I blink out of my fog, and realize James is biting his lip. My sweet, funny friend is in love. He deserves this and more. My chair scrapes over the floor as I jerk to my feet. James watches me with clear trepidation that turns to surprise as I lean across the table and cup his cheek in my hands before giving him a big, smacking kiss.

"I'm so happy for you," I tell him.

He laughs a little, letting out a gusty breath. "Jesus, I thought you were going for a *Godfather II* kiss of death reenactment or something."

I sit back in my chair. "What, the 'I know it was you, Fredo. You broke my heart.'"

"'You broke my heart!'" James intones with feeling.

We laugh like loons, but inside my heart truly is breaking a little. Change is rushing up like a rising tide against me, and I am unmoored.

FINN

Since I really don't want to mope around the apartment, waiting for Chess to come home from her night out with James, I decide I'll go out to dinner too.

I call Jake, who informs me that Dex, Rolondo, and one of the tight ends, North will be joining us. Oh, and we'll be eating at Rolondo's house. I really don't care what we do as long as I'm out.

Like me, Rolondo lives in a condo. His is in the Central Business District. Located on the fifteenth floor, the place looks like something straight out of Versailles with French style woodwork painted pale gray, mirrored walls, and ornate crystal chandeliers.

"Jesus, Ro," I say, as he leads me into a white kitchen with black and white checker pattern floors. "I feel as though I should have dressed for the occasion.

Dex is leaning against a counter and drinking a beer. "'Londo has always been particular about his place. And, by particular, I mean fussy as all hell."

"A man's home is his castle," Rolondo intones.

I accept the beer Rolondo hands me. "I don't think you're supposed to take that literally."

Dex snickers just as the doorbells rings again.

"Jealous bitches," Rolondo says before he goes to answer the door. But his voice echoes in the hall. "You keep it up and see if I share my ribs."

"Shit," Dex mutters. "That's his mom's recipe. You don't want to miss out on those ribs."

I don't doubt that. The kitchen is fragrant with the scent of slow roasted meat and spices. My mouth waters a little.

It's weird. I'm almost at a loss of how to act. Jake and I are tight. But I haven't hung out socially with the others very much. Dex is stiff too, clutching his beer like he wants to crush the bottle.

I don't know him well enough to be certain, but he seems low. Given that there's a bounty on his virginity, and the press has been hounding him, I'd say he has a right to be. Funny thing is, I know without a doubt that the big guy is not a virgin. Not after the way he talked about his woman's panties.

It pisses me off the way the press has been treating him. To make matters worse with Dex, someone stole his phone and put nude pictures of his girl up on social media. When I think about someone doing that to Chess, the level of rage I feel scares me. I don't know how he deals with it.

In the hall, I hear Jake blabbing about something and North's voice joining in. Rolondo leads Jake and North into the kitchen.

"Shit, it's like a wake in here." Jake glares around. "You two fighting or something?"

Dex straightens, his brows lifting. "No. The fuck, Ryder?"

"Don't listen to him," I tell Dex. "He lives for drama."

"Nope. I just happen to have four—"

"Sisters," we all say as one.

"We know," I add with an eye roll. "We all know."

Jake wrenches a beer out of the fridge and snicks the cap off, glowering. "I do not repeat myself that often."

"Keep telling yourself that," Rolondo mutters, as he checks on something in the oven.

"Fuck," North leans in. "Is that macaroni and cheese?"

"And cornbread," Rolondo adds.

"I'm hanging at your house more often." North is new, having signed at the beginning of this season. The lucky bastard was a free agent at the time and a superstar. Since our team was desperate for a good tight end, he basically got to write his paycheck.

Then he promptly got hurt and has only just gotten back to being healthy. Something we all need, since he's capable of making great plays.

Rolondo goes about finishing dinner, ordering Dex to get the plates since he's been here often, Jake to cut the cornbread, and for me and North to get the hell out of the way.

"Why do they get special treatment?" Jake grouses.

"Manny cuts a finger," Rolondo says, "and he throws shitty passes, and it looks bad on me when I try to catch them."

"And North?"

"It's his first time here. Stop asking questions and cut the damn bread."

Laughing, I help Dex with the silverware, and we're soon eating the best Southern style home cooked meal I've had since I can remember.

"Damn, Ro," I say between bites of tender ribs, "if you're in doubt about what to do after retirement, you could easily find work as a chef."

He grunts, sucking a bone clean. "Me, Dex, and a couple of our friends from college have been thinking about opening some restaurants. Get in it early so we can learn what we're doing."

"No shit?" I glance at Dex who shovels macaroni in his mouth without looking up. "Could be fun."

Rolondo's gaze slides to Dex, and his expression turns thoughtful, but he doesn't linger. "Yeah. Never too early to plan."

"I hate thinking about the future," Jake says, grabbing another piece of cornbread. "Change sucks."

"Change will happen whether you like it or not, man." North takes a pull on his beer. "Resist all you want, but it will get you."

"Like the Boogeyman, eh?" Jake says with a snort.

"I think about it," I say. "The future."

"Scares the shit out of me," Rolondo admits. "Not playing ball. But what can you do? Such is life."

"Not everything good in life revolves around football," Dex says in a low voice. He glares around the table when we all go silent and stare at him. "Please tell me you chuckleheads know this."

North sits back in his seat. "What, you mean women?" He rolls his eyes. "Try again."

"Finding someone to spend your life with matters," Dex insists in his quiet way.

North snorts. "Met a woman, fell hard. So hard, I insisted we get married. Wanted to lock that shit down, you know." He flicks a crumb off the table. "Had two good years before she got bored and fucked my teammate. Make that three of them."

"At once?" Jake asks, almost as if he can't help himself. But then blanches when North gives him a death glare. "Sorry, it just came out… That's fucked up, man."

North sighs. "Maybe she did. Who the fuck knows."

Rolondo leans in. "So you think that because your wife ended up being a cheater that it's all bullshit?" He shakes his head. "Man, do not give her that power."

"I'm not." North scowls. "I'm just saying…" He makes an agitated sound. "I don't know. Just don't put all your hopes on a woman."

"I'm not," Rolondo says succinctly.

"Or a man," North adds.

Ro' shrugs but doesn't look convinced.

I, on the other hand, am not liking this conversation. My chest is getting tight, and I find myself blurting out what's on my mind. "Chess and I got together over the bye week."

"What? Just now?" Rolondo's brows lift high. "I thought you've been hitting that since the beginning."

"Hey." I glare at him, and he holds his hands up in peace.

"Sorry, sorry. I thought you were having relations with Ms. Copper since you met her."

I roll my eyes, and he laughs.

"Anyway," I continue. "She has her insurance check so she can get a new place but—"

"Let her move out," North cuts in. "For the love of all that's holy, just let her go and take it slow."

Yeah. No.

"I get that you're coming off a bad relationship, but I don't see the problem with Chess staying. I want her to stay."

He utters a long-suffering sigh. "You ever live with a woman?"

"I've been living with her for a while now."

"Yeah, but you haven't been fucking—having *relations*—with her until now."

Jake snickers, and I flip him off, as North keeps talking.

"Being roommates is one thing. You start sleeping with her and suddenly she's going to expect more. Girlfriends have rights." He holds up a hand and starts counting off on his fingers. "The right to know where you're going. Where you've been."

"I don't mind telling her those things. I want her to know."

North's gaze is relentless. "The right to complain when your job keeps you away."

"That's true," Jake says. "They do complain."

"When have you had a relationship?" I scoff.

"I've dated. They always complain. Hell, hookups complain when you roll out of bed to gear up for practice."

Rolondo nods. "Fellas be talking about how their wives give them shit all season. And you don't even want to know about training camp woes they'll lay on your shoulders. Especially if you have kids."

Frustration claws up my throat, and I run a hand over my face. "You guys are supposed to be making me feel better, not telling me this."

"Oh, is that what we're doing here?" Rolondo asks with a laugh.

I look at Dex who is still brooding. "You're living with Fiona. Help me out."

He stares at me for a long moment. "I don't regret living with Fiona for a second. I love it."

"See," I say to the doomsday crew, while gesturing toward Dex.

"But," Dex continues in that maddeningly methodical way of his. "I think she wants to cut and run on me."

"What?" Rolondo and I say at the same time.

Dex looks completely blank as he picks at his thumbnail. "She's depressed about all this shit, and instead of turning to me, she's retreating." It's almost ponderous the way he tries to lift his shoulders in a shrug. "So I guess there's truth to what they're saying. This life isn't easy on our loved ones. Not by a long shot."

I slump back in my chair, as the guys start peppering Dex about his girl. My mind drifts to Chess. We always talk things out. Our relationship is built on communication; we had that down pat before we even touched each other. Chess wouldn't retreat.

Yeah, but she's been hesitant about you this whole time. She's one step from freaking even now. How is she going to be for the long haul? When you're gone more than you're around. Do you blame her? Who would want that?

Heartburn hits me in a rush, and I rub at my chest. Fuck, why did I go out with the guys? Ignorance truly is bliss. The future is a dark, murky place I want no part of anymore.

North glances my way, his gaze knowing. "You're thinking about it now, aren't you?"

"Fuck you," I say without any heat. I know he's only looking out for me. I still hate him a little at the moment.

"Don't listen to all of this shit," Dex says in a low voice. "I have friends who are in good relationships, happy relationships."

"Are you happy?" I can't help but ask.

He strokes his beard, clearly thinking about how to answer, which doesn't bode well. We all fall silent, waiting.

"I'm in flux," he finally says. "I'm in love with a woman, and she is my joy. And that scares the shit out of me."

The table is silent as we all take in his words. North nods slightly, looking so mournful my heartburn rises again.

"Am I happy?" Dex repeats. "Yeah. I'm happy as much as a clueless guy can be. Am I at peace? No, not yet. But I'm working on that."

"I'm depressed," Jake announces, shoving his plate back from his place. "This conversation is depressing."

"We can't always be talking about the newest Zelda expansion pass," I say, pushing my plate back too.

Jake rolls his eyes but then looks at me. "What are you going to do?"

"I asked her to stay with me. I can't take that back." *I. Don't. Want. To.* "So I guess I'll proceed with caution and hope for the best."

Sometimes I really fucking hate that I can read people so well, because my guys clearly think my new plan is crap. They're kind enough not to say it out loud, but the damage is done. By the time I head home in a cab, I'm popping antacids, in a foul mood, and slightly drunk.

CHAPTER 17
♟CHESS

Finn isn't there when I get home. And I have to laugh at myself because I'd expected him to be. After all my huffing about independence and the chokehold of living with someone, I hate that I come home to an empty place. Oh, irony, you bitter bitch.

I find his note on the kitchen counter.

> *Went to Rolondo's house for dinner. Didn't want to text and interrupt your friend time.*
> *See? Totally giving you space. ;-)*
>
> -F

At the bottom of the note, he's drawn a smiling stick figure of a guy wearing a crown and holding a football and… I lean closer, peering at the drawing in the dim light, then let out a spurt of laughter. "Sick, sick man."

Stick figure Finn also has an enormous stick dick. And it is clearly happy.

Grinning wide, I hold the note to my heart in a moment of complete sappiness then secure it to the stainless steel fridge with a *fleur-de-lis* magnet. Happy dick King Finn can now rule over the kitchen.

His note has cast out some of my sorrow. But not enough. It's too quiet in the condo, the hum of the fridge highlighting the fact. I help myself to a glass of red wine and take it to my room.

Changing into pjs, I eye the bed with trepidation. Finn's room is just down the hall in the far corner of the apartment. I've seen it. Of course I looked. But I've never really been in there. It felt like a threshold I'd dared not cross, as if entering it would make the temptation of Finn more real.

Picking up my glass of wine, I head for his room. It ridiculous how my heart rate kicks up as if I'm trespassing. The room is dark, illuminated only by the light coming in through the massive arched windows facing the river and the one looking toward Jackson Square.

Creeping like a thief, I make my way across the wide space and flick on a bedside lamp. Like my room, his has a fireplace on one wall, but his room is double the side of mine and painted a rich, deep red. The color is too dark for me, but it feels cozy, like a cocoon. A king size bed of weathered wood and natural linen padding takes up one wall, while a sleeping couch takes up the other.

The TV is arm-mounted over the fireplace and I can imagine Finn pulling it out and making it face the bed so he can lie down and watch his beloved sports highlight shows.

It feels strange now that I've never visited him in here. He's certainly popped his head into my room enough times to see what I was up to. Although, I always got the impression that he'd been vaguely disappointed not to find me naked. The imp.

I turn on the other bedside lamp and look at the artwork on the walls. There isn't much, a few abstracts on the wall above the couch, a large black and white abstract with a splash of gold paint running through it over the bed. On the wall next to the bed, there is a large, framed picture of Haystack Rock in Oregon. A bit of landscape, which, I realize with a little jolt was featured in *The Goonies*.

I stare at the picture and another frisson goes through me. Of all the pictures to have. Dust has settled on the edge of the white frame, so I know it isn't new. It's been there a while, sitting right where Finn could look at it while lying in his bed.

I turn away and investigate his bathroom. "Jesus."

It is a palace. All white marble, with a huge freestanding tub that could hold two people and a glass walled shower that could accommodate three. The toilet has its own room, and throne jokes run through my head as I close the door.

Over the tub hangs a glass chandelier fashioned to look like a sailing ship, a bit of unexpected whimsy that I love.

In all the pretty, he's left his brush on the counter next to three tubes of various men's hair products, and his toothpaste lays open by the sink. I fight the urge to cap it and put it back in the little gray cup that holds his toothbrush. I'm not here to tidy.

The closet is just as impressive. Dark gray walls, white woodwork. Rows of dark suits, polished leather shoes, and then an entire wall of athletic shoes. He has drawers and drawers of casual clothes. A section devoted to athletic wear and gear. The place smells like him, lingering with the cologne he sometimes wears. The space is so big that he's only taken up half of it.

The other half could be yours. Look at all those empty shelves and lonely rods, waiting for clothes to hang on them.

I swallow a sip of wine and then leave his closet. I don't stop until I'm in my own, smaller room. I love this space. It's comfortable, with a bathroom that, while perfectly done, is small enough to find in most homes.

Finn's space is like a dream. Big and bold, it speaks of the highest echelon of wealth and privilege. His sheets are fine linen. His duvet cover is cashmere. I can't even afford a cashmere throw. I glance at the cream-colored throw at the end of my bed and snort. It is cashmere, and it is Finn's.

Am I really freaking out over Finn's money? Or is it just a convenient excuse? I think about James and New York. James won't be here anymore. My sounding board is leaving me.

With a sigh, I plop onto my bed and wrap myself in the throw. "I'm a goddamn mess who is talking to herself."

I decide to ignore my brain and settle down with a good book that proves increasingly hard to read. My concentration is shot, and my self-pity is ridiculously high.

I'm close to maudlin by the time Finn finally comes home. My heart gives a little leap when I hear him open then close the front door. He's here. Finn will understand. He'll give me a hug and let me cry on his shoulder. He'll tell me everything is going to be okay.

He walks right by my room, not even glancing my way, even though my door is open and the light is on. Mouth agape, I watch him pass.

For a moment, there is only silence in my room and the sound of him tromping into his. And then the yelling starts.

"Chess? Chessssss! Chester!" He's so loud, I fear the neighbors will call the cops.

"Jesus," I mutter, then call out. "What?"

Footsteps stomp, and then he appears in the doorway, a big scowl on his face. "What the fuck are you doing in here?"

He sounds so disgruntled, I want to laugh. "Ah…getting ready to sleep?"

This clearly does not appease. "Why are you doing that in *here?*"

"Because it's my room."

It's as if he's sucked a rotten lemon, his mouth twisting, his nostrils flaring. "This is not your room. It's the guest room." Sheer disgust and outrage drips from his lips. And he raises an arm to point down the hall. "*Your* room is that way."

He stands, arms crossed over his chest, like some king waiting for an explanation. And I roll my eyes. "Excuse me for not presuming—ack!"

Finn scoops me up, puts me over his shoulder, and heads for his room. "Don't even start with that. We're together now. My bed is your bed."

"Put me down, asshole!" The floor is way too far below.

"I will. Once we're in *our* room." He gives my butt a light slap.

"Jesus, you really are a caveman."

"I prefer the Tarzan and Jane scenario," he says easily. "I'd look great in a loincloth, don't you think?"

"God, the ego on you." However, I silently agree.

Chuckling, he weaves a bit, which freaks me out, and I clutch the waistband of his jeans. "If you drop me, I will kill you."

"I'm not gonna drop you." He enters the bedroom and stops. "No, I lied. I am totally dropping you."

With that, he plops me down onto his bed, more gently than I would have imagined. I don't even bounce. I do, however, sit up and glare. "You crazy asshole."

He just stands there grinning. "Stick and stones, Chess."

"That doesn't even make sense."

Finn scratches the back of his neck and frowns. "Huh. I guess it doesn't." With a shrug, he flops onto the bed next to me, and the entire frame groans in protest.

I roll onto my side and really look him over. His skin is rosy and his eyes are glazed. The goofy, crooked smile is back in place. "Hey," he says. "Hey, Chess."

"What?"

"What, what?" he asks back, and then snickers.

I frown. The scent of beer and roasted meat emanate from him. It isn't a bad smell but not the norm. "Are you drunk?"

Supine on the bed, Finn lets out an expansive sigh. "Yeah."

I bite back a laugh. "Well, at least you're honest about it."

"Kind of hard to hide it." He turns his head and eyes me. "Let's fuck."

The laugh I've been fighting escapes, shocked and a bit breathless. "Yeah, let's not."

I only mostly mean it. Whenever Finn says fuck like that, my body reacts. Needy, but true.

His blue eyes are big and pleading. "But I want you."

"I'm not big on having sex with drunk men."

"Don't knock drunken sex till you try it." He gives me a leer that looks more cross-eyed than anything.

I snort. "Sorry, but no."

"You think I'll complain later that you took advantage of me?" Finn flicks the edge of his teeth with his tongue. "I promise you I won't."

"Maybe I'm afraid you won't remember my name in the morning," I tease.

"Not possible," he murmurs. "You're always on my mind." He giggles then. An actual giggle. "It's like that Willie Nelson song." He starts singing "You Were Always On My Mind" with an awful twang, but he gives into more giggling laughter halfway through the first refrain.

"I thought that was an Elvis song."

"Whatever the case…" He takes a big breath and sings, "give me one more chance to keep you satisfied…"

"If you don't stop crooning like Willie, I'm going to leave," I warn with a grin.

Finn's face goes blank for a second and then he tries his best Elvis instead. He gets out two words before we both crack up. We lay on the bed laughing full out for a good minute before he catches my gaze with his. The last vestiges of my self-pity melt away, and there is only Finn and this moment where we're both panting and teary-eyed with laughter.

His expression turns tender. "I fucking adore you."

God, my heart. I can't take it. I trace the curve of his eyebrow. "You've grown on me too, Mannus."

"I'm like fungus that way," he agrees happily.

Leaning in, I kiss his forehead. He tries to catch my mouth, but misses and gets my chin.

"Okay, big boy," I say, rising to my knees. "Let's get you undressed."

"For sex?" He blinks up at me with hopeful eyes.

"For bed."

"Have you always been this mean?" he pouts, kicking off his shoes. One hits the bathroom door with a thud. Which is impressive since it's all the way on the other side of the room.

"Yes."

"Okay." Finn sighs and stretches out his arms like he's about to make bed angels.

"Clothes, Finn."

"Right. And she claims she doesn't want me."

Helping Finn out of his clothes isn't easy. He's freaking heavy when he isn't trying. And then there's the loopy grin he won't stop giving me. It's adorable and annoying all at once. Especially when he gets tangled in his shirt. I finally free him and then tackle his jeans.

"Lift your ass so I can get these off."

"You say the sexiest things, Chester."

I roll my eyes and tug when he complies. His jeans and boxer briefs come off as one, and I'm left holding them while staring down at the glory that is his nude body stretched on the bed. And it is glorious, no doubt about that.

He gives me a heated look through lowered lids. "You're staring at my dick."

"It's hard."

So hard. The thick rod points straight upward. My sex tightens in response.

Finn skims a hand over his length. "It's a Chess related condition. Wanna help me out with it?"

Yes. I want to suck it like a lollipop then sink onto it and… *Down girl. No, no, no.*

"You're relentless," I say, tossing his clothes aside.

"Also a Chess related condition."

"Mmmhmmm. Come on. Get under the covers."

"Not until you undress too."

The firm set of his chin tells me he's not going to let this go. With a sigh, I pull off my clothes, aware of his observation. It's the way he watches that really gets to me, though. He clearly likes what he sees. The tenderness in his expression, as if he's drinking me in, memorizing every line of my body and cherishing it, makes my heart clench.

I shake off the feeling and stand by his side. "There. Now we can both go to sleep."

"You are so fucking beautiful," he says.

I clear my throat, but my voice is still raspy. "You're beautiful too."

He doesn't seem to hear me but keeps gazing at my face as if I'm an answer to an old riddle. "How did I get so lucky finding you?"

"Must be your Irish blood." I move to take his arm and help him up when Finn strikes.

He rolls over to pin me to the bed, and the tip of his penis touches my opening, where it is slick and wanting. We both pause, staring at each other, our breathing erratic. I know he feels how wet I am. I give him a weak smile. "It's a Finn related condition."

The words are barely out of my mouth when he groans and pushes in swift and deep. We both groan then, my back arching at the sudden invasion. A second's pause and then he's fucking me with steady but hard strokes.

I stop thinking and move with him, my hands gliding over his firm muscles. He feels so good the way he fills me up, the way he works me. "We weren't supposed to do this. You're drunk."

"Your fault." He grunts. "You let me feel your pussy. Game over, babe."

"You stuck your dick in my pussy." I moan. "It's your fault."

Sweat rolls down his temple, and he swivels his hips in a way that hits all the right places. "If you want to get technical, I stuck my dick in your pussy after I felt—"

"Shut up, and fuck me, Mannus."

A shudder goes through him, and then he's pounding me into the bed. So very good.

His lips graze my cheek. "I love this. I fucking love this."

I do too. So much. Nothing is like being with Finn. I wrap my legs around his waist and nuzzle the damp hollow of his neck. He shudders when I lick him there, suck on his smooth skin. I want to bite him, clamp my teeth and let him ride me.

"Fuck, Chess. Tell me this is real. That you're not going to get bored and have a threesome without me."

The words take a second to sink it. But I rear back and glare up at him. "Finn!" I slap at his side to get his attention.

He pauses, deep inside me. I can feel the pulse of his dick and it almost distracts me. Almost. I give his shoulder a little shove. "You did not just say that."

This is why we shouldn't be having sex when he's Chatty Kathy drunk.

Gazing down at me, he grinds his base against my clit just once as if his body is independent from his mind, then he groans.

"Sorry," he manages. He blinks down at me and takes another breath. "That was stupid… I don't think you… It's just North's wife fucked three other guys, and Dex's girl is depressed. Jake thinks everything is crap, and Rolondo's warning me about training camp woes…"

I have no idea what he's talking about, but his expression is aggrieved and distraught. My hand strokes his back. "What kind of crazy-sauce dinner was this?"

"An awful one," he laments, slowly starting to move again. God, he knows how to fuck.

My lids flutter, and I run my hand down to his firm butt.

"I got heartburn and wanted to go home to you," he complains. "But they kept talking about *relations* and giving me beers."

I fight a snicker. And he grumbles some more, frowning at the memory.

"Poor baby," I whisper, pulling him down for a kiss.

His mouth meets mine. It's a bit sloppy but intense, as if he wants to devour me, and my pulse quickens, heat surging. I wiggle beneath him, and he starts thrusting in hard, grunting pumps that feel so good, I whimper.

"Tell me we'll try," he demands inside of a kiss. "Tell me I won't be crying in my macaroni."

My lips twitch, but I cup his cheeks, and kiss him deep. "We'll try. No crying in macaroni, Finn."

"No," he agrees. And then he's all business, moving with skill and precision. I'm coming before I even know what hits me. My reaction sets Finn off.

I'm pretty sure he comes, but I'm too distracted by the second orgasm. It hits me so hard, I lose track of things. By the time I settle back on Earth, my throat is sore and I've called Finn a god several times over. I may have used other terms. I can't remember.

Sweaty and panting next to me, he gives me a lazy, pleased look. "I'm glad we got that settled, Chester." His lips brush over mine. "Hush now, your fuck master needs his rest."

Right. I'd called him that. I'm too exhausted to do anything more than drape my limp arm over his slick chest and drift into a well-earned sleep.

FINN

Morning is not my friend. We have a dubious relationship at best; I get up early because I have to, not because I enjoy it. But right now? I feel like a truck ran over me in my sleep.

I blink, trying to clear my vision, and notice the slim form of Chess standing by the bed. She's grinning down at me with an expression that's kind of evil. "Good morning, starshine."

Licking my dry lips, I manage to roll onto my back. "Do you think," I rasp. "We could both pretend I'm perfectly fine right now?"

Chess's grinning mug hovers over me. "Now, why would we want to do that?"

I try to glare but my eye pulses, and I groan instead.

Chess smiles so wide, her cheeks puff up. She takes a step back, and only then do I notice the cup of steaming coffee in her hand.

"Please say that's for me."

"I don't know. Can you sit up?"

With a grunt, I haul my sad ass up and slump against the headboard. The room tilts for a second, and I take a deep breath. "Coffee."

Chess sits on the edge of the bed and hands me the cup. She is a goddess because the coffee is strong and black with exactly the right amount of sugar.

"Oh, that's good."

She snuggles closer, resting her head next to mine on the padded headboard. "You okay?"

"Me? Please. I have the metabolism of a god."

"Right."

I take another snip of coffee and pinch the bridge of my nose. "What time is it?"

"Twelve."

"What?" I lift my head up too fast. Mistake. "I missed first breakfast and elevenses?"

Cool green eyes study me. "Exactly how many beers did you drink last night?"

"It wasn't the beer," I mumble into my cup. "Absinthe might have been involved at some point. Jake's a fan."

She stays silent, and I turn my head to face her. "Seriously, can we pretend this didn't happen?"

"Do you remember everything?"

I remember that I'm naked. And my dick stirs. His memory is crystal. "Yes," I say, randy dick getting harder. "I'm generally a doofus when drunk, but I don't forget things. Unfortunately."

She smiles then. "You were kind of a doof."

"I'm sorry." I so am. Chess dealing with me as a drunken moron was not how I'd wanted our first night back home to go.

"It was cute." Her head moves to my shoulder.

I finish my much-needed coffee in two quick gulps and put the mug on the side table. Settling more comfortably on the bed, I tuck Chess into the crook at my side. "I sang, didn't I?"

Chess laughs and strokes my lower abs. "Elvis and Willie Nelson."

"Jesus."

"You know, if you colored your hair black, you'd make a pretty good young Elvis." She blinks up at me. "Do you know 'Hound Dog'?"

"Cute."

"'Jailhouse Rock'?"

"Now, Chester, 'Don't be Cruel'."

She pauses and then snickers. "I see what you did there."

I roll over until I'm on top of her. "Oh, noes, I'm 'Stuck On You.'"

"Oh, god, stop," she laughs, her sweet tits brushing against my chest.

I work my way between her legs and settle in. "Do you 'Surrender'?" I give my hips a small thrust, loving the way she squirms beneath me. "'It's Now Or Never.'"

"No," she declares hotly between her laughter, but her hips rock against my dick, urging me on. The thin fabric of her panties taunts me further.

I nuzzle her neck, and she shrieks. So I nuzzle some more. "Man, you're a 'Hard Headed Woman.' 'That's All Right', mama, no need to get 'All Shook Up'…"

"Argh! The cheesiness, it burns. It burns." Green eyes glare up at me.

I grin wide, our noses nearly touching. "What? You want 'A Little Less Conversation'? Totally understand. I'll just hang out here and be your 'Teddy Bear.'"

"I give, I give," she wails.

Grinning in triumph, I rest my head beside hers, my body bracketing her smaller one. "Don't mess with the master."

Her hands find their way to my back to stoke my bare skin. I hum with pleasure. Chess runs a finger down my spine. "Who knew you were such an Elvis fan."

"It's my mom and dad. They used to play Elvis songs on Sunday nights when they cooked together. Pet me some more."

Chess hums, a happy noise. "Your parents are too cute."

"Did I mention they sang along?" I grimace. "I swear, that alone was responsible for half my teen angst."

"My parents sang show tunes. They loved duets."

"Fuck. You win." I settle onto my side and bring her with me. If I linger any longer on top of her, my dick will get ideas that, frankly, my weak stomach and pounding head can't handle at the moment.

Chess resting on me feels so good, I'm happy to stroke her hair and doze. But my brain won't turn off. "Hey," I murmur. "How did your dinner with James go?"

Instantly, she tenses, which makes me tense too. I lift my head to peer down at her. She's frowning.

"Okay," she says.

"That is the worst 'okay' I've ever heard, Chess."

With a sigh, she flops onto her back and blinks up at the ceiling.

"Chess?"

"James is moving," she blurts out. "To New York to live with Jamie."

Hell.

"Because he's in *love*." She makes the word sound like a curse.

"And that's bad?"

Chess glares at me. "No. Yes." A choked sound escapes her. "I hate change. I fucking hate it."

"Babe." I rest my hand on her belly, giving her that small comfort. She's tense as a coil, her body trembling. "I'm sorry he's moving."

Tears form at the corners of her eyes, but she glares up at the ceiling unblinking as if she's willing them not to fall. "He's leaving me."

"He's not leaving you. He's just staying with Jamie."

"Not helping."

Yeah, I got that.

"You can still visit him. Hell, I'll buy you tickets to go every weekend, if you want."

Chess gives me a wobbly smile, but then her expression crumples and she starts to sob. Panic runs through me. "Come here." I gather her up. "Chester. Baby, don't cry."

"I'm not," she wails, clutching my shoulders and burrowing her face in my chest.

"My mistake," I murmur, wanting to smile despite the fact that her pain hurts me too. I've never met a woman less willing to admit weakness. She's as bad as a football player that way.

Gently I rock her as she sobs, her body wracking with it. I stroke her back, the long strands of her hair. She clings tighter. "Everything is changing," she cries. "My house is gone. My stuff. My best friend is leaving. Everything is gone."

I'm here. I'm not leaving.

But I don't say a word. This isn't about me. I just hold her.

"Fucking Jamie," she grumbles through her sobs. "Fucking seducer of best friends."

I can't help it; a snicker breaks free. Because I've met Jamie via one of Chess and James's FaceTime chats. Seductress she is not; more like a cross between Tinker Bell and Urkel.

Chess stills, clearly having heard me laugh. Instantly, I feel like a shithead. She's hurting and…

A snort leaves her. And then she's laughing too, the sound raspy and thick with tears. "Oh, my god, I'm such an asshole."

Smiling, I cuddle her closer until there isn't an inch of space between us. "You're upset. If Jake left town to shack up with a cute geek, I'd be irate too."

With a sigh, she sags against me. "I like Jamie."

"I know you do."

She doesn't say anything, and I don't either. The rapid beat of her heart thumps against my ribs. I smooth my hand down her back. After a while, she stirs.

"I'm not a crier," she mutters against my damp chest.

"Okay." I kiss her temple.

"I'm not. I don't even like sappy movies."

I run my fingers through her hair. "Me either."

"I hate James."

"Do you want me to kick his ass?"

I can feel her smile. "No. I love him."

For a sharp second, I actually want to kick James's ass, resenting him for getting those words from Chess. I pull back and look down at her tear-swollen face.

With a grimace, she wipes her cheeks. "I need a tissue."

"I'll get you one." My voice is oddly thick.

I move to get up, but she stops me with a touch to my arm. "Thank you. For being here."

My hand feels heavy as I cup her cheek. "You're going to be okay, Chester."

She leans into my touch but her expression is mulish. Stubborn as ever. "How can you know that?"

I give her a small smile, my thumb brushing her damp cheek. "Because I'm making it my job to see that you are."

CHAPTER 18
FINN

For the first time in my life, I spend the entire day in bed with a woman. I don't know what that says about me. Have I led a shallow life? Or have I simply been waiting for Chess?

I don't dwell on it; I'm having too much fun.

After Chess settles down, we take a shower. Showering together should be a house rule. At least when I have nowhere to go, because it's not an experience I want to rush. I thank my foresight for asking my contractor to put a built in bench in my massive shower. I can comfortably sit there, thighs spread wide, and let Chess ride me while hot water rains down on us.

Perfection.

After the shower, it's right back to bed. We settle in, and I let Chess pick out a movie for us to watch. "I'm going to order a pizza," I tell her as she scrolls through the movie menu.

"I want meatballs on it."

"Meatballs?" I shake my head. "That's just overkill. Order sausage like a normal person."

"Meatballs. And onions."

"No onions."

Chess gives me a long look.

"I'm giving you meatballs," I say.

She snickers, and I roll my eyes.

"No onion breath, chuckles," I tell her over her laughter.

"Fine." She flips down a row of movie titles. "And extra cheese."

"A given."

I call in our order and then toss the phone aside. "You're picking *Ocean's Eleven*? Excellent."

Chess rests her head in the crook of my shoulder as the movie begins to play. "Why do you sound so surprised by my pick?"

"I thought you'd choose a chick flick."

"Because that's so me," she drawls.

"You don't like sappy movies. Chick movies aren't always sappy. They can be mushy too."

Chess tweaks my nipple and grins when I yelp. She rubs my abused flesh. "*Ocean's Eleven* is a chick flick, you know."

"It is not. It's a total guy movie."

"Is not."

"Is too. They are a band of brothers who devise a clever plan to steal the impossible, while forming an emotional, but manly bond in the process."

Chess lifts her head to meet my gaze. "Manly bond, eh?" Her smile unfurls. "You do realize that the whole plan was for Danny Ocean to win back the love of his wife, don't you?"

"Pfft. Subplot. It was all about the guys."

"Denial is strong in this one." Her expression borders on pitying. "And have you actually looked at the cast? It's like a man candy buffet of sexy goodness."

I glance at the screen where Brad Pitt is now talking to a dapper George Clooney. I'm comfortable enough in my manhood to admit that Clooney can work the hell out of a suit. I frown. "I think we should pick another movie. Let's put on *The Magnificent Seven*."

"Mmm… More man candy."

"You are killing movies for me, Chester."

She grins wide and then reaches to kiss me. "You're cute when grumpy."

I grunt, but it's all show. I am fucking putty in her hands.

Chess runs a hand over my chest. We keep touching each other. I do it because I can't seem to stop. Idly, I wonder if it's the same for her.

"Why do you keep calling me Chester," she asks, watching her hand glide over my skin.

"Why do you keep letting me?" I counter.

"I honestly don't know. I hate my name."

She has good reason; I can't think any woman would want to be named Chester. But it bothers me that she hates a part of herself.

Chess's gaze narrows. "Answer the question."

"All right, bossy boots." I turn toward her, resting my head in my hand. "I call you Chester because the second I learned that was actually your name I started falling for you."

A soft light fills her green eyes. But her expression remains dubious. My girl needs brutal honesty to believe anything is true. So I give it to her.

"There you were, this gorgeous, fierce Amazonian warrior, glaring hate-fire at me. And you had the most ridiculous, unappealing name—"

Her mouth falls open. "Asshat!"

Laughing, I evade her pinching fingers. "Unappealing, yet *endearing* name."

Chess launches herself at me, poking my ribs because she knows I'm ticklish. Curses and dire threats leave her mouth. I catch her hands in mine and easily tumble her back onto the bed.

She huffs and glares, as I straddle her hips and cage her in.

"Dickhead," she mutters, but there's no anger to it. Her lips quirk and then she lets out a laugh, as if she can't help it. And I love that about her, this gruff girl with the fierce armor, who can't help but laugh at my teasing.

She smiles up at me, and my chest suddenly hurts. Ink black hair spread out like a fan on the sheets, bottle green eyes glinting with happiness, pretty pink mouth smiling wide, she's the most beautiful women I've ever seen.

"Oh, fuck, Chester Copper, I'm so gone on you. There's no coming back from it."

I kiss those candy lips. "Haven't you figured it out?" I say against them. "Every time I call you Chester, I'm saying I adore you. I fucking adore every part of you."

She makes a soft noise in her throat, her gaze running over me like warm honey. "Finn… You don't fight fair."

"I never will when it comes to you, Chess. You're my girl and I'm your guy. Fate knows it. I know it. Now get with the program."

I move to kiss her again when the doorbell rings. I'm tempted to ignore it. But Chess knows me too well.

"Go get our pizza," she says. "I'm starving."

My stomach growls, agreeing with her. I give her a quick kiss, and the jump off the bed to find something to put on. I grab a pair of pajama pants and hop into them. The doorbell rings again.

"Fuck, I'm coming already," I say, not bothering with a shirt since the pizza guy is clearly impatient as all hell.

It rings a third time as I'm opening the door. "Man, it's a good thing I'm hungry or—"

I freeze, my mouth hanging open. Britt stands in the hall, swathed in some fuzzy cape thing and a cloud of expensive perfume. "Britt?"

She moves right past me, her long legs striding with purpose. "Did you forget about our meeting up?"

In a fog, I close the door and follow her into the hall. "Meeting?"

Britt turns and steps into my personal space. "Finn, I've made a terrible mistake."

I hold my hands up. "What are you talking about?"

Britt halts but then stands tall. "About us. I think we should try to be together."

"Britt, we were never—"

"But we could be," she says, her gaze searching my face. "Fate brought us together."

"And it broke us apart," I snap without thinking, then grimace when I see her flinch. "I'm sorry. I didn't mean it that way."

"You did. And I understand." Her hand lifts as if beseeching me. "That's why I think we could be good for each other."

"I'm not getting what you mean." Sweat breaks out on my skin. I glance toward the bedroom where Chess is waiting for me. I should warn her that Britt is here. But I don't want to make this any worse.

Britt stands in front of me. Too close. "Maybe we could heal, if we…" She lifts her hand again in a helpless gesture. "Had another one…"

Like that, my heart breaks for her. "Oh, honey, no." I clasp her shoulders and find them trembling. "No, Britt."

But she doesn't seem to hear me. Before I can say a word, she presses against me, her mouth seeking mine.

♟ CHESS

Finn is taking too long with the pizza, and frankly I'm too starving to wait for him to bring it in here. Sex with Finn makes me hungry. Grinning at the idea of placing a bed next to the kitchen, I pull on one of his oversized jerseys. The silky material skims the sensitive tips of my nipples as it settles over me and falls to my upper thighs. The fact that I even notice my nipples makes me laugh a little.

God, he's turned me into a hedonist.

That stupid smile is still on my face when I waltz out of his bedroom and run straight into a model-sized nightmare.

I halt, my heart clenching, my muscles seizing.

Britt Larson is in my man's arms, her face tucked into the crook of his neck. That. Is. My. Crook.

I don't know if I make a sound or Finn is just that attuned to me, because he instantly turns his head and catches my eye. A look of horror pulls at his face. And for an agonizing second, I'm paralyzed with fear.

Then I start thinking again and realize he's also looking at me as if I'm his lifeline. "Chess." He holds up his hands behind Britt's back in a plea.

Britt stiffens. Ice blue eyes glare at me though a veil of pale hair. Immediately, she lurches up. "You said you weren't with her," she accuses Finn.

Excuse me? I feel my brows lift.

Finn on the other hand detaches himself from Britt's grip. "I wasn't at the time. But I wanted to be." His tone is firm. "And now I am."

While I'd like to feel all warm and mushy about that, I'm standing in nothing but a thin jersey, my hair a tangled mess. All fine and good when rolling around in Finn's bed, but not when facing a model swathed in couture and wearing knee-high Jimmy Choo boots. I turn to go change when Britt burst out crying. A full out ugly cry of someone who has completely lost it.

Finn makes a helpless gesture, his gaze pinning me to the spot. His desperation is palpable. But it's Britt who has my sympathy. I should be annoyed that she's thrown herself on my man. But she's so distraught, I just can't be.

Giving Finn a look that says, *comfort her and I'll be right back*, I hustle into my bedroom to grab some leggings. It takes a few seconds, yet I still find them standing in the hall, Finn awkwardly petting Britt's head while she sobs.

"Here." Gently, I take hold of Britt's trembling arm. "Let's sit down."

I lead her to the couch and, when she plops onto it in a miserable sprawl, I sit next to her and stoke her back. "Could you get us some water and tissues?" I ask Finn.

"Sure." Finn all but leaps into action, clearly happy to be doing something other than dealing with a crying woman. Can't blame him; he's had to deal with me crying earlier. Two women in a row is probably a nightmare for a guy.

"I'm so sorry," Britt says through her tears. "I didn't mean to cry like this. I don't usually… God, this is embarrassing."

"It's all right," I say. "Everyone loses it at some point, and it's usually in the worst place possible. Murphy's Law and all that."

She pushes her hair back from her face and gives me a considering look. "You're being very kind. I don't know if I would as understanding in the same position."

"And what position is that?"

Britt grimaces. "Another woman throwing herself on your boyfriend."

Finn takes that moment to come back into the room. His steps stutter as if he's aware he's walked into a potential bomb, but can't quite make himself turn tail and run. Silently, he hands Britt a box of tissues and a glass of ice water.

Finn and I exchange a glance. He comes to stand by me, putting his hand on my shoulder as if I'm the one who needs soothing. Or maybe he's worried I'll be pissed. I give his hand a reassuring squeeze and then focus on Britt.

Delicately, she blows her nose and then takes a drink. "I really am sorry, Finn. I didn't think. I…" She starts weeping again.

"Talk to me," he says in a quiet voice.

"I don't know what to say," she wails, wringing her tissue in her hands. "I can't think straight. I can't sleep. I cry all the time. I thought coming to see you would bring me comfort." She snorts out a sad laugh. "Obviously a grave mistake."

"It's not a mistake," he says. "I want to help you."

Britt rolls her eyes, as she blows her nose, louder this time. "Don't patronize me."

He winces and glances my way again. And I blink back at him, a little shocked. He hadn't been lying when he said he was crap with women. Because he is terrible at this. At least with Britt. And yet he's always been wonderful with me, effortlessly perfect.

Perfectly imperfect.

Britt speaks again. "I miss her, Finn." She starts to sob, quietly now, her shoulders shaking. "I didn't even want her in the beginning. Can you believe that?"

Finn rubs his hand over his face, and he suddenly looks exhausted. "Yes."

Britt looks up at him with eyes that sparkle with pain and something deeper. "She would have been so beautiful, don't you think?"

He swallows hard. "Of course she would have."

This is too personal. I'm an intruder here. I move to go when Finn grabs my hand and holds it tight. His fleeting look is clear: he expects me to stay. I settle back with some reluctance, and he threads his fingers through mine as he sits on the arm of the couch. His warmth presses into my shoulder, as if he needs me to brace him. "We will never forget her. But, Britt, we have to find a way to move on."

She looks appalled and disgusted in him, and Finn blanches as if struck. My heart hurts for him, because he's right. It isn't callous to want that.

"I can't," she grits out.

My thumb strokes the back of Finn's hand. "Look," I say to Britt. "We don't know each other, and I understand that this isn't the greatest way to meet. But have you thought about going to talk to someone?"

Britt jerks her chin, her gaze darting away. "I don't need that. I'm not completely broken."

"It's not a sign of weakness to seek help," I say. "I did once."

Finn twitches with surprise, but he doesn't say a word. His hand, however, holds my mine a little tighter.

"I had to deal with some things a few years ago," I tell her, ignoring the jitters that start up in my belly. They always do when I talk about that time, so it isn't a surprise. "And I had a hard time coping for a while. I know it isn't the same as your loss—yes, Finn told me. But I know how depression can consume you."

Britt stares at me, her eyes wide and a bit glazed. I know that look too. I used to see it in the mirror. There are days I still do. She licks her reddened lips, as if nervous. "And it worked?"

"It helped a lot. I went to a counselor. It was a safe space where I could talk, get things off my chest."

She bites her bottom lip, her fingers clenching, and I put my free hand on hers.

"If you don't like it, you don't have to continue."

With a sigh, she stands. "I should go."

"You don't have to," Finn assures. And I'll give him credit, even though he'd been a mess when she arrived, he sounds sincere now.

But Britt shakes her head, her gaze darting to Finn. "I was obviously interrupting something."

It's only then I truly notice that Finn's wearing a pair of low-slung pajama bottoms and nothing else. Which must be a testament to my distraction because he looks delicious.

Finn looks down at himself, and skin colors a little, going a rosy-deep gold hue. "Right."

He puts his hands low on his hips, then seems to realize that only highlights his muscles, because his hands drop to his sides. He shifts his weight as if not knowing what the hell to do.

I stand as well. "If you'd like, I can get you the contact info for the person I saw."

"Thanks. But I'll find someone." Britt gives me a tight smile, but it's clear she wants to bolt. I don't blame her, and I'm not going to stand in her way. Sometimes, you have to lick your wounds in private.

I back away, letting her pass.

"Give me a second," Finn says to me, and leads Britt to the door.

They stop in the hallway, heads bent, talking in low voices. From an artistic standpoint, they look beautiful together, her light to his dark. I swear, their combined fame has a glow to it. Something about them makes you keep looking, even if you don't want to.

I never expected to be with someone like Finn. He will never fully be mine. I will always have to share him with the public. I'm okay with that. I'm proud of Finn. But seeing him standing with Britt pulls my thoughts down darker, less secure roads that I'm definitely not proud of.

It's bothered me before, but now those old insecurities are suddenly on display in all their ugly glory. I don't want to see them anymore than I want to view Britt and Finn as a pretty pair. But I can't look away.

I want to be back in bed, wrapped up in sex and Finn, where the real world is a distant murmur and the present is nothing but pleasure and warmth. I want it so badly that if feels like desperation. And that scares me.

CHAPTER 19
⬢ FINN

"When are you going to move your stuff into our room?" I ask Chess as she stands in the guest bathroom doing her makeup.

Chess pauses, eyeliner in hand, and looks at me through the reflection of the mirror. "What does it matter where my stuff is? We sleep in the same bed."

Technically, I suppose she's right. But it's been two weeks since we've returned from California. And call me an impatient man, but every time she veers off into this room to get dressed, I find myself worrying.

The whole scene with Britt arriving on my doorstep hasn't helped matters. I'd been afraid Chess would freak. But she'd treated Britt with compassion and a kindness that humbled me.

Even so, Chess has been withdrawn at times. I don't know if it's because of James leaving or it's something more. And not knowing worries me too.

"It feels significant," I tell her.

"Significant?" She runs the liner over her lid, a sweep of deep green done with a precision that fascinates me.

I love watching her do personal things no one else gets to see. And I know it's the same for her. Every time I shave, Chess appears in the bathroom and sits on the counter as if settling in for a show.

"Yeah, significant," I repeat. "As in, you're keeping this room as some sort of safe zone."

Chess blinks at me as if I've spoken in a foreign language. But I know her too well now, which means I know when she's stalling. I cross my arms over my chest and wait her out.

Slowly she sets her eyeliner down. "Sometimes I hate how perceptive you are."

"It's my job to read people."

Chess turns around and leans against the counter. "You're the first man I've ever lived with."

"You're my first too." I give her a brief smile. "I like that about us, truth be told."

"Caveman," she says with a laughing huff.

"So we've established."

Chess bites her lip with a bemused expression. "Don't you ever experience any moments of doubt?"

Maybe that should insult me, but it doesn't. We're more alike than she realizes.

"Of course. It scared the hell out of me when I realized that what I was feeling for you went beyond simple attraction or friendship. But Dex once reminded me that we have zero hesitation on the football field, and to hesitate in life is stupid."

"Stupid?" She raises one delicate black brow.

"Well…" I grin. "More like a waste of energy better spent on other things."

Chess pushes off the counter and walks toward me. Heat coils low in my gut, my abs flexing tight in response. She wraps her arms around my neck and lifts up on her toes. Her kiss is sweet affection and lingering appreciation.

My hands slide to her peachy butt and give it a squeeze. Chess makes a small noise in her throat and leans into me, her tongue licking my lower lip like it's candy.

A surge of lust goes through me, hot and thick, but I can't help smiling against her luscious lips. "You wouldn't be trying to distract me now would you, Chester?"

She gives me a little nip that goes straight to my cock, then pulls back enough to meet my eyes. "I don't think you realize how irresistible you are, Finnegan."

Her fingers trace lazy circles on my neck, and my lids lower as I dip down for another taste. She hums in pleasure. And we get a lost in soft, unhurried kisses before she speaks again. "Let's say distraction is an added side bonus."

I chuckle, then give her ass a light slap.

Chess yelps and glares. "One day, I'm going to spank your ass, Mannus, and we'll see who's laughing then."

"Kinky, I like it."

Chess cups my cheek. "Want to help me move my stuff?"

Smiling wide, I give her a swift kiss. "Okay, but let's give this guest bed a nice sendoff first."

She yelps as I wrap my arms under her butt and lift her high. We make it to the bed but just barely.

"I think we should change the mattress before you invite your parents for a visit," Chess says, as she hangs up a black dress. "Doesn't feel right, imagining them sleeping on it after what we just did in there."

I snicker and put down a hamper filled with her clothes. "I don't know, I kind of want to put up a commemorative plaque. 'On this site, Finnegan Mannus gave Chester Copper five orgasms and reduced her to tears of pleasure.'"

"I believe you were the one tearing up."

"It was an emotional moment."

She takes the basket from me. "Which drawers can I take?"

The closet is a large square with shelving on two walls, hanging racks on the other two, and a massive waist high dresser in the center.

"I've filled up the left side of the closet. Why don't you take the right? Let me just clear out some old stuff from this drawer."

"Sounds good."

From a top drawer, I start taking out a mess of old ticket stubs and college game day programs—nostalgic shit I can't seem to get rid of—and set them on the top of the dresser. "I'm thinking we should probably put a mirror in here. You know the kind that women use to put on earrings and shit? My mom has one in her closet—"

Chess make a soft sound, and I glance back. But she isn't even looking at me. Her eyes are on the dresser top, her skin pale and her expression haunted.

It takes me a second to figure out what she's looking at but when I do, my heart gives a painful lurch. Scattered among the papers, is a sonogram with the word "Peanut" scrawled across the top in vivid red pen.

The air in the room goes thin. I can hear my heart pounding, like it's trying to break free. But I can't move.

Chess's hand slips into mine. "Finn."

My fingers convulse, gripping hers tight.

With her free hand, Chess reaches out, her fingers just dancing at the edges of the picture. "Can I?" she whispers to me.

Dully, I nod.

She handles the flimsy piece of paper as if it was precious glass, bringing it closer to look at the image. A shiver goes through me. I don't want to touch it. But I can't look away.

"I forgot I put it there," I whisper—to Chess or to my baby's image, I don't know. I'd tossed it so carelessly into a draw to sit in the dark. With a shaking hand, I take the picture from Chess.

It's an old-fashioned sonogram that only shows an outline, not the more modern, high-tech version that renders a perfect image. "Britt was superstitious about seeing the baby's face before she was born," I tell Chess with a voice that sounds like chunky gravel. "Said some things should be a surprise."

"Honey…" Chess rests her cheek against my arm.

"I don't even know if I regret that decision or not."

Chess wraps an arm around my waist and hugs herself against my side. I turn into her warmth and take a deep breath. "I'm okay," I tell her. "I am. I just get sad sometimes."

"I know," she says, stroking my stomach.

My thumb touches the little image.

Chess speaks again in a low, hesitant tone. "I could frame it for you, if you'd like."

For a long moment, I stare down at my baby girl. "No." I clear my throat. "I don't think I can manage that… But she needs a safer spot to rest."

"Of course."

I take another deep breath and gently place the sonogram on top of the dresser, away from all the mess, before turning back to Chess and wrapping her in my arms. She hugs me tight.

"I feel bad for Britt," I mumble into Chess's hair. "But I'm sorry if it got too intense when she showed up."

Chess looks up at me. "Don't ever be sorry about something like that." Her green gaze searches my face. "It's okay, you know, to be friends with her. Maybe you can give each other something no one else can."

"God, please don't say that."

"Say what?"

"That I have something no one else can give her. I hate the idea of Britt hurting, but I don't think I'm the one to help her. She seems to think…"

I hesitate, and Chess frowns. "What?"

"Before you walked in, Britt started saying that she thought we were meant to be together." I run a hand over my face. "She's kind of messed up, Chess. She was talking about having another baby with me. I think she wants to…recreate…"

I can't finish.

"Shit," Chess whispers.

"She needs help, Chess. But I can't give it to her. I tried to tell her that there will be other chances. She'll find someone and have kids one day. We both will."

If I hadn't been looking right at Chess, I would have missed her flinch. She's good at hiding it, giving my hand a squeeze as she puts on a brave face. "You will."

Chess lets my hand go and opens a drawer to fill it with socks.

I stand there in heavy silence. "Something I said upset you."

She glances my way. "Of course I'm upset. Your pain is mine."

I believe that. I feel that. It's a comfort I never expected but appreciate. Even so. "That's not it, though. Something hurt you personally. What is it?"

The line of her slim shoulders tense. She opens the next drawer. "I'm fine, Finn. Really."

I take her hand and halt her movements. "Chess, come on. Something has been bothering you since Britt showed up here. You think I can't see it?"

A glimmer of panic lights her eyes before she glances away. "Now isn't the time to talk about this."

Breaking free of me, she heads out of the closet.

I follow her. "There's never a right time to talk about painful shit. But I'm here." Catching up to her, I clasp her elbow, and she halts. I move closer, until my chest is pressed against her back. "Talk to me. Please."

I'm tall enough to see her eyes flutter closed, and the pain that etches her face. "I can't have them. Children. Babies."

It's the last thing I expected her to say. "What?"

Her breath shudders. "I'm basically infertile."

Shit. Every comment I've made about having kids swims through my head. It had to have been a slap in the face for Chess. But she let me ramble and cry on her shoulder. "Honey…"

She moves away from me and starts pacing. "I found out during the whole latex fiasco. I've always had bad periods, horrible cramps, whatnot. I thought the latex issue was related to wearing… Anyway, they did a whole checkup thing and discovered that I had cysts in my uterus."

She talks faster and faster. "I had them taken out. But it was so bad that there was significant scarring, and the docs told me that I have little to no chance of becoming pregnant. Deformed uterus, and all that."

"Chess…"

She talks over me, the pitch of her voice rising. "And it isn't as if I'd been going around dreaming of babies or anything. But when the choice is taken away from you…" She shakes head, blinking rapidly.

Before she can move again, I grab her hand and tug her onto my lap as I sit on the couch. Her posture is rigid but she turns to face me. "It isn't the same as what you went through, but I know how it feels to lose something you didn't even know you wanted."

"I'm so sorry, Chess." I tell her, cupping her cheek.

She leans into my touch, and her hand comes up to rest on my chest. "It is what it is."

"Yeah, but you've had to listen to me go on and on—"

"Hey," she cuts in softly. "I want to listen. I want to be here for you."

I nod, but before I can reply, she talks again.

"But you want something I can never give you."

The words swell between us. And I go still. "What do you mean?"

But I know.

Chess gives me a sad smile. "You want kids. You know that now. And I can't have them." Her lids lower, hiding her eyes. "I think about that and what it means for the future of us. And it scares me."

"Chess—"

"Let me say this. I know my worth. I know that who I am is the sum of all of me not the parts that aren't perfect. I know that if I want children, I can adopt or find a surrogate. There are options. I've had all these conversations with myself already."

Her hand glides over my chest in a slow, steady circle, as if I'm the one who needs soothing.

"And I know that we've just gotten together and thinking about this stuff is kind of jumping the gun. But we're living together now, saying… emotional things to each other." She flushes pink. "And it feels weighty. Like it's more than just casual dating."

"Because it is." How can she doubt that?

Chess's fingers curl into the fabric of my shirt. "Which means we have to go into this relationship knowing the facts. I don't want to be a regret. I don't want you wondering somewhere along the way if you made the right choice."

"You think I'm not going to want you because you can't have kids?" I don't know if I'm hurt or insulted but it doesn't feel good. It feels a lot like pain and panic.

Chess shakes her head. "This isn't something you can just declare in the moment."

The hell I can't. But I bite my lip. Instinct is telling me that the more I push, the more she'll push back.

"And maybe…" She hesitates, licking her kiss-swollen upper lip. "I don't want to wonder if you're regretting things. When I found all this out, I made a promise to myself that any relationship I went into would be the right fit for me as well."

For a second I just stare at her, trying to process what she's saying. My words come out rough and halting. "Were you planning on finding a guy who didn't want kids? Is that it?"

Her green eyes go wide, and then she glances away. Guilty.

Something hot and itchy swells in my chest. "I don't know what to say."

"You don't have to say anything."

That hot thing grows, climbing up my throat. "I think I do. You're basically dooming us before we've even started."

Chess's eyes snap to mine. "I'm telling you how I feel. You wanted to know. Well, this is it. I get scared. I think about these things. I don't fucking want to. Believe me, I'd rather laugh and make love, and have my biggest worry be whether we get meatballs or onions on our pizza—"

I silence her with a kiss. Pressing my mouth to hers so she can feel me.

Chess stays stiff for a second then relaxes, her hand spreading wide on my chest. I pull back and look her in the eye. "I'm sorry, okay? I did ask. And I'm glad you told me."

She rests her forehead against mine. "You keep apologizing. Don't. It isn't your fault that I can't turn off my brain when I'm with you."

How fucking ironic: the only time I can turn off my brain is when I'm with Chess.

Gently, I set her aside. I feel a headache coming on and my joints are stiff. "Let's get this closet filled. Then I need to go for a run."

She looks at me for what feels like forever but is really only the blink of an eye. When she talks, her voice is subdued but understanding. "Putting away clothes is something I can do myself. Why don't you go for a run now?"

I don't argue. I leave her to it and head out. I run for a long time, but I don't find any answers while I'm gone.

♟ CHESS

What if I've made a mistake?

The thought tumbles around in my head with relentless persistence. I told Finn something intensely personal. The only other person who knows is James, who found out because he was at the studio when I came back from my appointment.

Maybe it was too soon to tell Finn. What guy wants to talk about conception or the lack thereof less than a month out from having sex with a woman? I probably sounded like a crazed, jock chaser. I wouldn't be surprised if he fears I'll be asking for a ring next.

God, he'd looked spooked. And then so freaking stubborn. Finn is a problem solver. He relies on instinct, whereas I like to think things out.

"Argh." I rest my head on the kitchen counter, letting the cool stone soothe my hot cheek.

I should have just told him the bare bones and moved on, had some fun with Finn without worrying about some shadowy future. And yet, I can't do that. I'm totally gone on this man. What did James call it?

Besotted. I totally am. If I let myself fall any further, it will wreck me if we don't last. I need for us to go in eyes wide open, or I will always worry.

Predictably, after I dropped my no baby bomb, Finn had been withdrawn. Oh, he had still reached for me as we got into bed, slid his hand down my pants and insisted that I'd be more comfortable never wearing clothes to bed again. He'd fucked me into oblivion, with quiet intensity that felt almost like desperation, as if I'd soon disappear on him. I'd felt the same and turned to him with a neediness that bordered on painful.

But it feels as though there's a rift between us now. And I put it there.

Finn had left early for his home game today. I'd expected him to ask me if I wanted a ticket to go watch. But he hadn't said a word, just gave me a light kiss on the mouth and said he'd see me tonight.

It hurt so much that I hadn't watched him on TV. I caught up on work instead.

Dinner at the kitchen table is lonely now that I know how it feels to share it with Finn. My dinner is finished and I'm still alone in a too quiet condo.

"Shit." I push myself upright and open my laptop. I don't know how to turn off my mind or stop from worrying. So I put my focus on work instead. Work is safe. Work I understand. I can control it.

I'm touching up a photo of Jake for the calendar when Finn comes home. I look up from my perch on the kitchen stool to find him limping along, his expression drawn and tight.

I know pain is part of his life. It still guts me every time I see him hurting. "Hey," I say, catching his attention.

"Babe." Finn moves toward me, going at a snail's pace.

Jesus, he's in a bad way.

I jump off my stool. "Bedroom."

His lips curl in a tired but pleased smile. "I like how you think, Chester, but you're gonna have to do most of the work tonight."

"My man, the eternal optimist," I say, fighting a smile. "But I was talking about getting you horizontal so you can rest."

He bends his head and gives me a soft kiss. "I like my plan better. But keep calling me your man. It soothes my weary soul."

I roll my eyes and put my arm around his waist. "Come on, hot shot, we can negotiate terms in bed."

Finn slings his arm over my shoulders and gives me a light squeeze as we slowly move to his bedroom—our bedroom now. "I love coming home to you," he says with a content sigh. "I have from day one. But now…" He glances down at me. "It makes it all worth it."

A lump rises in my throat, and I press my lips to the side of his chest, just breathe him in for a moment. He smells of soap, the clean cotton of his shirt, and the warmth of his body. "I'm glad you're home."

Once inside the bedroom, I grab a remote and turn on the gas fireplace. It flares to life, soon to send warmth radiating into the cool room. The bedside lamps give the bedroom a soft, golden glow. And I realize why his decorator did his room in warm tones and luscious fabrics. This place is a haven for his tough days.

"Want some dinner," I ask him.

"Downed a cheeseburger and some fries on the way home." He heads straight toward the bed.

"No soaking bath?"

"Had an ice bath after the game, then a hot shower." Finn toes off his sneakers. "I have no interest sitting around in more water."

Gingerly, he moves to pull off his shirt, and I help him. My breath catches as we lift the shirt past his ribs. "Jesus, Finn."

His sides and back are red and covered with a patchwork of nasty bruises.

"Ugly game," he says flatly. "Got sacked a few times."

I rest my hand on his lower back, barely touching him, and he shivers. But when I try to snatch my hand away, he stops me by covering his hand over mine. "No," he says. "It feels good when you touch me."

"Finn..." My heart aches, as I brush my lips over his shoulder blade, my other hand slipping around to his front to stoke his stomach. We stand in silence, Finn breathing slow and deep, leaning into me as I pepper soft kisses across the back of his shoulders.

I hold him as if he's fragile.

In this moment, he is. And I resent every hit that he's taken.

Another tremor goes through him and slowly, slowly, he disengages from me, turning to sit on the side of the bed. "Come here," he whispers, taking my hand.

"Don't you want to lie down?" I ask as he settles me on his lap.

"Gotta do this is stages," he says with a grunt, then arranges me to his liking.

"Baby..." I wrap my arms around his neck and rest my forehead against his. "You are killing me."

Finn touches my cheek, his blue eyes searching mine. "You worry for me, Chester?"

I run a finger over his jaw. "I ache for you, Finnegan."

His hand slides into my hair, and he pulls me close. Our kiss is slow, easy, deep. There are words in the kiss: mine, yours, always. His lips cling to my lower one is a soft suckle before he pulls away to meet my gaze. "I don't like the idea of you hurting. Especially if it's for me."

"Not something you get a say over," I tell him, kissing his temple.

He makes a noise, half a laugh, half an objection, and his hand trails down my cheek to my collarbone.

We're quiet then. I play with the short ends of his hair, kiss his cheek, his jaw, anywhere I can get. Finn strokes my neck, watching his fingers move along my skin as if the sight soothes him. I'm accustomed now to seeing him hobble home from a game. But this is different. He seems soul weary.

Cold fear and hot regret surge through me at the thought that I might be responsible for his mood.

"What happened," I ask him, as he finds the top button of the soft cotton work shirt I'm wearing.

He flicks open a button. "Dex totally lost it today. He's been on and off all season, but some dumb ass lineman tried to fire him up and he fell for it." Finn ducks his head and kisses the side of my neck. His breath is hot against my skin. "Don't blame him, but everything went to shit after that."

I rest my hand on the top of his head. "Why did he lose it?"

Another button slips free. Finn's fingers trace his progress. "Press got compromising pictures of his girl. Dude started making comments about her tits—*breasts*."

"That would do it."

Finn grimaces. "My control of the game is falling apart."

"I'm sorry." I smooth my hand over Finn's hair in an absentminded stroke.

"And it's all on me, Chess. Doesn't matter who's at fault. If we can't get the job done, I look bad."

His cheek touches mine. We're so close, I feel the sweep of his lashes when he blinks.

"The pressure gets to me sometimes," he says. "I tell myself that it's all in my head. To ignore it. But some days are harder than others."

"Maybe you don't ignore those fears but just face them," I say in a low voice. "Let them play out in your head and then let them go."

Finn sighs. "I know I won't play forever. But it's one thing to retire, walk away with your head held high. Getting cut? Never finding a new team? How do I face people then?"

"You face them head on, because you, Finn Mannus, are fucking brilliant with or without football."

"Chess…"

"This is a rough patch, Finn. But I believe in you. In who you are as a man, not just as a football player. You're not going to fail, because you'll never give up. That's the only failure in life."

The curve of his lashes cast shadows on his cheeks. "Everything is right when I'm with you."

He sounds so forlorn that I kiss his closed eyes. "You're here now. Let me take care of you."

"Couldn't wait to get home to you." Slowly he starts unbuttoning the rest of my shirt, placing soft, reverent kisses down my neck as he goes. It feels so good, my skin pulls tight with heat and pleasure.

His breath hitches when he finds out I'm not wearing a bra, but he doesn't part my shirt, just kisses my neck and the little hollow between my collarbones. His tender care lulls me into a languid haze, and I lower my head to his shoulder.

"Sometimes…" He presses his lips to my skin. "I hate that you've seen my guys naked."

My hand rests on his biceps, my fingers tracing the hard curve there. "Going all caveman on me, Mannus?"

"Yes." He runs the backs of his knuckles down the center of my chest to my belly. I shiver in response, arching my back just a bit. My breasts swell with heat, my nipples tightening. I want them exposed. I want his hands on them. But he keeps my shirt where it is, barely parted, revealing only my cleavage and the little indent of my navel.

His hand spreads out on the small curve of my belly. "I hate that you've seen their dicks."

I huff out a laugh. "But I only want yours."

"Mmm…" Slowly, he glides up toward my ribs.

My lids flutter, that touch so wonderfully tender but intent.

The tip of his thumb brushes the sensitive curve of my breast. I go still, silently willing him to move higher. But I don't ask. Not yet. It's too good, the way he teases me. He stays there, rubbing the underside of my breast with gentle fingers.

A sound escapes me, low, needy.

"Still hate it," he mutters, kissing my neck. His hand gently cups me, feeling the slight weight of my breast. I shift in his lap, and the hard swell of his cock presses against my ass.

"Get over it," I murmur, half-heartedly. His fingertip has found my nipple. He circles it, skims the sensitive tip.

Mouth against my neck, Finn laughs, and the vibrations tickles my skin. "I suppose I'll have to find a way." He kisses his way down to the rise of my breast while his finger continues its slow torture, barely touching.

As if he's taking an illicit peek, he lifts my shirt and draws it away from my breast. "What do we have here?" He kisses my nipple, giving it a small suck.

I squirm, hold the back of his head so he can't get away. He chuckles again, licks my breast from curve to tip, as his free hand roams to find my other breast. Warm hands kneed me. His mouth is hot and wet.

Lust rushes through me like a fever. I rub my thighs together with impatience. But he ignores that. His hand plumps my breast, holding it firm as he tugs on my nipple with his mouth.

"Finn," I warn—*beg*—I'm not sure which.

He nuzzles the hollow of my throat, as his fingers pluck at the sore tips of my breasts. "Love that sound. You whimpering my name."

I do it again and he slides the shirt off my shoulders. His mouth finds mine. He kisses me, abuses my nipples, until I'm whimpering again, wiggling in his lap with need. Finn and I might have our fears, but here, in this way, we are perfection.

With a last kiss, he lays me back on the bed and then grasps the waistband of my leggings and panties. "Lift," he orders. I raise my butt and he pulls. I'm left in only my knee-high pink socks with ridiculous Christmas elves on them.

"Take them off," I say, lifting my foot.

But Finn just grins. "Oh, no, I love these." He grabs the arch of my foot and gives my toes a kiss before lowering my leg.

He looms over me, his chest bare, track pants riding low on his hips and not hiding the rise of his hard cock. Gorgeous as hell. But battered and bruised. I don't want him to feel more pain.

"I thought you said I had to do the work tonight."

His smile is lazy, as he looks me over. "You do. Spread your legs for me, Chess."

Hands on my knees, I do as he asks. A guttural sound rumbles in his throat, and his gaze settles on where I'm swollen and wet. "Good girl."

It should piss me off what he says, and the way he says it, as if I am in fact his good little girl. But I picture myself stretched out on his bed, my thighs spread wide, pink knee-highs on, and it feels illicit, so hot that I tremble, lift my tits a little higher in the air.

"So pretty," he murmurs, then settles himself between my legs. He sets his big hand low on my belly, holding me still, his thumb touching my clit. It distracts me, and when he kisses my sex like a man starved, I yelp, my body twitching.

But he doesn't let me get away. His hand keeps me in place as he goes at me. He licks my sex as if it's warm candy.

"Finn…" I can't take it. I throb.

Over the length of my body, his eyes meet mine. "Pinch those tight, little nipples," he orders between kisses.

My breath grows short, as I lift my hands to my breasts. The first pinch on the aching tips has me moaning.

He grunts in approval. "Give them a tug. Nice and slow."

I do, and my back leaves the mattress as I gasp.

"Good," he says, his thumb toying with my clit. "Good girl."

It shouldn't get me so hot, but it does. My lids flutter, my thighs fall further open even as I writhe. And his gaze slides from mine to focus between my legs. That he's staring there makes everything more sensitive. I revel in the exposure.

His finger comes up to trace the lips of my sex. He finds my opening and toys with it, dipping in just enough that I feel it but not enough to satisfy. I whimper, and his gaze flicks to mine before sliding back down. That thick finger sinks in. In and out. Just the tip. Not enough.

"Finn…"

I'm panting harder, my thighs trembling.

He plunges in deeper then pulls back out, and his finger travels downward. He touches the entrance to my ass, and a strangled sound leaves my lips. But he doesn't move away. He strokes me with the slightest of movements.

When he talks, his voice is rough, but his tone is almost conversational. "You ever taken it in here?"

"No," I whisper, watching him.

That finger, slick with my desire, pushes just a little. And I nearly choke. It's so sensitive there, my entire body seizes. He notices and hums low in his throat. He plays with my ass, making me whimper.

"Would you let me take you here one day, Chess?"

It feels so good, wrong, dirty, intense. "Yes," I say on a garbled breath as sweat breaks out over my skin. Without thought, I push back at his touch, and his finger slips inside me.

I cry out, my hips bucking, and he sinks further. Finn makes a noise in his throat, and his mouth latches onto my clit. His finger pushes deep, pumping a little.

It undoes me. I'm coming, pinching my nipples so hard they hurt. It's not enough. I fuck myself on his finger as he sucks me. My orgasm breaks so hard and fast, I collapse, boneless and breathless onto the bed. He lets it ride with soft playful pecks of his lips until my breathing evens.

Slowly he withdraws his finger and gives me one last kiss before rising up.

"I'm dead," I moan, shivering lightly.

"You're still breathing." Finn's gaze is fierce and hot as he slides down his pants. His cock is angry and dark.

I shiver again, a pulse of want going through me. "Barely."

He climbs on the bed and leans against the headboard, his knee brushing my shoulder. "Get up here and sit on my cock. This won't take long."

He is evil. Evil. And I love it.

Holding his gaze, I roll over and get on my hands and knees. Avidly, he watches me crawl his way. My breasts sway with the movement, and he runs a hand over his swollen dick. His pecs twitch, his nipples tight beads. I lean in and lick one, as I straddle his hips.

We both groan as I sink onto him. I'm so slicked up, so well attended that he slips right in. Still I feel it. I feel it at the back of my throat and along the soles of my feet. I feel it in the cool heat that races over my skin.

His hands grip my hips, tilting me forward. I catch myself by holding his big shoulders, and he takes the opportunity to swoop in and draw my nipple into his mouth to suck it hard and greedy.

As if by mutual consent we start fucking, him thrusting up into me, me pushing down to get him deep. It is frantic and fast. His fingers sink into the soft flesh of my ass, pulling at it, moving it. He's so strong, I'm bouncing on his hips, our bodies meeting with loud slaps.

"Fuck, Chess," he pants. "I can't. I can't..." He breaks off and tries to kiss me.

But our movements are so violent and uncoordinated that our mouths barely meet. I wrap my arms around his neck. The walls of my sex clamp down on his dick, and he makes a strangled sound, his body jerking.

"Get there," he pleads, thrusting harder.

But I'm too weak to do anything more than hang on. His hand slides down. No, he can't. He can't. I won't survive. But he does it. He pushes his finger in deep and rough. And I come again on a wail.

He comes with me this time, making sounds that are almost pained.

We crash in a heap, me slumped on his chest, Finn sagging against the headboard. His arm bands around me, and he cups the back of my sweaty necks as we lie there and regain our breath. His heart is a fast beat in my ear. Too late I remember his injuries.

"Let me get off you," I say, trying to move.

His grip tightens. "No."

Not wanting to struggle, I let him hold me, and he relaxes. He turns his head and rests his lips against my temple. "Do you have any idea how much I need you? You make everything better."

Emotion clogs my throat. I blink rapidly, my cheek pressed to the wall of his chest. My arms wrap around his shoulders. I want to pull him into me, protect him from the world. "I thought…" I clear my throat. "I thought I might have messed things up."

Finn stills, and then slowly smoothes his hand over the back of my head. "You didn't. It's good to talk."

I nod, but don't say a word.

His touch is lazy, fingers carding through my hair. "My whole life, I've lived with my eye on the future. Every day, working for it. Worrying about it." His hand comes to rest on my nape. "I'm tired, Chess. With you, I can rest."

The beat of his heart is fast and strong against my cheek. Warm fingers tighten on my neck in entreat. "Can we rest for a while? Just be?"

There is true yearning in his voice, and that plea goes straight to my heart. From the beginning, Finn had been clear about what drew him to me; I turned off all the white noise in his head. It had been flattering, seductive to be his sole focus. It still is.

And it isn't one sided. I did not know what true joy was until Finn. Every emotion I'm capable of having amps up with him. I feel. I live. I breathe. The world is more real when he is there.

He wants to just be. Not think. I don't know if I can. But, for Finn, I'll try.

With a smile that feels too weak, I place a kiss on the center of his chest. "Yes," I say against his skin. "Let's just be."

CHAPTER 20
♟ CHESS

"So, how are you getting along?" I ask James on the phone. I know Jamie is a programmer and has a tiny efficiency walk-up on the Lower East Side, but Manhattan is ridiculously expensive. James will have to get a job quickly.

"I'm waiting tables at this cute *osteria* in SoHo."

I'm not surprised; James waited tables through college, and the money will probably be more than he earned with me.

He gives me the name of one of New York's biggest chef's Italian restaurants. Leave it to James to understate.

"We're so eating there whenever I visit," I tell him, rubbing some coconut oil onto my arms. My wrist is healed, the cast removed, but my skin is pale and overly sensitive where it used to be.

Swathed in a towel, I've taken over the bathroom, refusing to let Finn enter while I get ready for tonight. He'd pretended to pout about it for a few minutes, but soon gave up and walked away with a fairly satisfied expression. Not that I blame him; I'd satisfied him very well all morning long.

"You got a deal," James says. "How about you? Things picking up?"

Sitting on a big ottoman in the massive closet, I rest my chin on my knee and study my toes, now painted scarlet red. "I need to find a work studio."

Finn's condo has three bedrooms, and he'd suggested I use one. But the room isn't big enough and the light is all wrong. Never mind the fact that I cannot violate his privacy by bringing clients in here. This space is his sanctuary, and though his willingness to offer it to me speaks volumes about his trust, I won't let him make that sacrifice. I need a separate workspace that I can comfortably bring people to.

Not for the first time, a pang of longing for my loft hits me. I breathe through it.

"I've been looking at a few places, but haven't found the right space yet." Most of them are out of my price range. Finn doesn't want me to pay rent, but I can't agree to that. The argument is ongoing and stubborn on both sides.

"You'll find something," James says.

"I miss my place." I hadn't meant to say it, but the words are out anyway. "At least the work space set up."

James is silent. "Have you told Finn? Maybe talk about finding some place new?"

Shrugging, I wiggle my toes. "We just officially got together. Asking him to move would be a total Psycho Sally play." And I've heaped more than enough baggage on his head.

James laughs. "Yes, but he asked you to move in with him. If you're not happy there, it will show."

Happy. My mind drifts, pulling up the image of Finn in bed this morning, stretched out on his back, all long lines, honed planes, and amber skin. He'd been warm and loose-limbed with sleep, the scent of sex and pheromones a seductive fragrance I couldn't ignore.

Finn was made to be worshipped. And he is mine. I'd slowly woken him with lingering kisses over that glorious body, nuzzling his warm neck as he gave a sleepy grunt, hooking his arm over my shoulders to draw me close. I hadn't been deterred. I'd made my way down, past tight little nipples that begged to be nibbled on, around the cute divot of his navel, to his cock that rested on the hard swell of his thigh.

And then I'd done exactly what I'd promised him; took him in my mouth, sucked him as he grew thick and hard, his body arching with a moan. "Oh, fuck, Chess. Don't stop."

As if I could. The feel of him in my mouth, heavy and fat on my tongue, stretching my lips wide. The way his brow furrowed, his mouth slack in a pant, eyes watching me with hot and helpless intensity. All of it worked like a drug to the system, filling me with wicked heat and covetous greed.

I'd worshiped at the altar of Finn Mannus's glorious cock, making it slick and swollen, caressing the tight ripple of his belly to keep him still. And I had moved my mouth-wet fingers down past his balls to stroke him where he'd once stroked me.

Tongue toying with the tip of his dick, I'd given his words back to him. "You gonna let me have you here?"

As if I'd touched him with a live wire, he'd lit up, his big body shuddering, his breath coming out in great heaves. He'd looked at me, his expression twisted with lust and pleasure, the small shock in his eyes mixing with dark interest. I'd pushed against his tight flesh, wanting to torment, and he'd pushed back, letting me.

"Yes," he'd rasped. "Fuck, yes."

I'd never experienced that level of trust before, that willingness to try anything, knowing that the giving and receiving of pleasure would be tenfold because you were with the person you wanted above all things.

"Chess? Hello..."

I come back to myself with a shiver, almost surprised to be sitting alone in the closet with a phone in my hand. Taking a deep breath, I try to recall what I'd been talking about. *Happiness.*

Will I be happy living here with Finn?

"Sorry. Dropped the phone." I lick my lips and find them tender. "I'm happy. It's just an adjustment period, fully moving in." I glance at the dress I'm wearing tonight. It's a black and white halter top sheath, not my favorite Grace Kelly knock off. That beauty went up in a blaze of glory. It hurts to think about it. But, Finn has already seen me in it. New is better. "Getting back to work with a big project would help."

"Speaking of that," James says. "I've been hesitant to ask, but…"

"But? When are you ever hesitant? Spit it out."

He huffs. "Remember Michael Harrison?"

"Of course." Michael is a photographer too. We went to school together. "How is he?"

"Busy. He's going to Milan next week, but he asked about you."

"Me? Why?"

"I had lunch with him. We caught up, I told him about you and the fire, and one thing led to another."

"You're rambling, James."

James makes a tisking sound. "He wanted to know if you'd take over a project for him."

"Go on." I get up to pace.

"It's huge, Chess. You know that old 'Got Milk?' campaign?"

"Sure."

"Think something in that style, but to raise awareness for prostate cancer. They're pulling together Hollywood's hottest male stars for a photoshoot."

Abruptly, I sit down again. "Why the hell is Michael giving that up? And how does he know they'll even want me?"

"Because when a fashion photographer gets personally invited to Milan by Armani, he doesn't say no. And the ad company agreed with his suggestion to use you as a replacement because they've seen the shots of Dex and Rolondo. They want something similar." His voice becomes almost giddy. "It's good money, Chess."

James names a sum that makes me a little dizzy.

"Fuuuck."

"Exactly," he says.

"And we'd be able to work together on this?" My heart is beating harder now, an excited flutter going through me.

"Well, if you want me to."

"Shut up. You know I would. Do you really think I don't know it was you who put this idea in his head?"

I can almost hear him smile. "So you'll do it? The project starts in two weeks. They need to know as soon as possible. It should run for about a month, maybe two, depending on scheduling."

"Where would I live?" I pace again, touching the edge of my dress then walking to the other side of the closet to brush a hand over the sleeves of Finn's suits.

"With the money they're paying, you could rent a place. But Michael has offered the use of his loft."

"Michael is being generous as fuck."

"Oh, please, Chessie. You know he's always had a thing for you. I'm not at all surprised he asked about you."

Halting, I stare at the wall of sneakers that is Finn's secret pride and glory. "He's not expecting… You told him about Finn, right?"

Finn. What will he say? I press a hand to my hot cheek and find my fingers cold.

"Yes, I told him," James says, exasperated. "And don't insult yourself. This is about your talent and people recognizing it."

I've trained myself not to put too much hope into a good thing. Plans change, promises fall through the cracks. You stand on the curb enough times waiting for parents who forgot about yet another school function and it's inevitable.

But I don't want to be ruled by my childhood. So I let myself get excited. "I'm interested. Of course I am."

"I'm so fucking excited," James bursts out.

I grin wide, wanting to jump around. But then I catch sight of Finn's shoes again. My smile dies down. "Don't say anything yet," I tell James. "I have talk…"

"To Finn," James agrees, as expecting nothing less, as if we're already a package deal.

We are. I'm living with the man. I flex my cold fingers, shaking them to get warm. "But I'll let you know soon."

Hanging up, I walk over to my dress. Happiness is a strange thing. One second, it surrounds you and you're swimming it in, gladly willing to let it consume you. Next second, thoughts roll in and it takes effort to hold onto your happy.

Finn is my happy. But he can't be the only source. I'll drown that way.

FINN

Chess has cast me out of the bathroom—out of the bedroom, really. It has been declared "woman's domain" as she gets ready for tonight. I like that she's claimed her space and ordered me out of it, because it means she feels at home.

And even though I'm stuck in a tux, my neck held too close by a stiff, white collar, I'm happy to wait on the couch and flip through TV channels. Every so often, I hear the hum of the shower, or the high-pitched whine of her hairdryer, and part of me really wants to peek.

I won't. Anticipation is better.

Tonight, we're attending a gala hosted by the Whett Foundation, the charity behind our calendar. Despite the fact that a bunch of football players are attending, the invite had been clear: it is a black tie event.

There had been much grumbling among my teammates. Personally, putting on a tux isn't any different then donning a suit for game day, so I'm not going to complain.

Down the hall, the bedroom door opens with a definitive snick, followed by the click of high heels. I get to my feet and make my way toward Chess.

I'm quicker than she is, and we find each other at the end of the hall.

The first sight of her makes me light-headed, the floor beneath me unsteady. "Wow," I say with a breath. "You look... You're fucking stunning, Chester."

Her cheeks pink, as she looks down as if inspecting herself for flaws. "I've never been to a black tie gala. I hope this is all right."

"It's perfect." I take a step closer, her perfume and warmth hitting my system like a drug. She staggers me. "You're perfect."

Her dress is floor length with thin straps holding it up. It skims over her like milk, the fabric white and black patterned lace that, when she moves, reveals tantalizing glimpses of skin beneath.

"Please tell me you're wearing something under that," I say. "I don't think I'll be able to function if I catch a flash of nipple."

She laughs. "It's lined. No nipple peeks for you."

"I'm almost sorry about that." Reaching for her, I slip my hand around her waist, but halt when I find smooth, bare skin. "Oh, now what do we have here?"

"That would be my back," she says with a straight face.

I haul her closer, my hand gliding up and down. "Your entire back." Glancing over her shoulder, I confirm it with a groan. The devious dress rests just above the rise of her peachy ass. "Jesus, Chester. You're going to kill me."

A small smile plays on her pink lips as she fiddles with the lapels of my jacket. "I'm pretty sure you'll want to live, if only to take this off me later." She straightens my bowtie, and her green eyes meet mine. "God, you're gorgeous. It's like I forget the impact of you, and then 'wham' weak knees and fluttering heart."

The way she just out and says it, her gaze sliding over me as if I'm hot fudge on a cold day, I get weak-kneed myself. My free hand cups her cheek, the silk of her hair sliding over my fingers. Without a word, I seek her mouth.

Her lips are a study of contradictions: soft yet firm, yielding then greedy. She sighs inside a kiss, small sounds of pleasure and want. It sends a fierce surge of lust through me. I take her mouth, own it, plunge in deep, feeding her my tongue with urgent strokes as if she's starving for it. And yet she's the one who owns me. I'm the one starving.

"I love kissing you," I say against her lips, never stopping, but taking more and more. Begging for it in return. Chess grips my lapels, holding on, tugging me closer.

My hand slides further along the curve of her back, down under the edge of her dress. A pained groan rips from me. More satin skin. "Fuck no," I plead, sucking her lower lip. "You're bare?"

I feel her smile. "No panty lines," she murmurs, breath hot and damp.

I grip her ass, kneading the firm flesh. "Fuck, baby. We're not going make it out."

Her teeth pull at my upper lip, as she reaches down to cup my dick, where he is hard and insistent against the seam of my pants.

Chess makes a sound of approval, stroking and giving me an impatient squeeze. "I want him."

"You have him." We tumble against the wall, me leaning into her. I don't know who is holding up whom at this point. Chess fumbles with my zipper, slipping her hand in to clasp my dick. She gives him a hello stroke.

Things get hazy. My hands go to the skirt of her dress, gathering the fabric, wrenching it up and up until I find the smooth length of her thighs.

"Hold on," I say, kissing her deeper, a little frantic now.

Her long legs wrap around my waist, gripping tight, pulling me in.

I find the wet heat of her, stroke the soft slickness with the tips of my fingers.

Chess shudders, her breath gusting out in a pant. "Finn. Now."

My forehead rests against hers. "Always."

It almost hurts, that first thrust. She so fucking tight and I'm so fucking swollen with need. I groan like I'm dying. Maybe I am. I'm so hot, I can't find a breath.

And she's arching her neck, whimpering and clawing at my shoulders. Her thighs spread wider, opening for me with a demand for more.

I know she expects a fast, hard fuck. I go slow, rocking into her, loving the way her body lifts a little when I'm balls deep, then sinks back as I draw out. With every push into the snug, slick well of her body, she makes a raspy noise in her throat, a bit helpless, a bit needy, like she's begging for it but doesn't want to. It gets me hotter, sweat rolling down my spine, heat flickering up my thighs, over my ass.

Her hand cups the back of my neck, and she kisses me. It's disjointed, sloppy. We're both breathing too fast, shaking too much for finesse. Somehow, it makes it better, earthier, everything boiled down to primitive fucking and base lust. I take her air then give her mine. The press of her fingers against my skin makes me shiver.

I'm claiming her against a wall, but if feels as though she's claiming me. I'm losing my damn mind. I'm afraid I might cry. Cry and fuck her and beg for something I don't fully understand. Every time I push into her, I'm begging for it. Every pull though her heat, I'm anticipating the next thrust.

I grip her ass and pump harder. "Chess."

She seems to understand better than I do because she strokes my hair, trying to calm even as her hips rise to meet mine with increasing need. Her eyes flutter closed, her lips parting on a gasp. And she is so fucking beautiful it tears me wide open.

We come together. I fill her up, until she's overflowing, warm wetness running back down over my cock. I'm supposed to be the strong one, her protector, but she is the one who holds me close, murmurs soothing sounds as I shake and struggle to pull myself together.

Something has changed, leaving me exposed and feeling out of control. And it scares the fuck out of me.

CHAPTER 21
♟ CHESS

The Whett gala is being held at a mansion in the Garden District. Set back from the street and surrounded by iron gates, the neoclassical mansion is surrounded by sprawling lawns and gardens. Inside, the scale of the place is immense, soaring ceilings, grand hallways, an enormous curved stairway built in the days when women wore hooped skirts that gently swayed when they descended those stairs like queens.

I don't want to glorify the past, but I can appreciate the hell out of the architecture.

With a warm hand on the small of my back, Finn leads me past throngs of guests and down the main hall.

"One day, I want a place like this," I tell him as we pass under a chandelier glittering twenty feet above.

Finn's brows quirk as he glances at me. "Really? I thought you'd want something a little less massive."

I tuck myself closer to him, as the crowd gets thicker. "Well, not this big. I'd get lost in here. But something with history like this. A house that's graceful and grand in its proportions. And I've always wanted to live in the Garden District."

We enter a reception room, done in shades of cream and gold, where they've set up a bar. Finn takes in the space, as if really looking at it for the first time. His hair is adorably mussed, the satin lapels of his suit jacket snagged and rumpled, having been crushed under my grip.

I probably look equally disheveled. Though we'd tried to tidy up, short of a shower and starting from scratch, there was no hiding the fact that we'd been messing around.

A warm hum of satisfaction moves through me. "Messing around" is a weak term for what we'd done. It had been the best sex of my life. Transcendent. Altering.

Finn's gaze clashes with mine now, and there's a subtle gleam in his eyes. He knows me too well. Thankfully, he has better restraint than I do at the moment. He keeps his voice light, his touch on my back gentle. "We could get one, you know? A nice sized place with a pool and a guesthouse. Fill it up with..."

He trails off, going pale under his tan.

I don't know if I hurt for him or me. Either way, the sensation isn't pleasant. I step away from his touch, my gaze drifting over the room filled with smiling faces.

"Chess," he says low and rough. "I meant friends and family."

No, he didn't. He shouldn't have to lie.

I give him a tight smile. "It's not quite the same, is it?"

The clean sweep of his jaw bunches. "It doesn't mean anything. We were just talking."

"About the future?" I shake my head. "We agreed we shouldn't be doing that, anyway."

Finn touches my elbow, leaning in to meet my eyes. "They were just words off the cuff."

"I know that." I tuck a lock of his hair back from his brow. "Let's just do as we promised. Let's just be. I'm okay with that."

"You taking me literally wasn't what I had in mind," he mutters with a frown.

Annoyance skitters up my back. "If you get to pick and choose what we focus on, then expect the same from me."

The space between us tightens as we lock gazes. But then he relents with a grunt and walks off to the bar. As soon as he's gone, my shoulders sag with remorse. I can't snipe at him whenever he accidentally touches a nerve. It isn't fair to either of us.

He returns with two glasses and a wary expression. "Here."

"Thank you." I take the glass. It's filled with something pale green bubbly. "What is it?"

"Tears of Regret." His mouth quirks. "I hear it tastes a lot like Champagne cocktail."

My hand trembles as I take a quick sip. "I'm sorry too."

He doesn't say anything but kisses the top of my head.

"I got offered a job in New York."

Finn pauses, his glass halfway to his mouth, then takes a long, audible swallow of his drink. "It must be good," he says, after catching his breath. "To put that look in your eyes."

I study the rim of my glass before taking another sip of my cocktail.

"Tell me about the job, Chess."

He listens as I fill him in on the details, both of us strolling toward the French doors that lead to a terrace. Outside, we find a dark corner, and Finn leans against the wall of the house.

"Sounds like a great opportunity," he says, giving nothing away. "How long would you be away?"

I grip the narrow bowl of my glass. "One to two months if all goes well."

He nods, glancing down at his shoes. When he looks up, his eyes glint in the moonlight. "Is this something you really want?"

Such careful control in his voice. It closes in on me like a vise.

"When James first told me, the answer was yes. But…" I lift my hands in a helpless gesture. "I don't want to leave you."

Finn gives me a small smile that doesn't reach his eyes. "I'm not going anywhere."

But I would. And it feels wrong leaving him right now. As if it will kill the momentum of us, when we've only just started.

"When would you leave?" he asks.

"In the next two weeks."

A grimace mars his features, though he clearly tries to hide it. "I won't be able to visit you," he says. "These last two games of the season are going to be intense. And if we win, I'll have to concentrate on the playoffs."

He sounds so apologetic, as if it's his fault I'm leaving. Sadness and a strange sense of panic roll around in my chest, rising up to clog my throat. From the second I'd thought of taking the job, I knew he wouldn't be able to follow. Something in his eyes tells me that he understands this as well.

"You'll make the playoffs," I tell him. "And I wouldn't have it any other way."

His smile is tilted and wry and fades fast. "I'm proud of you, Chester."

I don't feel anything but a need to cling, a weakness I don't want or like.

Our conversation comes to an abrupt halt when Jake strolls into our quiet spot. "Manny. Copperpot. Why are you two hiding back here?" He glances between us, noting the distance. "I'd approve if someone had a hand in someone else's clothes, but no way am I letting you guys get away with trying to escape the stuffed shirts."

"Did you just call me Copperpot?"

Jake is all innocence. "What? Me? No. Who?" He hooks my arm over his elbow. "Now, come with me. The guys want an official ruling on whose dick is the biggest."

I laugh, as Finn pushes himself off from the wall and glares. "I *will* kick your ass, Ryder."

"You'll have to catch me first, and we both know I'm way faster."

Jake leads me away, with Finn following. And I don't protest. It's a relief walking into the crowded, noisy party where I don't have to think.

Just be. Just be. I can do that. I have to.

FINN

"I don't know about you guys, but I look fucking sharp in this suit." Woodson runs a hand down the front of his tux. "I'm getting laid tonight."

You have to love Woodson's corn-fed, Iowa boy brand of optimism and child-like honesty. I laugh as he waggles his brows with hopeful glee.

"You're married, aren't you?" North asks him with a look that clearly states he's skeptical of Woodson getting any play.

"Cynicism is a bitter taste that rests on the tongue and destroys the appetite," Woodson intones.

North snorts. "You read that in a fortune cookie."

"Did not." Woodson grins. "I saw it on the side of a bus."

"No way."

"Believe what you will, bitter boy. I, on the other hand, am going to hunt down my wife. Convince her to get an early start."

North and I groan.

"Those who talk too much do too little," I tell Woodson.

"Let me guess," he says. "Fortune cookie?"

"No, a simple Finn Mannus truth."

Woodson scoffs and then goes in search of his woman. He trudges over the grass toward the house, leaving North and I sitting on a low stone wall that edges the pool area. Up in the distance, I catch a glimpse of Chess's dress. She's talking to Meghan, our PR director.

"Ten bucks says she'll have a headache," North says.

I flinch, thinking he's talking about Chess, but then I realize he means Woodson's wife. "You really are a cynic."

"I prefer realist." North turns my way. "So how about you, Manny? You ready to buckle down and finish out this season with some wins?"

It's my turn to snort. "Is this some sort of pep talk?"

"Yeah, I guess it is." North rests an elbow on his knee and gives me a look. For a bizarre second I have the image of The Thinker coming to life to give me a lecture. Weirdly, that image doesn't die when North speaks again. "We win these last two games and we're in the playoffs."

"I know this well." I dream about it. Have nightmares about it. Who the fuck on our team doesn't know this?

"You seem distracted, is all."

I stare at North. And he stares back.

"I heard you talking to your girl earlier."

I rub a hand over my face. "Fucking hell."

He merely shrugs. "Don't talk in public places if you don't want to be overheard."

I think about who else might have heard. The prospects aren't pleasant. "You're a nosy fucker, you know that?"

"I like you, kid."

"Kid? You're only five years older than me."

His smile is thin. "It's not the years. It's the mileage."

"Jesus, don't quote Indiana Jones. I beg you."

North laughs. And for one shining moment, I think I'm clear. But he quickly sobers. "Look, these are the years that define your career."

"Oh, hell…"

"If you don't make your mark now, give it your all, then you're done. The next college hot shot is just around the corner, waiting to take your place."

North points a long, bony finger at me. "Don't fuck this chance up by dividing your attention between football and a woman. Love is great, and you think it means forever, but it's not worth risking everything you've worked for."

"I'm not trying to fuck it up. I'm trying to have it all."

"Impossible. Something has to give. You want a woman? Find one who wants to be a player's wife. The kind of girl who will give you babies, put you first, and never complain when you're gone. The kind who will be there when you come home. Otherwise, it's going to fuck with your head. Put that shit aside and focus on your career for now.

Once you're established and have a few rings on your fingers then worry about women."

I glance at the gaudy as fuck Super Bowl ring on North's hand. He doesn't usually wear it, but I'm guessing it's a go-to accessory for galas, a nice piece of bragging rights. It's a weird bit of irony that football players dream of wearing a ring better suited to sit on some Vegas pimp's finger. But we do. We all want those ugly ass rings.

North stands and looks down at me. "Tell me this, what occupies your thoughts more? Football or the girl?"

My jaw ticks.

"Here's a hint." North leans in. "The answer should always be football."

A true football player lives, breathes, and dreams of the game. I've had that pounded into me since I put on my first peewee helmet. Anything less than total devotion to the sport and you're an amateur.

North's voice cuts through the thick haze that's settled over me. "Besides, if you play well. I play better. And I want to kick ass this year."

I cut him a look. "I'm glad we had this talk. We should do it again sometimes."

Ignoring my sarcasm, he gives my shoulder a slap and walks off toward the house.

I should get up too, go inside, find Chess and mingle. But I don't move. Everything feels sluggish and heavy. I'm also thirsty as hell, my throat dry and tight. "Fucking North."

"I think he was trying to be your friend."

Chess's voice startles me, and I lurch to my feet just as she walks out of the shadows.

"Hey." I shove my hands in my pockets. "You heard all that?"

Her lip quirks, as she hands me a cold bottle of beer. "Enough. What was it North said? Don't talk in public if you don't want to be overheard."

So she heard it all. I take a long pull on my beer and try to run through all of North's lecture. None of it is puts Chess in a good light. "North is coming off a bad marriage."

Chess stands beside me. "I heard. Megan says he got married too young. Before he could know his own mind."

"Jesus, gossip is rampant in this organization. With everyone doling out advice like they're Dear Abby."

Amusement lights her eyes. "It's a wonder you've survived."

I snort and take another drink. Something uncomfortable buzzes between us. I don't know what it is, but I don't like it. Knowing she'll follow, I start to walk toward the pool house. It's dark and abandoned right now. That doesn't stop me from trying the door.

Thankfully it's unlocked, and I walk in. Chess is a step behind me, a small wrinkle forming between her straight brows. "We're not having sex in here," she says. "That would be cliché."

"I'd like to say I have better game than that. But we both know I'd be up for sex anywhere you wanted it."

My joke falls flat, as Chess strolls around the darkened room. There's just enough light to see her shadowy form and the glint in her eyes as she turns back toward me. "Then why are we here?"

"Something's going on with us," I blurt out. "Everything feels off since we got here."

Chess walks back toward me, until she's illuminated by the outdoor sconces that flank the pool house doors. "I feel it too."

"Then talk to me."

Chess lets out a tired sigh. "I don't know where to start."

"At the beginning."

Slowly, she shakes her head as if trying to clear it. "Finn, you're my best friend but—"

"No, I'm not," I cut in.

Chess gapes at me. "You're not," she repeats, pissed.

I want to kiss her. I refrain. Barely. "I have a best friend. It's Jake."

Her delicate nostrils flair. "Fine. Then James is mine."

"I know this." I take a step closer.

"Well, I'm glad we got that cleared up." She sneers. "Asshole."

I grin, which really pisses her off. I ignore that too and take another step. "I know Jake is my best friend because I don't want to fuck him."

"Lucky for Jake," she mutters, glaring up at me.

"I don't miss him the second he's out of my sight," I add.

Her eyes narrow, her gaze darting over my face in growing confusion.

I'm so close now, the tips of her breasts brush my chest when we both take a breath. "I don't need to hold him, need to see him just to know that he's okay, that he's comfortable and happy before I can relax."

The anger in her eyes mutes to something softer.

I touch the curve of her jaw, my thumb brushing her lower lip. "We are not best friends, Chess. We are more. You are my everything. The reason I get up each day."

She melts toward me. "Finn..."

My hand slides to the nape of her neck, and I hold her steady. "So don't come at me with this, 'we're best friends' bullshit when you want to use it to drive me away."

She freezes, her chin firming in stubborn resistance. Does she think I am blind?

"You are *not* doing whatever this is under the guise of friendship."

Her head jerks back, trying to get free. I don't let her. My hold is gentle but firm.

Her glare is fierce. "Let me go, Finn."

I can't. It'll break my heart.

"Talk to me," I rasp.

Her cold hand wraps around my wrist. "I heard everything he said."

Guilt has me flinching. "Look, North is..."

"He's right." Her voice is soft but emphatic. And it is a kick to the gut.

"He believes he's right."

Chess frowns. "Do you know how many times I've heard James bitch that one of his favorite athletes is starting to suck because he's lost his focus in a relationship?"

"Are you saying I suck now?" My head pounds, a dull thudding at my temples.

"I'm saying that, aside from that kind of gross and misogynistic bit about players' wives in the middle, North was making a lot of sense. And you know it."

The pounding in my head gets worse. Something bitter burns its way up my throat. "I can't fight you too, Chess. I need you on my side here."

"I am on your side." She moves to touch my cheek but stops short. "I just think that if we take a step back—"

"Fucking hell. Just stop with your damn logic and listen to me!" I throw the bottle against the wall and it shatters. Chess flinches as I round on her. "I'm hanging on by a thread. A fucking thread. And you're either trying to end us with talk of babies that we may or may not want, or you're being some sort of goddamn sacrificial lamb on the altar of football! Do you want me to choose football over you? Is that it?"

She blinks back at me with glossy eyes. "No. You shouldn't have to choose."

"Then don't make it a choice."

"Do you think it was easy to hear all that?" she snaps. "While knowing that, by having me in your life, I make it that much harder for you to succeed?"

"Your faith in my ability is heartening, Chess. Truly fucking inspiring."

"Goddamnit, Finn, this isn't about my faith in you, it's my lack of faith in me. I am a bad bet!"

"And yet I'd put all my money on you," I shout. "I'd do it in a second. But you won't do the same for me."

She flinches but that stubborn chin of hers remains firm. Like she's already committed to her plan. "Finn—"

"No." I back away, holding up my hands to ward her off. "You know what? I want you to go. Take that job in New York, stay there and find yourself. Because North is right. It's too hard as it is. Going into this with doubts will just set us up to fail."

She stares at me as if she's been frozen, and I wait for the denial, for her to tell me I'm wrong. Slowly, she starts to breathe, her chest lifting and falling with the effort. Her rage gathers, and it is a beautiful thing to watch. Her glare is like justice and judgment all rolled into one, and it is directed at me.

"All right, I'll go. But let me tell you this." Her voice rises, growing harder. "My parents always followed their hearts. They never stopped to think or work out the consequences of their actions. Not once. It was always instinct and emotion over logic and planning. Well, guess what? I got left behind." Her small fist punches her chest with a hollow sound. "I suffered. Not once did they consider the effects their actions would have on me."

She blinks rapidly, and her voice changes again, cracking. "I'm sorry if I worry. If I weigh pros and cons and ignore my heart sometimes. But I can't be like them. I can't be like *you*. I won't. When I choose forever, I want it to be forever. I *need* that."

I've made a grave mistake. I've pushed her too far when I should have yielded. "Chess…"

"No." Her hand slashes through the air. "We've said enough. My head hurts and don't want to fight."

"I don't want to fight either," I whisper. Her head hurts, after all. "It's bullshit, all this worrying."

She visibly flinches. "I've lost everything that is safe and familiar to me. My home, my place of work, my best friend. And I've replaced it with you. You ask me to have faith in us while you protect yourself. All I want is one simple thing."

The stale air of the room presses in on me. "You want me to predict the distant future. I can't do that. I can barely focus on tomorrow." What if North and Chess are right? What if I can't divide my attentions and succeed?

It's a testament to how well she knows me because it's clear she sees my fear. Chess gives me a sad, defeated look. "You can't give it to me because you're thinking now about what he said, aren't you? And the answer isn't what either of us wants to hear."

My heart pounds too hard now, my whole body throbbing in time with the rapid beat. Sweat breaks out on my skin. "I'm sorry, Chess. Just…" I swallow past the panic. "Give me a little time…"

Her gown rustles as she moves past me, not looking me in the eye. "I'm going to New York." She pauses at the threshold of the doorway. "And while I think about taking a leap of faith and following my heart, maybe you think about how you're going to make your life work. With or without me."

I let her go on ahead to give her some space. It's a mistake. By the time I return to the party, she's left it when Meghan. And by the time I get back home, she's gone.

CHAPTER 22
♟ CHESS

I left Finn and New Orleans like a thief on the run. I'm not proud of it. I should have said goodbye. But panic took hold, and I needed to see a familiar face that wasn't Finn's. I went to New York, my hometown, and to James, my oldest friend, thinking that maybe distance would make it easier to breathe again, and to figure out what the hell just happened.

Finn doesn't call or come storming after me, demanding we talk things out.

Did I expect him to? I can't say. It's horrible to admit that I'd wanted him to maybe show even a little bit of resistance. But he let me go.

A week out, I get a text from Charlie, asking for my address. Since I'm not trying to hide, I give it to him. Charlie sends me the bulk of my clothes.

I cry myself to sleep that night.

Weeks pass. I throw myself into work. And I guess Finn does too. He wins one game and then the next. I cry again when I watch him celebrate on the field with his teammates, the sight of his smiling, victorious face too much to bear. But I'm not a total masochist, and when they go to interview him, I turn the TV off.

Two days after they officially announce Finn and his team are in the playoffs, a New Orleans gossip e-mag I subscribe to shows a picture of Britt and Finn walking into a restaurant, Finn's hand protectively on her arm as they shy away from the camera. Another grainy image of them sitting at a table for two follows.

I cry myself to sleep for a second time.

Do I think he's with Britt now? My heart says no. My brain keeps flashing to the image of them together, and I am sick with bitter jealousy. Part of me thinks I deserve this. It's my own fucking fault for leaving. Another, far angrier part of me says, fuck that noise.

Ironically, every other aspect of my life is fantastic. Michael's SoHo loft is so prefect it makes my bones hurt with envy. I remember that he's from New York real estate royalty and probably doesn't have to work a day of his life if he chose not to, and I feel a little better about myself. And I'm grateful all over again that he offered me this opportunity.

The project is a dream come true. Every day, I look forward to working. I meet established Oscar-winning actors who flirt shamelessly, and young Hollywood A-listers who act like overgrown boys, which, unfortunately reminds me of Finn and his guys.

I keep waiting for someone to throw attitude or be a dick, but it doesn't happen. It's as if the stars have aligned and fate is telling me this is exactly where I need to be.

I hate fate.

I'm sitting in the sun-drenched living room of Michael's loft, curled up on his oversized Italian leather couch, and eating a New York bagel with apple cinnamon cream cheese, when Finn calls.

I should have known he'd hunt me down when I was the most content I'd been since leaving him. Face prickling with heat and heart pounding hard, I stare at the phone, his name lit up on the screen, as if it might up and bite me.

I don't want to pick it up. But the damn phone won't stop. It rings and vibrates, making the coffee table rattle. My fingers dig into my thighs. Finn.

Answer it, you weenie. It's just Finn, for fuck's sake, not Satan.

Grumbling, I snatch the phone up.

"Hey." I sound like I've been eating glass.

"Hey." The timbre of his voice, rough and unsure, lodges between my ribs and digs in.

I close my eyes and bring my knees to my chest as if I can protect myself.

Finn clears his throat, but doesn't speak.

"I should have called you."

"I wanted to call you."

We speak over each other, and he huffs out a small laugh, before his voice lowers to something hard and tight. "You left me."

A shard of guilt goes through my heart. "I said I was leaving."

"But not like that. Not without saying goodbye."

"I'm sorry."

"It hurt, Chess. We deserved more than that."

A lump swells in my throat. "I know. It was shitty."

Finn doesn't say anything for a long moment. But when he finally speaks, it's a strained rush. "I took Britt out to dinner."

Hearing the words from his mouth makes it more real.

"I saw pictures of it." I lick my lips and taste salt. Another fat tear runs down the side of my nose, and I bat it away.

Finn makes a sound. "I was afraid of that."

I don't know what to say to that, so I stay silent.

He sighs, long and tired. "I wanted you to hear it from me."

A wave of dizziness comes over me, and I rest my head against the couch pillow.

"I'm trying to be her friend," he goes on. "Like you suggested."

As if he's trying to appease me? I don't feel appeased. I'm miserable. I swipe at my eyes. "That's good. She needs a friend."

That it's the truth doesn't make it any easier for me to picture them together.

Silence descends.

"How's work?" Finn blurts out, as if forced.

"Good. Great. Tomorrow I'm photographing The Avengers. Well, the guys, that is."

A choked sound comes through the phone then abruptly cuts off. "Naked Avengers?"

I almost smile. "They get to hold their weapons. Iron Man is wearing his glove."

"Oh, well at least his hand is covered," Finn grumbles.

My lip twitches. But it's not enough. Our easy flow is broken. And we fall silent once more.

When Finn speaks again, his voice is so low and hoarse, I almost don't hear it. Almost.

"I miss you."

My heart kicks against my ribs, and I clutch the phone. "I miss you too."

Tell me to come home. Tell me you need me.

"You were right, though," he rasps before clearing his throat. "I needed to get some clarity. Figure out what's important."

Something inside me cracks. I think it's my heart. I draw in a ragged breath. "Me too." *Don't cry. You're fine. Fine.* "This job has been a dream come true. Really, really. Good."

That's descriptive. You don't sound at all like you're falling apart.

He pauses. "I'm glad. You deserve….good things."

Neither of us says anything. And then Finn tries again. "We made the playoffs."

"I heard. I'm… so happy for you."

Someone in the background yells for Finn. I close my eyes, knowing my time is up. He speaks at stronger now, but more distant. "I've got to go."

I feel every cold mile between us.

"Yeah. Me too. I've been so busy…" I swallow hard.

"That's good. I'm glad."

God, we're horrible now.

"Good luck, Finn."

It's so quiet on his end, I think he's hung up. But then he speaks, his voice soft and full of regret. "Sleep well, Chess."

It's only after the line is dead and I'm back at work that I remember he'd said the same words to me before. On the night we met, when I'd left him at my apartment door, intent on walking right out of his life.

FINN

The door to my condo opens. I don't bother looking up from the TV. I know it's not who I want to see. Keys jangle and then Charlie walks into the room.

"Manny," he says, glancing at me then the TV. "What are you watching?"

"*Singles.*" My voice sounds as if it has been dragged over rust before breaking free.

Charlie takes a seat next to me. "Never seen it."

"You're missing out on the glory that is Cliff Poncier and Citizen Dick."

"Citizen Dick?" He makes a sound of amusement.

I cut him a glance. "They were underrated."

"If you say so."

We watch for a few minutes. Every time Steve and Linda are on screen, my chest hurts. *You broke his heart, Linda.*

Yes, I am a fucking masochist.

"This looks like a chick movie," Charlie says out of the blue.

"According to Chess, every movie is a chick movie." It isn't easy saying her name out loud, but I refuse to make her a ghost.

He's silent for a moment. "I guess she has a point."

"She usually does." Fuck. I need some antacid.

Charlie turns my way. "You talk to her lately?"

"Yes."

I don't expand on the disaster that was our phone call. The conversation had been so stilted it was like pulling teeth just to get the words out.

His stare is a weighty thing. "You going to go get her?"

When she's in the middle of her dream job? With The Avengers? How the fuck do I compete against Iron Man? Or—*fuck*—Thor?

"She isn't lost, Charles."

He pulls a bottle of green juice from his backpack and hands it to me. "It's about time to get going for the game."

Normally, I'd drive myself. But this is a playoff game. When Charlie asked me if I wanted a ride to the stadium, I realized, that he really wanted to drive me. He wanted to be a part of this. He deserves to be. So I have myself a chauffeur, even if he's a nagging one.

"We have at least fifteen minutes to spare." Because it's in my hand, I open the bottle and take a drink. I'm not going to say I love the green health drink because I have working taste buds, but it does send a nice shot of energy running through my system.

"Let's spend them at the stadium," Charlie says.

Charlie doesn't like living on the edge. With a sigh, I heave myself up. "Fine. Let's go win us a football game."

Charlie stands too, turning off the TV with the remote. "We'll work on your enthusiasm levels in the car."

I'd like to think I'm a good actor. But apparently, my performance today is lacking. Despite digging deep and pulling out all the enthusiasm I can muster, as soon as it's halftime and we've received all the instruction we're going to get, Jake plops down next to me on the bench and elbows my ribs.

Pads keep me from feeling much but it gets my attention. "What?"

He takes a bottle from a passing ball boy and squirts water all over his head before looking me over. "You've been playing better than you ever have."

He's right; I'm the best I've ever been. Each time I go out on the field, I become a machine, playing as if I have something to prove. The sad truth is, I *am* trying to prove something. Not to myself. It's for her. Always for her.

But in the twisted way of things, with every win, I feel worse, the distance between Chess and I bigger. Because what the fuck am I really proving here? That she and North were right? That she was just a distraction? That I don't need her?

I do. I fucking do.

"Thanks for letting me know," I say to Jake, as if I don't care. "I appreciate the pep talk."

He gives me a sidelong look, but keeps a smile on his face. We might be in the relative privacy of our locker room but someone is always watching when we're in game mode, and neither of us wants to spook the team. "Wise ass. You're playing great. But you have dead eyes."

"Not liking the direction of this pep talk, Ryder." I swipe a bottle from a basket near me and take a long drink. "Did Charlie put you up to this?"

"He noticed it too?"

I look over the locker room as if I'm on top of the world. "Now is not the time."

"Your avoidance game is killer. It's never the right time."

God, Chess had accused me of the same thing.

My smile aches at the corners. "Well, it certainly isn't right fucking *now*."

Guys are milling around, some getting their limbs stretched by the trainers, some hydrating. We've all got our game face on, counting down the minutes before we go back out.

North sits his ass down on my other side. "What we talking about? Winning? Because I love winning. It's, like, better than losing, you know?"

"Easy there, Nuke LaLoosh," I mutter.

He winks. "So?"

Jake leans past me. "Manny's girl has decamped to New York, and he's depressed. But he doesn't want to talk about his feelings."

"Fuck me." I groan, ducking my head under the pretense of putting my bottle down so no one can see my grimace.

"Your girl left you?" North sounds surprised.

I don't know why, since he all but pleaded with me to see the light and concentrate on my career. And since I really don't want to fucking hear that again, I simply blot my face with a towel and speak past it. "We're thinking things through while she's on a job."

Every man knows that when a woman has to think about things it isn't good. North is no exception. "Sorry to hear that, man."

"You?" An incredulous snort escapes me. "Seriously?"

He gives my thigh a slap before he stands. "If her absence is responsible for that dull look in your eyes, then yeah."

"Told you," Jake says. "Dead eyes."

North shakes his head as if he's disappointed in me. "When did I ever say anything about being miserable? If she makes you happy, then work the rest out." With that, North trots off.

I stand as well, wanting to pace. No, really, I want to chase after North and smack his head. But I don't. I put my hands low on my hips and pretend I'm watching the clock count down. "That fucker lectures me about focus and now he's sorry."

Jake gets to his feet and mimics my pose, all smiles and "we're fucking owning this game" on his face. Then he turns, his shoulder pads blocking out the rest of the room. Sweat and water bead on his face, his eye black is smeared. "Screw North. He doesn't know you for shit. And you're right; I don't want to talk about this either. I'd rather be exchanging high-fucking-fives and or spewing a 'Win one for the Gipper' speech. Because we're here. In the playoffs."

He leans in, his voice low and intense. "The fucking *playoffs*."

He doesn't have to tell me what that means. Every football player understands where this road leads. I open my mouth to talk, but he doesn't let me.

"You should be ecstatic. Instead, you're a walking sack of misery."

His words hit like a physical blow to my gut. I grit my teeth against the urge to yell. Not just yell but to scream and rail. Because fuck it all, I've done everything I could to get to this moment. Including letting Chess go, and this is what he has for me?

Jake faces my rage without flinching. "I'm not trying to bust your balls."

I glare, unable to keep my happy face. I don't trust myself to speak.

"Call her," he says. "Plead, beg, whatever the hell you have to do to get her back, so you can snap out of this funk from hell."

My reply comes out so sharp, it's almost a shout. "She thinks…" I take a breath, and lower my voice. "This isn't on me, all right? She made everything complicated when it should have been easy."

"Easy?" Jake makes it sound like a bad word.

"Yes, easy. She's worried about the future. That we'll eventually want different things. That one day I'll resent her and want some model wife instead." I throw up a hand. "As if I'd want anyone else but her."

Jake's brows lift. "Wife, huh?"

Heat flushes my neck. "When you know, you know."

"Does *she* know you know?"

I blink back at him.

Jake huffs, glancing around to see if we have time, before zeroing in on me again. "Did you say, 'I don't give a rat's dick about having anyone else.'"

"A rat's dick?" I choke on a laugh.

He rolls his eyes. "Did you tell her you love her, you moron?"

Behind us, Coach yells for guys to huddle up.

The sad truth embeds itself like glass in my throat. "It might not be a matter of *me* loving *her*."

I regret the words as soon as I let them out. It's easier to pretend that I walked away. Admitting that I might not be the man Chess ultimately wants hurts so much I can't breathe past it.

Jake stares me down. "They don't call it risk because it's safe. Tell her anyway."

He gives me a slap on the shoulder pads and walks away.

I follow, my mind set. I'm going to lead my guys and win this game. I don't need Chess to succeed at football. Whether she's in my life or not, I am who I am on the field.

It's off the field that I need her. And I'm going to find my girl and prove that to her too.

CHAPTER 23
♟CHESS

James and Jamie take me to an Irish Pub in lower Manhattan. It's cozy and wonderfully warm, especially after walking six blocks in the icy wind to get there.

"I can't feel my fingers," I say rubbing my hands together.

"We should have taken the subway." Jamie's nose is bright pink.

"The walk was bracing," James insists. "And you two are wimps."

Jamie takes off her fogging glasses and wipes them. "Pretty sure someone was whining about frozen balls in danger of falling off and shattering on the pavement."

"That was a vivid description," I add. "Maybe you should check your pants, James. Make sure everything is accounted for."

"My balls have already checked in." James unwraps his scarf and leads us through the crowd. "And they're demanding a drink."

"You talk to your balls?" I ask with a laugh.

"All guys do, Chess. Have I taught you nothing?"

"I thought they talked to their dicks."

"They're kind of a package deal, darling."

We settle into a booth by an empty stage. James snuggles up next to Jamie, and I'm left by myself on the other side. Again comes the horrible, internal coldness running along my side. I don't mind sitting alone. I've done it for years. But I can't shake the feeling that I'm not whole. I'm missing a part of myself. And it's annoying. Another person can't complete me. I do that for myself.

"So who has final say," Jamie asks James. "Balls or dick?"

James settles back into the booth and rubs his beard in contemplation. "Hmm. Dick can definitely act alone. He's been known to perk up and want to investigate a situation, while Balls are shriveling and shouting 'run away, fool!'"

"That's because balls have a sense of self-preservation," I say, shrugging out of my coat. "Dick is basically a brainless knobhead."

Jamie laughs.

"True," James says. "But as to the ruler of my package?

"Let me guess," I put in. "Mr. Hand?"

"Har. That might have been the case a few months ago, but now the supreme ruler is Jamie, so she really shouldn't be laughing at poor Dick."

Jamie flushes pink and leans into him. "Aw, that's so sweet."

I suppose it is, in a weird way. Doesn't stop me from wanting to leave the table so I don't have to watch them cuddle.

You had that, you moron. And you had to think about "things."

It really sucks when your conscience starts to hate you.

"*I would have whispered sweet dick jokes in your ear too,*" Finn's voice says in my head.

"*I know you would have. You never could pass up an opportunity to talk about your junk.*"

"*Neither could you, Chester. I'm pretty sure you're obsessed with my junk.*"

It really, really sucks when you start having conversations with a man who isn't there.

The waitress comes up to take our order. "We're having a special on Guinness tonight. And the chef's specialty of the evening is steak and kidney pie."

"I'll have a Harp and a pie," I tell her.

"Guinness for me," James says. "And the fish and chips."

"I'll have the pie too," Jamie orders. "Oh, and a white wine."

"*What did I tell you?*" Finn's ghost whispers in my ear. "*Women like to order white wine. Even when they're in a pub.*"

"*Isn't there a lamp you could go haunt?*"

"*I'm a quarterback, Chess, not a genie.*"

"What's that smile about?" James asks me, cutting into the ridiculous and probably unhealthy conversation going on in my head.

"The impending promise of hot food," I lie.

He looks at me as if he knows better, but thankfully he doesn't say anything.

Our drinks arrive and, while we wait for our food, a band comes out and begins to play. It's a full Irish band, complete with a flute player, two fiddlers, and even an accordionist. And they're good.

Soon, the bar is filled with lively music and people clapping along. The singer is a young woman with curly hair and a voice like a pixie. We eat our food as they play.

And it is almost perfect, soaking up good music and good food with good friends. I can see myself in the future, having more nights like this. I will have a good life. I know it. I can feel it in my bones. And a sense of peace comes over me. I'll be okay.

No matter what I do, I'll be okay. But is *okay* enough?

The band finishes a song and the singer accepts a pint of Guinness from a waitress. She takes a long drink before setting it down on a stool by her side. "I love the film *Some Kind of Wonderful*," she says in the mic.

The crowd whistles their approval.

She nods, her curls bouncing. "The end is especially lovely. You remember it?"

As one, we all shout, "You look good wearing my future!"

Laughter rings through the small space.

"Aye, so romantic." The singer grabs her tambourine. "We're going to play a little homage to *Some Kind of Wonderful* and Lick the Tins, who did a brilliant cover for the flick."

I'm smiling, but a niggling feeling begins to start up around the edges of my heart.

The band begins to play a lively, Celtic version of "Can't Help Falling in Love," and my heart clenches. Oh, God, I truly am haunted.

Around me, people start to sing along, an utter wall of sound rolling over me, insisting that some things were meant to be. And I can't stand it. I can't stand that Finn isn't right here with me, laughing in my ear, demanding that I take his hand, that we could be fools together.

He'd been doing that since the beginning. He'd always known. He'd been trying to tell me what we were to each other all along. I just hadn't listened. He might be stubborn, and his refusal to give in a little still pisses me off. But he is mine.

A sob breaks free. And I'm stuck between laughter and crying.

James looks at me sharply. "What's wrong?"

"The song. Elvis. He's everywhere."

James frowns, leaning in so we can talk over the ribald singing. "And that makes you cry?"

I shake my head, tears running down my face. "I love him."

"Elvis?" Jamie asks, confused.

"Finn. I love Finn. Doesn't matter where I go..." I lift my hands helplessly toward the band. "He's my fate."

James smiles softly. "Your perfectly imperfect."

"I have to tell him."

"You will." James reaches across the table and puts his hand on my trembling one. "Do you want to step out and call him?"

"He's playing a game right now." I wipe my cheeks. "I should do it in person."

"Okay." James gives me a squeeze. "We'll get you home as soon as we can."

Home. I need to go home. The heat of the room and the music press in on me.

"I have to get out of here," I tell James. "I can't breathe. I need to see Finn. I have to..."

"It's all right," James says. "Don't panic."

My fingers are clumsy as I fish my wallet out of my purse and pull out some bills. "I'm going to take a walk."

James grabs my wrist. "You're not going out alone."

"I grew up in this city, James. I'll be okay."

"Doesn't matter," he insists. "We're coming with you."

He tosses some more money onto the table then sets his empty glass on the pile to secure it. But I can't wait any longer; I'm halfway across the room by the time James and Jamie catch up to me.

I stumble outside and draw in a deep breath of icy air. It burns going down but I suck in another breath. James and Jamie stand beside me.

"You all right?" Jamie asks, resting a hand on my arm.

"Yeah." I give her a weak smile. "Sorry for the drama."

Beneath the lenses of her glasses, her eyes crinkle. "It's pretty emotional, falling in love."

"I shouldn't have left him. I should have stayed."

James pulls out a cigarette and lights it. "If leaving meant you finally realized without a doubt that he's the one, then don't punish yourself for it." He takes a drag then lets out a puff of smoke. "Consider it time well spent."

"I hurt him."

"Something tells me he'll forgive you." James winks at me, then laughs. "My grumpy Chessie bear is dating the quarterback. Will wonders never cease?"

"I think James is a bit jealous," Jamie teases.

"I'd like to point out that I had a crush on Manny before Chess met him, and before I met you." James flicks the tip of his cigarette. "Now it would be too weird to keep him in the spank bank. I'd start picturing Chess's disapproving face and…total bone kill."

"You're not supposed to have a spank bank now," I say. "You have Jamie."

"When I enter my bank, Jamie is always there to watch," James retorts with an evil grin.

"TMI," Jamie huffs, pinching him. "You're going to give Chess indigestion."

"Well, she's killed prime fantasy material for me so we're even."

I know Jamie is embarrassed on my behalf, but I also know James is trying to distract me. He's doing a good job of it. We exchange a secret smile between us, one that's gotten us through a lot of tough times. Gratitude fills me, and I want to hug my best friend. He gives me a little wink in silent reply.

"I'd flip you off," I say with false annoyance, "but it's too cold."

I tuck my icy hands under my arms.

"Come on." James snuffs his cigarette on the side of the building then tosses the butt into a nearby trashcan. "Let's find a bar and watch your boyfriend play."

Three doors down, we find a bar that, no surprise to anyone, is showing the game on multiple TVs. Patrons are yelling at the screen and I see that the score is seven to fourteen, and New Orleans is down. Given that Finn's team is playing against New York, everyone is ecstatic.

We get our beers at the bar and then James finds us a seat by the door, facing one of the TVs. We sit down as Finn and his offense trot back on the field. I can't see his face behind the helmet he wears, but just the sight of the number ten on his jersey has my heart clenching.

Although his team is currently losing, he moves with authority, bringing his guys in for a huddle. They're on their home turf and the crowd chants for Finn. The commentator on the TV spews on about the offense having not been at their best in games past and how Finn has struggled throughout the season to regain control.

"That's why our defense is gonna kick your ass, Manny," a guy at the bar shouts.

I know it's not personal; it's part of the game. But it feels personal. I want to yell at the guy to either put on a uniform and try it or shut the fuck up.

James reads me well. "Easy there, tiger."

My fingers grip the edges of my chair. "I'm fine."

On the screen, the next drive begins. I don't know much about football. Next to nothing really, but watching Finn makes my breath catch and pride swell through my chest. He is beautiful in the way rare and powerful things are.

Finn catches the ball hiked to him by Dex, and then he dances back, his guys protecting him. To me, it's a scramble, the defense scurrying around like mad ants trying to get him, the offense scurrying like mad ants running this way and that. All the while Finn remains the center of calm.

He cocks his arm back and throws, heedless of the big barn of a guy hurtling toward him. The ball flies through the air like it's on a string. But my eyes are on Finn. Unfortunately, the camera follows the ball as it shoots downfield toward Jake.

The guys at the bar shout. Jake arcs in the air like a ballerina, catches the ball, and lands in an inelegant heap as a bunch of defenders tackle him. But he keeps the ball.

"Right through traffic!" James slams his fist on the table in victory as the rest of the bar groans.

I grin wide. The camera goes back to Finn who jumps once and then pumps his fist. As Jake runs back to the huddle, Finn smacks him on the butt in congratulations.

"Come on Defense," bar dude shouts, doing that annoying rapid clap thing.

I ignore it and watch Finn. This time he passes the ball off to North who doesn't get very far, much to the bar's delight.

Doesn't matter. I can sense the difference in Finn's game. He has a rhythm going, a confidence about him. He's playing to win. I'm so proud of him that I have to bite my lips to keep from shouting my encouragement to the screen, because, it's not like he can hear me. And yet, some small, shitty dark corner of my mind feels distress. Because he is playing better now. Without me in his life.

It could be a fluke. But they haven't lost a game since I've been gone.

The announcer babbles on about Finn being in the zone. He is. This is what he does best.

And you love him. And if he knew that, he'd be...

My thoughts scatter because Finn has the ball again. This time he scrambles back, guys homing in on him.

At the bar, the crowd shouts at the defense to take him down, knock his ass flat. But Finn isn't an easy target. He evades like the pro that he is.

My stomach clenches, my heart kicking my ribs. A lineman hooks Finn around his waist. My fingernails dig into the wood. But Finn swings around, somehow slipping out of his grip.

James shouts.

Finn zings a pass to North, who takes off toward the end zone.

James jumps to his feet. Somehow I'm on my feet too and we booth cheer as North races along.

"Touchdown," James cries, throwing up his arms. I laugh and pump a fist in the air.

"Man, shut up," someone says behind us. We ignore him and wiggle our hips.

Finally, they show Finn on the sidelines, helmet off, as he sits on a bench next to Jake and they laugh about something. Sweat slicks his hair and his cheeks are ruddy. But his smile is big and infectious. He's so damn gorgeous, my fingers ache to touch him. It hurts my heart to look at him, but I don't dare blink.

It nearly kills me with they cut away to the other team.

"Here comes Baylor," annoying bar dude says, clapping. "Kick some ass, Battle."

"Is he any good?" I ask James as New York's quarterback takes the field.

"Yeah." James looks disgruntled. "He was Manny's rival in college. Finn was drafted the year before Drew Baylor. And you should know this, missy."

"We don't exactly talk about football all the time."

James grins. "Right. Too busy licking his fine—"

"James!" Jamie gives his arm a slap. She's been quiet up until now, clearly not in her element. "Stop it."

He cackles but then gives her a swift kiss. "I'm just messing with Chess."

"You're being a pig."

"Yeah, that too."

Unfortunately, James is right. Drew Baylor is good. He reminds me a lot of Finn in the way he moves and in the size and shape of his body. The main difference seems to be that while Finn has a more playful demeanor, clearly joking with his offense and even the defensive linemen who try to tackle him, Baylor is all gruff business.

I don't like watching him play, because it means Finn might lose. Part of me wants to leave now, go book a flight home and just be there. But it feels like a betrayal not to watch Finn finish this game. He has no idea that I'm watching, so it shouldn't matter but it feels like it does. As if I'm supporting him, even though I'm nearly two thousand miles away.

I hate that distance.

New York doesn't manage to score and, after a nice punt return, Finn is soon back on the field. They're tied now, and tension coils in my gut. *Please win. He needs this. I need this for him.*

For three plays, I sit on the edge of my seat, as Finn and his offense battle their way down field, gaining some yards, losing others. Another drive, and I'm fairly twitching. The ball snaps. Finn catches it, steps back, he pump fakes one way and then, as if on cue, lets it fly. James screams as the ball soars.

Guys at the bar scream too, lamenting.

It's to Jake again. He jumps high, his body stretched to its limit. I bite my lip hard. Jake catches the ball and, in the same instant, a safety slams into his lower half. Jake flips head over heels, still clutching the ball. He lands head first onto the field, his helmet snapping toward his chest.

He crumples. And doesn't get up.

My heart stops so hard and fast, the room spins. Refs blow whistles.

Medics rush onto the field.

"Jake."

I know this man. I've laughed with him. Eaten with him. He is Finn's best friend.

Finn, who, when Jake doesn't get up, runs over to be with him. His helmet is off and he stands back just enough to let the medical staff work. His eyes never leave Jake, who lies lifeless in the end zone, his arm still wrapped around the ball.

I stand in the middle of the bar, my fists balled at my side, thinking he'll get up. It will be like Jerry McGuire, and Jake will soon be dancing around in the end zone. But he doesn't. They call for a stretcher.

Finn grasps the back of his neck with both hands and begins to pace. The camera zooms in on him. A strangled sound leaves me. Because the look in Finn's eyes has ripped open my heart. Although his expression is tightly controlled, I know him. Terror, agony, helplessness, it's all there, swimming in those blue depths. He's crumbling inside.

I grab my coat, slinging it over my shoulders. "I have to go."

James rises. "Chess."

"No," I shout, then take a breath. "No waiting. He can't be alone like this. I won't let him be alone anymore."

James nods. I don't wait to see if he and Jamie follow. I run straight out the door. The night is bitterly cold. My breath leaves in white puffs that obscure my vision. A cab comes down the block on the opposite side of the street. Without pause, I whistle high, lifting my arm.

It starts to slow, and I run to meet it.

Call it sixth sense, call it self-preservation, but the second I step out onto the street, my body tenses all at once. I feel the danger before I see it. Or maybe I hear it.

Someone shouts my name, unhinged and desperate. But I don't turn that way. I turn toward the rushing sound at my side. All I see is a blur before impact. Something hits me so hard, my brain registers it as sound: shattering light bulbs, dropping from a great height. Stars sparkle behind my lids.

I think of Fred slamming into me in a smoke filled hall, and for a second I don't know where I am.

Finn's frowning face flashes in my mind, and then there is nothing.

🏈 FINN

What the fuck just happened? What the *fuck* just happened!

The thought cycles through my skull as I pace the halls in the bowels of the stadium. It had been a perfect pass, a sweet forty-yard spiral straight into the end zone. Jake had caught it. Perfect catch. A thing of poetry.

That ball had landed in his hands, and I swear I felt the contact. We'd been connected in that play, one mind. Fucking poetry.

And then he went down.

Panic skitters up my throat. I can't breathe. I'm going to be sick. I halt and bend over, resting my hands on my thighs as I take deep breaths.

We deal with injuries all the time. Pain and football go hand in hand. But neck injuries, spinal damage. It's the thing you don't even want to think about. Not just career ending but life altering. He could die.

The ground beneath me sways. I grip my thighs tight.

Breathe. Breathe.

A door opens with a squeak. I don't look up as footsteps approach.

Charlie stops beside me. "Been looking for you."

I'd done my part. Finished the game. Bucked the fuck up and buckled down to win it. Nothing less would satisfy any of my guys. The fact that Jake had been joking at halftime about a "Win one for the Gipper" speech, almost made me lose it a couple of times.

But I'd held it together. Kept my game face on through the post game interviews where reporters clamored to know how Jake was doing. I'd wanted to know too. It fucking killed me, not knowing, waiting to hear what the doctors had to say.

Was he paralyzed? Would he play again?

"You hear anything," I ask Charlie, as I stare at the floor.

"I don't know much. But they think he'll be okay."

My knees sag. "Okay?"

Charlie knows what I'm asking. "No spinal damage."

I let out a gust of air. "Okay. Okay." Standing straight, I face Charlie. And then I'm hugging him. He pounds my back, and I pound his, both of us breathing too hard. I let him go with a final squeeze then step back and rub my eyes.

"Coach wants to see you," Charlie says when we head back toward the locker room.

"Now? Jesus."

I find Coach Calhoun waiting for me. "You hear about Ryder?" he asks without preamble.

"Charlie told me."

He nods, the relief in his eyes clear. "We need to talk about a few things. Got a minute?"

It's not really a question, just Calhoun's way of being polite, which is rare in and of itself.

"I was planning to go see Jake."

"He's under sedation."

"That's good. He needs the rest. Still plan to go."

"Nobody but family is getting in to see him tonight."

"I'll get in."

His eyes narrow. "We've hired guards to keep everyone out. You're not getting in."

Our stare stretches. It's a delicate thing, saying no to your coach. If you don't have a good reason for it, you're accused of not being a team player. Management does not find that amusing. Press gets wind that you're being uncooperative—and somehow they always find out—and suddenly there's talk of "problems" between the player and the coaching staff.

Politics suck. But there's also respect. I respect the hell out of my coach. Enough that I can wait a few minutes more to go see Jake.

I let out a silent sigh. "Your office?"

Appeased, he relaxes too. "Won't take too long."

I haven't taken a step when my phone rings. I reach to turn it off, but it's Chess's ringtone. Until now, I haven't let myself think of her; it's hard enough worrying about Jake. But the wall is crumbling. I need to hear her voice, to see her. Hell, I need *her*.

Calhoun shoots me a glance, as Cindy Lauper's *Goonies* song plays on. Gritting my teeth, I ignore the call. It feels fundamentally wrong to do it. But twenty minutes isn't going to kill either one of us. Twenty minutes, I promise myself.

We're almost at Coach's office when Chess calls again. Hell.

"You ever heard of turning that thing off, Mannus?"

He's one to talk. Gossip has it Calhoun brings his into the shower with him.

"Give me a second." I pull the phone from my pocket. "I'll tell them I'm in a meeting."

The second I answer, I know something is wrong. It isn't Chess's voice coming at me in a rush. It's James. "Thank fuck you finally answered."

"What's wrong? Why are you using Chess's phone?"

"Chess is hurt. She's in the hospital…"

Had I felt panic with Jake? That was nothing to this. Everything stops. Black spots dance before my eyes. I can't breathe. I can't fucking breathe.

This isn't fear. This is terror.

"Mannus? You there?"

"What hospital?" I manage.

James gives me the name and then takes an audible breath. "She's okay. Just…I think she'd want you here when she wakes up."

Wakes up? A weird sound comes out of me. I clench the phone. "I'm on my way."

My fingers feel numb as I hang up. In fact, my whole fucking face feels numb. "I have to go," I tell my coach, who stares at me as if I've lost it.

"Now? Who was that? One of Ryder's sisters?"

"No. My girl. She's..." *Don't lose it.* "She's in New York. I've got to go."

"You're going to New York?" His voice rises. "We have meetings tomorrow."

Already, I'm texting Charlie, telling him to book me the next flight out and fuck the expense. Any flight. Now.

"Mannus," Calhoun snaps. "You listening?"

I meet his gaze head on. "Yes, Coach. Meetings. I'll attend every single one of them. As soon as I get back from New York."

He stares at me, his mouth open.

I should feel bad. Worry, maybe. I don't. I was the number one draft pick of my year. And for the first time, I'm playing that card. "My girl is in the hospital. She *is* my family. And I'm going to be with her."

It's as if Coach is moving in slow motion but he finally nods. "Give Ms. Copper my best."

I don't answer; I'm already running down the hall, my whole fucking life waiting for me in New York.

CHAPTER 24
♟ CHESS

Hospitals are horrible. Especially waking up in one. I threw up and they scanned my brain for internal swelling or bleeding. That scared the shit out of me. Apparently, I have a concussion. Which means I spent the night being checked on in intervals that felt too short and were really annoying since it meant I couldn't sleep. I really wanted to sleep.

It's morning now. My head weighs a metric ton and throbs as if someone is steadily kicking it. But the nausea is gone, and I'm no longer dizzy. I've been allowed to shower and put on my street clothes. Yeah, a hospital shower with antiseptic smelling shampoo that turns hair into straw.

Lying on the bed to wait for James, I've been drifting on and off, sheer exhaustion pulling at my lids. They're releasing me with instructions that James watch over me for the next twelve hours.

The hollow feeling in my chest grows. I don't want James.

The door opens, another nurse coming to poke at me. But it isn't a nurse. Emotion punches into me, a fist to my aching chest, a sharp squeeze of my tender heart.

Finn.

He looks about as good as I feel, eyes blood-shot, the skin bruised beneath them, his hair matted on one side and sticking up on the other. I soak in the sight of him like water on parched earth.

His blue gaze darts over me as if he doesn't know what to focus on first, or that he can't yet take in the whole of me. Tension rides his body, making it visibly tremble. And then his eyes meet mine. He looks haunted, ripped apart.

I swallow with difficulty. "Hey."

When he speaks, his voice is a ghost of its former self. "Hey." He takes a step into the room and closes the door behind him. "I got here as soon as I could. Flights were scarce."

He's here, that's all that matters to me. I should sit up, make myself appear strong and capable and all that. But, unless someone comes to wheel my ass out of here, I'm not moving until I have to.

"I think I was hit by a guy on a bike." Everything's kind of hazy but I remember two wheels and a handlebar.

The grooves around his mouth deepen. "You were."

He moves like an old man, making his way to my side. I watch him come, little tremors quaking in my belly. I want to hug him so badly my arms twitch, but they're too heavy to move.

He sits in the chair by my bedside, his body too big for its stingy frame. Up close, he looks worse, careworn and exhausted. I empathize.

"Is the guy okay?" My memory is fairly shitty right now. Apparently, concussions can do that to a person.

"Couple of scrapes. Broken wrist." Finn's expression is blank, barely a flicker of movement. He glances down at my hand resting on the bed.

"How ironic. Mine just healed."

The corners of his mouth pinch. "Love that you can joke. Two times, I've had to hear you were in the hospital." Blue eyes pin me to the spot. "That's two times too many."

"It's not like I planned this."

He grunts.

"I'm not even a clumsy person. Both times they ran into me."

"Haven't you ever heard of looking both ways, Chester?" He

actually glares.

"It was a one way street. Who thinks to look for rando bikers going the wrong way?"

"You do. From now on. Jesus." He wipes a hand over his mouth. "My heart can't take another call like that, okay?"

"Okay. I'm sorry." I am. Not for getting hit, but for putting that look of abject fear in his eyes.

Finn scowls. "Don't be sorry. How do you feel?"

"Fuzzy." I blink down at my body. The inside of my elbow has a bandage on it from where they put an IV in earlier. A saline drip that had provided cool relief and, later, some very exceptional painkillers. One thing to love about a hospital, I guess. "I can't remember what I look like. Give me a damage report."

His throat works on a swallow. "A few scrapes and bruises on your right temple and cheek."

"That's not so bad."

"Debatable."

This is not the reunion I'd planned. Finn is here, and clearly worried about me, but he's distant and fairly humming with some emotion I can't figure out. My memory clears a little more and a bolt of horror hits me. "Oh, shit."

Instantly, Finn jolts as if pinched. "What? Are you hurting? Talk to me."

"Jake. How is he?"

Finn settles down with a scowl then rubs a hand over his face. "He sprained his neck. And, like you, has a concussion. He's out for the season but, all in all, he got lucky."

"I saw it happen. I was so scared."

Finn pales, and his lashes lower. "Me too."

"I know. I should have been there."

Finn glares down at his fists.

I want to touch him, stroke away the stiffness along his neck and shoulders. But he looks as if one touch will shatter him, and I don't know what to say to bridge the gap between us. "Did you win?"

The muscle on his jaw bunches. "Yes. We weren't going down without a fight."

But there's no emotion in his words. He keeps glaring at his fists as if he's thinking of punching something. I don't know what to do.

"You were magnificent," I tell him with a soft voice.

He grunts.

"Are you mad at me?"

"Yes."

It lashes like a whip.

I bite my lower lip, look away, blinking hard.

None of the harshness leaves his voice. "I'm trying not to lose it."

Guilt pulls at my heart. He witnessed his best friend get knocked out on the field. Jake could have died, and I know how much that affects Finn.

"I can't believe you're here." My voice is a thread, reaching out for him.

Silence greets me instead. The force of his stare is a heavy hand on my chest. I turn to face him.

Wide eyes filled with outrage and anger glare back at me. "You think I'd be anywhere else than at your side?"

"Jake—"

"God…" Finn laughs but then, without warning, his eyes well up and his lips twist. I stare in shock as his chin quivers and he lets out a harsh exhale that ends in a strangled sob.

"Hey," I whisper.

His chest heaves, a horrible pained movement, and he leans in, resting his head on my belly. "Fuck, Chess," he says on a choked breath. His arm slings around my hips, fingers clutching my side. "You have no idea what it does to me to see you like this. I cannot stand seeing you hurt. I can't."

I stoke his hair. "It's okay. I'm okay."

"It's not okay." He lifts his head and looks at me with eyes that are wet. "I got that call from James telling me I needed to get to the hospital because you were there, and my life fucking stopped. Do you understand? Your life stops, mine does too."

My heart swells in the hollow cavity of my chest. "Oh, Finn. Come here."

But he doesn't listen. He sits back in his chair, his expression resolute and hard, as he wipes his eyes. "So, yeah, I'm mad. You left me. And you got hurt. You can't get hurt. And you can't leave me again, Chester. I won't survive."

My big, strong man waits for an answer, his body tense, silvery trails of tears running down his cheeks. He's left his heart wide open for me, without shame or hesitation.

My vision wavers, and I blink to clear it. When I'm able to speak, emotion garbles my words. "Take my hand."

Shaking, I hold out my own, waiting.

Finn's brows pinch, his gaze darting from my face to my hand. I meet his eyes and hold his gaze. Does he know what I'm asking? Does he understand? Emotion bounces between us, and then, all at once, his expression clears. A small smile unfurls, as he reaches out.

His warm, rough palm presses against mine. Our fingers thread. Something inside me settles into place with a silent click.

I give Finn's hand a squeeze. "I was coming to find you. To tell you that I loved you."

He lets out a breath. And then he's crawling into bed with me, tucking my body around his hard strength. Soft lips brush my temple. Finn cups my cheek with infinite care. "I love you so much, it scares me."

I lean into his touch with a sigh. "That was my problem too. But I'm not scared anymore." My fingers toy with his longer ones. "I think no matter how my life played out, I would have found you. I would have loved you."

His eyes squeeze shut and when he opens them, they are shining. "You're my fate, Chess. I've known that since the beginning. I was meant to be yours."

"I told James that you were my fate."

He gives me a knowing smile. "Some things were meant to be."

I huff out a laugh. "That song... A band started playing it, right in the middle of my dinner. Every person in the place was singing along. How am I supposed to ignore a sign like that?"

He laughs. "You don't."

I lay my head on his shoulder, and we both rest. The steady beat of his heart soothes me. Finn strokes my knuckles with an idle touch.

"I'm sorry I left the way I did," I finally say.

Finn stirs. "I wasn't hearing you when you said you were afraid. Not the way you needed me to hear it, anyway."

He turns his hand so that my palm rests on his and he's now holding me. "You think I need to father a child to be happy, because of what I lost. And it was easier for me to brush that aside with quick assurances than to really ask myself if that was true."

A tremor goes through me, and he tightens his grip as if he knows I want to pull away. Finn's voice is steady and sure, but taut with a hint of wryness. "Football is easy, if you want to know the truth. Easy in the way that I'm gifted. I can do it well. And if I fail it's all on me. I can control that."

Long fingers curl over mine. "I never really lost anything that mattered to me until the baby. I couldn't control that. It changed me, made me afraid. And what I feel for you is fucking terrifying. Because I can't control you either. I can only love you and hope for the best, that you'll love me back, that I can keep you safe and happy."

"I am happy," I whisper, turning further into his body, to press close. "You've always made me happy. I panicked. But I shouldn't have. Because you are worth any risk."

He lets that absorb, pressing his lips to my head. "You have no idea how happy I am to hear that, Chess. But I owe you an answer. Because I panicked too. And I should have taken that same risk."

Nerves pluck at my belly. I don't know why; he loves me. I love him.

I know my worth, and I know he sees it too. But some feelings cannot be changed, no matter how much you want to ignore them. I go still, letting him say what he has to. And maybe it's hard for him, because he takes his time, measuring his words as if they have weight.

"Thing is, when I lost my child…I lost someone to love. I didn't realize it until then, but I needed that. I needed love in my life. Someone who makes all the effort worth it." Finn shifts on the bed to that we're face to face. "I love you, Chester Copper. More than anything. It isn't a matter of that being good enough; it is essential. You take yourself out of the equation and the rest has no meaning."

I don't know who moves first. Our kisses are soft and sweet, apologies mixed with promises. After a lingering press of his mouth to mine, Finn strokes the sensitive side of my neck with the backs of his fingers. "You want to adopt a child, employ a surrogate, do both, that's what we'll do. But I don't need that. Not now."

"I don't need that now either. I'm happy with it being just us."

His cheek brushes mine. "Whatever we choose, we'll do it together. As long as we're together, Chess."

"Together." It is a word ripe with possibilities, and I cannot wait.

EPILOGUE
♟ CHESS

In the spring, Finn bought me a house for my birthday. And I let him. It was surprising how liberating it felt, not worrying about what kind of message that sent or if I'd be trapping myself by allowing him to spend so much money. I'd placed my life in his hands and he'd done the same. Every day the threads of our lives grew more intertwined, and we were stronger for it.

We chose a house on Third Street in the Garden District. Built in the 1850s, it was a Greek revival style with double galleries along the front and the back of the house, and surrounded by wide lawns, with a pool tucked in the back. We painted the stucco a pale violet to represent New Orleans' purple, with white for the trim. The high iron gates—which we needed for privacy—were a glossy dark green. And I was in love, true love with the massive old house.

When I found out that Dex's girlfriend, Fiona, was both an interior decorator and furniture maker, I went to her for help. While Finn was at training camp, Fi and I started decorating. Between the two of us, we chose an ebony stain for the floors and clean white paint for the walls to let the architecture shine. We kept the furniture comfortable but with modern lines, set up a home gym and movie room, an art studio in the attic, and a photography studio in an outbuilding near the back of the property that had its own entrance, and I loved the space more than my old loft.

Was the house too big for Finn and me? It didn't feel that way. We filled it with friends and family and love. In the summer, we hosted James and Jamie's wedding. I ended up getting drunk and inelegantly bawling during my best woman speech. Finn consoled me by taking me skinny dipping later that night when all the guests had gone. He'd been right, drunken sex with someone you love really was fun—in a sloppy, no-holds-barred, wake-up-the-neighbors kind of way.

By the time fall arrived, our house was our home, and I loved Finn with a depth I didn't know I was capable of.

"I can't believe I thought this was a good idea," Fi grumbles as she stands before the mirror in my dressing room. We're close friends now, and I'm only sorry we didn't meet sooner.

I take in the little green dress, so short it barely covers her bum, and the shimmery pink tights with matching ballet flats. "You look cute as hell."

Fi scowls and flicks one of the iridescent wings strapped to her back. "Cute? I'm a masochist, is what I am. My whole life I've been compared to Tinker Bell. And now I'm dressing up like her, for fuck's sake."

Petite with killer curves, a button nose, big green eyes, and wispy blond hair, Fiona definitely looks the part.

I grin wide. "Embracing your inner Tink gives you power over her. Isn't that what you said?"

"Shut up."

"Dex will lose his shit when he sees that dress."

She grins too. "That's the plan."

"What is he going as?"

She winks, an evil glint in her eyes. "A lumberjack."

I can't help laughing. Mainly because I know Dex will be grumbling over whatever he wears. "Oh, man. Talk about hot lumberjack porn."

"I know. I think my panties might go up in flames when I see him." She fluffs out her tiny skirt. "What about Finn?"

Downstairs, the catering staff I hired is setting up for the Halloween party Finn and I are hosting. We'd done most of the decorations ourselves, but the caterers will put the finishing touches on things.

"He won't tell me. It's supposed to be a surprise. And speaking of…" I walk to the garment bag hanging by the mirror. "My costume is one as well."

"Finn picked out your costume?" Fi gives me a look that's part amused, part afraid. "And you trusted him? What if it's a carrot?"

I snort. "All the things you could have come up with and you pick carrot?"

"Felt nice and random."

I press a hand against the bag, prolonging the moment, because I know it will be good. "Finn would never dress me as a carrot. No, he was downright giddy when he left this for me with strict, do not look until you're getting dressed instructions."

"Well…" Fi waves a hand. "Let's see it."

Taking a breath, I slowly unzip the bag. Shimmery white tulle pours out as if it's been waiting to spring free. My breath kicks up a little.

"What is it?" Fi asks behind me. "An angel costume?"

With trembling hands, I part the edges of the bag. *He couldn't have. He didn't…*

A happy laugh bubbles up and bursts free as my vision blurs. "He did." I press my hand to my mouth, still grinning wide. "He did."

The midnight black bodice is soft velvet with a deep v-shaped neckline. The skirt is frothy snow white tulle, layers and layers of it that rustle and bounce at the touch of my hand. Black vines snake out from the bodice to lie upon that pristine skirt.

"Wow," Fiona whispers at my side. "That's…"

"Grace Kelly's dress from *Rear Window*." Another messy, sobbing laugh escapes me. "He actually got me a new one." Only this version is so much better than my old, sadly destroyed knock-off dress. This is a masterpiece, a truly authentic copy of Kelly's iconic dress, down to the slim patent leather belt and the even deeper v-shaped neckline in the back.

I explain to a confused Fiona about how I'd worn a dress like this before, how Finn recognized it, and how I'd lost it in the fire.

"And he had a new one made for you." Her gaze is dreamy as she touches the short sleeve of the bodice. "Touchdown, Mannus."

There's even a bag filled with a pearl bracelet cuff, strand necklace, and cluster earrings.

Fi helps me get ready, pinning my hair back in a swirly chignon, and I hunt down a pair of strappy black heels.

My dress swishes and sways as I walk down the stairs. But I don't find Finn waiting for me. In fact, he conspicuously absent by the time the party is in full swing. I'm surrounded by friends, but no Finn.

I don't know if I should be worried or annoyed.

Searching for him is slow going, as costume-clad guests stop me every few feet to compliment my dress. Finally, I reach the back garden where Finn has ordered a dance floor to be placed beneath strings of little ghost-shaped lights. A band is set up at the far end and is playing a cover of "Werewolves of London."

I catch a glimpse of Jake's face at the edges of the crowd and head his way.

"Jake, have you seen—What the hell are you wearing?" I squeak out with a laugh.

Bland as can be, Jake glances down the length of his body before answering. "A bunny suit."

Rolondo, Dex, Fiona, and Charlie are with him, and they all start to crack up.

"He looks like a pink nightmare," Dex intones.

Jake raises a fuzzy, pink middle finger in his direction.

I bite down on my grin. "You lost a bet, didn't you?" And here I thought Fi was way off with her carrot worries.

Jake's lips purse. "Yes." He brightens a little. "Though I can't entirely say I'm disappointed."

I have no idea why. He really does look like a pink nightmare. All six feet two of him. It feels good to tease Jake, though. He walked through hell to get back to full strength.

"Look," I say, snapping out of my bunny-induced daze. "I'll give you a carrot if you tell me where Finn is."

Jake's smile turns smug as he nurses his beer. "Oh, I think he'll show soon enough."

I glare but the music stops and someone turns on a mic. There's a small whine of feedback and then *he* speaks.

"I'd like to thank you all for joining Chess and I tonight."

Slowly I turn toward the sound of Finn's voice. But I can't see him anywhere. The band is smiling, one of them moving behind a xylophone, of all things.

Finn keeps talking. "It means a lot to us that you could be here. And I was wondering if my pink bunny friend could help me out here."

Everyone laughs, and looks at Jake, who is grinning like a loon. "Sure thing, asshole!" he shouts back with good cheer. Jake holds a pink arm out to me. "Ms. Copperpot."

Bemused, I take his arm and he guides me farther onto the dance floor. People part for us. And then the band begins to play with the kitschy pluck of a ukulele.

The music barely registers before Finn steps out from behind the big live oak next to the dance floor, and he begins to sing. A laugh of pure joy rises up from me.

Most people go for the iconic Vegas Elvis with his white jumpsuit. But not Finn. He's young Elvis, hair slicked back, neat wedge sideburns, his black leather jacket with the stiff, high collar framing his face. Finn's blue gaze zeroes in on me as he croons "Can't Help Falling in Love." It is such cheesy goodness that I'm laughing, even as tears leak from my eyes.

Slowly he walks my way, tossing the mic to Jake, who picks up where he left off. Jake is surprisingly good.

Finn stops before me, close enough that my skirts surround his legs. A small smile plays on his lips. "Hey, Chester."

I'm fairly certain I'm beaming. "I always knew you'd make a great young Elvis."

His gaze stays on my face. "You're more stunning than Grace Kelly."

"Sweet talker."

Finn holds out his hands. "Dance with me?"

My palms slide over his. "Always."

The band plays on, our friends singing along with enthusiasm. But I only have eyes for Finn as he takes me in his arms and we begin to sway. All is right with the world when I'm with him.

"I love you, Chess," he whispers against my cheek.

I snuggle closer. "I love you too."

A hum of acknowledgment rumbles in his chest. "And I was wondering…"

He lets my hand go. Slowly we stop dancing, and I stare up at him with my heart in my throat. Finn's smile wobbles, but his eyes are wide open, looking at me with that same connection we had the first time we met. Only now it's stronger, so much stronger.

I'm hooked by that blue gaze. I'll never tire of it. I'm so drawn in at first, I don't notice that he's holding something.

But his gaze darts to his hand, and then I see it. Winking under the tree lights is a large emerald cut diamond ring.

I don't cry. I grin so wide it hurts my cheeks.

"Whether you wear this or not," Finn says in a thick voice, "I will hold your hand through life. I will love you forever. But it would be an honor to be your husband—"

"Put the ring on me, Finn," I say in a shaking rush. "I can't wait to be your wife."

The ring slides on cool and solid. We're still laughing and kissing when our friends finally swoop in to congratulate us. Only then do I notice James and Jamie are here too.

Much later, when the excitement has died down, Finn and I sit on the porch swing just outside of our room. Finn holds my hand, his thumb fiddling with the diamond on my finger.

"Just think," I tell him as we rock. "I'll soon be Chester Mannus."

He tries admirably not to snicker. But he doesn't hide his smile. "I think it's a lovely name." His voice grows husky. "Really, the best name I've ever heard."

With a sigh, I rest my head on his shoulder. "Me too."

Below us, people are still swaying on the dance floor. Sometimes, I think of that older couple we saw at the beach, dancing beneath the holiday lights, content to just be with each other. I see my future in them, but I don't dwell there. Now is where I live. And that, too, is surprisingly easy to do.

THANK YOU!

Thank you for reading *THE HOT SHOT!*

Reviews help other readers find books. If you enjoyed THE HOT SHOT, please consider leaving a review.

I like to hang out in these places: Callihan's VIP Lounge, The Locker Room, Kristen Callihan FB author page, and Twitter

Would you like to receive sneak peaks before anyone else? Or know when my next book is available? Sign up HERE for my newsletter and receive exclusive excerpts, news, and release information.

Want to see how the Game On series began?
Read The Hook Up

The rules: no kissing on the mouth, no staying the night, no telling anyone, and above all… No falling in love

Anna Jones just wants to finish college and figure out her life. Falling for star quarterback Drew Baylor is certainly not on her to do list. Confident and charming, he lives in the limelight and is way too gorgeous for his own good. If only she could ignore his heated stares and stop thinking about doing hot and dirty things with him. Easy right?

Too bad he's committed to making her break every rule…

Football has been good to Drew. It's given him recognition, two National Championships, and the Heisman. But what he really craves is sexy yet prickly Anna Jones. Her cutting humor and blatant disregard for his fame turns him on like nothing else. But there's one problem: she's shut him down. Completely.

That is until a chance encounter leads to the hottest sex of their lives, along with the possibility of something great. Unfortunately, Anna wants it to remain a hook up. Now it's up to Drew to tempt her with more: more sex, more satisfaction, more time with him. Until she's truly hooked. It's a good thing Drew knows all about winning.

All's fair in love and football…Game on.

THE GAME ON SERIES
The Hook Up —Book 1
The Friend Zone – Book 2
The Game Plan —Book 3

ABOUT THE AUTHOR

Kristen Callihan is a New York Times and USA Today bestselling author. She has won a RITA award, and two RT Reviewer's Choice awards. Her novels have garnered starred reviews from Publisher's Weekly and the Library Journal, as well as being awarded top picks by many reviewers. Her debut book FIRELIGHT received RT Magazine's Seal of Excellence, was named a best book of the year by Library Journal, best book of Spring 2012 by Publisher's Weekly, and was named the best romance book of 2012 by ALA RUSA.

When she is not writing, she is reading.

You can sign up for Kristen's new release e-mail at www.thehookup.kristencallihan.com

ACKNOWLEDGMENTS

To Kati Brown, Jovee Winters, and Sahara Hoshi, for early reads and encouragement. Sarah Hansen for always making my kickass covers. Sara Lunsford for copy edits. Kylie Scott for some much needed moral support. Danielle Sanchez for her awesome PR efforts. For the readers who are always so awesome, and the bloggers who are always so supportive.

Printed in Poland
by Amazon Fulfillment
Poland Sp. z o.o., Wrocław